Lynda La Plante

GOOD FRIDAY

ZAFFRE

First published in Great Britain in 2017 by
ZAFFRE PUBLISHING
80–81 Wimpole St, London W1G 9RE
www.zaffrebooks.co.uk

A CIP catalogue record for this book is
available from the British Library.

Hardback ISBN: 978-1-78576-281-9
Trade Paperback ISBN: 978-1-78576-328-1
Ebook ISBN: 978-1-78576-329-8
Paperback ISBN: 978-1-78576-330-4
Open Market Edition ISBN: 978-1-78576-334-2

1 3 5 7 9 10 8 6 4 2

Typeset by IDSUK (Data Connection) Ltd

Printed and bound by Clays Ltd, St Ives Plc

Zaffre Publishing is an imprint of Bonnier Publishing UK,
a Bonnier Publishing company
www.bonnierpublishing.co.uk
www.bonnierzaffre.co.uk

This dedication is to my son, Lorcan

Author's Note

During 1974 and 1975 London was subjected to a terrifying bombing campaign carried out by Active Service Units (ASU) of the Irish Republican Army (IRA). Over forty bombs exploded, thirty-five people were killed and many were seriously injured. In one day alone the IRA planted seven bombs at locations across central London. Some were defused, some were not.

On 6 December 1975, four armed members of the ASU took two elderly Balcombe Street residents hostage after a botched machine-gun attack on a Mayfair restaurant. A tense stand-off with the Metropolitan Police Bomb Squad ensued, but after six days the siege ended when the IRA men surrendered and released the hostages.

After several days of intense interrogation, the 'Balcombe Street Gang' were charged and remanded in custody to stand trial for multiple bombings and murders. The press portrayed the arrests as a major victory for the Met's Bomb Squad.

It was the lull before the storm. The bomb squad received information that another ASU had come to London. Both police and the public lived in fear: where and when would the IRA strike, and could they be stopped in time?

Prologue

In March 1976, Jane Tennison successfully completed her ten-week CID course at Hendon and returned to Bow Street whilst awaiting a transfer to another station as a fully fledged detective constable. DI Gibbs had moved on, but she was still under the strict, watchful eye of DCI Shepherd, nicknamed 'Timex' due to his almost obsessive timekeeping schedules.

It wasn't long before Jane's posting as a DC came through and to her dismay she was offered a place at Hackney. She requested a private discussion with Shepherd to ask if she could remain at Bow Street. Although she knew that he could be tricky and controlling, she nevertheless admired his tenacity.

Shepherd knew, intuitively, the reason behind Jane's appeal. Several officers who had been stationed at Hackney at the time of the abortive bank raid, which had tragically killed DCI Leonard Bradfield and WPC Kath Morgan, had been transferred. Jane gave no reason for her request, but encouraged by her previous performance at Bow Street, DCI Shepherd agreed that she could return there.

Jane was in a catch-22 situation. Although Shepherd had agreed for her to remain with the CID at Bow Street, he gave her very little opportunity to prove herself and she was becoming increasingly frustrated. She was due to attend a court appearance for a drunk driver. Usually this kind of case would have been handled by a uniformed officer, but Jane had been driving an unmarked CID car when the drunk driver had driven straight into the back of it. He had been belligerent and quite abusive.

On arriving at the court she was annoyed to find that there was a backlog of cases being heard, so she went to get herself a coffee. As she headed back to the waiting room she was almost sent flying by a DC bounding through the door.

'God, I'm sorry,' said DC Brian Edwards, then, recognising her, gave a wide smile.

'Jane! It's good to see you!'

'Hello, Brian. You got a case here this morning as well?'

'Yeah, Flying Squad job. Committal hearing on a three-hander for armed robbery.'

'You're on the Flying Squad?' Jane tried to hide her surprise. Edwards was young, and almost as inexperienced as she was.

'Yeah, it's completely changed my life. The blokes on the squad are a great bunch of guys. We work all over London investigating armed robberies. The adrenaline buzz when you nick an armed blagger on the pavement is incredible.'

'Congratulations! I must say, you look good.'

Edwards had always been rather untidy and scruffy looking, with his thick curly hair worn long, and his shirt always hanging out of his trousers. Now he was wearing a trendy leather jacket, a white T-shirt, and dark trousers with side-zipper boots.

'Are there any women on the Flying Squad?' Jane asked.

'No way. I doubt they'd ever bring in a woman. It's tough work, Jane, and we get results.' Before she could respond to his arrogance and chauvinism, Edwards glanced at his watch, 'So, what're you here for?'

'Just a traffic offence. A drunk bloke rammed into me whilst I was driving the CID car.'

Edwards laughed. He turned to look over at two men dressed in similar clothing to him, as one gestured for him to join them.

'See y'around,' Edwards said, as he sauntered over to them.

By the time Jane got to the CID office three hours later she was in a foul mood. Edith, the CID's clerical officer, who had worked alongside Jane since she started at Bow Street, smiled warmly when she saw her.

'Everything go all right in court?'

'Yes. Guilty, banned for two years and a hefty fine. When you think how much paperwork I had to do to get him into court . . . He wore a smart suit and tie and said it was out of character, blah, blah . . . Considering the lip he gave me, he got off lightly.'

'Well, you've got a load of shoplifting crime sheets on your desk from DCI Shepherd. There's been a slew of clothes nicked from Oxford Street stores today.'

'Shoplifters? That's a uniform crime investigation, not CID!'

'Not when they all happened within an hour of each other. Shepherd reckons it's an organised gang who sell the stolen goods on market stalls.'

'Well, that sounds a lot more interesting than the stuff I usually investigate.'

Edith sipped her tea. 'He wants you to get statements from all the shops, and an inventory of exactly what was stolen, along with the value.'

'Oh my God,' Jane muttered.

'Don't shoot the messenger,' Edith retorted, resuming her typing.

Jane began to sift through the crime sheets and statements on her own desk. 'I met DC Brian Edwards at court. Remember him from the Susie Luna murder?' Edith looked blank. 'The rapist, Peter Allard? He got a life sentence, and –'

'Oh yes, I remember. Long time ago, now . . . Over a year . . .'

'Edwards is on the Flying Squad now.'

'Really?'

'He said they never take women on the Squad.'

'Well, I doubt any decent woman would want to be on it.' Edith's tone sharpened. 'They're a bunch of chauvinistic bastards! Ever since that TV series came out, *The Professionals*, they act like they're film stars, the lot of them, think they're God's gift . . . There've been a lot of unpleasant rumours about corruption too, but far be it from me to name names . . .'

Jane processed the Oxford Street reports for the rest of the day, drawing up charts of the shops, times of the thefts and a description of the suspects. She then filed everything methodically, just as DCI Shepherd liked, but she was finished by three thirty. She sat drumming her fingers on her empty desk and at four o'clock decided she would approach DCI Shepherd. It was ridiculous that she was sitting around when she was now qualified to investigate more serious cases.

She knocked on his office door and waited.

'Come in.'

Jane walked in and stood by his desk. Shepherd gave her a cursory glance.

'What is it, Tennison?' Shepherd's pale blue eyes and boyish looks belied not only his age but also his professionalism.

'May I speak freely, sir?'

'Yes, of course. Sit down.'

She drew a chair up in front of his desk.

'I don't feel that my time here is being utilised properly. I've gained a lot of experience since I've been here, and I know that you are aware of my participation in previous cases – like the apparently non-suspicious death that resulted in two murder convictions.'

Shepherd didn't answer right away. He paused for a moment, then picked up his fountain pen, unscrewed the top, examined the nib, then slowly screwed it back together. 'Yes, of course, I am aware of the case you are referring to . . . Katrina Harcourt and . . . er, Barry Dawson . . . correct?'

'Yes, sir. I was also part of the investigation of the rapist Peter Allard when the body of Susie Luna was discovered, and –'

'Yes, Tennison, I'm more than aware of those investigations, and the part you played in them. But I don't see why you're bringing them up now, all these months later?'

'Sir, I'm grateful that you agreed for me to return to Bow Street, but now that I've passed my CID course and been made detective I'm concerned that my training is not being used to its full potential.'

'Really?'

'Yes, sir. I was wondering if there was any possibility that I could apply for a transfer to the Flying Squad?'

Shepherd laughed. 'Tennison, with your length of service and experience there is absolutely no possibility of your being transferred to the Flying Squad. You are welcome to apply but I doubt the application would be taken seriously. But let me think about what you've said and we can talk in due course about some possible alternatives.'

Edith was getting ready to leave when Jane walked into the CID office and sat down at her desk in a glum mood.

'I'm off home now,' Edith said.

'Edith, do you think DCI Shepherd's got it in for me? He keeps his distance from me, and I get all the dross. I'm investigating dead-end crimes that none of the other detectives are allocated. I know that he was very complimentary to me, and agreed for me to return to Bow Street . . .'

'As I keep on telling you, Jane, the Met really don't like giving women the kudos they deserve. They're old-school, and Shepherd is as well . . . although he maintains that he's a forward thinker, in my opinion he plays by the rules – and those rules don't include female detectives.'

On returning to the section house Jane sat on her bed, feeling thoroughly depressed. She had been thinking of moving out and renting a flat of her own now she was earning a sufficient salary. She had saved a considerable amount living at the section house. The time was right for her to be independent.

Later that evening she called her parents and told her father that she was contemplating moving. Mr Tennison encouraged her to think about buying rather than renting. He even offered to help by paying the deposit, saying that in the long run it would be much better for her to own a flat and pay a mortgage, as it would be an investment.

Jane's morale was boosted. If she couldn't improve her working schedules at Bow Street, she could at least change her personal lifestyle, and be more independent.

DCI Shepherd didn't approach Jane after their meeting, so she carried on working on the low-level investigations she had been assigned to. She was disappointed, but at least she now had another focus, spending her days off looking at possible flats. She was unsure how she was going to manage financially, as she had only just bought a second-hand VW Golf. However, Jane's father actively encouraged her and produced a list of areas that he felt would be suitable.

'I don't want to jump the gun, Daddy. This is really going to stretch my wages . . . so far I haven't seen anywhere suitable.'

'It takes time, dear, and you won't be jumping the gun. I'll look into everything with you. If we find a place that needs fixing up you can call on your brother-in-law, Tony, to help with the carpentry, and I can do the decorating.'

Mrs Tennison was not quite as enthusiastic and was anxious about Jane moving into a flat on her own and taking on such responsibility. She had even suggested that Jane might want to go back and live at home with them again. She constantly worried about Jane and felt that, if she wasn't living at home, it was safer for her to be in secure accommodation like the section house, along with other police officers.

'It sometimes feels like I imagine a school dormitory would be, Mum, with no privacy . . . and I hate the communal bathrooms. I really want to find my own place.'

'Well, in my opinion, if you get your own place there'll be no incentive for you to meet someone, get married and set up a home together. Just like Pam and Tony did.'

After years of being compared to her sister, Jane had learnt not to argue with her mother, or to listen to her opinions. Mrs Tennison was still unable to cope with Jane's career choice, and would far rather that she had been more like Pam and had chosen a safe 'homely' job. She had always been prone to anxiety, and if she had known of the horrors that Jane had been subjected to during her training and at her various attachments since then, she would be even more neurotic.

On her days off, Jane and her father scoured the estate agents' windows, viewed endless properties and made arrangements for a mortgage. She had a file of estate agents' particulars and spent her breaks in the canteen having coffee and sifting through them all. Edith was very supportive of Jane buying her own flat, although she was quick to dismiss one property after another as being too far out of the West End, or in an unsatisfactory area. Edith owned her own small terraced house in Hackney but constantly complained that the neighbourhood was going downhill and that it was not a good investment for her future. Her elderly mother suffered from dementia and she was dependent on social welfare carers to be able to look after her. Jane had once asked Edith if she had considered placing her mother into a care home.

'I wouldn't dream of it! She might be the bane of my life but she's my mother . . . even though she often doesn't know who I am, and she's a constant worry, but when she is lucid it makes it worthwhile. I'm sure if you were ever in the same situation, Jane, you would do the same.'

Jane nodded in agreement, although the thought of losing one or other of her parents and having to care for them by herself was too much to even contemplate.

As she was pondering, DCI Shepherd summoned her into his office.

'Detective Tennison, I have been giving your request for a transfer some serious thought. You are, as I have said to you before, far too inexperienced a detective to join an elite squad like "The Sweeney". But they have a sub-division known as the "Dip Squad" . . . if you do well there it could be a stepping stone towards the Flying Squad. They're quite keen for a female to join them, and I can get you up on an attachment, if their DCI agrees.'

'What exactly is the Dip Squad, sir?'

'Well, they deal with professional pickpockets . . . there's shed-loads of them descending in force from overseas, most notably Italy, Chile and Colombia. The Dip Squad are working right now with teams along Oxford Street, Regent Street and Piccadilly, as well as teams covering underground stations at Victoria, Embankment and Oxford Circus. So, how does that sound to you?'

Jane wasn't at all sure, but at the same time if this might be a possible route to the more glamorous Flying Squad then she knew she should accept.

'Thank you very much, sir.'

Shepherd stood up, dismissing her. 'Good. I'll let you know as soon as I get confirmation.'

Jane was beaming when she went back into the CID room and Edith swivelled around to look at her.

'I may be transferred to the Dip Squad.'

Edith shrugged and turned back to face her typewriter. 'Rather you than me, dear . . . it's a dreadful, dirty little office and they don't even have any clerical staff. Oh, by the way, I meant to show you this.'

Edith handed her an advert from *The Job*, the Met's official newspaper.

'I think it sounds really interesting . . . an ex-clerical worker based in Scotland Yard is offering her flat for sale. Good location, just off Baker Street, a minute from the Underground. It's got two bedrooms, and I think it's a very reasonable price.'

Jane jotted down the information. As she was off duty that after-noon she arranged to go and see the flat in Melcombe Street. She walked the short distance from Baker Street underground station and liked the location as it was so close to Regent's Park. Melcombe Street was a small turning, with a row of shops on one side and narrow three-storey houses opposite. There was no front garden as they were built back from the pavement, but the houses were white-washed and looked well kept. The door to number 33 was freshly painted with a row of brass bells on one side. She rang the bell for the top flat and waited.

After a short while a very pregnant woman opened the door and introduced herself as Mrs Taylor. Jane could immediately see why she wanted to sell the flat. She followed the woman up three flights of narrow stairs, and reaching the top floor, Mrs Taylor had to stand and gasp for breath.

'Are you all right?' Jane asked, concerned.

'Yes, I just get so breathless. I used to run up these stairs before I was pregnant . . . they never bothered me. But I've only a month to go and it feels like I'm carrying a sack of coal in front of me!'

Jane followed her into the hallway of the flat. It was mostly all white walls, newly painted. She showed Jane a small, well-equipped kitchen incorporating a dining area with high stools. Straight opposite was a bathroom with new bath, washbasin and toilet. It had fresh, flowered tiles, and a heated towel rail.

'My husband has just finished doing this place up. We've moved to our new house in Barnes so we're ready to sell and can exchange right away.'

Jane loved the flat. Although it was small, it was clean and bright, and the two bedrooms, one much larger than the other, were freshly painted and decorated with Laura Ashley wallpaper.

'That's it!' Mrs Taylor said, as Jane looked around the larger bedroom, which had fitted wardrobes.

Jane had hoped for a larger flat, with a communal sitting room. But this flat wouldn't need anything done to it, and she could rent out the smaller bedroom straightaway.

Jane enquired whether any of the furniture was included.

'Yes, everything! I mean, I'll be taking the bed linen, cutlery and china, but I'm leaving all the furniture as is. And it comes with a new washing machine, fitted fridge and cooker.'

Jane rang her father as soon as she returned to the section house and told him that she thought she had found the flat she wanted to buy.

Whilst she was at work the following day her father went to view it, and during her lunch break she called him to see what he thought.

'Well, you can't swing a cat in it . . . I mean, there's no dining room or sitting room, and it's quite a walk up. Your mother had to have a breather halfway.'

Jane hadn't realised her mother was also going to look at the flat. She doubted that Mrs Tennison would approve and was starting to feel disappointed, as her father continued discussing the finances.

'You know it's only a twenty-two year lease?'

'Yes, Daddy, but I think the price is fair, and it includes all the furniture . . .'

'There's no garden. It's a top floor and there isn't even a small balcony.'

'Yes, I know that . . . but it's close to Regent's Park.'

'And it's a bit too bloody close to that siege that went on in Balcombe Street, which is just up the road you know, Jane?'

'Yes, I do know that, Daddy, but the IRA are hardly likely to target the same area twice and the IRA gang were arrested and are awaiting trial . . .'

'Your mother wants to talk to you . . .'

Jane sighed, certain she would get a negative response.

'I like it, dear,' her mother said. 'It's so clean, and has lovely big windows so it's very light and airy. But don't you think it's going to be too small? I mean, you said you were going to need two bedrooms. You could make the big one into a sitting room, because otherwise you have nowhere to sit and watch the TV so, taking that into consideration, I think it will be too expensive to just be there on your own . . .'

Jane was forced to listen to her parents' pros and cons regarding the flat, as they handed over the phone from one to another. Eventually Jane had had enough.

'I like it and I prefer it to any other flat I've seen. I know it may be small, but it's ideal for me. I don't need much space.'

'Where will you park your car?' Mr Tennison asked.

'There's residents' parking outside the house, and when I don't need the car I can park it in the small lane behind your flat.'

'Well, that's fine by me. It's in a good position for the underground station and then Marylebone Station is just up the road. But I doubt you'll be able to rent out that small bedroom.'

Jane was becoming increasingly argumentative and now insisted that she wanted to go ahead.

'Well, it's £24,000, and with that short lease I'm not sure it's a good prospect. But I'll talk to the mortgage broker in the morning. We've made a file of your income and future earnings, and if I put down £10,000, let's see what they think about it.'

'That's very generous of you, Daddy.'

'Well, you'll eventually have to pay me back, but if you really want this flat then in the end it's your choice.'

As she put the phone down Jane felt relieved and grateful to her father.

'Everything all right, luv?' Edith asked.

'My father's OK about me buying the flat. I can't wait to move in and have my own independence . . . no more section house rules and regulations . . .'

'Well, don't get too excited yet, Jane, everything has to be signed on the dotted line before the purchase goes through.'

'I know, I know . . .'

'And then there's the police regulations to follow: your move must be approved by a Chief Super, neighbours have to be checked out for criminal records . . .'

'Yes, I know, Edith.' Jane sighed, wishing she hadn't said anything in the first place.

'And you need permission if you want to get married.'

'I've no intention of getting married yet, Edith, but I might take in a lodger.'

'Well, you'll need permission for that as well.'

'God, this job wants to know the ins and outs of everything, even my personal life.'

Edith put her straight, tapping the side of her nose. 'Listen, dear . . . it feels like they want to know the colour of your knickers, but just make sure it's all reported in line with police regulations.'

As she was about to leave the station, DCI Shepherd called Jane into his office again. He was quite abrupt, saying that he had been in talks with the team and the DCI heading up the Dip Squad at Vine Street Police Station, and she could start there immediately, from the beginning of the following week.

'You'll work with a splendid officer, DCI Church. There's about ten or twelve officers on his team and you'll work shifts, 9 to 5, mostly, or 2 to 10. I've arranged a six-month attachment and at the end of it the DCI will make the decision regarding whether you will continue with them or not.'

He stood up. 'Good luck, Tennison. I hope you'll find this attachment more to your liking. I've arranged for your replacement, a male officer, to start next Monday. You can spend the rest of this week completing any outstanding reports and paperwork.'

'I really appreciate this, sir. If my replacement needs me to go over anything whilst I'm still here then I will be only too pleased to do whatever is necessary.'

He shook her hand. 'I am sure he will be quite capable, Tennison.'
'Yes, sir.'

Instead of feeling excited by the prospect of joining the new team, she felt a little nervous and wondered if perhaps she had been overenthusiastic. DCI Shepherd's attitude had not been very positive, in fact the reverse. She had also noted that he had made it clear her replacement would be a male officer. But it was too late to change her mind now, so she concentrated her thoughts on arranging the final details of her mortgage with the bank and making the purchase of the flat.

Jane's last day finally arrived and Edith bought her a housewarming/leaving present of a tablecloth and matching napkins. It was thoughtful of her but Jane doubted she would ever use them, as the folding table in the kitchen had a Formica top.

'I'm going to miss you, Jane.' Edith said.

'I'll miss you too, Edith. You've always been such a good friend to me, and I hope we'll stay in touch.'

'I'm sure we will. Please keep me updated on how it's all going with the Dip Squad. When do you start?

'Next week. And tomorrow I'm picking up the keys to my new flat so it's going to be a busy weekend.'

Edith watched as Jane filled up a cardboard box with her personal items. She suspected that Jane would be in touch sooner than she expected, because from what she had heard about the unit, Jane was in for a big change. The Dip Squad sounded like a bunch of hooligans.

The next morning, Jane unlocked the door of number 33 and walked into the flat she now owned. Her parents were helping her move and she could hear them panting their way up the stairs with suitcases of clothes and the few boxes of personal items that she'd accumulated during her time at the section house. Jane walked into the small kitchen. The previous owner had put fresh flowers in a jam jar on the kitchen table, and had left milk, sugar and a loaf of bread on the side. She'd also left Jane a note wishing her good luck and hoping that she would like living in the flat as much as she had.

Eventually her parents left and Jane was alone for the first time in her new home. She carried her suitcase into the bedroom and sat down on the bare mattress on the bed. She hugged herself, feeling sure she had made the right decision.

CHAPTER ONE

Jane arrived in plenty of time at Vine Street Police Station, in the heart of London's West End, for her nine o'clock meeting with her new DCI. The Vice Squad also worked out of Vine Street, but on a different floor, while the much larger Flying Squad was based at Scotland Yard. The duty sergeant directed her downstairs. She walked past the station cells and charge room area, then down the old stone steps and into the darkened basement. A door was ajar with DIP SQUAD printed on a card pinned on it. She hesitated and then knocked. Getting no reply, she gently pushed the door open, to reveal a large, dank, squalid room. A string of worn desks, typewriters on a couple of them, ran across the room, and along one wall was a row of battered filing cabinets. The only window, high in the wall, was tiny and covered in cobwebs. It looked as if it had never been opened.

'Are you WDC Tennison?'

Jane whirled around to face a tall, angular man wearing a full-length leather coat, polo-neck sweater and baggy trousers with a thick leather belt at the waist, walking out of a small office in the corner.

'Yes.'

'Bit early, aren't you?' He shook her hand. 'I'm DCI Jimmy Church. Take a pew and let me fill you in.' DCI Church spoke with a northern accent and chain-smoked, lighting one cigarette from the other as he moved around the room. He picked up an overflowing ashtray and emptied the butts into a waste bin as he spoke. 'The team are usually out nicking dippers, so this office is often empty. We work all over London, but we bring any arrests back here to Vine Street to be processed and charged. The team here consists of me, plus two detective sergeants who each have a team of four detectives working with them. We don't have any clerical staff, so we take reports for typing up to the main Flying Squad office at the Yard. Bit of a drag, but it's only a fifteen-minute walk. Or we use the one unmarked car we have.

'Oh . . .' Jane said, trying to take it all in.

Church turned at the sound of voices and heavy footsteps coming down the stone steps outside the office.

'Here come the lads!' He grinned. Jane was astonished at how much more youthful Church appeared when he smiled, his heavily lined face immediately lighting up.

The officers, who were all male, piled into the room. All of them wore worn-looking jeans and bomber jackets, and most had long hair and sideburns. They spread out sitting on the odd chair or perched on one or other of the desks. She recognised DS Stanley, who she'd worked with before, but the others were new to her.

'This is WDC Joan Tennison everybody.'

'It's Jane,' Jane said, as Church cocked his head to one side.

'Sorry. *Jane* Tennison. OK, that little wiry DS over there, who looks like the cat just dragged him in, is Stanley –'

'We worked together a long time ago at Hackney,' Stanley said, nodding to Jane. He still wore fingerless gloves and was even scruffier than she remembered, looking as if he had slept in a park somewhere.

'And that's DS George Maynard.' Church nodded at a well-built officer who was putting a stick of chewing gum in his mouth. He was dressed in a huge duffel coat, dirty trainers and jeans.

'Maynard plays drunk better than a drunk,' Church added.

Jane smiled at Maynard and was rewarded with a cursory nod.

Church gestured with his lit cigarette towards the rest of the group. 'You can get to know the other reprobates later.'

Jane doubted that she would be able to remember all their names on her first day and realised that the Dip Squad, like the glamorous Flying Squad, had no female officers apart from her.

She wondered if the Dip Squad might not be such an attractive proposition after all.

'Right, before we get into what's going down today, let me remind you all that the forthcoming Scotland Yard Detective Squad's big annual black-tie dinner dance is only a couple of weeks away . . . Good Friday, 16 April, at St Ermin's Hotel. You can't miss it – it's in Caxton Street, right opposite Scotland Yard. If you don't have your tickets booked then you'd better get onto it, or you'll lose out.'

Jane watched as a few of them handed cash over to Church. A couple said they would pay by cheque.

A young DC held his hand up. 'It's a bank holiday, isn't it, Guv? Only I was booked to go on a fishing trip . . . can't they change the date?'

'Don't be an idiot, Mead! It's always on Good Friday because it *is* a bank holiday, and the squads are at minimum strength over the holiday weekend. Just cancel your bloody fishing trip . . . it's a right knees-up, and worth getting your dickie bow out for.'

Church handed out some crime reports detailing theft incidents on the Underground and in the busy shopping areas around Oxford Street and Regent Street.

'As you can see, the descriptions of possible suspects are pretty poor and most of the victims didn't even know they'd been dipped until it was too late . . .'

Jane was flicking through the crime reports, trying to take in all the information, then realised that Church had stopped talking and, along with everyone else in the room, was looking at her.

'Sorry?'

'Tennison, just concentrate and read the reports in your own time.' He addressed the room again. 'This bunch are obviously professionals, possibly from abroad. They're working in a group of around four to six people, and their marks tend to be the wealthier-looking members of the public.'

He turned to Jane. 'D'you know what a "mark" is Tennison?'

'The intended victim, sir,' Jane replied.

'Correct. Now, start counting to ten . . .'

Jane felt embarrassed and suspected she was about to be the butt of an initiation joke.

'Come on, don't be shy,' Stanley said, nudging her.

She started counting aloud and as she reached number six she felt someone push her from behind, causing her to stumble forward. Stanley grabbed her left arm to catch her, and she heard several chuckles from the other officers. She turned around to face the huge DS Maynard.

'What did you do that for? It's not funny.'

'Carry on counting,' Maynard said, with a serious expression.

'What?'

'From where you left off.'

'Um . . . four, five . . .'

Church interrupted. 'You'd got up to six.'

Jane looked at him. 'Had I? Sorry . . . six, seven . . .'

Maynard pushed her gently on the shoulder. Jane turned back to him sharply.

'Would you please stop pushing me!'

Maynard was holding up her warrant card.

'Is this yours?'

Confused, Jane hurriedly unzipped her handbag to discover that her warrant card was missing. As Maynard handed it back to her, Stanley asked, 'What's the time?'

Jane glanced at her left wrist and found that her watch was missing.

Everyone laughed as Stanley held up her watch, swinging it like a pendulum.

'Tick tock . . .'

Jane was shocked. 'How did you get that . . . and my warrant card?'

Church took her watch from Stanley and pulled up her shirt sleeve to replace it on her wrist.

'Your mind can only properly focus on one thing at a time. Clever pickpockets distract their marks whilst simultaneously lifting their wallet, purse or watch. The targets don't notice at the time because they're too focused on the distraction. It takes a thief to catch a thief, Tennison, and we practice what the bad guys do . . . but only on each other. It keeps us on our toes. I like to think of myself as Fagin, and these reprobates are my little pickpockets.'

There was a unanimous groan from the squad. Stanley jovially twanged his red braces and launched into the song from *Oliver!*, 'Consider yourself . . .' Church gave him a good-natured swipe across the head.

'All right, all right, Dodger, just calm down. I'm going to need you all to step out to the yard and do a little bit of "bump and lift" work for Tennison to observe. I'll organise some teas all round and a few sandwiches whilst we're out there.'

Jane was, in fact, observing how attractive DCI Church was, and noticed how much respect he had from the squad.

As they herded out of the room, a tall, baby-faced officer stood beside Jane.

'Don't worry, I'm pretty new to all this as well. I'm DC Dunston, but they all call me Blondie.'

Jane thought he might be trying to distract her, and held her handbag tight to her side and checked her watch.

'What's bump and lift?' she asked.

'Sounds like a dance, doesn't it? It's the action Stanley and Maynard pulled on you earlier. Maynard distracted you with the push and when Stanley stopped you falling you thought he was helping you. He put pressure on your upper arm, again distracting you, then with his free hand he flicked your watch strap undone and slipped it from your wrist. At the same time, Maynard unzipped your handbag and took your warrant card.'

'It all happened so quickly.'

'That's the way the dippers operate on the streets. This type of theft is a combination of distraction and misdirection, which gives the pickpocket just enough time to make the lift and walk away. If you think Stanley and Maynard were fast, the real dippers are like lightning . . .'

Jane nodded. 'I'm certainly going to be wary when I'm out shopping from now on.'

They headed up a heavily worn stone staircase towards the back exit to the station yard.

Blondie continued, 'There's a lot to learn about the different distraction techniques and hand movements they use. There's bump, grab and slip, fake lifts, oops sorry, and –'

'Is there some sort of manual that I can read?' Jane asked.

'No manual as such, but I've made my own list of distraction techniques and methods that the pickpockets use. You can have a copy if you want,' Blondie offered as he held the back door open for her.

'Thanks, that would be really helpful.'

'The difficult part to follow is when one of the gang makes a lift and passes the goods to a "runner", who then makes off with the property . . . sometimes they'll pass a wallet or purse three or four times . . . it can be like a "guess who" game, and sometimes you end up stopping a suspect who's empty-handed.'

They reached a small, stone-flagged yard surrounded by a high red-brick wall, with paint-peeled double gates and a run-down bicycle shed next to a row of aluminium dustbins.

'It's all much more complicated than I ever imagined. Do the suspects resist arrest?'

'Sometimes. You need to be careful of the pickpockets who carry small razor blades to cut a rear pocket or handbag open. The cut is made against a wallet or handbag so the mark usually doesn't feel a thing.'

Jane remembered an old case she'd been involved in.

'At my previous station we had a bag-slasher who was using a switchblade. Is that the kind of weapon your pickpockets would use?'

'Most pickpockets avoid using switchblades or flick knives ... I know of only one occasion where an officer was cut, and that was just on his hand, by a razor blade. All in all, it's interesting work and nicking a good team of pickpockets is really rewarding. Keeps Church happy if we get good results.'

An officer appeared with a tray of polystyrene cups and shouted 'Tea's up'. Maynard started to hand Jane a half-filled cup of tea. As she reached out to take it, he said. 'We're all having a break now, but here's a word of warning: when you're out working never be caught with a cup of anything in your hand. Let me show you why.'

Maynard gently bumped into Jane, causing some of the contents of her teacup to spill out. She immediately reached into her pocket for a tissue to mop it up, but Maynard produced a large handkerchief and started to pat down her jacket.

Stanley interjected. 'Oh, come on, Maynard. Let's get on with the real demonstrations. Tennison, just take it that you never carry any drinks whilst you're on the job ... it's the easiest way for a pickpocket to distract and pinch the contents of your coat or jacket pockets whilst they are patting you dry.'

Church clapped his hands saying that the break was over, and it was time to demonstrate the various methods of distraction and misdirection. Although he was serious about the training there were several funny moments when officers, who took turns playing the mark, were oblivious to the fact that their wallet had been stolen. This was usually achieved by Stanley, who was the most adept at 'dipping', concealing his hand movements with a folded newspaper.

Jane was not the only victim. The team seemed to take great pleasure in removing Blondie's wallet, not once but three times. When Stanley accidently dropped some loose change on the floor,

Jane, without thinking, bent over to help pick up the coins. Whilst she was kneeling on the ground, Maynard stole Jane's purse from her handbag.

'I know what you've done,' Jane said, raising her eyes upwards.

Maynard held his huge hands up, saying, 'Search me! Search me!' Jane watched as Stanley made a rugby pass of her leather coin purse across the yard, to be caught by Church on the other side. He held it up.

'OK, fun's over. Let's get back inside.' Church handed Jane her purse.

Inside, Church showed her a covert radio, which they would be using when they went out on the streets.

'You have to learn how to listen. Stick with Stanley today to learn the basics. Here's a list of the radio terms you need to memorise for future jobs.' Church handed her a rather dirty page of typed radio terminology. Jane barely had time to glance at it before he continued, 'You'll be going on a surveillance operation this morning. We work it that when the suspect is in position and looks ready to jostle and do the business, such as nick a wallet or whatever, we move in so he's surrounded and nicked as soon as he commits the theft. But, in this instance it's an ongoing case: we're looking out for our suspect's pals as they're working in a team, and we need to act fast to see who he's palming off the gear to. I won't be satisfied with just bringing in one of them. We all have concealed radios, so we cross communicate during the follow, and when the arrest takes place, we've got a wagon on standby. If it's a good arrest, often the intended victim hasn't a clue what just happened. Are you with me?'

'Er, yes, sir, I do understand . . . I had to study powers of arrest in my probation. I'm just wondering if you're going to use me as some kind of decoy, being that I'm the only female on the team?'

Everyone laughed at Jane's remark as Church picked up the report sheet he had been handing out.

'Before we can use you as a decoy, you need to get up to speed on exactly how we work, Tennison. I hope there'll be plenty of opportunities in the future for us to use your feminine attributes . . .

'We've got this guy in our sights and he's been nicking gear left, right and centre. Yesterday, Stanley was able to confirm that it's a three-man unit. So, we're going to use all our tactics to nab the lot of them. First up, we need to find today's victim. The thieves seem to work around midday at Oxford Street underground station or during evening rush hour. That means access to shoppers with money . . . you got that big exclusive store, Liberty, on the corner, and tourists shelling out big money all along Regent Street.'

'Do you have any surveillance pictures or mugshots of the suspects I can have?' Jane asked.

Again, there was laughter amongst the team.

'That's not how the Dip Squad works, Tennison! There're loads of mugshots in that big album on the desk, far too many to carry round with us. It takes time, but we memorise photographs and descriptions, then go by eyeball on the street. You've got to understand that these guys work in a team. You can see them stalling or distracting a victim . . . they could have a newspaper concealing their hands, or you can have one of them acting like a helpful stranger whilst their mate is nicking gear out of the victim's handbag. They can get a watch off your wrist and you wouldn't feel a thing. Give her a description of the bloke you got a look at, Stanley.'

'I'd say he could be Spanish or Italian. He had dark, greasy hair, with shifty eyes and bad acne. He wears a big double-breasted overcoat and thick crêpe-soled shoes. He can move like lightning.'

Church clapped his hands. 'OK, Stanley, take our new girl out with you and your guys and meet up back here when you've got them bang to rights.'

Accompanied by Stanley, Maynard and two other officers, Jane left the squalid office. She thought they would be using a patrol car to drive to their destination but instead they caught a bus. She was now beginning to have severe doubts about what she had got herself into. The Dip Squad acted like day trippers. They laughed and joked with each other at the bus stop, and when they got on board and herded up the stairs to sit on the top deck, Stanley squashed into a seat beside her. He had overpowering BO and looked so scruffy that Jane had a moment of horror that someone she knew might get on the bus and wonder what on earth she was doing sitting beside a tramp.

'You seen anything of Spencer Gibbs since his Hackney days?' Stanley asked, rolling a cigarette.

'Not for a while. He was at Bow Street, we worked together on a murder, but he was transferred whilst I was on my CID course.'

'I heard he was getting pissed every night.'

'No, he wasn't. I mean, you were there . . . you know the terrible events at Hackney hit him badly. He was very close to DCI Bradfield.'

'Yeah, that was a bad time – and as for that lovely Kath Morgan . . . At least we got the bastards. Clifford Bentley went down for thirty years. He'll die inside. Good riddance.'

Jane nodded as Stanley licked his cigarette paper.

'So, what brings you to the Dip Squad? What fuck-up got you foisted on us?'

She straightened in her seat.

'No fuck-up, actually . . . I asked to be transferred. I was told that it could be a way into the Flying Squad.'

Stanley laughed. 'Yeah, and pigs might fly, sweetheart! You're only with us because we need a good-looking stooge to attract dippers. Added to that, the blokes on this unit are ahead of you in the pecking order. Well, most of them. Some got moved to the Dip Squad from the Sweeney because of one screw-up after another . . .' He saw the disappointment on her face and added in a gentler tone, 'We get better overtime in the Dip Squad, anyway.'

Stanley lit his roll-up, then stuck it in the side of his mouth as he checked his radio's speaker and told Jane to double-check hers.

'A lot of our equipment is bloody useless and outdated. Flying Squad gets the new gear and we get their hand-me-downs.'

Jane glanced at him. 'How come you're with the Dip Squad?'

'Rapped over the knuckles, darlin', for being a naughty boy. Besides, I like Jimmy Church – I rate him. But a word of warning: don't get on the wrong side of him . . . and his sidekick, DS George Maynard, is also a piece of work. You think it's his duffel coat making him look well built, but he's solid muscle underneath it, and he can throw one hell of a punch.'

Jane was desperately trying to take it all on board, and wasn't sure how to respond. Stanley turned away from her as if he didn't want to talk anymore, his roll-up cigarette still stuck between his lips, getting damper and smaller. Why on earth had she left the relative comforts of Bow Street?

After half an hour they piled off the bus in Regent Street and made their way towards Oxford Circus underground station. Jane thought they could have walked there faster. The four of them kept their distance from one another as they looked up and down the street for any suspects. Stanley was next to Jane when he spoke over his radio.

'Looks like a male suspect from our mugshots heading down into the Underground. Early twenties, tanned face, dark-haired, unshaven, wearing a leather coat.'

Jane pressed her radio earpiece further into her left ear, and checked the mouthpiece was securely attached to her wrist – the wires were hidden along her jacket sleeve and attached to the radio in her pocket.

Stanley nudged her. 'Radios are bloody useless in the Underground, we go by hand signals, just stick close to me, OK?'

Jane nodded as she followed Stanley down into the Underground. They flashed their warrant cards to the ticket guard, who let them through, and moved on to the escalator, with the other two officers close behind. The southbound Central line platform was so crowded with passengers waiting for the next train, it was hard to see through the throng of people as they moved along the platform, keeping their distance from the suspect.

Jane glanced around cautiously and saw the suspect moving in behind a well-dressed man in an unbuttoned camel coat, carrying a briefcase. The man had just taken out a thick wallet and checked something before replacing it inside his coat pocket. Stanley looked at his colleagues, nodded, then touched his eye with his index finger and discreetly pointed to the suspect.

One of the other officers repeated the same signals to Stanley and Jane as a young, tanned, dark-haired man with acne wearing a leather coat slipped in casually to stand beside the target. Jane spotted him glance almost imperceptibly to his right, where an older, grey-haired man in an expensive-looking black raincoat was also moving slowly towards the target. Each undercover officer discreetly confirmed they had eyeballed these three men as possible dippers.

Even though she was watching for it, Jane almost didn't see the dip. As the unshaven man in the leather coat jostled the victim and lifted his wallet, his two sidekicks moved in, ready to palm it. Stanley and his team stepped in to collar them. The victim, surprised by their sudden appearance, dropped his briefcase. An approaching train screeched in the tunnel, and Jane found herself being pushed backwards by the crowd towards the tracks. She teetered on the edge of the platform as a train thundered towards her. Stanley saw her at the last minute and dragged her to safety.

As the train came to a halt and passengers began to stream onto the platform, it became clear that the pincer move had gone astray. The other officers chased after the two younger suspects but the grey-haired man in the black raincoat managed to get onto the train. The doors closed behind him before Stanley or Jane could fight free of the crowd.

Stanley turned to the badly shaken Jane.

'What the hell do you think you were doing? Haven't you got any bloody sense? You should never stand with your back to the tracks!'

'I'm sorry. I thought they were going to steal his briefcase when he put it down on the platform . . .'

'They were after his wallet, Tennison! I thought, after seeing all those demos in the yard earlier, you'd understand what we were doing? Thanks to you, we've now lost the guy who was probably running this show . . . that grey-haired man in the black raincoat was our prime suspect.'

Stanley ran his hands through his hair in frustration. His expression cleared a little. 'Well, I expect the team have arrested the other two, and I am sure they'll have retrieved the stolen wallet. No thanks to you, Tennison. DCI Church is not going to be a happy man.'

Jane was crestfallen. 'Sorry, Stanley.'

'We'll get the victim back to the station and take his statement.'

The pickpockets' mark, Clive Hughes, was from a wealthy family. His wallet held over a hundred pounds, as well as quite a few credit cards. Jane asked him to tell her exactly what had happened, but he hadn't noticed anything untoward, or felt a thing, and he had no idea how they had managed to steal his wallet.

'Can you describe any of the men who were standing next to you just before the train arrived and we moved in to make the arrests?'

'No.'

'Did you feel anyone bump into you?'

'Not really. The platform was busy and people were all squashed together.' He paused, then smiled.

'There was an attractive girl in a mini skirt and low-cut top in front of me. She turned to look at me as if I'd done something to upset her. I felt rather embarrassed . . .'

'Embarrassed? Why?'

'Well, it was as if she thought I had deliberately brushed up against her . . .'

'Did you brush up against her, Mr Hughes?'

'No! I didn't. I don't know why, but I said I was sorry and she gave me a warm smile.'

Jane thought about the incident at the underground station. Church had said at the briefing that the dippers usually worked in groups of four to six, yet they had only seen three men acting suspiciously and jointly making the theft. She wondered if the team had been distracted by concentrating on the three men.

'Can you describe the woman to me in a bit more detail?'

'D'you think she might be part of the gang that stole my wallet?'

'I don't know for sure, but it's possible that she deliberately distracted you while the others moved in to make the lift.'

'Oh, my goodness! She was about 5'6", very young-looking, maybe late teens, with long dark hair. She was tanned . . . sort of olive-skinned. She was wearing a black mini skirt and low-cut white blouse, with a hip-length fur jacket, which was undone.'

Jane glanced up from her notebook. Clive Hughes seemed to have a detailed recollection of the girl.

'Her fur jacket was undone?'

'Deliberately, I suppose, to reveal her cleavage.'

'Did she say anything to you?'

'No, not a word.'

When Jane returned to the Dip Squad office, Stanley and Maynard had become frustrated. Their suspect, who had been wearing the heavy leather coat, was refusing to talk. However, they had discovered hidden pockets throughout the lining of his coat containing watches, jewellery, wallets and other trinkets that had all been stolen. Blondie Dunston was instructed to list all the stolen goods, while the younger dark-haired suspect with acne was given a good grilling. Stanley was slapping him around the back of the head.

'I know you can speak English otherwise you wouldn't be able to find your way around the Underground or buy a ticket . . . so, stop fucking us about, and tell us where the guy in the black raincoat has pissed off to.'

'*No hablo ingles, Señor.*'

Stanley looked at Maynard.

'If we know where he's from we could get an interpreter in.'

'That's just going to waste more time . . . he's pissing us about. Aren't you?'

'*Yo no hablo inglés, Señor.*'

'Is he Spanish? He sounds Spanish,' Maynard muttered.

'*Español*?' Stanley asked.

'Colombia,' the suspect replied.

Stanley pushed his face in front of the young man. 'Oh, a lying thief *and* a drug dealer then!'

'*Yo no soy traficante de drogas . . . Yo no soy un ladrón.*'

Maynard slapped him again. 'Stop speaking the Dago language . . . Speakee de English so we understand. *You* understand?'

Stanley raised his hand to slap the suspect, but Jane interjected. She had witnessed her male colleagues physically assaulting prisoners before but she never understood why they resorted to violence – it never seemed to get them the information they wanted.

'Colombians speak Spanish. He said he's not a drug dealer or a thief.'

There was silence in the room. Both men turned, looked at Jane with surprise and spoke in unison.

'You speak Spanish?'

'A little. I did it for A level, but it's been a few years now . . . I'm nowhere near fluent.'

'Well, I'm sure he can understand you, so start asking what we need to know . . .'

'You'd be better off getting an interpreter,' Jane replied.

'We need answers right now. If we get an address there could be tons of nicked gear there. We'd clear up loads of pickpocket thefts, and it'd be a good result for the team. We need to find the older guy in the raincoat. Thanks to your near miss with the train, he got clean away.'

Maynard, like Stanley, was annoyed with Jane. He turned to the suspect.

'You obviously just understood what my colleague said about being a drug dealer so I'll ask you again, you piece of shit . . . where is all the nicked gear and where's your older mate?'

Jane moved in between the suspect and Maynard. She spoke slowly.

'*Cuál es su nombre*?'

'Miguel Hernandez.'

'Miguel . . . um . . . *sabemos que había una señorita joven contigo.*'

The suspect reacted, looking nervous, and avoided eye contact with Jane. Stanley nudged her.

'Whatever you just said got to him.'

'I told him we know there was a young woman working with him.'

'What're you talking about, Tennison? It was three *men*!' Stanley shouted. 'And thanks to you one of them got away.'

Jane handed Stanley Clive Hughes' statement.

'Read the last paragraph, Stanley. I'd say the woman is part of the gang and was used to distract the victim so the others could dip him.'

'You saying we're all blind?' Maynard asked, angrily.

'No, I'm saying the platform was so busy we were all concentrating on the mark and the three male suspects . . . so we missed the female.'

Jane bent down and, placing her fingers under the suspect's chin, raised it so she had direct eye contact with him.

'*Estos hombres seguirán lastimándote . . . dime dónde está la mujer y el otro hombre y se detendrá . . .*'

The suspect looked Jane in the eye and was close to tears. She had told him that the officers would continue to hurt him, but if he told her the whereabouts of the girl and the other man they would stop. The suspect said nothing and sat looking up at Maynard as he stepped forward with his hand raised. Miguel winced in anticipation but Jane held up her hand to stop Maynard.

'Let him talk . . .'

There was a brief pause, then Miguel looked at Jane.

'*Gracias, señorita.*'

'*Habla usted inglés*, Miguel?'

'Yes, I speak leeetle English.'

'Good. Was there a girl with you?'

'*Sí* . . . She my sister, Regina. They say if we no help them then they hurt us.'

Jane pulled up a chair to sit next to Miguel.

'We can help you and your sister, but in return you have to help us.'

It wasn't long before Miguel revealed that he and his fifteen-year-old sister, Regina, had been brought to London by their uncle, Andres Hernandez, on the promise of employment and somewhere to live. Andres had subsequently taken all their money, and their passports, and was now forcing them to steal for him.

After further lengthy, and tedious, interrogation, Miguel was put into a cell whilst DCI Church was given an update. As he listened to them and glanced through their notes he looked up at Jane.

'Well, that was a right fuck-up this afternoon, wasn't it, Tennison? On your first day you nearly get swept under a train and we lose our number one suspect! Have we got an address for this uncle?' Church asked Stanley.

'Yes, it's in the interview notes. Miguel said that the uncle owned the house they were living in. It's in Shepherd's Bush, not far from the flyover and near Portobello Road. If these guys are professional dippers, then Portobello Market would be the perfect location to offload their stolen goods. When we ran a check on the uncle, Andres Hernandez, it turned out he's wanted for aggravated burglary and a brutal sexual assault eighteen months ago. So, we've already got a file on him . . . he's a nasty customer. Miguel is terrified about his uncle finding out that he's talking to us . . . he's very concerned for his young sister's safety.'

'I don't believe a word these dagos say. That girl's probably not even his sister,' Maynard retorted.

'I disagree,' Jane replied. 'I think Miguel is telling the truth, and if his sister is only fifteen then she's vulnerable and we need to find her.'

Church interjected. 'We've now got grounds to get a search warrant, and find this girl . . . as well as a shedload of nicked stuff. This is sounding much more promising. Perhaps your first day hasn't been such a total disaster after all, Tennison.'

'Thank you, sir . . .'

'Don't thank me yet. Go back to your boyfriend and get him to give us a diagram of the floorplan of the house in Shepherd's Bush. Then he can show us where it is.'

Church turned to Dunston and handed him the interview notes.

'Blondie, get over to Bow Street Court and get a search warrant from the magistrate for the address Miguel Hernandez gave us . . . then we'll pay this uncle a surprise visit.'

CHAPTER TWO

By early evening the whole team were in Shepherd's Bush. Miguel's information had brought them to a rundown premises situated above a seedy Moroccan café. From where she stood across the road with the rest of the Dip Squad, Jane could see it was lit inside by red paper lanterns and decorated with a garish Middle Eastern carpet. The charity shop next door had been boarded up. A notice hanging on the graffiti-daubed boards read NO JUNK MAIL – OPEN AT WEEKENDS ONLY.

Two patrol cars pulled up by the group. Handcuffed, Miguel sat fretfully in the back seat of the front car looking out at his uncle's building.

Stanley leant through the front passenger window to talk to Church. 'According to my Moroccan friend who runs the café there, an older man entered the premises at around 4.30 p.m. As you can see, there are lights on in the first and second floors. There's a back yard, but it belongs to this junk shop . . . and is full of junk. Fire safety would have a field day here . . . there's no fire escape or back exit. The only way in and out is through the front door.'

Church turned around to look at Miguel in the back seat. 'When you open the main front door and go up the stairs, is there another door at the top of the stairs?'

Miguel looked blankly back at him.

'Front door . . . stairs . . .' Church mimed a stair-climbing action with his fingers. 'Second door?'

'No . . . only front door,' Miguel replied.

Church opened the passenger door and climbed out of the patrol car.

'Stanley, see if you can gain entry. Jane, Blondie, Maynard . . . I want you to follow me.'

He instructed the other Dip Squad officers to wait in place outside until the first group had gone in. Stanley jemmied open the front door. The threadbare brown carpet on the steep wooden stairs muffled the sound of their steps as they moved upwards. When they reached the top of the staircase they could hear the muted sound of a television set.

Church shouted: 'Go, go, go! This is the police! Stay where you are! I have a search warrant for these premises.'

A startled man appeared in the doorway of a room at the end of the corridor and quickly retreated as Stanley, Church and Maynard rushed towards him. Dunston pushed open the nearest bedroom door, with Jane behind him. The scene that confronted them shocked Jane to the core. Regina was tied to a bed, naked and gagged, her hands bound together to the metal bedstead and her legs tied apart so they were open. The man who had escaped from them in the Underground was having sex with Regina. He quickly rolled off her, hampered by his trousers and underpants, still halfway down his legs.

Jane was sickened by what she saw. Enraged, she ran at the semi-dressed man, kicking him as hard as she could in the groin. He collapsed in agony onto his knees, raising one hand in a plea for her to stop, but she kicked him again. Dunston pulled Jane to one side.

'That's enough, Jane. He's scum and ain't worth getting in trouble over.'

Dunston quickly handcuffed the suspect, dragging him out of the room. Jane went swiftly over to the bed to untie Regina, who was writhing in terror and attempting to scream through her gag.

'Bloody hell – it's all going on in here,' Maynard said. He and Stanley were standing in the doorway, taking in the scene. 'Church has just arrested Andres Hernandez at the end of the corridor.'

'Get out . . . Get out!' Jane screamed, still struggling with Regina's bonds. Released from her gag, the girl was in floods of tears.

'Back off, you two!' Church said sternly behind Maynard and Stanley.

When Jane released her, Regina didn't move; she was clearly in a state of shock. Jane sat on the bed next to her and gently wrapped a blanket around the young girl's shoulders.

'It's OK,' she said. '*Está bien*, Regina. You're safe now. We are police officers . . . *policía, somos la policía.* Those men won't ever touch you again . . . *Esos hombres no te tocarán nunca más.*'

Regina was in no condition to speak, but Jane could tell from the way she clung to her that the girl knew she was safe in Jane's arms.

Back at Vine Street, Church wanted everything done by the book. He, like Jane, had been shocked by what Regina had been subjected too. He was not a man who revealed his emotions easily, but he took time to talk to Miguel and reassure him that his sister was safe.

Jane took Regina to the medical examination room and called for a female police doctor to examine her. She made the girl a hot cup of coffee and left her safely with a uniformed WPC whilst she returned to the Dip Squad office to start making out her report.

Church was sitting at his desk and glanced towards her.

'You all right? Dunston told me you lost it in there.'

'Yes, sir . . . I just . . . She's only fifteen years old, sir . . . I shouldn't have reacted like I did.'

'No, you shouldn't have. But the offender hasn't complained; it's done and forgotten as far as I'm concerned. Anyways, I had a word with the Deputy Assistant Commissioner to ask him to personally contact the Colombian Embassy. They are going to send an embassy official to the station to speak with Miguel Hernandez and see if we can secure temporary safe accommodation for her with the family of a resident diplomat.'

'Can we arrange for her brother to see her?'

'He's being held in the cells, Tennison . . . I might be able to get her off any charges, but I can't do anything about him.'

At that moment, Stanley walked in carrying a large evidence bag.

'Guv, we've finished searching the Hernandez flat . . . We found drug paraphernalia, a lot of money, stolen credit cards, as well as two more addresses for premises we believe Andres Hernandez also owns.'

'Bloody hell! We're going to have paperwork coming out of our ears with this one.'

'Not necessarily, Guv,' Stanley responded. 'Take a look at what we found under the floorboards.'

Stanley pulled a bundle of passports out of the evidence bag, splaying them out like a deck of cards in front of Church. 'These belong to fourteen different girls, all under the age of sixteen. This has to be handed over to Vice now . . . it's no longer Dip Squad territory.'

'Nice one, Stanley. Thank Christ for that. Vice can deal with all the paperwork now. We just need to follow procedure with the arrested suspects for the pickpocket charges, then they can go up in front of the magistrates. And we don't need to worry about Regina's rapist after you dealt with him, Tennison . . . that's one hell of a right foot you've got. But you'd better stop making a habit of this . . . I know what happened when you were a decoy.'

Jane had a flashback to the time when she had been acting as a decoy in London Fields, Hackney. A man had attacked her, with intent to rape, and she had never forgotten the feeling of violation.

'You'd better get on with completing your report and you can make the bail objections at court tomorrow morning.'

As Jane and Stanley left Church's office she felt flattered to have been trusted with this task, but at the same time wasn't at all sure how to make out the objection to bail, as she was not certain exactly what it should be.

'Stanley, this bail objection . . . could you just fill me in on what's required?'

'Sorry, luv, I'm off to the pub to celebrate. Ask Blondie. He'll tell you what you need to write. Oh, and photocopy these girls' passports for our records; they might also be dippers.' He handed her the wad of passports and walked off.

Jane copied the passports first and left them on Stanley's desk with the copies. With Dunston's help, she spent the next hour writing out the report for the arrests they had made. She thanked him, and as it was now after eight in the evening, she said she would head off home.

'I wouldn't if I were you. The team will be expecting you at the pub. I'll walk you over there . . . and be prepared for getting some stick.'

'Do you know what time I should be at court in the morning?'

'No, but call in first thing. Just make sure you've got all the paperwork.'

Jane hesitated. She was unsure whether she could take police documents home with her, but as Dunston didn't appear concerned she picked up all the reports and put them in her briefcase.

The favoured watering hole for the Dip Squad was the Snug Bar at the Dog and Duck, an ornate Victorian building with lavish interior tiling and grand gold-leafed mirrors. As Blondie Dunston had predicted, she was the butt of all their jokes. DCI Church laughed as Stanley relayed how Jane had nearly been 'squashed like a fly under the oncoming train'.

'Well, Tennison, you know the train drivers on the Underground get time off for a jumper. Here you go, have another glass of wine on me.'

Jane took the stream of repetitive jokes about how she had fouled up on her first day and almost ended up under a train. Whilst they were all getting plastered, especially Stanley, she made her escape.

Jane was exhausted after her first day, but on returning to her flat she immediately felt better. It made such a huge difference to have a place of her own to go home to. She had just run a bath, and was wearing her dressing gown, when the phone rang. The sound took her by surprise, but then she smiled, realising that it was her own phone.

'Jane? It's Edith. How did your first day go?'

'It could have been better . . . I think I'll have a lot to learn. It's very different from Bow Street. I was on an arrest of two pickpockets, and I'll be taking the case to court tomorrow.'

'Oh, jolly good. Now listen, I know you advertised a room in *The Job*. Have you had any takers?'

'Well, I've been out all day and didn't get back until quite late, so there's nobody yet.'

'Listen, dear, you really need to monitor any applicants. And if there are no takers then you should put an advert up at one of the colleges close to your flat. You don't want anyone too old, or too young, and you need to make a list of questions to ask them, especially about their diet . . . God forbid you should get a vegan moving in! And check if they have boyfriends. You don't want a man moving in at weekends as well, because that's what happens . . . You need to make firm rules, no visitors . . . it's best to make sure they are single and employed. And you must get references, as well as six weeks' rent in advance. Plus you'll need to declare any lodgers to the Met, as I told you . . .'

Jane tried her best to absorb all of Edith's suggestions and, when she could get a word in edgeways, promised that when she had time she would make a list to have ready when interviewing any applicants.

'I'm glad you called, Edith.'

'That's all right, dear. Truth be told, I miss you. A very young DC has taken over from you, and thinks he knows everything . . . Smart Alec type.'

Jane was eager to go and have a bath but Edith seemed unwilling to end the call.

'How's your mother?' Jane asked

'Oh, much the same. I had porridge all over the kitchen this morning . . . she really is such a trial. Now she won't eat the dinner

I brought in . . . it's cold salmon with salad, and she wants mashed potatoes and gravy . . . Anyway, dear, it's been good to talk to you. Just you remember to be careful about who you let your room out to. Remember the IRA were only just around the corner from you, in that terrible siege . . . they killed an officer last February as well, you know. So make sure that whoever you are considering as a flatmate gets vetted by the Met.'

'I will. Thank you for calling, Edith.'

Jane replaced the receiver and went into her bathroom. The truth was that she enjoyed being on her own, and liked the freedom of being able to walk around naked if she wanted to. But the mortgage wouldn't pay itself – she would have to rent out the spare bedroom. She decided she would take Edith's advice and check out the nearest colleges in the morning, and perhaps even put an advert up in the local newsagents.

CHAPTER THREE

Jane ate breakfast in her dressing gown, then put on a suit and a clean, pressed shirt. She coiled her hair into a pleat and, on looking in the mirror, was satisfied that she was smart enough for her court appearance. It wasn't even seven yet, so she thought she would contact the Dip Squad at Vine Street to find out if they had a more accurate time schedule for her to be at the court. She dialled the number for the station, but the phone rang without anyone answering. She wasn't sure whether she should go to Vine Street or straight to Bow Street Court, so decided to wait and then try calling again. Whilst she was waiting she put together an advert, writing it out neatly on two cards – one for the newsagents and, remembering Edith's advice, one to pin up at one of the nearest colleges.

It was almost seven forty-five when she called the station again. This time the phone was answered by a gruff voice, which she recognised as Stanley's. Jane asked him if there had been an allocated time for her court appearance.

'Christ! I dunno, Tennison.' Stanley sounded groggy. 'They don't sit until after ten, so just make your way over there. It could be hours before you get called so you'll just have to wait it out.'

Jane had a strong suspicion that Stanley had spent the night in the office sleeping off a hangover. She thought he had a nerve talking about Spencer Gibbs' drinking when it was obvious he had been hitting the bottle himself.

Jane went into the newsagents and paid fifty pence for her advertisement card to be displayed in the window for one week. As she walked to Baker Street tube, she decided that, as the magistrate's court was close to Bow Street station, she would pop in and maybe have breakfast with Edith in the canteen.

Jane took the Circle line from Baker Street and changed at King's Cross St Pancras to take the Piccadilly line to Covent Garden. From there it was just a short walk to the Bow Street station.

It was eight thirty when Jane arrived at Covent Garden station, right at the peak of the early morning rush hour. There were groans from the other passengers when they saw that the lift wasn't working, but Jane didn't mind as she wasn't in any great hurry. She followed the throng of people walking up the 193 steps of the spiral staircase, trying her best not to bump into the people heading down the stairs in the opposite direction. Behind her was a woman with a pushchair and a baby in her arms.

'Can I help you?' Jane asked.

'Oh, yes please, thank you, love. These lifts here are always out of order.'

Jane carried the pushchair, and as there were so many people up ahead of her, they moved very slowly. On reaching the top stair she unfolded the pushchair so the woman could put her baby in the seat. Jane paused at the ticket barriers to search her handbag for her warrant card. The area surrounding the faulty lift was heaving with people moving in both directions, and a guard was on duty checking and taking tickets. Behind Jane were queues of passengers waiting impatiently to show their tickets so they could leave the station, and she found herself being pushed forward.

The guard shouted, 'Please do NOT push! We apologise for the lifts being out of order and ask for your patience. Please proceed in an orderly manner through the ticket barriers!'

Jane made her way through the ticket barrier and out into the packed foyer.

'Excuse me, sir, you forgot your bag.'

Jane turned to see an elderly woman pointing to a rucksack that had been left on the floor next to the ticket box.

'Hey, you left your bag!' the woman repeated. Jane followed her gaze and caught sight of a man wearing a hooded winter coat, walking away with his head down. Instead of turning to acknowledge the old lady he pushed people out of his way as he hurried towards the Long Lane exit.

'I just saw him put it down!' the woman said loudly.

Jane hesitated. Was it just a mistake, and the man had simply not heard the woman calling out to him? She hurried after him, in the hope of stopping him and reuniting him with his bag.

'Excuse me, sir! I'm a police officer and . . .'

The man kept on moving quickly through the throng of people and Jane picked up her pace as she called out for him to stop. Just as he reached the exit, Jane managed to grab hold of his sleeve. He half turned towards her and she had a momentary glimpse of his profile, but he twisted out of her grasp, batting her away. He pushed people aside as he ran out of the station. Jane stumbled backwards, and then turned to look for the abandoned rucksack. She could feel the panic rising as she realised it had gone, but then calmed down as she reassured herself that the old lady must have been mistaken and the real owner had picked it up.

Jane turned around in a circle, searching for anyone carrying the rucksack. Then she saw the ticket barrier guard holding it against his chest, heading towards the guards' office. She immediately sensed that something was very wrong. For a second she was paralysed with fear, but then she started pushing people aside and screamed at the guard to put the rucksack down, shouting for everyone to evacuate the area. Some people began to run. But it was too late.

The sound of the explosion was horrific. A ball of flame mixed with shattered glass and metal filled the air, followed by dense smoke which consumed the lift and ticket area.

A huge man blocked Jane and unintentionally shielded her from the blast and flying debris, but his weight pushed her to the ground. Jane was completely dazed, and her ears throbbed with a high-pitched whine. A thick cloud of black smoke quickly filled the air, making it hard to breathe. There were screams of terror from people trying to escape and the pitiful cries of those who had been injured was like a terrible nightmare.

Choking, Jane staggered to her feet, pulling a handkerchief from her pocket to cover her mouth. The ticket guard's body had been blown apart, and amongst the mass of gasping, terrified people, Jane could make out the body of the old lady lying on the ground. She was badly injured, her leg virtually severed below the knee. Jane stumbled towards her but stopped as she spotted the overturned pushchair that she had carried up the stairs. The woman lay face down in a pool of blood with what looked like a severe head injury. Jane looked around frantically for the baby. She turned the pushchair over, but it was empty. She looked around anxiously and suddenly heard muffled cries from near the woman's body. She had to push her way past people who were still desperately trying to get out of the station. Jane bent down and turned the woman over. The baby was beneath her, covered in its mother's blood. Jane felt for the woman's pulse – she was still alive. She eased the infant out from underneath its mother's body and held it in her arms. There were no obvious injuries.

It wasn't long before uniformed officers were at the scene and herding terrified people out of the station, and Jane shouted that she was a police officer. She put the baby into the pushchair and took one of the baby's blankets, folding it to place beneath the mother's head. A man bent down to assist her as more officers entered the station, and in the background she heard the sound of ambulances and fire engines approaching.

Now she was sure that the baby was safe and that the mother was being looked after, Jane made her way towards the old lady. She was bleeding profusely from her injured leg. There was too much blood. Jane took off her belt and used it as a tourniquet, wrapping it tightly around the old lady's thigh. She was conscious but in great pain.

'What's your name?' Jane asked.

'Daphne. I'll be all right, love,' the old lady murmured. 'You go and help the woman with the baby.'

Jane looked back and saw two ambulance attendants lifting the young woman onto a stretcher. She called out to let them know that it was the mother of the child in the pushchair. One of the attendants acknowledged Jane and rushed over to lift the baby into the ambulance with the mother. Then she used all her strength to tighten the belt some more around Daphne's thigh.

'Did you see the man who left that rucksack?'

'Yes, I called out to him . . . I saw him,' she whispered.

'Would you be able to recognise him again?'

'Yes . . .' she gasped, and her head fell forwards as she passed out.

Jane knew they had to get Daphne to hospital quickly as she had lost a lot of blood.

'Over here!' Jane shouted to an ambulance man who came over and knelt beside the victim. 'I made a tourniquet the best I could to try and stem the blood flow.' As they lifted Daphne on to a stretcher, she added, 'I'll come with you.'

She shouted to another police officer that she was going with the old woman to hospital. She climbed into the ambulance next to her as she was being given CPR. Daphne's eyes flickered open and she reached for Jane's hand.

'Don't leave me. Please don't leave me . . . I have no one . . .'

Jane was unable to question her further. The ambulance man placed a mask over Daphne's face and instructed Jane to sit further away so they could monitor the old lady's breathing.

They arrived at St Thomas' Hospital on the south side of Westminster Bridge in Lambeth. Jane waited in the A & E department as they began working on the old lady's injuries. It was mayhem. More and more injured people were being brought in and doctors were being called down from all the other wards to assist. The area was filled with the sound of pained cries and weeping, nurses and doctors rushed between the cubicles, and gurneys were hurriedly wheeled up to the operating theatres. Jane watched helplessly as the devastating aftermath swamped the hospital.

A young woman doctor swished back the curtain surrounding the cubicle Daphne had been wheeled into. Jane jumped up and made her way towards her.

'I am DC Jane Tennison. Could you give me an update on Daphne's progress?'

'We need to amputate her leg. It'll be touch and go if she survives . . .'

'Did you get her surname?'

'No. She's been unconscious ever since she came in . . . Excuse me, I'm needed in the cubicle next door.'

Jane watched as the gurney was wheeled out to go up to the operating theatre. Daphne seemed so tiny and vulnerable lying beneath her blanket. As Jane turned to leave, the young doctor pulled aside the curtain from the cubicle next door. A nurse came out carrying the baby Jane had placed in the pushchair after the explosion. The child was screaming, wrapped in a bloodstained sheet.

'She's fine, doctor . . . but I'm afraid the mother . . .'

The doctor leaned over the bed and slowly drew up the blood-soaked sheet to cover the young mother's face. Jane put her hands over her ears; sounds were becoming distorted. The baby crying, the screams and shouts . . . It was a while before Jane could move away from the panic-stricken scene surrounding her. Hospital staff attempted to identify the incoming injured as yet more victims kept on arriving. The nurses and doctors moved with a weary efficiency; this was not the first bomb they had had to deal with and they were used to managing the aftermath. Jane knew there was nothing she could do at the hospital. She would only be in the way if she stayed.

The traffic outside the A & E department was chaotic with ambulances. The road leading to the hospital was almost at a standstill due to the explosion and Jane had no option but to walk to Bow Street. Her mind was frozen, and she kept stopping to take deep breaths to calm herself down. It was impossible to make sense of such terrible violence, of the murder of innocent people who had been going about their everyday lives.

Jane knew that the man who had unintentionally shielded her must have suffered serious injuries, or most likely had been killed. She could still hear the cries of the baby in her head like a tormented echo, and tried to understand what it would mean to the young woman's husband and her family. She had to force herself to keep on walking, unaware that her clothes were covered in thick, filthy plaster dust. One sleeve of her jacket was torn, and her face and hair were covered with blood and dirt.

'I should get to court . . .' Jane muttered. She kept on walking, in an almost zombie-like manner, until she reached Bow Street Magistrates Court. By now it was midday. She entered the court foyer in the hope of seeing someone from the Dip Squad, but the area was empty. She went to the door leading to the police officers side of the court, and when the sliding hatch opened she showed her warrant card.

On seeing the state that she was in the court sergeant opened the door.

'Dear God! Are you all right, luv?'

'Yes . . . I'm sorry I'm late but I got caught up in the explosion at Covent Garden and then I had to go to the hospital with some of the injured –'

'Well, the court cases have all been put off for the day.'

'I'm here for the bail objection to –'

'Come with me, luv. Come on, now.'

The sergeant led her into a police waiting room and explained that because of the bomb incident her two prisoners had not been brought into court, and they were still at Vine Street Police station.

Jane sat in a daze as he brought her a cup of tea and then produced a small hip flask of brandy. He poured a nip of it into Jane's mug and a larger one into his own.

'Did anyone from the Dip Squad turn up for the hearing?' Jane asked.

'No. Tell me, are you new to that team?' The sergeant seemed to sense that Jane couldn't process the morning's events and let her change the subject.

'Yes, it was my first day yesterday.'

'So, you nicked those two pickpockets, did you?'

Jane turned away from him. It was difficult for her to even contemplate what had occurred on her first day. It was a lot more than two pickpockets. It made her think about Regina and the whole unpleasant discovery of what the young girl had been subjected to. On top of the shocking events she had just been through, she felt nauseous at remembering the sight of Regina stripped naked and being sexually abused.

The sergeant saw she was having difficulty talking, so he wagged his finger and said, 'I'll bet that Dip Squad bunch were all out on the piss last night to celebrate.'

She nodded. She'd left them in the bar drinking, celebrating not so much the arrests, but the news that they'd be able to hand the paperwork over to the Vice Squad.

Jane took a long sip of the tea and felt the brandy warming her, although her hand was still shaking badly.

The court sergeant was white-haired and overweight, with a long service history and experience. There was nothing he didn't know about the various squads but he had no notion about what had happened the previous night.

'When that lot make an arrest, they act as though they've clobbered old-time villains like the Krays. Arresting the dirtbags who are nicking stuff is hardly worth the aggro, but you gotta do what you gotta to do to try and protect the public from them. I was nicking dippers while most of the squad were still at school. Those squad lads are all too big for their boots ... they usually draw straws for who's going to remain sober to be in court the following morning. I'd say, as you were on your first day, they gave you the short straw . . . this morning they'll all have hangovers, and the magistrate is a teetotaller who gets nasty if he even smells a whiff of alcohol.'

Jane smiled wanly as she drained her mug and handed it to him.

'Thank you for your time . . . and I appreciate that nip of brandy.'

The sergeant tapped his bulbous nose. 'It's between you and me, luv . . . and if you want some advice, you call in UC – uncertified sick – and get home now. You've obviously had one hell of a morning and you may think you've got it all sorted, but then it comes back and hits you like a sledgehammer. Go home.'

Jane was escorted out of the court, but she had no intention of going home. She hailed a taxi to take her to Vine Street and sat back trying to compose herself. At least she had stopped shaking.

CHAPTER FOUR

The Dip Squad team gathered around a small colour TV. The basement office had poor reception, and Stanley was holding up the aerial trying to get a decent picture. The other men were all yelling different instructions, and eventually he stood up on a chair.

'How is it now?'

'Just stay up on the chair,' Jimmy Church said.

On the screen the news reporter was standing outside Covent Garden station. He announced that the IRA was suspected of being responsible for the bomb, even though the usual coded warning had not been sent prior to the explosion.

They all remained silent as they listened to the reporter confirming that there had been many fatalities and a huge number of people injured. Church gestured for Stanley to get down from the chair.

'Bastards!' Stanley snapped.

'Do we know how many fatalities there are yet?' asked Blondie.

'Not yet,' Church said. 'They haven't released any information, but it was rush hour at Covent Garden. I'm guessing there will be quite a few.'

There was an uneasy tension in the room. Church spotted yesterday's arrest reports on his desk.

He wasn't exactly changing the subject, but at the same time, work had to commence. 'The Hernandez case: did Miguel get to see his sister, Regina?'

'Yeah, he was taken over to St Thomas' hospital around midnight, but she was heavily medicated. The doctor at the hospital wanted to keep her in overnight for observation. Miguel's back in the cells upstairs, but even if he pleads guilty, with no previous against him, he'll make bail. The leather-coated yob, Matías Agatha, probably likewise,' said Dunston.

'What about the uncle, any word on him?'

'All I know is he seems to have friends in high places. The Vice Squad will keep us updated,' Stanley confirmed.

There was a pause in the room as the television reception cleared up just as the one o'clock news came on. It began with a broadcast of new footage from the bomb scene.

'Dear God, that was some explosion.' Church looked at his watch. 'Where's Tennison? Anybody seen her this morning? Stanley, call the court and see if she showed up.'

'I already did, sir . . . she wasn't there.'

Despite his hangover, Stanley had felt concerned when Tennison failed to show.

'Well, does anybody know where she is?'

'I took a call from her early this morning,' Stanley said. 'She was asking about what time the magistrates got into court.'

'But you just said you contacted the court and she hadn't showed.'

'That's right, Guv, but she sort of implied that she was on her way there.'

Church was looking really concerned. 'Has anyone called the section house, or her parents?'

At that moment, Jane walked into the room. Everyone stared at her. It was obvious from her dishevelled appearance that she had been at Covent Garden.

'Where the fuck have you been?' Stanley exclaimed, not intending to sound angry.

Jane snapped at him, 'I spoke to you earlier this morning, so you should have known precisely where I was. You stitched me up with the court case and I nearly got killed because I was at Covent Garden –'

'Come on, I was just being facetious . . . just calm down. You're here and obviously safe. It was just bad luck that you were in the wrong place at the wrong time. We were all really worried about you . . . but you aren't dead, so everything's OK . . .'

'Shut up, Stanley,' said Church. He gestured for Jane to follow him into his office.

Jane glared at Stanley and looked coldly at the rest of the shame-faced team. She tossed her briefcase onto a desk and went into DCI Church's cramped office. Slamming the door behind her, she said, 'I called here before I left for the court, and I was at Covent Garden underground station –'

'Sit down, Tennison.' Church pulled out a chair, tipping off a bundle of files onto the floor. 'We were concerned about you. You should have called us from the court to say you were OK. We were told you hadn't turned up.'

'Nor did the two men we arrested yesterday.'

'I know . . . I know that. But we were not to know what had happened. Stanley called the section house, and I was about to contact your father to find out where you were.'

'I was at the underground station when the bomb went off, and I was so close to the explosion. There was an old lady called Daphne, who I'm sure saw whoever it was that left the device . . . but she was badly injured. Afterwards I did what I could to help the other injured people, and I accompanied Daphne to the hospital.' Jane was speaking so quickly she barely stopped to draw breath. 'I wanted to see if she could give me any details, but she was unconscious and was taken up to the operating theatre. So, I went to the court much later than I was told to be there.'

Jane found herself hyperventilating, the stress of the events catching up as she tried desperately to process the explosion and aftermath while at the same time her words tumbled out about the court case, arrests and all the events of the past twenty-four hours.

'All right . . . all right. Now, I'm going to get you a cup of coffee, and maybe you should call your parents? Use my phone. This has been all over the news, so if you use that underground station a lot, it's best to let them know you're OK. Then you're to go home and take the rest of the day off.'

When Church left the room, Jane tried to calm down. Eventually she picked up the desk phone and dialled her parents. The number was engaged. Just as she replaced the receiver DCI Church walked in carrying a mug of coffee.

'Here you go. I put a couple of sugars in it, but I didn't know if you needed them so I haven't stirred. Bad scene, eh?'

She looked at him. DCI Church's gentle manner confused her. There was such compassion beneath the simple enquiry. For a moment she thought he was going to embrace her but instead he patted her shoulder. 'Tell me about it when you are ready, but don't bottle things up. If you want to talk about it further, I'm here and the whole team is here for you, too.'

She turned away, desperate to change the subject.

'Will the two men we arrested be in court tomorrow morning?'

'No idea. Don't waste a moment thinking about them.'

'I was thinking about the young girl, Regina.'

'She's being well looked after. And the Vice Squad are now handling that douchebag Uncle Andres. It seems he has contacts – he's already organised his own legal representation.'

'But what about all the passports, the young girls the same age as Regina?'

Church could feel the panic behind her innocuous enquiries, so his response was quiet. 'It's not our problem ... it's down to the Vice Squad sorting it.'

He left her in the office to finish the coffee. It was strong, soothing, but her hand was shaking again so she stayed sitting for a while. It was not until she had drained the mug that she felt a bit more in control. She stood up and dusted down her jacket, examining the torn sleeve. She felt much calmer as she walked out into the main office. There was no one around and Jane picked up her briefcase. She had no intention of going back to her flat.

St Thomas' hospital was quieter now than it had been that morning. At the main reception desk, Jane enquired of a receptionist with badly dyed hair about Daphne's condition.

The receptionist scowled at Jane, replying through tight, plum-red lips, 'Lots of people came in with severe leg injuries this morning. Unless you have a surname I can't help you. I have been on duty since six and my phone has not stopped ringing.'

Jane stood her ground, holding up her warrant card. 'I'm very sorry, but I am a detective with the Metropolitan Police and I would like you to take my enquiry seriously.'

The bad-hair job scowled even more as she snapped, 'I have been taking everybody seriously all day! If you want any further information I suggest you contact the duty sister on the intensive care ward.'

'Do you have the name of the duty sister?' Jane asked, tight-lipped. Only then did she notice that in fact the receptionist seemed close to tears and she felt sorry for her.

'Yes . . . it's Mitchell. I'm sorry I can't be more helpful but we are inundated, and it's been a terrible time.'

Jane headed up to the intensive care ward and approached the nurse's desk. A male nurse was writing on a file.

'Excuse me, I need to speak to Sister Mitchell.'

'You're talking to him. . . I'm the charge nurse. What can I do for you?'

'I accompanied a lady called Daphne here this morning. Her leg was severely injured in this morning's bombing. I'm trying to find out how she is.'

Mitchell glanced down a page on his clipboard and turned it over.

'I've got an elderly woman called Daphne who sadly had to have her leg amputated. She's currently in a drug-induced coma in the intensive care unit. We have no surname for her yet . . . Are you a relative?'

'No, I'm a police officer, WDC Tennison.' Jane showed him her warrant card. 'I was with Daphne at the time of the explosion. Would it be possible for me to see her?'

Mitchell beckoned her to follow him to the ward of curtained cubicles. He eased back the curtain of one of the middle beds. Jane was shocked to see just how small and frail Daphne looked. She had breathing tubes in her mouth and nose, a drip attached to her left arm and a protective cage over her injured leg.

'And you didn't find any ID on her?' Jane asked.

'No, nothing . . . we know her only as Daphne. No one has made any enquiries about her . . . Only time will tell if she'll survive.' Mitchell waved his arm, taking in the ward. 'We've got a lot more victims in a really bad condition.'

Jane could hear moans and sounds of weeping from the curtained cubicles. As they stood looking down at the old woman, who seemed so vulnerable and tiny, a voice made them turn.

'Excuse me . . . I need to talk to the doctor in charge here.' A tall man wearing slacks, an open-necked shirt and a tweed jacket, stood behind them. He was a big man, with a tough, square-jawed face and broad shoulders.

'I think they're all tied up just now . . . Are you a relative of one of the patients?'

'No.' The man peered past Jane. 'Is that elderly woman one of the bomb victims?'

Jane moved from the bedside, astonished at the man's rudeness. 'Yes, she is, and she's in a coma.'

'Who are you?' He glared at Jane.

Offended by his brusque manner Jane showed him her warrant card.

'I'm WDC Jane Tennison. Can I ask who you are?'

He gave a cursory look at Jane's warrant card before he took out his own.

'I'm Detective Chief Inspector Crowley, Bomb Squad.' He moved towards her. 'What can you tell me about this woman?'

'I only know her first name's Daphne. I accompanied her from the underground station in the ambulance. I believe she may have seen the man who planted the bomb.'

'Why wasn't I told earlier about this witness?' he bellowed.

'Please keep your voice down,' said Mitchell.

'You a nurse, are you?' Crowley asked abruptly.

'Yes, I'm the charge nurse on this ward and patient care is my responsibility. So, please let me show you where you can continue your conversation.'

He ushered them into a small side room with a couple of easy chairs and a coffee table. Crowley stood with his back to the window, which had a green blind drawn over it, as Jane sat down in one of the comfortable chairs. Mitchell remained standing by the door, which he left slightly ajar. He spoke quietly as he gave the details of the old lady's condition.

'How long will it be before I can talk to Daphne?' Crowley said brusquely.

'I'm afraid I'm unable to say. You will need to speak to a doctor.'

'I want her moved to a private room as soon as possible. Go and talk to whoever is necessary to find out when I can speak to her.'

Mitchell nodded and walked out, shutting the door behind him. Crowley opened a notebook, flicking over pages.

'So far, we've got a host of injured people unable to give detailed accounts, but one witness heard an old woman shouting about a rucksack being left unattended –'

'That was Daphne, sir. I was standing almost beside her when she first called out about the rucksack. I believe she saw the suspect leaving it.'

Crowley sat down in the other chair. For a moment it appeared that he could hardly take on board what Jane had said. When he spoke, his voice was very quiet, clipped and unnerving.

'You believe she saw the suspect leaving it?'

Frightened by his manner, Jane nodded.

'Right . . . Start from the top, will you?'

'Has the IRA claimed responsibility?' Jane asked.

'Not yet. There was no coded warning prior to the bomb explod-ing but it has all the hallmarks of an IRA attack. So, tell me exactly what you were doing at Covent Garden station.'

Crowley had exceedingly thick, bushy eyebrows and small, thick-lashed piercing blue eyes. He stared at Jane without blinking as she nervously began to explain exactly what had happened to her that morning.

Almost as soon as she'd started, Crowley held up a finger for her to stop speaking. 'So, you were intending to have breakfast at Bow Street police station where you were previously stationed with a colleague? Your intention was to then continue to the Magistrates Court?'

'Yes, sir, which is why I was at Covent Garden station.'

'Right,' he said curtly. 'We now have you at 8.30 a.m. at Covent Garden underground station.'

'Yes, sir, I was heading up the stairs –'

Again he held up his finger. 'Why were you on the stairs?'

'Because we were told on the platform that the lifts were out of order.'

'So, you are moving up the stairs at Covent Garden underground station . . .'

Crowley's unflinching eyes bored into her as he gestured for her to continue. Jane's mouth was dry as she described helping the mother and baby up the staircase.

'I was looking in my handbag to show my warrant card to the ticket collector when I heard a woman's voice calling out to a man that he had left his rucksack. That was Daphne.'

Crowley pursed his lips. 'So are you saying that Daphne had a good sighting of the suspect and may possibly be able to recognise him again?'

'Yes, I believe so.'

Now Crowley really unnerved her as he clenched his fists. 'Why the hell didn't you inform the Bomb Squad earlier about such a vital witness?'

'I wasn't sure if she'd got much of a look at him. That's why I came back to try to see her. She was unconscious in the ambulance, so I couldn't question her then. I told a uniformed PC that I was accompanying her to the hospital and I assumed the information had been passed on. When I left earlier I had to go to Bow Street Magistrate's Court regarding a two-hander, but when I got there it was closed. So, I made way to the Dip Squad office, and –'

Crowley interrupted her. 'Yes, yes . . . no need to go into details about where you were, or what you did afterwards. What's important is whether you saw the same suspect?'

'Yes, but I only had a side view. I did go after the suspect to stop him. I caught his sleeve and said I was a police officer, but he pushed me away and ran on.'

'Christ! Why the hell didn't you report this before now? If we'd known at the outset then we might have had got some vital information, like the suspect's bloody description . . .'

'I'm sorry . . . I was still in shock. All I can remember is that he had dark stubble, and dark hair, and was wearing a thick, greyish raincoat. But it was just a flash really . . . I mean, I didn't see his whole face –'

'Yes, all right . . . but you should have contacted the Bomb Squad at the earliest opportunity. We'll need a full statement from you about exactly what you saw, as well as the old lady's possible closer look. It'd help if we knew exactly who she is.'

'She told me at the scene her name was Daphne, but there was no ID on her when she was brought in. Her clothing must be here somewhere, so we can check that to see if the hospital missed anything. Maybe her handbag will be found in the debris . . .'

'Even in a coma Daphne is still a threat to the IRA, and people like them usually try to eliminate anyone who could cause trouble. They shot a TV personality for daring to offer a reward for information leading to the Balcombe Street ASU's arrests. The old girl needs to be heavily protected . . . if she got a good look at them I guarantee they'll want her, dead or alive. I'll get an armed officer to be on guard outside her room, as soon as they get the poor bloody woman moved. I want you to stay with her until the guard arrives.

'I'm sorry if I sounded off on you,' he added, towering above Jane as they both rose to their feet, 'but it's been one hell of a day. If you can just keep an eye on her until I get organised, and hold the fort here . . . I'll arrange for a direct line number for you to contact my office. You can ring with hourly updates on her condition, but let me underline to you that she could be targeted . . .' He hesitated. 'Do you understand what I am saying, because you are also going to be a possible witness? You need to be very diligent about anyone making enquiries about the victim, relative or otherwise. Get their ID and don't allow anyone to see her unless it's been authorised by me or my team.'

A knock on the door announced Mitchell's return. He told them Daphne would be moved within ten minutes to a private room. A doctor would also be monitoring her, as she was still in a coma.

Crowley glanced at his watch as Mitchell left the room.

'I'm going to organise the armed officer now. I hope to God you haven't mentioned this to anyone else? Just stay put and I'll get you brought into my office at New Scotland Yard in the morning so I can take a formal statement from you.'

'I have to go to court in the morning, sir. I should also contact my DCI about where I am, as he gave me the afternoon off . . .'

'Just sit tight with the old lady. I'll contact your squad. What's the DCI's name?'

'Jimmy Church.'

'Oh, right . . . I'll talk to the doctor first and then contact him. I've got to shift and get things organised.'

He walked out, leaving Jane speechless.

While Daphne was moved to a private room, Jane went back through the ward, through the double doors and into the corridor to find the ladies. Looking at herself in the mirror above the washbasin, she was shocked at her dishevelled appearance. Her face was filthy and her hair was full of plaster and dust. She washed her hands and face, and pulled down the towel to dry herself. She took a comb from her handbag and did her best to tidy up her hair. There was nothing she could do about the rip in her jacket sleeve, and she was also minus her belt, which she had used as a tourniquet.

Refreshed and calmed by the cold water, she returned to the ward to find Mitchell looking for her. He led her out of the ward, to the far end of the corridor, and through a second set of double doors. The private rooms were situated along this short corridor, a fire escape door marked the end.

'She's in here,' said Mitchell, showing her into one of the rooms. 'We still haven't had any response but considering what she's been through it might be a while.'

Daphne lay unmoving in a single bed, wired up with drips and covered in a lightweight white blanket. Her childlike hand rested on top, the cannula held in place by two plaster strips. Between the bed and a small chest of drawers was a wingback chair, with a trolley on the opposite side of the bed.

Jane sat down beside her and gently touched her fingers, talking softly to her in the hope that Daphne could hear her voice, and that it would be a comfort to know someone was with her. Even though there was no response, Jane continued to hold her hand. Suddenly, Daphne's hand moved, and Jane jumped to her feet. She was about to go and find someone when Mitchell appeared. Jane explained what had happened. Mitchell moved to Daphne's side and checked his patient, then turned to Jane.

'It was probably just an involuntary muscle twitch. I came in to let you know that an armed officer is here.'

They left the room together. The armed officer had placed a chair outside and was already sitting down. He looked a bit surprised when Jane asked to see his warrant card, but showed it to her with a grin.

As Jane walked back down the corridor with Mitchell, she thanked him for his help.

'Where are you off to now?' he asked.

'I probably should go and see my parents in Maida Vale. Apparently one of the team I am working with called them, but I think they must have been concerned when they heard about the bomb – Covent Garden station is close to where I worked until last week.'

'Can you wait a few minutes? I'm going off duty and could walk you to the tube.'

Ten minutes later he joined her, having changed his nurse's tunic for a T-shirt, with a raincoat over the top. Together they left the hospital. Jane was grateful Mitchell was with her to show her the way. She also liked the fact that he took her elbow and guided her across the road. He was rather pleasant-looking, tall and broad-shouldered with sandy hair and a lovely gentle manner.

'What's your first name?' she asked.

'Michael. And yours?'

'Jane. How long have you been a nurse?'

He smiled. 'A long time – ten years. I usually get disparaging looks when I'm asked what I do. Most people assume that nursing is a woman's profession, and automatically think I must be homosexual. I think air stewards get the same reaction . . .'

Jane laughed. 'Well, if it's any consolation I'm probably regarded as being a woman in a man's world most of the time. The male officers refer to us as "plonks", or even worse, "a bit of skirt".'

'How long have you been in the Met?'

'Nearly four years. Before that I worked in my dad's office but I wanted to do something more challenging than surveyors' tedious paperwork. It's odd, you know . . . I can't remember the exact moment when I considered joining the police force. I think it may have stemmed from an article I read in the newspaper about the Met; it said the role of women within the organisation was changing, and that female officers were being fully integrated with the men on shift work.'

'So, it wasn't exactly a calling . . .'

'No, not really. I think it was more of an opportunity to get out from behind a desk, stand on my own two feet and do something rewarding. My parents, especially my mother, didn't approve. What about you?'

'I don't often tell people this, but when I was eight my dad had a brain tumour. He was an incredibly fit man . . . used to have me out playing football with him every spare minute, even after a hard day's work in the printing factory. But then he became frail and dependent . . . he couldn't even feed himself. My mum was forced to go out to work, so I used to wash him and cook for him – it's awful to be on a liquid diet for so long. His speech gradually went but I could understand what he needed. When he was lucid he used to give me this look . . . "Thank you, son," he'd try to say. So, I became a nurse.'

Mitchell shook his head. 'I dunno how you got all that background from me.' He turned to face her. 'I'm going over to the pub now to have a few well-earned beers with some of my colleagues. Do you want to join us?'

Jane hesitated. For a few minutes she had forgotten about the awful things she had seen that morning. Mitchell had been easy company and she had enjoyed talking to him.

'No, I really should get home and see my parents . . . but thank you.'

'OK. Just go straight on down here and the underground station is on your right.'

They shook hands and parted. She had only walked a few yards when he called her name and hurried back towards her.

'Listen, would you like me to phone you when I find out more about Daphne?'

'Oh, yes, please.' Jane took out her notebook out of her bag, wrote down her home phone number and tore out the page to give to him. 'Thank you, Michael.'

'Good to meet you, Jane. Have a safe journey home.'

Jane walked away, smiling. He was so nice and she hoped she would hear from him again. Michael had been honest about why he had chosen his career, but she hadn't been as open with him. Jane hadn't told Michael about how she'd had to fight her mother's opposition to her joining the police because she hadn't wanted to share what had happened to their family. It was something from her childhood that she kept to herself. Jane's brother, who was also called Michael, had drowned when he was a toddler. He had been given a fishing rod by her father, and had been too impatient to wait for her father to take him fishing. He had squeezed through the hedge in their garden to go next door, where he knew they had a fish pond.

Sitting on the train as it rattled towards Maida Vale, Jane closed her eyes as she recalled what she remembered of the awful tragedy. They had found her brother face down in the pond. His lifeless little body had been carried home and when the ambulance arrived, accompanied by police, her mother had become hysterical, refusing to allow them to take Michael from her arms. There were uniformed officers everywhere, asking questions as if there had been a crime instead of a tragic accident. This began her mother's deep-seated hatred of the police, because she felt they had blamed her for her son's death. She only recovered from her breakdown when her younger daughter, Pam, was born, but for years afterwards the sight of uniformed police officers made her freeze with anxiety. At the time of her brother's death, Jane had been too young to understand why the police were involved. She now knew they were just doing their job, but their manner of dealing with the situation should have been more caring and understanding.

Jane sighed. She wasn't sure why she hadn't opened up to Michael, when he had been so honest with her. Truth was, Jane never went into depth about her life with anyone as, like her father, she was always protecting her fragile mother.

Shaking off her thoughts, Jane got off the train at Warwick Avenue and walked along Clifton Gardens towards Maida Vale. She passed a row of shops, the *Evening Standard* displayed outside showing the headlines about the IRA bomb. She didn't stop to buy one and instead turned onto Maida Vale, passing the large Clarendon Hotel on the corner. From there it was a short walk to Clive Court, the big building where her parents' flat was situated.

Jane had her own key but she rang the doorbell first. When no one answered she used her key to open the front door.

'Is that you, Pam? We've still had no news. I called Scotland Yard but they didn't have a report and –'

'It's me, Dad . . . it's Jane!' she called, shutting the door behind her.

Her father came hurrying down the corridor from the bedroom, his face ashen.

'Jane! You've no idea what you've put us through today! Didn't you get any of my calls?'

Jane put up her arms to hug him, but he was white-faced with anger. She was so shocked that she stepped back as her mother came running down the hall.

'She's here . . . she's here . . . she's all right,' he said.

Mrs Tennison let out a cry, then her legs buckled beneath her and she collapsed in the hallway. Mr Tennison quickly gathered her up in his arms.

'It's all right, darling . . . she's safe . . . she's here . . . Come on now, come and sit down on the sofa. Jane, help your mother, quickly.'

As Jane guided her to the sofa, Mrs Tennison burst into tears.

'I'm so sorry, Mum. I tried to call but it was engaged, and then I got caught up in the . . . I'm so sorry.'

'You should be! We've been at our wits' end because we knew you often used that Covent Garden station. We've called everyone we could think of . . .'

Just then Pam arrived, using her own key to let herself in. On seeing Jane, she threw up her arms.

'I don't believe it! We thought you were dead, for God's sake! This bombing's been all over the news and it's in all the evening papers . . . Why didn't you call?'

'I'm sorry . . . I'm so sorry . . . I tried but this number was engaged. I was at the station when the bomb exploded . . . But I was so lucky . . . I wasn't hurt.'

'I can't cope with you being a police officer . . . it's too dangerous,' Mrs Tennison exclaimed, as her husband handed her a small schooner of sherry.

'Mum,' Jane said, doing her best to reassure her, 'the bomb wasn't aimed at police officers. The injured were all innocent . . . one man saved my life because he shielded me from the explosion; he saved –'

'I don't want to hear the details!' her mother snapped. 'Your work brings you into contact with murderous people like the IRA. We've been worried sick about you since the day you joined up.'

Pam sat beside her mother as she sobbed again. It was a difficult half hour until her father suggested that she should get something to eat. He eventually persuaded her mother to go and lie down and by this time Jane was completely drained.

'Are you going back to your flat?' Pam asked, as they went into the kitchen together.

'I don't know . . . I'm totally wiped out.'

'Maybe you should stay the night here and talk to Mum in the morning? I'll make you a sandwich and a cup of tea.'

'What I'd really like is a hot bath . . .'

'Well, you go and have one. I'd better be going back. Tony was worried about you as well.'

Jane nodded and sat down on one of the breakfast stools. She wasn't hungry but Pam had buttered two slices of bread and was peering into the fridge.

'So, what happened? I mean, were you in the thick of it?'

'Yes, I was right there. It was dreadful. I haven't really got my head around it. One minute I was walking out through the ticket barrier, and the next –'

'Will a ham sandwich do? And there's tomatoes and lettuce?'

'Yes . . . thank you.'

'Or there's some cheese?'

Mr Tennison walked in. 'Your mother's lying down,' he said. 'She's taken a sleeping tablet. I don't think I'll bother waking her up now – she can sleep in her clothes tonight.

'Jane wants a bath, Daddy . . . she's staying here tonight. I'm going to go back to Tony. I've made her a sandwich. Do you want one?'

Jane didn't have the energy to argue about staying, and found it difficult to even start a conversation as her father and sister were talking across her as if she wasn't there. She got down from the stool and said she would run herself a bath, and eat her sandwich later.

Her bedroom was almost as she had left it, with her old towelling robe hanging on the back of her door. As she slowly undressed she could hear Pam and her father talking in the kitchen.

'She said she was just coming out of the ticket office when the bomb went off,' Pam said. She heard her father reply that he would talk to Jane after her bath.

Jane almost crept to the bathroom, not wanting to face either of them. She locked the door and sat on the side of the bathtub, watching it fill. She poured in some bubble bath and watched as the water became frothy. When it was almost to the overflow, she turned off the taps, slowly stepped into the water and lay down, submerged in the warmth with her eyes closed.

The sudden realisation of how lucky she was not to have been maimed or killed at the Covent Garden explosion hit her like a massive wave crashing against rocks. She didn't know the names of the dead, not even the young mother or the man who'd saved her. After controlling her emotions all day, she began to tremble and then started to weep. She placed a wet flannel over her face, pressing it down over her mouth to stop anyone from hearing her cries. Her breathing turned to small gasps.

'You're OK . . . you're OK . . .' she repeated to herself. As she sat up, there was a knock on the door.

'Are you all right in there?'

'Yes, Daddy, I'm fine. I won't be much longer.'

'Pam's gone, and I've made you a hot chocolate. I'll put it with your sandwich, on your bedside table.'

'Thank you.'

Jane sighed and closed her eyes. She started to weep again, trying to muffle her sobs so that her father wouldn't hear. Eventually she forced herself to get out of the bath, wrapped a big, soft towel around herself and unlocked the door. She went into her bedroom and opened one of her drawers, taking out an old, long nightgown. Everything had been washed and pressed as if awaiting her return. Jane sat on the edge of her bed and sipped the now tepid chocolate. Pam's sandwich was a bit soggy and unappetising. The bread was thick with butter and slathered with mayonnaise, with tired lettuce leaves and thick tomato chunks.

It was after ten and she was beginning to feel as if she could go to sleep, when her father knocked on her door and inched it open.

'You all right, darling?'

He edged further into the room. Jane's hair was still wet and she used the hand towel from the bathroom to rub it dry. She was sure her eyes would be red-rimmed from crying and she didn't want him to notice.

'You can always talk to me, Jane . . . you know that, don't you?'

'Yes, Daddy.'

He was uneasy, even a little embarrassed, as he sat beside her on the bed.

'Your mother will be all right in the morning. You know how nervy she can get, and what with worrying about you she got herself into quite a state.'

'I am so sorry, Daddy. I really did try to call you. I went to the hospital with this old lady called Daphne . . . She was badly injured . . .'

Mr Tennison gave her a sidelong look. He could tell she had been crying and he patted her hand.

'It must have been one hell of a day for you, sweetheart.'

'Yes, but it didn't hit me until I was in the bath . . . I sort of relived it all . . . the explosion, and the awful aftermath. At the time I controlled my fear enough to help as many of the injured as I could, in particular the old lady.'

'Well, I'm very proud of you. I understand what you must have been through. I lost many friends in the D-Day landing in Normandy. There were awful explosions and terrible sights – the injured and the dead . . . So I know what it feels like to have that fear. It was felt by all of us, but you eventually learn how to supress it and cope. Fear is in the mind of every soldier in battle, and only fools fail to admit it.'

Mr Tennison put his arm around Jane. She had never felt so close to him.

'What you did today, sweetheart, was beyond the call of duty. You were brave and totally selfless. In the morning, I'm going to talk to your mother and try to make her understand that she should be proud too, and not afraid of the job you do.'

She hugged him and he kissed her cheek.

As he opened her bedroom door he turned and said softly, 'It's good you came home . . . good we had this time together. Now, try to get some sleep.'

He closed the door quietly behind him, and Jane lay back on her pillow. She felt safe in her old bedroom and knew how much it meant to her father that she was here. She had not expected that she would be able to switch off, but only a moment later she was in a deep and dreamless sleep.

The following morning Jane woke up and realised that it was already after eight. She was just getting out of bed when her mother knocked on her door and walked in. She was holding Jane's washed and ironed shirt, and had pressed and repaired her suit.

'I woke up early and Daddy and I had a long talk. I've got everything ready for you to go into work . . . unless you don't feel up to it.'

'I do. Thank you so much, Mum.'

As her mother hung up the clothes on the hook on the back of her bedroom door, she asked, 'Would you like an omelette and some bacon?'

Jane was near to tears. She walked over to her mother and held out her arms.

'That sounds just perfect . . . and I'm so sorry again for not getting in touch sooner yesterday. Please forgive me.'

Mrs Tennison gave Jane a small, tight smile as she hugged her.

'Let's not go back into that again, shall we? The fact that you are safe and sound is all that matters . . . I am proud of you. Get dressed and come and have breakfast, just like we used to.'

Alone in her room again, Jane knew that nothing could ever be just like it used to be. But what was important was the love she had felt from her parents, a love she reciprocated. She felt so lucky to have her family supporting her.

They ate breakfast together then Jane left with her father to walk to the station. Mr Tennison went into their local news-agent's to buy his usual paper and Jane continued to the station in Warwick Avenue.

Mr Tennison was folding his newspaper to tuck under his arm when he caught sight of the front-page headline about the Covent Garden explosion. He walked out of the shop and opened the newspaper, stopping in his tracks when he saw the black-and-white photograph of Jane, her hair matted and face smeared with what was obviously blood. He thanked God that they didn't have their newspapers delivered. If his wife had seen what he was looking at, the lengthy conversation about Jane's work and her promise to be supportive about their daughter's career would have disintegrated into hysteria. As he passed a dustbin he threw the paper in it.

CHAPTER FIVE

Jane took the tube to New Scotland Yard. The Underground was busy, everyone refusing to let yesterday's explosion change their way of life. She was impressed by London's resilience to the IRA attack. Only a day after the horrific explosion everything was up and running, and throngs of people were still using public transport to get to work.

As requested by DCI Crowley, when Jane arrived at New Scotland Yard she showed her warrant card and was told that the Bomb Squad offices were on the seventh floor. She took the lift and walked along the corridor until she came to DCI Crowley's office.

Jane knocked on the door and it opened sharply. Crowley gestured her in.

'This is WDC Jane Tennison,' he announced, and waved an arm at the other man in the room. 'Commander Gregson.'

Gregson rose from his seat behind a modern desk and shook Jane's hand. There were numerous files neatly laid out alongside a telephone and notebook, with a large leather-edged blotting pad and a row of pens. The commander was austere and slim and wore an immaculate suit, unlike Crowley, whose clothes were crumpled. He looked as if he had been up all night.

'Take a seat, Tennison,' said Crowley, as he sat down himself. 'How are you feeling after the bombing incident?'

'I'm fine, thank you, sir. I'm here to give a statement about it.'

'You read the papers this morning, WDC Tennison?'

'No, sir.'

Gregson looked at Crowley and drew a file towards him.

'There was a photojournalist who was exiting the station at the time of the explosion. He took a fair few photographs of you tending to the injured, and of you getting into the ambulance. You accompanied an elderly woman to St Thomas'?'

'Yes, I did, sir.' Jane looked from one man to the other. 'Is there a problem with me going to the hospital, sir?'

'No, but what is a major problem is this.'

Gregson passed over a copy of a tabloid article. The heading read:

IRA BLAMES WOMAN POLICE OFFICER FOR COVENT GARDEN EXPLOSION

Shocked, Jane couldn't speak. There was a large photograph of her getting into the ambulance at Covent Garden station.

Gregson lit a cigarette.

'I'll give you the gist of the article: the newspaper received a phone call from a man with an Irish accent using a code name known only to the newspapers and the Bomb Squad. As you probably know, we usually get a call, with a coded warning before an IRA bomb goes off, thus giving us time to try and evacuate civilians and reduce any possible casualties.'

'I don't understand . . .' Jane said, feeling her stomach churning.

Crowley pulled at his tie.

'The caller told the paper that the plan was to make the coded call after the bomb was left at Covent Garden. But he says that an off-duty policewoman tried to apprehend their Active Service Unit member, and when she grabbed his arm she triggered the detonator he was holding in his pocket.'

'That's not true! Yes, I followed him as he left the station, but I barely touched his sleeve before he swiped my hand away – the bomb went off at least a minute later. By then I'd already. moved back into the ticket area of the station.'

Crowley got up and put his hands on her shoulders.

'It's all right, just stay calm. No one is blaming you, Tennison. The IRA will know there's a big public outcry coming down because they didn't give a coded warning. The IRA look for a way to pacify their sympathisers, especially the ones in the US who support them, and they'll be worried about losing their backing.'

Crowley looked at Gregson, who stubbed out his cigarette.

'They needed a scapegoat, so they're using you.'

'But if I hadn't warned people, there would have been more fatalities.'

'It's possible the suspect set the bomb off early in a panic. Whatever happened, it was a blatant act of terrorism, an attempt to bring mass fear to the streets of London.'

'The press has been onto us,' Crowley interjected, glancing at Gregson. 'They're trying to find out if the IRA's allegation bears any truth. They've been asking us to name the police officer concerned. We've said that the matter is under investigation and the primary fact is that the IRA detonated the bomb and murdered innocent civilians.'

'But where does that leave me, sir? I don't know what I would do if the public thought that I was to blame in any way.'

Gregson moved to sit on the edge of the desk and face Jane.

'Our concern is that someone might identify you from the photographs in the newspaper and reveal your identity to the press. I have every intention of countering the allegation and want the public to be aware of what scum the IRA are. I want this to cause unrest amongst their supporters. To that end . . .'

He paused to light another cigarette and inhaled deeply before he continued.

'I want you to appear in a police press conference here at the Yard, stating what happened and the carnage you found yourself surrounded by. You've got nothing to be ashamed of, and we're not going to allow the IRA to blame the Met for this.

Jane drew in a breath, her heart racing.

Crowley could see she was worried. 'We want the public to recognise the brave side of policing and see what underhanded lies the IRA will spread to further their cause. I want you to describe in detail the event, and I will make an appeal for assistance from the public. Your actions may make someone step forward with vital information to help identify the suspect.'

Jane didn't have the chance to reply, as there was a knock on the door and DCI Church walked in, apologising for his late arrival.

'It took longer than I anticipated to brief all my officers on their new surveillance duties in the aftermath of the explosion.'

Gregson shook Church's hand, and Crowley acknowledged him with a nod. Church, seeing that Jane was shaken, rested his hand on her shoulder.

'Are you all right, Tennison?'

She nodded. Gregson turned to sit down behind the desk.

'DCI Church is aware of the newspaper headline,' Gregson told Jane, and then added for Church's benefit, 'I have just explained that we are organising a press conference this afternoon, using WDC Tennison as the front person, and –'

'Hang on a minute,' Church inerrupted angrily. 'Have you also explained the risk Tennison is taking if she does this?'

'We were just about to do that when you came in, Jimmy. The press conference will no doubt piss the IRA off. There is, of course, a danger of a reprisal from them, against Tennison . . .'

Church leant forward. 'Does Tennison also have the right to refuse to participate in the press conference?'

Jane looked from one man to the other; Gregson stared at her. 'I believe you are agreeable to taking part?'

Jane didn't have time to reply as Crowley gestured with his hand.

'Remember, all of you, that mainland UK police officers are not considered legitimate targets for the IRA.'

'So, what does that make civilians?' Church asked, facetiously.

The three men talked across Jane as if she wasn't in the room, becoming more argumentative as they spoke.

'Listen, the reason the terrorists give coded warnings is to minimise civilian targets. They give a warning very close to when they intend the bomb to be set off to delay any bomb disposal teams discovering the device. They consider themselves to be an army, not terrorists, and they want to instil fear in the public.'

'Jesus Christ, you sound like you're on their side!' Church snapped.

'I fuckin' resent that!' Crowley shouted back.

Gregson rose to his feet. 'Come on, now, let's desist with this petty bickering. It is WDC Tennison's decision and hers alone. So maybe we should all just let her have some time to think about it.'

'I want to do it,' Jane said firmly. 'On the condition, and with your assurance, that my family will be protected.'

Gregson eagerly shook her hand. He was keen to get everything organised.

'Thank you, WDC Tennison. I'll green light the press conference for this afternoon at the Yard. In the meantime, DCI Crowley will brief you on what you should say. He will also take a detailed statement from you about yesterday's events, and your brave part in trying to apprehend the suspect.'

As Gregson left, the room fell silent for a moment. Crowley looked over at the still-angry DCI Church, then glanced at his watch.

'Let me arrange for some refreshments whilst you discuss your squad's new detail with Tennison.'

Crowley walked out and DCI Church moved around the desk to sit in front of Jane.

'Commander Gregson has ordered the Dip Squad to utilise their skills by patrolling the Underground and main West End shopping areas, to look for possible IRA bomb suspects. We're already attending yesterday's scene looking for any explosive devices left nearby, but the bomb squad have their own forensic unit and have gathered evidence to be sent over to the lab at Woolwich.'

Jane looked up at him. 'Do you know if anyone found Daphne's handbag at the station? I mean, the other witness?'

Church shook his head. 'Nobody's mentioned it to me if they have. The Dip Squad's involved because they're trained to detect any suspicious movements or body language. Crowley has his teams out searching for possible safe houses, and they'll be setting up raids utilising armed officers to carry them out.'

'Will I still be working with the Dip Squad?'

'Just don't jump the gun, Tennison. This morning Crowley requested that you be assigned to a desk job with the Bomb Squad, until the IRA Active Service unit's members are arrested.'

'But I want to be on active duty!'

'There's no way that can happen.'

'Why not? I'm doing the bomb squad a big favour by agreeing to be at the press conference, so why should I be grounded?'

'You won't be able to change their minds. But I've come up with another possible placement, if you agree with it. Crowley can get you attached to the Forensic Explosives Laboratory, which is part of the Royal Armament Research and Development Establishment over at the Royal Arsenal in Woolwich. It's a secure site patrolled by Ministry of Defence police, so you'll be safe there and out of harm's way.'

'I don't know . . .'

'Look, I had to twist his arm to do this, and he may change his mind depending on what happens in the press conference. But if you agree at least you won't be stuck behind a desk.'

'How were you able to twist his arm? I thought what goes on at the Royal Arsenal was supposed to be secret?'

'I know the detective sergeant there. It's a terrific unit. They do all the bomb-related forensics and are funded by the MOD.' Church laughed gently. 'Better facilities than our dump! No matter what they ask you to do, show you're keen and offer to help, then they will take you under their wing. When this is all over you'll walk away with some good forensic knowledge about bombs and explosions, which would be a plus if you ever fancied joining the Bomb Squad. So what do you think?'

Jane thought about it. Being stuck behind a desk was not appealing. 'I accept. Thank you.'

Church looked pleased. 'Well, since Crowley is now off somewhere filling his stomach, what do you say to grabbing a bite in the canteen?'

'He said he needed me to make a statement?'

'Plenty of time for that. Come on.' Holding the door open for her, he added, 'Oh, by the by, have you ordered any tickets for the big dinner dance?'

It was clear that Church was changing the subject, but Jane was glad of the distraction.

'I don't think I want any tickets,' she said as they walked down the corridor towards the lifts.

'It would be a good way for you to meet everyone. There aren't many posh nights out with the Dip Squad and Flying Squad lads, along with all the different CID squads based at the yard . . . and everyone can bring a partner, wives, girlfriends, boyfriends . . .'

'I don't have one,' she said, as he pressed the button for the lift.

'Well, you can come solo. Or one of our team can escort you and be your chaperone. At the end of the day, Tennison, they're all just detectives having a good night out.'

In some ways, Church was relieved Jane was single as it was one fewer person, who would have been close to her, to worry about. The lift doors opened and they both stepped inside.

'As far as I can see, a good night out for them involves getting pissed out of their heads.'

'Well, I'll put two tickets aside and maybe in the interim you'll find a good-looking bloke to take with you.'

Jane smiled. 'I doubt that will happen.'

'With your looks and figure there's no reason you shouldn't. Let's see what happens in the next few weeks. And I'm a good dancer, so you could always come with me!'

Jane smiled as they stepped out of the lift to head to the canteen. Jimmy Church was quite the charmer and for the moment Jane forgot about the consequences of her decision to do the press conference. Which is just what Church intended.

CHAPTER SIX

Jane bought a ham sandwich and a coffee but she was too nervous to eat. Church remained affable as he wolfed down his bacon sandwich. He asked her about her parents and Jane told him about their fears for her safety.

'I should have called them yesterday. I did try, but the phone was constantly engaged. I feel really guilty about not getting through to them. Pam, my sister, also came over as she had been worried about me, and she suggested I spend the night at my parents''

'Do you get on with your sister?'

'Yes, sometimes . . .'

'But she doesn't live with your parents?'

'No, she's married, they have a flat in Kilburn.'

'What does her husband do?'

'Tony? He's a carpenter. Pam runs a local hairdressing salon.'

'Do they have kids?'

'No, but they're keen to start a family.'

Church checked his watch as he drank his coffee. Jane was completely unaware that he was making a mental note of who might possibly need protection.

'I'm not having a go at you, Jane, but you should have contacted the Dip Squad office to let us know where you were last night. If you are off duty and not at your usual place of residence, you need to call it in. We should always know where to contact you in the event of an emergency.' He lit a cigarette. 'And what's this I hear about you moving out of the section house without leaving a forwarding address?'

Jane was shamefaced. 'I'm sorry, but I only just moved into my flat. I did mean to leave my new address and phone number at the office.'

'That was against police regulations, Tennison. Give me your contact details so I can make sure we have them on file for future reference.'

Jane jotted down her new address in her notebook, then tore out the page and passed it to him. He tucked it into his wallet, checked his watch again, and suggested it was time she went back to see Crowley.

Jane sat opposite Crowley as he handed her a prepared press statement.

'I drafted this from what you've already told us about the events at Covent Garden.'

Jane read through the document and glanced up.

'You make no mention of Daphne, or why I was at the hospital?'

'Of course not – we need to protect her identity. How does everything else read?'

'Well, it's concise and correct, apart from the fact that it's missed out the part where I tried to stop the suspect by grabbing his sleeve.'

Crowley sighed. 'That's because, Tennison, the IRA are saying that the bomb went off because you tackled the bomber. We don't want to acknowledge that possibility in any way, shape or form. I'm not asking you to lie . . . we simply don't want to draw attention to the issue.'

'What should I say if the press asks about it?'

'Don't worry about it. Commander Gregson will be by your side and he'll fend off any dodgy questions. Just read through it again so you feel confident that you'll be able to handle it.'

Jane started to read the statement again as Crowley picked up his phone and dialled an extension.

'Can you get DS Dexter to come into my office to take WDC Tennison's official statement? Thanks.'

He replaced the receiver and sat drumming his fingers on the desk as Jane carefully finished reading through the press statement. A few moments later there was a gentle knock on his door.

'Come in,' Crowley barked. 'This, Tennison, is DS Alan Dexter. He's one of the Bomb Squad's most experienced bomb disposal experts and has saved the day on more than one occasion.'

Jane looked up as Dexter walked in and nodded politely at her. He had an athletic build, about six feet tall, with blond hair combed back from his angular high-cheekboned face. He was wearing a casual soft leather jacket over a black polo-neck sweater and jeans. Dexter picked up a high-back chair, carried it over to the desk and confidently sat astride it, leaning his elbows along the back.

Dexter turned to Jane. 'DCI Crowley has already briefed me about your involvement. Your reaction under immense pressure at the scene was admirable.'

Jane blushed.

Dexter took out a packet of Henri Wintermans Café Crème cigars and lit one.

'Dexter is aware you grabbed the suspect, but it's imperative at the press conference that we use the fact you shouted at the suspect to stop, he assaulted you and made his escape, then the bomb went off. You could not have caused the detonation. Do you understand, Tennison?

'I understand, sir. But I am also very sure of the fact that his hands were not in his pockets . . . he swiped my hand away from him causing me to stumble and fall backwards. It was at that point that I saw him, but only his side –'

'I want you to look at a surveillance photograph.' Crowley interrupted.

He opened a drawer and removed a thick photograph album which was marked HIGHLY CONFIDENTIAL – SPECIAL BENCH SUR-VEILLANCE, dated March 1976. He flicked through the album and stopped at a photograph with an exhibit mark on it. He showed Jane this picture, a shot taken at a distance, of two young men standing outside a café. One man was holding his hand up as if to hail a taxi.

Dexter remained silent, smoking and occasionally looking towards Jane. He had very blue eyes, which were hooded and heavily lined, as if he'd spent endless hours in the sun, squinting against the glare.

'Is one of these men the suspect you chased at Covent Garden?' Crowley asked Jane.

Jane carefully examined the photograph, then shook her head.

'I can't be sure. I didn't really get a good enough look at him. All I can remember is that he had dark, collar-length hair and he might have had a thin beard or heavy stubble.'

'Think . . . what about his height, and his clothing?'

'Er, he was about 5'8" or 5'10", and he was wearing an overcoat – a type of donkey jacket or labourer's coat – and dark trousers. The coat might have had a hood, or he wore a top with a hood underneath the overcoat . . . maybe even a woollen hat.'

'Take another look. The man on the right is wearing a dark jacket, has dark hair, and is the right height. Do you think it could have been him?'

Jane took her time looking at the photograph. 'I honestly don't know, sir . . . it might be him, but I can't honestly say for certain. Neither of the men leap out at me as being people I have seen before.'

Dexter leaned forwards, stubbing out his cigar. He turned to Jane.

'You must have had a pretty traumatic experience, Tennison, and you might even be suffering from a mental block. I've seen it many times before after people have gone through an event like this.'

He had a soft, cultured voice, unlike the brusque and impatient Crowley, who leaned over Jane and snapped the album shut, startling her.

Crowley grabbed his jacket from the back of his chair. 'Dexter will take your statement. I've got some business to deal with.' He swung his jacket over his shoulder and marched out of the office, slamming the door behind him.

'I'm a bit confused. I thought I had already read and checked my statement? Am I now making another one?' asked Jane as she held up the statement Crowley had given her before Dexter arrived.

'That's your statement for the press conference, but I need to take a full and detailed statement from you. This one's for the trial, when the suspects are arrested and charged.'

'Oh ... I'm sorry, it's all been such panic. Have I upset DCI Crowley in some way?'

Dexter smiled at Jane. 'Don't worry about Crowley. He's obviously under a lot of pressure. His bark is always worse than his bite. Maybe in a couple of days you'll have a clearer recall and might remember more about the suspect. For now, you've done a fantastic job.'

'Did any other witness at the tube station see the suspect?' Jane asked.

'No one else can give a good description, or they're too frightened to come forward. God forbid that Daphne dies, because we're depending on her to give us more details.'

'Does Crowley think the man in the photograph is an IRA bomber? If he does, why doesn't he arrest him?'

Dexter stood up and moved around the desk, putting his hands in his trouser pockets.

'This is in the strictest confidence, Detective Tennison, but it might help you to understand the pressure Crowley is under . . . I'd appreciate it if you kept it between the two of us. That photograph was taken by a Special Branch officer. One of the men in the photo is an IRA informant and the one hailing a taxi is believed to be part of an IRA Active Service Unit, or ASU, who has just arrived in the mainland to initiate a bombing campaign in London.'

'But why hasn't he been arrested?' Jane asked.

She could see that Dexter was apprehensive about answering. He took his time lighting another cigar.

'Because we don't know who or where he is yet. We couldn't risk putting an undercover officer in that café or putting a wire on our informant. Although we had surveillance officers following the black cab, they lost the suspect. We don't know if he sussed that he was being tailed, but later that night our informant was found hanged in his bedsit. It was staged to look like suicide.'

'No wonder Crowley's under pressure,' Jane responded.

'That's not the half of it. The shit hit the fan after our informant's death because he'd already passed us information that suggested the IRA were building up a sophisticated and extremely secure network of operatives and logistical teams in the country. He was about to give us details with names, dates, times and places. Some of his contacts are what we call "sleepers" . . . you know, appearing to be good and valued citizens until they're needed. The informant wanted a whole new identity in another country before giving up everything he knew and Crowley had it all in motion . . . he was just waiting for approval. Anyway, we've got nothing now.'

Jane shook her head as Dexter sat behind the desk.

'Commander Gregson got a dressing-down from the Home Secretary, and in turn he gave Crowley a bollocking just before the Covent Garden explosion. So it's obvious why Crowley was hoping you'd recognise the man in the photo. The only positive lead from the photo is that the informant was associated with him and then murdered.'

'I'm sorry, but I literally only saw the man for a second.'

'It's not your fault. Now, I need you to walk me through exactly what happened so I can take your official statement.'

Jane began once again to go through everything she could recall. Dexter glanced up only once, when she was describing finding the small child beneath the body of her mother. He held up his pen every now and then, for her to slow down whilst he wrote every word, and then nodded his head for her to continue.

'Hang on a second. Can you just go over the description again of the suspect?'

'Well, as I've said, I didn't get a good look at him, just his profile. I remember he had dark hair, perhaps stubble on his face, but I can't really recall his features at all.'

The copious detail of the statement covered page after page, and it took a further hour and a half before it was concluded. Repeatedly Dexter questioned her about the possibility that she might be able to identify the suspect. Jane continued to assert that she doubted that she could, then she surprised Dexter.

'I remember his rucksack.'

'You mean you can describe it?'

'Yes. A gym instructor had one that was similar. It was made of a thick, grey cloth with a brown . . . maybe leather . . . bottom.'

'How come you can remember details of the rucksack but you can't recall the suspect's face?'

'I remember the face of the ticket collector and the way he was holding the rucksack before he was blown up and killed.'

Dexter eventually passed over the written statement to Jane, and stood up to stretch his long legs.

'Read it carefully, just in case I've missed something. And let me know if you have any questions.'

Dexter paced around the room and lit another cigar. Jane skimmed through the statement as she could sense his impatience. Then he leaned in close, handed her a pen and asked her to sign it. He wore a soft-smelling cologne, which mingled with his cigar smoke but was not in any way offensive. Quite the contrary. Dexter was a very attractive, relaxed man, and Jane noticed his clean, manicured hands.

'How many bomb scenes have you dealt with?' Jane asked as he put the signed statement in a neat pile on Crowley's desk.

'More than I care to think about,' he replied, returning to sit beside her. He gave her a side-on look. 'You were stationed at Hackney when that explosion happened, weren't you? That's one I'll never forget . . . that terrible scene around the bank vault. What made it a lot harder was the fact that two fellow officers were killed. It was impossible to tell who was who from their charred remains. Once it became clear it wasn't an IRA job, we withdrew and let the locals deal with the aftermath.'

Although it had been three years ago, Jane had never known what state the bodies had been in inside the bank. She still felt emotional whenever she remembered Kath Morgan and Len Bradfield, but it didn't hurt as much as it had just after the explosion. It was as if the bomb at Coven Garden had helped exorcise some of those demons. More than anything she now realised that death could result from simply 'being in the wrong place at the wrong time'.

The door banged open as Crowley returned. He handed Jane a signed authorisation to work at the Forensics Explosives Laboratory.

'I've spoken with the senior scientist at Woolwich Arsenal and they are expecting you at nine tomorrow morning. Now, you'd better wait in the canteen. I'll send someone to collect you when the press conference begins.'

Dexter stood up, waiting for her to stand. 'It won't be long, I'll see you up there in a minute.'

Jane felt as if both Crowley and Dexter were impatient for her to leave. She didn't know exactly where the lab in Woolwich was, but decided it was best to ask for the details later.

As soon as the door closed behind her, Crowley sat at his desk and nodded to Dexter.

'So, what do you think?' Crowley asked.

'Well, I laid it on thick about the IRA cell and trusting her with sensitive information, et cetera, so she must be aware of what scum the IRA are and how important an ID will be.'

'Yeah, well I hope to Christ she doesn't back down . . . especially after that situation with the Balcombe Street ASU. Their defence barristers are throwing a lot of shit at us and saying that we beat a confession out of the wrong guys for the Guildford and Woolwich pub bombs.'

'Shit, give me a break! The politicians and top brass wanted a quick result, and we got it for them. They confessed, so the end justified the means.'

'I know that. If the old girl in hospital croaks, Tennison is all we've got to ID the suspect . . . She'll be our only useful witness.'

'We both know the man in the surveillance photograph is part of the ASU, but we need to keep our fingers crossed that the old lady survives. She'll be a lot easier to persuade into making a positive ID of our man than Tennison.'

Crowley opened a drawer and took out a file.

'This is WDC Tennison's police file. She's a blue-eyed girl, trustworthy. She's never been in any trouble . . . plus she has a Commissioner's Commendation. In my opinion, if we can influence her to make a positive ID on the man in the photo, the case is cut and dried . . . it won't even matter if he denies it in interview.'

Dexter read through the report as Crowley rocked back in the chair.

'Did she sign her statement?'

'Yep, it's in front of you.'

'She wasn't aware of the addition?'

'No, but I doubt she'll remember if she did or didn't say it. I deliberately kept it long-winded. I even allowed her to check it over, but she just skimmed through it.'

Crowley picked up the pages and flicked through them, reading. After a while he looked up and smiled, quoting, '"I think I might recognise him if I saw him again . . ." Good, that's good. I hope to Christ she doesn't challenge it in court. I want you to keep up the Mr Nice Guy act. Get closer to her, take her out and get her on our side.'

'OK if I shag her?'

'If your girlfriend doesn't mind.'

'She's long gone. How about hypnosis?'

'I'm sure you can get her into bed without resorting to that.'

'Ha ha, very funny. I meant we could use hypnosis to try to trigger a better recollection of the event from her. If it works, we don't need to manipulate her into saying what we want.'

'Let's see how we go with the artist's impression.'

Crowley looked at his watch, and then back to Dexter. He waved his hand in front of his face.

'Jesus, those filthy cigars stink! I'm going to get a call any minute about the press conference. Give the hospital a ring and see how the old girl is.'

Dexter shrugged and handed back Jane's police file. Crowley flicked through it while Dexter put in a call to the hospital to enquire about Daphne. He was relieved to be told that she was still alive, although she hadn't woken from the coma. The hospital had now identified her from a handbag found in the debris at Covent Garden station. It contained her pension book with a library identification card and some photographs. Her name was Daphne Millbank, a widow aged seventy-five, but they hadn't yet been able to contact any living relatives.

Dexter informed Crowley, who then picked up the phone, patted it with the flat of his hand, dialled an internal number and waited before it was connected.

'Is the artist's sketch of the suspect bomber ready? I need it before the press conference . . .' He put the phone down.

'They're bringing a copy up now,' he told Dexter. 'Go buy Tennison a coffee in the canteen . . . sweet-talk her out of any nerves. I'll come up to get you both when it's time for the press conference.'

There was a knock on the door. A uniformed officer entered and handed Crowley a large manila envelope. As the officer left, Crowley looked at Dexter and tapped the envelope in his hand.

'This will lead us to the man we want. We get him and we'll get the whole ASU.'

Dexter didn't look so confident. 'Are you sure you're doing the right thing?'

'Like you said, Dexter . . . the end will justify the means.'

CHAPTER SEVEN

Dexter joined Jane in the canteen. He tried to reassure her but she was apprehensive, constantly looking towards the double doors, waiting for Crowley to call her to the press conference.

'You've got the press statement, the one Crowley made out for you?' he asked, trying to cheer her up. 'Maybe just skim over it, so that you feel confident. And put some more sugar in your coffee. It'll give you an energy boost.'

Jane added two heaped spoons of sugar to the milky coffee and stirred it.

'There'll be a lot of press and cameras in there, but don't be nervous. You want to make the public understand the carnage at the scene, just like you did when I took down your full statement, all right?'

He gently patted her shoulder, taking a sneaky look towards the canteen entrance.

'OK, he's here . . .'

Crowley gestured for them to follow him, disappearing back out of the doors as Dexter and Jane both got up from the table.

'I need the loo . . .' Jane said.

'There's a gents off the canteen corridor . . . I'll stand guard outside for you.' Dexter drew her chair back as she picked up her bag and the statement.

Halfway down the corridor they stopped for her to pop into the gents. She went into one of the cubicles alongside the urinals and locked the door behind her. She felt as if she was going to be sick, and had to take deep breaths.

Crowley went to the conference room. While Dexter waited outside the toilet for Jane he was approached by DCI Church.

'Where is she?' Church asked.

'Taking a leak.'

'For a moment there I thought she might have got cold feet and left.'

'No, she's up for it and remarkably calm under the circumstances.'

'Look, I've asked one of my team to be at her flat to look out for her tonight. He can stay until we know how this is going to play out. It may be a good idea to organise an armed special patrol group unit to sit outside her address and make sure she gets to and from work safely.'

Dexter nodded. 'SPG's a good idea.'

'We'll also have to check out her family,' Church added. 'I've got her parents' address . . . and she has a sister who's married, living elsewhere.'

As Jane came out of the gents they both turned to her and smiled. It was obvious that they had been talking about her, and Church departed as soon as they saw her.

'Let's go,' Dexter said, taking her arm.

Crowley was waiting in the anteroom with Commander Gregson, who was now dressed in full uniform. Dexter wished Jane luck, and then walked out.

'Be prepared, Tennison . . . there's a room full of journalists and a lot of cameras, but I'll be right by your side,' Commander Gregson said, checking his watch. 'We don't want to keep them waiting any longer.'

Jane followed the Commander and Crowley out of the anteroom and through the double doors that lead into the conference room. Despite Gregson's warning, she was unprepared for the frenzy of camera flashes as they all went off in unison, creating a strobe light effect that made her feel quite dizzy.

The large room was crowded with journalists armed with notebooks and small portable cassette recorders, as well as a television crew. The three officers made their way to a raised platform, upon which stood a long table with three chairs placed behind it. The Commander sat in the middle with Crowley to his left and Jane on his right. She focused on placing her statement on the table in front of her and tried to stop shaking.

The buzz in the room quietened as the Commander slowly rose to his feet and spoke in a loud, clear voice.

'I'd like to thank you all for attending this press conference. As a result of yesterday's callous bombing carried out by the IRA at Covent Garden tube station, five people were killed. There are also several people still in hospital on the critical list with life-threatening injuries. Many of the survivors will be scarred both mentally and physically for life. I want to make it clear to the press and public that the IRA have lied: a police officer was in no way responsible for causing the detonation of the bomb at Covent Garden. It was the merciless act of a cowardly IRA bomber, who, fearing arrest by a brave police officer, set the bomb off without warning.'

There was a flurry of questions from the press. How could they be sure that it wasn't an accidental detonation caused by a police officer? Didn't the IRA usually give coded warnings before their attacks? Gregson indicated Tennison with a gesture of his hand.

'This is WDC Jane Tennison, a fine example of a brave Metropolitan police officer who risked her own life in the line of duty.'

The sudden flash of cameras made her blink. Gregson continued.

'Like everyone at the tube station, she didn't expect to suddenly find herself in the middle of such a traumatic incident, one in which her own life was threatened. Even after the explosion, and despite being blown to the ground herself, she kept calm and rendered first aid to the wounded and dying. WDC Tennison has bravely come here today to answer your questions and tell you what happened.'

He nodded to Jane to stand as he sat back down in his chair. The cameras started flashing again as the reporters shouted out a barrage of questions. Gregson raised his hand and said loudly that they were to ask questions one at a time, and he pointed to one of the journalists to speak first.

'How are you feeling about the terrible event?'

'I am obviously still very shaken, but I have had a lot of support from my fellow officers. There was someone who was in front of me when the explosion occurred and if I had not been shielded by him, I would have had severe injuries, or could even have lost my life.'

'What made you suspicious of the bombing suspect?'

Jane carefully answered the question, avoiding making any reference to Daphne. She explained that she heard someone calling out 'you've left your bag,' and then she had noticed a man moving quickly away from the ticket area.

A sullen-faced journalist interrupted before she could continue. 'Do you feel you are in any way responsible for the explosion? If, for example, you had not approached the subject and attempted to stop him but had waited for him to leave, then maybe a coded warning would have been sent? Then the area could have been cleared and the bomb diffused?'

There was an audible gasp around the conference room and many looked at the man in disgust. Jane was visibly shocked but stood her ground.

'No, I am not responsible. I was there, and you weren't. Everything happened very quickly, and I didn't have time to consider other options. At first I thought the rucksack might have been left innocently, but when I challenged the suspect and said I was a police officer he pushed me aside and ran off. Both of his hands were empty, and not in his pockets.'

'If you grabbed him, maybe that was what caused the bomb to go off?' he persisted.

Gregson rose to his feet and looked over at Jane to sit down.

'This young woman risked her own life knowing the suspect might be an IRA bomber and armed. The suspect assaulted her, ran off, and seconds later the bomb went off. The forensic lab is working flat out to determine if the bomb was on a timer that went off prematurely or was detonated by a radio-controlled device. WDC Tennison followed the correct procedure under the circumstances and we are all very supportive and proud of her. Due to WDC Tennison's tenacity and forethought we now have an artist's impression of the suspect. I would appeal to anyone who recognises this man to contact the bomb squad at Scotland Yard.'

This was the first Jane had heard of any artist's impression. Her description of the suspect had surely been far too vague.

Crowley gave the signal for a large screen behind the table to be turned on, which showed the projected image of the drawing of the suspect. Jane swivelled around in her chair and quickly realised that it was a sketch of the suspected IRA man hailing the taxi in the surveillance photograph Crowley had shown her. She was shocked that this had been done without her knowledge.

There was a frenzy of flash bulbs again, and some of the photographers were up on their feet, desperate to get a good picture. Gregson continued describing their suspect as being 5'8" or 5'10", aged between twenty-five and thirty. He pointed out the man's collar-length hair and said that he was wearing a dark overcoat, perhaps some kind of hooded sweatshirt beneath.

'I was apprehensive about WDC Tennison being here at the press conference because she saw the suspect's face and would therefore be able to identify him upon his arrest. I am aware this places her in danger from the members of the IRA ASU who committed this atrocity. However, WDC Tennison was asked if she wished to appear in front of you today to aid our appeal for public assistance, and it is to her credit that she has put the investigation and the public's safety before her own.'

There were loud murmurs of agreement and a few people clapped as Gregson signalled for her to stand. Crowley also rose to his feet.

'I thank you all for your time and would respectfully ask you to remain seated until we have left the conference room.'

The same sullen-faced journalist held up the paper Jane had seen that morning, and pointed at the photograph of her on the front page.

'Why were you getting into the ambulance? Were you injured?'

Gregson raised his hand. 'Fortunately, as you can see, WDC Tennison was unharmed. She rode in the ambulance to accompany a mother who was badly injured and who, sadly, subsequently died. Thankfully her young child was saved.'

Jane was quickly ushered out between Crowley and Gregson, back into the anteroom where DS Dexter was waiting. He gave Jane the thumbs-up. Trying to keep control of herself, she asked if she could have a private word with the Commander.

'I'm sorry, Tennison . . . I have to dash. I've got a meeting with the Home Secretary and I'm already running late. If you have any questions, DCI Crowley can help you.'

Gregson hurried out of the anteroom as Jane turned angrily to Crowley.

'Why did you issue that artist's impression without consulting me, or warning me that it was going to be shown?'

'When there's been a terrorist attack we have to move fast, before memories fade. We needed something to reassure the public that the investigation was moving swiftly. If the sketch helps to identify the man, then that will be a bonus.'

'But you used me, and I feel as if I lied in there.'

'No, you didn't. You told me the man in the photograph we showed you looked familiar, or similar, to the suspect you saw at Covent Garden.'

'No, I didn't say that . . . you're twisting my words!'

'Either way, let's hope we get a result. Now, I've got to go. You did very well, Tennison.'

Stunned, Jane could only watch as Crowley walked out, slamming the door behind him.

Dexter smiled at her. 'Are you all right?'

'No, I'm not! I didn't realise Crowley was even going to show an artist's impression . . . Were you in on it as well? Did you know?'

Dexter shrugged. 'Come on, why would I confide in you about the ASU and the informer if I knew what he was going to do?

She shook her head, bewildered. 'Sorry for sounding off at you. I'm just . . .'

'Under the circumstances I don't blame you. Now, I don't want to alarm you but Church is arranging for a couple of armed plain-clothes SPG officers to keep watch outside your flat . . .'

'Oh my God!'

'Don't worry, Jane. It's highly unlikely the IRA would try anything, especially now the heat is on to find their ASU.'

'Then why do I need armed protection?'

'It's more of a deterrent than anything else . . . and the bonus is they'll keep the press away. Your neighbours will be very envious . . . and your boyfriend will behave himself.'

'I don't have a boyfriend,' Jane snapped, unable to appreciate his jokey manner.

'Sorry, sorry.' He paused briefly. 'Well, that gives me the opportunity to ask you out for a drink. Unless you fancy a spot of dinner?'

Jane smiled. She *did* find him very attractive.

'Thank you for the invitation, but I'm exhausted and tomorrow is my first day with the forensic team in Woolwich. I really need an early night.'

Dexter opened the door and gestured for her to go ahead of him.

'I don't even know how to get to the Royal Arsenal,' she added, walking out with him.

'Well, you can take a train, but if you've got a car I'd drive. Oh, and a word of advice . . . don't wear anything new. You'll probably be sifting through rubbish bins full of rubble from Covent Garden, so you'll get covered in dust.'

They took the lift down to the ground floor and as they were walking to the exit, DCI Church hurried to join them.

'Press conference went well, Tennison. Do you mind if I have a quick word with Dexter?'

Jane didn't have time to answer before the two men moved away together.

When he was sure they were out of earshot, Church said, 'Listen, Al, I've organised one of my team to keep an eye on Tennison, plus Crowley's agreed to the armed SPG officers outside her flat.'

'There's no need to be secretive, I've already told her about the armed protection. It's spooked her a bit, but I was going to take her home and reassure her it's for the best.'

'I had no doubt Mr "Sex on Legs" would be volunteering to "reassure" her. She's vulnerable at the moment, so you just back off,' Church hissed. He saw Jane looking over and changed the subject. 'By the way, Dexter, do you want tickets for the big black-tie do? We've still got a lot of spaces.'

'Yeah, put me down for two. I'll sort out a cheque later.'

'That's what everyone's saying. I need it soon or you won't get a table. Don't leave it too long or I'll take you off the list.'

They walked back to join Jane. Dexter gave her one of his smiles and jerked his thumb towards Church.

'Jimmy's driving you home. If you don't mind, let's take a rain check on drinks and dinner.' He walked off.

'If you wait here at the entrance,' said Church, getting out his car key, 'I'll bring my car up from the underground car park . . . Just stay inside until you see me draw up.'

Jane did as he instructed but was astonished when a back-firing Ford Anglia pulled up. She hadn't envisaged him driving a wreck. He leaned over to open the passenger door and Jane climbed in beside him. As she tried to close the door it got stuck and she had to pull it hard to make it shut.

'Right, Baker Street . . .' Church said, grinding the gears as they moved jerkily away in a cloud of exhaust fumes. The interior of the car was almost as decrepit as the rest of it. The seats were torn, and the ashtray was overflowing. Church gave her a small sidelong glance.

'These are just the wheels we use for undercover,' he said unconvincingly. 'My own car is an E-Type.'

Jane laughed. Grinning, Church continued, 'The engine's in good shape. If you really put your foot down she'll do seventy. That's if your foot doesn't go through the floor.'

They hit rush-hour traffic, so it took a while to get down the Euston Road. Jane directed him to take a turning into Regent's Park and to come out through the gates nearest to Baker Street. As the traffic eased she could feel the tiredness begin to make her eyes droop.

'I'm exhausted,' she said, as he drove out of the park and headed down Melcombe Street. 'That's it . . . just stop over there,' she added.

Church stopped the car and pulled on the handbrake. He opened his door to get out and help her.

'There's no need, I can manage,' Jane said.

He ignored her and walked around to the passenger door. He had to heave it open as it was stuck firm. As Jane climbed out he took her elbow and they walked the few steps to her front door.

'Right . . . delivered safe and sound. One of the squad will be over later to check on you, and those are plain-clothes SPG officers in the unmarked car over the road.' He nodded in their direction and did a thumbs up to indicate Jane was the officer they were there to protect. They nodded back.

'You've been really kind,' Jane said to Church. 'I appreciate it.'

'Any time. Just call me if you need anything.'

Jane turned on the hall lights. They were on a timer and often switched off before she had had time to reach the top floor. She was so tired that her legs felt heavy as she walked up the stairs. Above her, she heard a light cough. Pausing, she listened carefully, then slowly continued up the stairs, stopping again when she heard a creaking sound from the landing above, outside her flat. Jane hesitated, feeling the panic rise as the timer lights cut out. She was now in almost total darkness and was about turn and run back down the stairs when she saw a man's legs in the hall above, and screamed.

'It's all right! It's me!'

Jane almost fell backwards as DS Stanley appeared, gesturing at her to stop screaming.

'What the hell are you doing here?' she demanded, gasping for breath.

'Looking out for you. The boss wanted one of us to keep you company, just in case there were any repercussions after the press conference. I was gonna wait for you to come home, but your neighbour downstairs let me into the building, so I've been sitting on your stairs.'

'I'm surprised she let you in,' Jane snapped, making her way past him.

'I do have a warrant card, you know, Tennison, and I gave her some bull about checking out your burglar alarm, and that I was expecting you back any minute. I've been sitting here waiting for you for over half an hour.'

Jane unlocked her front door and Stanley followed her inside, picking up an overnight bag he had left on the landing.

'There's SPG outside. Surely you don't need to be here all night?' Jane asked.

'I can doss down on the sofa. It's just an extra precaution . . . and I'll take you to work in the morning.'

'Just for the one night?'

'Depends . . . this is nice . . .'

'I don't have a sofa, but there's a small spare bedroom along the corridor, on your right.'

Jane was now very tense, and also angry. She watched Stanley saunter along the narrow corridor and push open the door to her own bedroom.

'No, that's my bedroom.'

'Just checking it out for safety.'

Jane took off her coat, watching as Stanley crossed to the window in her bedroom, which overlooked the road below. He shone his torch twice to signal to the still-waiting Church that he was inside and all was well.

'This is really very nice . . .' he repeated, as he walked out. Now that she'd calmed down, Jane forced herself to offer him a cup of tea.

'Lovely . . . and if you can rustle up a sandwich that'd be great,' he replied, as he went into the spare room. Jane grimaced. She wished she could ask him to take a bath, as he smelt terrible. But instead she went into the kitchen and put on the kettle.

After a few minutes, Stanley joined her and perched on a stool.

'Nice little place . . . compact, though, and a hell of a long walk up. Do you have a TV?'

'No, I don't. I've only just moved in.' Jane buttered two slices of bread and took out a packet of ham from the fridge.

'You having one?' Stanley asked, rolling up a cigarette.

'Yes, but I can only make one at a time. Do you want mustard?'

'Yep, and two sugars in my tea.'

Jane took out some cups and made the sandwiches while the kettle came to the boil. Stanley watched her preparing the tea as he finished assembling his roll-up and put it down in front of him. They eventually sat next to each other and used the same teaspoon to remove the teabags from their cups, placing them on a saucer.

'When I've finished this,' said Jane, 'I'm going to have a bath. Perhaps you might like one after me?'

'No, I'm OK, thanks.'

Stanley was wearing filthy jeans and an old torn T-shirt, both of which looked, and smelt, as though they hadn't been washed in weeks. She had a lot of questions she wanted to ask, uppermost was why DCI Church had wanted Stanley to be in her flat.

'Do you think that there could be repercussions about what went down at the press conference?' she asked Stanley.

'Possibly.'

'Does that also mean that it might affect my family?'

'It might, but that'll be taken care of . . . it depends what reaction we get after today.'

'Should I warn them?'

'I wouldn't. Why put the frighteners on them when it might not be necessary? If it is, then they'll be well protected, but it's best not to sound the alarm bells. This is a good sandwich,' he mumbled through a mouth full of food.

'Is DCI Church married?' Jane asked.

'He was. Got divorced a few years ago. He had a right time of it . . . she was a real bitch and went off with an electrician who was rewiring their house. Actually, she didn't leave . . . she stayed and Church moved out. But he doesn't like talking about it. I've probably said too much, but he's a really good guy. I like him.'

Stanley lit his roll-up as Jane took their plates to the sink.

'What about DS Dexter from the bomb squad. Do you know him?'

'Course I do, everyone knows Al. And if you're interested in him, he's not married.'

'I'm not interested in him, for heaven's sake!'

'Well, that's probably a good thing because he's got quite a reputation with women. If you ask me, out of the two of them Jimmy is the better man.'

'I was only asking because I work with them, that's all! Tell me about you, Stanley, are you married?'

'I certainly am. And I've got two kids, aged four and eight. My wife, Alison, is a gem. She has to put up with a lot but never complains.'

Jane smiled. Considering the state of him she reckoned Alison had to be special.

'Does she know you won't be home tonight?'

'Yeah, she understands it's the job. Listen, you go and take your bath and I'll clean up in here, and then go and have a kip.'

Jane left Stanley to make himself another cup of tea, and went to run her bath. She completely submerged her body in the perfumed, bubbly water, then surfaced and washed her hair. After a long while she thought she should perhaps get out and make up the spare bed, but when she emerged wearing a dressing gown, with a towel wrapped around her wet hair, Stanley was already in the spare room.

'Oh, I was going to put some sheets on the bed.'

'Don't bother, I'll just lie on top of the cover. I'm in working gear and don't want to mess up the bed. You just carry on as if I wasn't here, and get a good night's sleep.'

'OK . . . just help yourself to another cup of tea if you want one.'

'Ta. Goodnight, then.'

'Goodnight, Stanley . . . I'm sorry, I don't know your Christian name?'

'Nobody ever uses it. I just go by Stanley.'

Jane checked the kitchen. It was neat and tidy, and Stanley had washed up the cups and the plate, which were now drying on the draining board. She closed her bedroom door and dried her hair. There was no doubt that she felt much safer with Stanley being in the flat. She was just about to climb into bed when the phone rang, so she hurried out to the small hallway to answer it.

'Hello?'

'Hello,' a woman replied. 'I'm answering your advertisement about a room to let.'

'Oh, yes.'

'I'm sorry to call late, but I work locally and would be very interested in viewing the room.'

'Could you give me a contact number where I can reach you?'

'Yes, I suppose my work place would be the best number as I'm there all day. I work in Madame Tussauds.'

'Oh, well this area would be convenient for you . . . but let me call you tomorrow.'

'Is the room still available to rent? I have to move out of the place that I'm currently living in.'

'Yes, the room's still available. Can I take your name and date of birth please?' Jane asked.

'Yes, of course . . . I'm Pearl Radcliff, born 25 October 1951. I have my previous rental details as well as references from where I've stayed previously.'

Jane wrote down Pearl's details and a phone number. She apologised that she couldn't arrange a viewing straightaway as she was unsure what her availability was, but said that she would call her back as soon as she knew.

'Oh, is there any chance I could come by tomorrow evening, after I finish work?'

Jane hesitated, then agreed that she would call her back when she returned from work to let her know if it was convenient.

'Who was that?' Stanley asked, standing in the doorway of the spare bedroom.

'It was in response to an advert I put in the local newsagents . . . I want to rent out the room you're sleeping in.'

'Are you sure that's wise with everything that's going on at the moment?'

'I need a lodger to help pay the mortgage. Besides, I don't see why I should change my plans because of what's happened.'

'Well, it's up to you. Bit small, isn't it? How much are you charging?'

'Why? Don't tell me you're thinking of moving in . . . I'm only letting it out to a female.'

Stanley shrugged and pointed to the phone. 'You make sure you check their background and get a good wad up front, as well as a deposit. You know you need to have it all vetted, as well as fill in a form at the Met? You'd be surprised how many people rent somewhere and have no intention of paying rent, or of ever moving out. I once let out a room to a photographer who paid two months' rent in advance . . . Eighteen months later he hadn't paid another penny, so I threw him out the window by the scruff of his neck, followed by his cameras . . . So, if you get a dodgy lodger you know who to contact . . . I'll sort it.' He patted his chest, unintentionally revealing a holster and weapon by his left armpit.

'Really? How do you go about doing that?'

'It's called the "Ways and Means Act" . . . getting somethin' done without sticking to the rules.'

'Thanks for the advice, Stanley . . . Goodnight.'

As soon as her bedroom door was closed Stanley went over to the small hall table and glanced at the notepad. He saw the name 'Pearl Radcliff' and the date of birth. Returning to the spare room, he jotted down the details. He'd do a precautionary check in case Jane didn't follow the Met's rules about vetting. Then he lay on the bed, smoking.

Jane was oblivious to the fact that, throughout the night, Stanley checked the flat over every hour, even going down to the front door and back up the stairs. He only had a couple of hours sleep and had used the bathroom, cleaned his teeth and washed his hands and face by the time Jane surfaced.

'Good morning! I've made a cup of tea and some toast for you . . . I've had mine.'

'Gosh, thank you. I might change my mind about having only a female flatmate . . . you're very domesticated.'

Stanley smiled and told her he was just going out to fetch some newspapers, giving Jane time to have her breakfast and get dressed. She handed him her front door key and he left.

Stanley crossed the road and headed into the newsagents. He bought a selection of papers before returning to the flat. He didn't go back up to the top floor, but sat on the stairs looking at the front page and inside coverage of the press conference. One of the headlines read BRAVE MET DETECTIVE STARED DEATH IN THE FACE, and under it was a picture of Jane and the artist's impression of the suspect. All the papers had similar headlines and articles about how she 'stood up to' or 'tried to arrest' the bomber, along with pictures of Jane, some at the Covent Garden explosion and others at the press conference. It concerned Stanley that the Bomb Squad's eagerness to trace the suspect now meant Jane could be easily recognised. After he had accompanied her to Woolwich he would talk to DCI Church again about the likelihood of retaliation from the IRA, as the articles made it clear that Jane could identify the bomber.

Jane was dressed and ready by the time Stanley returned. Letting himself in with her key, he put the newspapers into his holdall and then stood in the narrow hall, ready to go. Jane was wearing an old skirt and a worn jacket with a polo-neck sweater. She also had on a pair of old hiking boots.

'I was told not to wear anything decent as I'll be sifting through the debris brought in from Covent Garden,' Jane explained, as she caught him staring at her boots. 'I want to drive there.'

'Right, we should get a move on. It'll take a good hour to get over to the unit. We'll have to go through the Blackwall Tunnel but as we're in good time we should miss the traffic.'

They left Jane's flat and walked some distance down Melcombe Street before stopping beside Jane's VW. Stanley put out his hand to stop her opening the door. Only once he had checked beneath it and walked all around the car did he give her clearance to get in.

'You've not registered this vehicle with us at the office?' he asked.

'I've only had it a few weeks. I mostly just use it at weekends, and will probably park it near my parents' flat.'

'That sounds sensible, since we get our tube fares paid anyway. It's a nice car . . . although yellow's not my colour, a bit on the bright side. I've never been in one of these. What did it cost?'

'It was second-hand . . . my dad got it for me at a good price. Now, do you want to map read? There's an *A–Z* in the glove compartment.'

Jane was impressed by Stanley's street knowledge, although his delivery left something to be desired as he often shouted out instructions at the last minute, not giving her enough time to indicate. She was not yet a proficient driver and he made her jump more than once as he swore and became annoyed when she missed a turning. He took her through back streets to avoid the congestion in central London, but as they neared the Blackwall Tunnel the cars were already bumper to bumper. By the time they entered the tunnel their progress was very slow. Stanley leaned back and went to sleep, snoring loudly, as Jane drove on, realising that even with an early start she was going to be late for her first day.

By the time they left the tunnel Stanley had woken up and barked another instruction as they arrived at an ornate brownstone building. A security barrier was in position and after seeing their warrant cards the MOD police officer pointed to the guard house and told them to book themselves and their vehicle in. They were issued with personal passes and a car pass. The estate was big and they drove over to the Royal Armament Research and Development Establishment, where the Forensics Explosives Lab was based.

They parked the car and after Jane had been authorised to access the lab, Stanley left, telling her that he would be at the Dip Squad base at Vine Street if she needed him. He disappeared before she could thank him, and she felt rather nervous. Not only was she late, but she was about to start working in a totally different environment from the offices she was used to at Hackney and Bow Street. As she entered the main lab she saw several white-coated forensic scientists at work on long trestle tables. Jane was relieved to see DS Lawrence, whom she knew from working on other cases. He seemed pleased to see her and walked towards her smiling.

'Hi, Jane, I was only told this morning that you'd be coming. You need to go see the head scientist first and he'll brief you on what you'll be doing here. His office is down the corridor on the left . . . and don't worry if you hear gunfire or explosions – they test the stuff out on the wasteland. Maybe we can catch up at lunchtime in the canteen.'

The head scientist was stern-faced as he took down her details and made her sign a non-disclosure form about working at the explosives lab. He appeared displeased at having her foisted onto the team, as she had no forensic qualifications. However, he knew the reasons for her being there and eventually told her to go and see the MOD police sergeant at a large hangar style building with a corrugated roof at the rear of the premises.

As Jane entered the building she could see a group of men and two women at work sifting through numbered dustbins filled with debris which she realised must be from the Covent Garden bomb site. Most of them were dressed in industrial style buff boiler suits, although a few were wearing white laboratory coats. Some of them were also wearing masks to protect themselves from the dust particles that permeated the room like a morning mist haze. There were numbered white groundsheets on the floor and numbered sheets covering trestle tables. Next to each groundsheet was a large numbered bin bag.

'You WDC Tennison?' a gruff-voiced man asked her bluntly.

Jane read the tag on his boiler suit breast pocket – *MOD SGT* – and produced her pass and warrant card to introduce herself. The sergeant went over to a metal cabinet and took out a boiler suit that he threw to Jane, followed by long rubber gloves and a mask. He explained that the staff in the boiler suits were police officers, and those in lab coats were forensic scientists. As Jane put it on, the sergeant told her she would be sifting through the debris for bomb shards and other material. Jane said that she didn't know exactly what bomb shards looked like. Irritated by her comment the sergeant shook his head and told her that was why the scientists were in the hangar.

'Your job is to sift through the contents of a bin using your hands and the sieves provided. As you can see, each dustbin is zone numbered and corresponds to an area at the bomb site from which the debris was collected. Put any fabric you find into the same numbered bin bag. Large fragments of metal on the same numbered groundsheet, and ditto with the small bits on the trestle table so the experts can examine them and decide what is potential evidence. Grab a clipboard and exhibits book from the cabinet and start on bin eight.'

It was after midday when DS Lawrence arrived with the head scientist. Due to the constant sifting, Jane was now filthy with brick dust, which had even got into her hair. The mask hadn't been much use; her mouth was dry and her nostrils itched from the dust. Lawrence came and looked at the debris she had sifted through and laid out on the groundsheet and trestle table. She had found a few large fragments of metal, a small belt buckle still attached to a thin piece of leather strap, two bits of coiled wire with metal on one end and the tattered bloody remnants of a man's shoe, the toecap of which had a small shard of metal stuck in it. As Jane listed each item in the exhibits book, along with detailed descriptions, Lawrence looked closely at the smaller items she had placed on the trestle table. She could tell from the look on his face that something had intrigued him.

'Do you think they could be important?' Jane asked.

'Well, from the size of them, that leather strap and buckle look like they could be from a rucksack fastener. The small pieces of metal are also interesting . . . What location was this stuff recovered from?'

'Zone 8,' she told him.

Lawrence looked at the clipboard he was holding, which contained details of each zone that debris had been swept up from. He tapped the clipboard then asked the head scientist to come over.

'Zone 8 was near the seat of the explosion,' he explained. As the scientist closely examined the wire and small pieces of metal, Lawrence added, 'He's an expert in identifying bomb fragments and examining debris for traces of nitroglycerine.'

The scientist used a magnifying glass to look more closely at the small metal fragments and wire.

'Who found these?'

'I did, sir . . . are they important?'

'Good spot, young lady. I'd say the wire and bit of metal attached to it are from a detonator. I need to look at some other stuff from zone 4, so bag these pieces up separately and I'll sign your exhibits book so I can carry out a further examination and explosives residue test in the lab.'

As the scientist walked off, Jane turned to Lawrence. 'I didn't have a clue what they were when I saw them, other than pieces of wire and metal that could have been from anything.'

Lawrence smiled. 'To be honest it's not my field of expertise . . . so I wasn't sure either. The same scientist you just spoke with attended the post-mortems and found other bomb fragments embedded in the ticket guard's body. It was tragic that he died that way, but the items recovered from his body could offer up vital clues about the origin of the parts used to make the bomb.'

Jane didn't need to ask what state his body was in, as she'd seen it for herself at the scene. She added the details to the exhibits book and packaged the items separately for the scientist before placing them on a trolley with other items of importance.

Jane accompanied Lawrence as he pushed the trolley laden with exhibits across to the chemistry lab in the main building opposite. As they walked along the corridor, Jane looked through the small door's window into a side room. She could see that the room was filled with heavily bloodstained clothing, and that many items were bomb damaged, shredded and burnt. They were labelled and pegged up on clothes lines, pools of dripping blood had gathered on the plastic sheets below from when they were initially hung up to dry. Lawrence explained that there were large heaters in the room to dry the clothes and remnants before they were examined. The awful state of the clothes and the bloodstained baby blanket, which she recognised, were evidence of the horrific injuries many of the victims must have suffered.

Jane made her way to the ladies to wash her hands and face. It was hard to get rid of the gritty powder on her clothes and even though she had been wearing gloves she could feel dust underneath her nails. Lawrence was waiting for her in the corridor to lead her up a flight of stairs to the canteen.

Lawrence sat down beside Jane as they placed their trays onto one of the dining tables. Jane was having meat loaf with vegetables, and they both had coffee. Lawrence seemed on edge, sipping only a few spoons of his soup before pushing it aside.

'You know, I wanted to be brought onto this case but it is so time-consuming, and some of the equipment here is archaic. I just read an FBI article on gas-chromatography and mass spectrometry testing. The Yanks have developed a *quadruple* capillary column GC-MS. It's an analytical workhorse for breaking molecules into ionised fragments using their mass-to-charge ratio. Mind you, they don't have the talented and highly trained forensic experts that we have.'

Jane laughed. 'Like you, you mean?'

Lawrence shrugged. 'I'm not blowing my own trumpet, but interpreting and finding the clues at murder scenes is my forte. Here, we already know that people were killed by a bomb; it's tedious work sifting stuff by hand, not to mention using eye verification for minute bits of a bomb.'

Lawrence's frustration was obvious. As he was talking, Jane spotted DS Dexter, who was in the line of officers waiting to be served hot food. He was wearing a checked shirt, casual fawn trousers and his tie was hanging loose. He was laughing with one of the canteen servers and on turning around with his tray he saw Jane, smiled and headed towards her table.

'Hello there!' he said. 'I meant to catch you in the lab but I was nabbed by Crowley, who was having a fit about someone who had parked a VW in a scientist's reserved parking bay and didn't have a permit displayed . . . probably one of the woodentops assisting in the debris hangar.'

Jane blushed and jumped up.

'You haven't finished your lunch!' Dexter said, surprised.

'I'll be right back . . . just forgotten something.' She rushed out, looking flustered.

Dexter dumped his tray down on the table and patted Lawrence on the shoulder. 'Hey, my man, how're you doing?'

'Been at it all morning, taking scrapings of blood and fibre lifts off smashed bricks, in between piecing together sections of body parts over at the Westminster Mortuary, so I've not got too much of a spring in my step, actually . . . Have a seat.' Lawrence buttered his crackers and loaded them with cheese.

Dexter's eyes rested on Jane's empty seat. 'She's very attractive, our new colleague . . . You worked with her before, Paul? Or has your legendary charm enticed her to dine with you today?'

'We were both at Hackney and then Bow Street. Nobody else was talking to her, so I brought her up for lunch. How come you know her?'

'From the Covent Garden attack. You know she was there?' Lawrence nodded. 'I helped her prep for the press conference at Scotland Yard. Crowley pushed her. He's made out publicly that she can identify this bastard bomber. Now, whether she can or not, it means she could be in the line of fire.'

'Christ, that's disgusting. I read about it in the papers today. I never brought it up with her, though. I know she was there when the bomb exploded, but do you really think she could be in danger?'

'Who knows? We've had no further contact from the IRA, and I would say they've gone underground – which is not a pun about them bombing Covent Garden bloody underground station . . .'

'Have you been over there?'

'Course I have . . . got to go back later. Just came over to see how the lab's doing at piecing together the bomb fragments. Be handy to know its construction in case we need to defuse any others this bomber plants.'

Lawrence acknowledged Dexter's comment with a nod. Dexter ate his steak & kidney pie quickly and moved on to a bowl of sticky syrup pudding swimming in custard. Lawrence sipped his coffee, feeling ill just watching the speed at which Dexter was eating.

'Why do you eat so quickly?'

'I'm hungry . . . I was up at the crack of dawn. So, are you trying to pull Tennison?'

'No, I am not!'

'Jimmy Church was looking after her last night.'

'My God! Don't tell me he's after her?'

'I meant he arranged her protection . . . he got Stanley to house-sit in her flat.'

Despite his concern for Jane, Lawrence couldn't help laughing. The infamous scruffy Stanley had never been one of his favourite undercover officers. Before he could question Dexter further, Jane returned.

'I don't think your food is going to be very appetising now. Let me get you something else,' Dexter offered.

'No, thank you . . . I'm fine. I'm not that hungry, and I suppose I should really be getting back to the lab.'

'What time are you leaving?' Dexter asked, and Lawrence raised his eyes to the ceiling. 'Just wondered if you wanted to have some better food this evening?' Dexter scraped the last of the custard from his bowl.

'Oh, I would have liked to but I've got someone coming to see me about renting a room in my flat.'

'OK, well . . . maybe another time. Are you here tomorrow?'

'Yes, for the next few weeks, I think. I'll just have to wait to be told.'

Dexter pushed back his chair as he wiped his mouth with a paper napkin.

'OK, I'm off . . . Good to see you, Paul, and maybe I'll see you tomorrow, Jane.'

She smiled as he walked off and Lawrence shook his head.

'Bit of advice, Jane: I'd steer well clear of him. He may be good at defusing bombs, but he's got a bad reputation when it comes to women. Thinks he's God's gift to the opposite sex. If you like, I can run you home tonight . . . I've got my car.'

Jane hesitated and then leaned forwards. 'So have I . . . it's the yellow VW and it was my car that Crowley was moaning about being parked in the wrong bay. I just went out to move it.'

Lawrence laughed. 'Good for you! Where are you living? You said you had a new flat?'

'I'm actually not that far from you . . . in Melcombe Street, near the Baker Street entrance to Regent's Park. Are you still living in the mews there?'

'Yes . . .' He paused. 'Well, another time. I can pick you up and we can come into the lab together.'

'Let me give you my phone number.'

Jane jotted it down in her notebook, tore out the page and handed it to Lawrence. As they left the canteen together she felt rather flattered. First she'd had attention from the 'ladies' man, Dexter, and now Lawrence.

Later that day, as she was signing out, she saw DCI Crowley waiting for her. At first Jane thought he was going to reprimand her for parking her car in a reserved space, but he didn't mention it. Instead he asked her how she had found her first day, and hoped it would prove to be a good experience for her. He didn't wait for her to reply.

'As far as your safety's concerned we haven't received any threats or warnings.'

'Well, sir, I doubt that the IRA would give a warning if they were going to murder someone!'

'This is no joking matter, Tennison . . . far from it. You need to be watchful and take precautions, and ensure that we are always aware of your movements.'

'Yes, sir. Am I to come back here in the morning?'

'No, not immediately . . . That's also why I wanted to have a word with you. The old woman you tended to after the explosion has been identified. Her full name is Daphne Millbank and she has come out of her coma. As you have a connection with her I want you to visit her at the hospital tomorrow morning and go over what she may be able to add to your statement. I have people there, and DS Dexter will also be with you. Afterwards he'll take you over to Covent Garden underground station and walk you through exactly what happened and then I'll see you back here.

'Yes, sir.'

'Right, off you go . . . and remember to take precautions. Just be wary of anyone you don't know contacting you, and keep a low profile until we can ascertain our position.'

As Crowley watched Jane walking away, he hitched up his trousers. There had been no communication from the terrorists since they had claimed responsibility; the press release had not flushed them out. Everything suggested they had gone to ground, but after years of experience on the Bomb Squad, he knew not to trust the quiet after the explosion. Jane was still in danger.

CHAPTER EIGHT

Jane had been caught up in heavy traffic and didn't arrive home until after seven. She parked her car in a space a short walk from her flat and as soon as she got inside she called Pearl Radcliff to say that she was at home if she wanted to come over to view the room. She had a quick bath and put on some casual clothes before checking the spare room to make sure that it was immaculate after Stanley's stay. As she was making herself a cup of tea the doorbell rang. Jane went to the intercom.

'Who is it? she asked.

'It's Pearl Radcliff.'

Remembering the advice about being cautious, Jane asked her to wait for a moment. She went into her bedroom and looked out of the window onto the street below. She could see a woman standing on her own by the front door and went back to the intercom.

'Come up to the top floor,' Jane said, pressing the door entry button and replacing the receiver.

She opened the front door to her flat and waited as Pearl came slowly up the stairs. As she appeared on the small landing, Jane greeted her.

'Hello, I'm Jane Tennison. Could I ask to see some identification?'

Pearl was a slim young woman, with short bobbed hair in a Mary Quant style. She was wearing a green beret and a dark green overcoat, and was slightly out of breath. She smiled at Jane.

'Quite a way up, isn't it? Will my driving licence be enough? I've got my passport as well, but I've never been asked to show it before . . . hold on a moment.'

Pearl rooted around in her large leather shoulder bag and then produced her driving license and passport for Jane to look at.

'Sorry if this sounds a bit officious, but it's just for security purposes.' Jane glanced at the licence in Pearl's wallet, then handed it back.

'Please come in.'

Pearl followed Jane into the flat as she shut the door behind them.

'I'll just show you around first,' Jane said, 'and if it's to your liking we can talk over a cup of tea. It's obviously not a large flat . . . The bathroom's here, and then this is my bedroom. The room for rent is this one.'

Pearl said nothing as she followed Jane. She peered into Jane's bedroom, then went into the small bedroom and walked around, looking inside the fitted wardrobe and the small chest of drawers, which had a mirror and glass tray on the top.

'Well, that's it,' Jane said. 'Apart from the kitchen.' As Pearl had not said a word she couldn't tell whether she liked the room or not. She walked into the kitchen. 'Fridge, washing machine and cooker are all new.'

Pearl nodded, still not saying anything.

'I'm charging ten pounds per week, which includes everything . . . so there will be no expenses on top of the rent.'

Pearl nodded, showing no reaction.

'So, what do you think?'

'Well, it's smaller than I had hoped. But it's very fresh and clean. My only worry would be that we'll be sort of on top of each other, unless we come to some arrangement.'

'Yes, I agree. Do you want to take your coat off and we can discuss how we can make it work?'

Pearl took off her coat and beret, and Jane put them both on a hook in the hallway. When she returned, Pearl was sitting on one of the breakfast stools. Jane put the kettle on and took out two cups and saucers, milk and sugar and a small teapot.

'What work do you do?' Pearl asked.

Jane hesitated, then said that she was a detective with the Metro-politan Police.

'Oh, gosh . . . Now I understand why you were so officious about seeing my identification. Do you wear a uniform?'

'No, I'm plain-clothes now.'

'Oh, that must be exciting.'

'It is. And you work at Madame Tussauds?' Jane asked, as she filled the teapot with boiling water.

'Yes. I've been there for a few years now. I run the ticket office and sometimes do the tours when we're very busy. We're always busy, but in the summer it can be exhausting, especially during the school holidays.'

Pearl was wearing a neat blouse and pleated skirt. She had on rather sensible lace-up shoes, but Jane presumed this was due to her having to be on her feet most of the day if she was doing tours. She had a nice soft voice, with a slight accent.

'Where are you from?'

'Originally Southport in Lancashire, but I came to London about eight years ago, to study at the polytechnic. I never finished the course though. It was economics and I didn't sort of fit in. Money was short so I did a few part-time jobs. Eventually I called it quits and worked as a receptionist for a couple of companies, whilst doing a secretarial course. Then I went for the job I'm in now. I never meant it to become full-time but I really enjoyed it, so I've worked my way up and it looks like I'll be staying put.'

They chatted while they waited for the tea to brew, establishing that neither had boyfriends, and that Pearl was an only child.

Pearl watched as Jane poured their tea, then helped herself to milk and sugar.

'You wanted to see my references. I've brought a few letters, includ-ing one from my present employer, and one from the landlady where I've been living for the past two years. I've got to move out as she's sold her house and they've already exchanged contracts . . . So, she wants me to leave as soon as possible.'

Jane smiled as Pearl handed her a stack of papers in a large envelope. She began to sift through them as they drank their tea. She carefully read the letter from her landlady, which said that Pearl had been a pleasure to have as a tenant, and confirmed that she had always paid the rent on time. The landlady had also given her phone number should further information be requested.

The letter from Madame Tussauds was equally commendable. Authenticated copies of Pearl's wage slips confirmed she was paid every week.

'I'm impressed.' Jane said, passing everything back to Pearl.

'I have to be methodical in my work, so I've tried to give you everything you might need.' Pearl neatly refolded the letters and placed them back in the large manila envelope.

'I noticed that you don't have a television,' she added. 'I've got a small portable set, if I could bring that . . . but I don't have too many personal belongings. As I said, I visit my parents regularly and as I've got to wear a uniform to work I don't have too many clothes. I'm rather careful as you can probably detect, but I've sort of been forming a plan for my future, which is why I really wanted to rent the room from you, as it's well within my budget.'

Jane cocked her head to one side. 'Can I ask what you're planning?'

'I would love to travel to Australia and New Zealand. I've got a cousin who lives in Sydney . . . it will obviously be a couple of years before I've saved enough to take a year out, but that's what I'm working towards.'

'I've never been travelling,' Jane said, pouring herself another cup of tea.

'I'd like to go backpacking . . . you know, really have time out. But it will be costly as I won't be able to get a visa to work there. So it will be a lengthy holiday. I haven't been on a proper holiday for as long as I can remember. Southport is such a lovely seaside place, so when I have my week's holiday that's where I go, and it doesn't cost anything more than the train fare.'

Jane lifted the teapot to ask Pearl if she would like another cup, but she shook her head.

'Are you seeing other people who are interested in renting the room?'

'I have had a few people applying, but I've been very caught up with work,' Jane lied, hoping she didn't sound too eager.

'Well, I'll really need to know quite soon. I could move in this weekend.'

Jane took her cup to the sink, and ran the water to rinse it out.

'Pearl, you seem to be perfect . . . but I really need to have a think about it. And whilst you're here we should discuss a few things that we need to agree upon before I make any decision.'

'Oh. I really thought I'd sort of covered everything you'd need to know about me.' Pearl looked downcast.

'You've been thorough, and I really appreciate it. But when you first came into the flat you said that it was rather small, and that we'd need to agree on how we can live together and not get on top of each other.'

'Oh yes, I completely agree with that. It's always best to get things out in the open at the very start, and not let them build up and become awkward.'

'Obviously, I'll have to ask for a deposit, as well as a month's rent in advance.'

'Yes, I'm happy with that . . . how much is the deposit?'

Jane thought about what Stanley had said about unpaid rent. 'Just a week's advance is fine. Is ten pounds OK?'

Pearl nodded. The sharp sides of her well-cut hair curved into her cheeks as she leaned forwards. She wore very little make-up, and had pretty, slanting, greenish eyes. Her nose was rather hooked and she had a wide mouth with small, neat, white teeth.

'I've never rented or shared a flat with anyone before,' added Jane, 'so I'm rather inexperienced about putting together a list of "dos and don'ts" ... but I think we need to discuss it before we finalise anything.'

'Absolutely. I can give you a cheque for the deposit, and if you want I can have my rent paid directly into your account every month ... whatever method you prefer.'

Jane picked up Pearl's cup and saucer and put them into the sink beside her own.

'I don't want any boyfriends staying overnight. I'm willing for you to have friends visit, or perhaps have dinner, but I don't want anyone staying. It's obviously a very small flat and I think it would be too inconvenient.'

Pearl cocked her head to one side and gave a slight smile. 'Does that also include you not having any men staying over?'

'Yes, it does. Also, we'll need a bathroom rota as there's nothing worse than wanting to get off to work and finding the bathroom is occupied.'

Jane continued listing everything she could think of, and was now jotting down details in a notepad. Pearl was very amenable to all her requests, and suggested getting a joint 'flat' diary so everything could be organised on a day-to-day basis.

Jane made a few more notes and finally they discussed cooking and how they would arrange their meals. Jane said she would call Pearl the following evening with her decision as she wanted to sleep on everything they had talked about. Pearl was clearly disappointed, but said she would wait for Jane to make contact. By the time Jane had cleared the kitchen and got into her nightdress it was after nine. Jane felt guilty about not calling her parents and was just about to dial their number when the phone rang and it was her father.

'I've just had that nice superior officer of yours, DCI Church, here, giving me advice about how your mother and I should take precautions following on from your press conference.'

Jane was surprised, and concerned for her parents. Church hadn't mentioned he'd be speaking to them.

'What did he say? Was Mum OK?'

'Your mother was out, so it was a private conversation between him and me. He said for me not to get anxious but they were keeping an eye on you, and he gave me some general advice about our own home security, "just to be on the safe side" were his exact words.'

'He should have spoken to me first.'

'How bad is all this, Jane? I mean, I don't want your mother being made even more anxious. She's been in a terrible state since the bombing and I daren't let her near a newspaper ... you're front-page news in all of them.'

'It's not that bad, Daddy. Church and the others are just being overprotective. Besides, I'm stuck in a lab at Woolwich which is guarded by MOD police, so I'm perfectly safe.'

'I'm sorry if I overreacted, dear. I'm sure you would have contacted me if you were worried about your safety.'

Jane knew it was the last thing she would do under the present circumstances. She quickly changed the subject and told him about her interview with Pearl Radcliff. She relayed all the questions she had asked, and told him about the letters of recommendation.

'So, is she moving in?' her father asked.

'Not yet. I just wanted to run it all by you first to see what you thought.'

'I appreciate that, dear ... but she'll be sharing with you, and the most important thing is what you thought about her. Did you like her?'

'Yes, I did. She's quiet and unassuming, and spends most week-ends visiting her parents in Southport, so she won't be at the flat and getting in my way. She's agreed to pay a deposit and a month's rent upfront.'

'Well, she sounds like the perfect candidate to me.'

'I suppose so. I said I would call her tomorrow to give her my answer.'

'You don't sound very sure. If there's anything you don't feel comfortable about then keep on seeing more girls. You should always go with your gut instinct.'

'I will. Thank you for all your advice, Daddy . . . I appreciate it.'

'That's what I'm here for, darling, and I love you. I'll call you soon.'

Jane replaced the receiver. Her father was right. She was feeling strangely nervous, and put it down to the fact that she had hardly eaten at lunch and had only had a cup of tea with Pearl. But she didn't feel hungry, just uneasy. She was not usually so incapable of making decisions and, as her father had said, Pearl did seem perfect. She just felt unsure for some reason, but couldn't think why.

Jane went into the bathroom and cleaned her teeth, then splashed cold water over her face and looked at her reflection in the mirror as she patted it dry with a soft white towel. She looked very pale and had dark circles beneath her eyes. The terrible sense of panic overwhelmed her without any warning. Her heart started racing, and felt as if it would burst through her chest. She was struggling to breathe properly and started gasping for air, as if someone was squeezing her lungs too tightly. She slowly slipped onto her knees and grasped the edge of the washbasin. The sound of her own hysterical sobbing frightened her. She was shaking uncontrollably. Her head filled with the screams of the injured and images of the bomb blast: her hand on the terrorist suspect's sleeve, his half-turned face, tying the tourniquet around the old lady's shattered leg, the blood, the dust . . . and then the awful sight of the naked and vulnerable Regina tied down to a bed.

Every recollection felt like a heavy blow to her body, and Jane curled up and wrapped her arms around herself to try to keep the images out. But they wouldn't stop, and she was scared. She even had visions of Stanley on her staircase, the drive through the

Blackwall Tunnel, and her yellow VW parked in the wrong space. Everything merged into a terrible, constant nightmare. Then there was the face of Pearl Radcliff, with her short hair and green beret, as if she was the epicentre to the nightmare.

Suddenly she had a flashback to the moment she saw the bomber, then the image quickly changed, replaced by the man in the surveillance photo, both images flickering in and out of her head like a blinding strobe light. The two men were completely different in appearance. In a rush of fear, she thought she could recognise the bomber if she saw him again.

Jane had no idea how long she had been sobbing for, and by the time she had calmed down enough to get to her feet she was drained and totally exhausted. Her whole body ached and she moved slowly out of the bathroom towards her bedroom. She had to keep her hand on the wall to steady herself as it felt as though she was going to fall again. Eventually she made it to her bed and lay face down. She was afraid to close her eyes in case the images returned. She was no longer sobbing, but tears were cascading down her face. Gradually the terror subsided.

Tonight, the horror of everything she had experienced had hit her with full force. She had been in denial, never allowing herself to show her fears and she now understood the cost of holding it together all day, and at the press conference. Anger drowned out the fear. Crowley had used her. She wanted to know why.

CHAPTER NINE

Jane had only had two hours sleep when her alarm woke her. After the torment of the previous night she felt strangely calm. She dressed quickly and applied some foundation and rouge to her face, then decided to apply mascara to her eyelashes and use a little brown eyeshadow. She wore one of her smartest and most expensive suits, over a white clerical-collar shirt with starched cuffs. It was only seven thirty but she hoped she would miss the heavy traffic she'd encountered the previous morning with DS Stanley.

Before leaving, Jane put in a call to DCI Crowley at the Yard, but was told he had gone directly to Woolwich from home and wasn't expected at the Yard until later. She then tried to call DCI Church. He wasn't in the Dip Squad office but Stanley took the call. He sounded his usual groggy self and Jane was certain he had more than likely slept the night in the office again.

'Everything all right?' he asked.

'Yes, but I wanted to ask a favour. I need a criminal record check on the girl who wants to rent a room in my flat. Her name's –'

'Pearl Radcliff . . . I've done it, she's clean, no record.'

It took a second or two to sink in before Jane realised the obvious. 'You've been snooping round my flat, Stanley. How dare you?'

'I was only thinking of you, Jane. Besides, you'd have had to check her out anyway . . .'

'That's not the point, Stanley. It's my flat, my *belongings*, and –'

'OK, it won't happen again.'

'Too right it won't, because I don't want you coming round to my flat anymore.' Jane put the phone down, seething.

She had miscalculated her travel time again, because if anything the traffic was even worse than yesterday. Her hopes of catching DCI Crowley before he returned to the Yard were looking slim, and she wondered if she should have gone straight to the hospital to see Daphne. By the time she had parked in the allocated area for assistant laboratory staff, it was after nine. She was pleased to see Crowley's car still there, but vowed that from now on she would take public transport, rather than drive.

Jane showed her ID pass again and was allowed entry to the lab floor. She then proceeded towards the small offices, hoping to find Crowley there. A clerical worker was just coming out as Jane approached. She told Jane that DCI Crowley was in the canteen having breakfast, but as Jane approached the lifts and the doors opened, Crowley stepped out holding a paper plate of sausages and a bread roll, with a mug of coffee in the other hand.

'Morning, sir.'

He gave her a surly glance, and would have walked past her if she hadn't asked for a few moments of his time.

'You told me to go to St Thomas' this morning, sir, to interview –'

'Yes, yes . . . I know. So, what are you doing here?'

Jane followed him along the corridor to his office, and held the door open for him as he had his hands full.

'Well, I needed to know what name Daphne would now be under as I assume, for security purposes, she wouldn't be using her own name?'

'There's an armed guard by her room. Her full name is Daphne Millbank. She's registered under the name "Patient C" and I am sure it is obvious that there will be no ID on her door. She has come out of her coma but is still very weak. I checked this morning and they said she's quite coherent, so the sooner you get there to speak with her, the better.'

After her flashback, Jane was certain that the man in the surveillance photo and artist's sketch wasn't the man she had seen at Covent Garden. She realised that if Daphne said the same she'd have further proof she was right.

'I have a copy of the artist's sketch of the suspect,' she said. 'I'll show it to Daphne and see if she recognises him.'

'I'd rather one of my team did that, as her description of the suspect is critical to the investigation. It needs an experienced bomb squad officer to go over the finer facial details. You just deal with her version of events and what she saw.'

Crowley carefully placed his sausages inside the roll, then opened a packet of HP sauce and squirted the contents over the sausages.

'I understand Church spoke to my father,' Jane said. 'Could I ask what protection is in place for my parents?'

'It's all in hand, Tennison . . . So far there's been only an ominous silence from the terrorists, and it is quite possible the suspect and his cohorts have gone to ground. It remains for you to be extremely vigilant and, as I ordered yesterday, you should go to the hospital and talk to the other witness.'

'Yes, sir. I'm then due to go to Covent Garden with DS Dexter, so should I return to work here afterwards?'

'Yes. Is there anything else, Tennison?'

'No, sir.'

Jane left Crowley's office. As she was walking past the lab, DS Lawrence approached her.

'Looking a bit smart for a day's work out in the rubble?' he said.

'I'm going to St Thomas' to interview the lady who saw the suspect.'

He nodded, then moved closer. 'Is everything all right with you?'

'Yes. Why, does it look as if it isn't?'

'No, to the contrary, you look terrific. Will you be coming back later?'

'Yes, but not until this afternoon.'

'See you then.'

Lawrence walked off, leaving Jane feeling a bit tetchy. She was getting irritated with everyone checking up on her and asking how she was. Blackwall Tunnel was just as bad as it had been earlier in the morning, and the City was bumper to bumper with rush-hour traffic. By the time Jane reached St Thomas' hospital it was nearly eleven. She made her way up to the ward and approached the nursing bay where she showed her ID and asked if Nurse Mitchell was on duty.

A stout nurse at the desk looked her up and down before telling her he was accompanying a patient to theatre.

'Oh. I'm really here to see a patient. She's under the name of Patient C.'

The nurse checked Jane's ID, then gestured for Jane to walk ahead of her. In contrast to the last time she had been here, the atmosphere was now strangely quiet and eerie. The dark green lino floors, the strong smell of disinfectant, combined with the almost echoing silence all made Jane feel uncomfortable. They eventually stopped to speak with a doctor who seemed irritated that Jane had not sought his permission before approaching his patient.

'She's quite remarkable, really. She's very intelligent, but she tires easily and is on strong medication for the pain, although she no longer requires a morphine drip. You'll see some deep bruises on her arms – those are from the catheters required for her surgery. She's been breathing on her own since last night. But she'll need a lot of treatment and care for some considerable time. You can have a few moments with her . . . the nurse will direct you.'

Jane followed the portly nurse past curtained booths busy with nurses, until they reached the double doors leading to the private rooms at the end of the ward. An overweight armed officer, who looked as if he was about to burst out of his uniform, sat outside Daphne's room reading the *Sun*. He immediately rose to his feet when he saw Jane, folding the paper and placing it on the chair. The straining belt around his rotund stomach had a radio hanging from a clip at his waist, and a .38 revolver.

'I'm WDC Jane Tennison,' she said, showing her warrant card.

The officer took her card and nodded.

'I'll bring you a mug of tea when I get a minute,' the nurse said to the officer. 'Two sugars, right?'

'Thank you, Nurse.' He passed Jane her warrant card back and then went to the closed door. He knocked lightly and then eased it open. Jane entered the room and the officer closed the door behind her.

The room was as bare as she remembered, and the blind was drawn. The bedside cabinet was covered with kidney bowls, pads and plastic cups. A draped protectivce cage had been placed over Daphne, covering her from the waist down. A glucose drip was attached to a catheter in her left arm, and there was a tube running from her bladder into a urine bag. Wires ran from her chest to a heart monitor, which bleeped steadily. She lay slightly raised on a pillow, her thinning white hair combed away from her face. Small, scabbed wounds stood out on her cheeks and forehead, and her thin arms were black with bruises and raised blue veins that tracked down to her small curled hands. She had her eyes closed, and Jane moved closer to be beside the bed. Not wanting to wake Daphne if she was sleeping, Jane gently stroked her hand. Daphne's eyes opened.

'Hello, Daphne. My name is Jane. I was with you at Covent Garden. I'm sorry if I'm intruding but . . .' She hesitated, as there was no reaction. 'Can you hear me?'

'I've got just about everything else wrong with me, but I'm not deaf.'

Jane smiled, then drew a chair from the wall to sit closer beside her.

'You've had such a dreadful time, but I've been told you're really recovering very well. If you feel up to it, I would like to ask you some questions. I understand that your full name is Daphne Millbank. My name is Jane Tennison.'

Daphne turned to look at her through watery, blue eyes. 'I remember you, dear . . . you saved my life. To be honest I'm not sure whether to thank you or not. You know they had to amputate my left leg? I can't feel a thing down there sometimes, but then it aches so much it's dreadful. It's going to make it difficult for me to play golf. Not that I was a regular, or even that good . . . but I keep thinking about it. At least I've got my teeth back. The nurse left them in a little cardboard box. I told her I needed a bottle of peroxide as I like to let them soak overnight so they look nice and white, but I have not been given it yet. How do they look to you?'

Daphne gave a wide, open-mouthed smile.

'Very white . . . they don't look like false teeth to me.'

'I know, my dear. Always get a good, private dentist. The NHS dentures never fit. These were made to measure and cost a fortune.'

'Can you remember anything that happened?'

'Not all of it . . . it's very hazy. I suppose it'll come back to me. They found my handbag, but I don't have my reading glasses. Maybe they got broken, but I can't read anything . . . Are you a nurse?'

'No, I'm a police officer.'

'I was a Wren in the last war . . . my husband was a pilot. What did you say your name was again, dear?'

'Jane.'

Although Daphne was talking relatively coherently, she spoke slowly and with little expression. She opened and closed her eyes as if the effort wearied her.

'Daphne, I don't want to tire you too much but do you think you could try to answer some questions for me? If you want me to wait a while I can do that, but it is rather important and time is really against –'

'Go ahead, dear. I was a Wren, you know, so I'm used to working under pressure. As you are here it must be important, and I was always a stickler for putting duty first.'

'I want you to try to recall everything that happened in as much detail as you can remember from the moment you arrived at Covent Garden station . . . what you saw, and how it all occurred.'

Daphne lay with her eyes closed. It took a while before she slowly recounted to Jane how she had noticed the rucksack, and had seen the man walking away. She had called out to him because she thought he had forgotten it, but he didn't take any notice. She had called a second time, but he'd walked towards the exit. Then she had seen Jane and heard her calling out to the man. Considering what she had been through, her recollection was very clear, but Jane didn't want to take her to the moment of the explosion. She patted her hand.

'That's good, Daphne. Can you describe what he was wearing?'

'Yes, a dark coat . . . and he had a scarf around his neck. He was a big man with longish, shoulder-length hair. He didn't have a full beard but he was unshaven.'

'Do you think you would recognise him?'

'Yes, I would, most definitely . . . because when I called out to him he turned to face me.'

Jane was deep in thought about what to do. Crowley had said he'd send someone from Bomb Squad to get Daphne's description but she wanted to know if Daphne recognised the man in the artist's impression that had been shown at the press conference.

'Don't you want to know what he looked like, dear?'

Daphne's question made up her mind. Jane rummaged in her bag and pulled out a crumpled press release showing the image of the man that Crowley had released to the press.

'Did he look like this, Daphne?'

Daphne couldn't lift her head so Jane had to stand close to her to show her the sketch. She pursed her lips and squeezed her eyes open and shut.

'I need my glasses. Can you hold it a little bit further away from me?'

Jane held the sketch in front of Daphne, until she gave a small shake of her head.

'No, no . . . that's not him. The hair's not right; he had more of a square face, thin lips, and a sort of flat nose, with bushy eyebrows. That sketch isn't right at all.'

Jane knew that this would put a spanner in the works for Crowley. It didn't mean that the man he suspected, in the surveillance photo, wasn't part of the ASU, but he clearly was not the actual bomber. And this confirmed that Daphne was a more important witness than Jane, as she had seen the bomber's full face.

'Thank you, Daphne, you have been extremely helpful, and I'll make sure you get some new glasses.'

'Thank you, dear. I'm being well looked after. I don't have any family, you know. My husband was a pilot, he was shot down over Dresden . . . never anyone else, no children . . .'

Jane listened as Daphne talked about her husband, until her voice became fainter, and when she fell asleep Jane quietly left the room. She headed down the ward and into the corridor, just as DS Dexter came towards her.

'Hi, Jane, I've been waiting for you. How did it go with the lovely Daphne?'

'Better than I could have hoped for. She's an incredible lady and has excellent recall of the suspect's face.'

As they went out of the hospital Jane told Dexter that she'd shown Daphne the artist's sketch and how Daphne had dismissed it, giving her a detailed description of the man she saw leave the rucksack. She added that she, too, was now almost certain the man in the surveillance photo was not the man she'd seen at the station. Dexter was very attentive and smiled.

Jane was frustrated. 'This situation has the potential to leave Crowley with egg on his face, as well as making me appear to be an unreliable witness.'

'I couldn't agree more, and the press will have a field day if it gets out. Listen, you did a good job with Daphne. Crowley will be pissed off, but he's got only himself to blame. He took a gamble releasing the artist's impression at the press conference, and so far it hasn't paid off. I know how to handle Crowley, so let me talk to him. In fact, I'll call him now. I can also order a car for us if you wait here . . .'

'I've brought my own car,' Jane replied. Dexter hesitated, slightly wrong-footed, and told her to bring the car around to the reception and he would meet her there. He waited for her to move off then made his way back to the nurse's bay and called Crowley to update him.

'It's Dexter. We've got a spanner in the works, sir. Daphne Millbank was shown the artist's sketch by Tennison, she said it isn't the man she saw and now Tennison's saying the same thing.'

'For fuck's sake, that's the last thing I need. Tennison disobeyed my order.'

'On the plus side, Tennison knows this makes her an unreliable witness. She's not likely to publicise that. You could always raise the possibility of two men working together and . . .'

'There's never been any reference to a second man,' Crowley snapped.

Dexter remained calm. 'I know that, but Daphne Milbank saw the man who left the rucksack, whereas Tennison saw a man who reacted to Daphne shouting "stop". It's natural to assume an accomplice would react as well . . .'

'Christ, don't complicate everything. We'll talk about it later.' Crowley snapped again and ended the call.

It was about fifteen minutes before Dexter walked back out of the hospital. He stood looking at Jane's VW, shaking his head.

'This is very subtle, Detective Tennison. Was this the only colour you could get? I mean, bright yellow? Nobody could miss you!'

Jane didn't react as Dexter climbed into the passenger seat beside her, and jerked the seat back to accommodate his long legs.

'What did Crowley say?'

'What do you think? He wasn't happy, said he'd talk about it later and slammed the phone down.'

'Do you want me to be there as well?'

'No, he's mad you disobeyed him. I'll handle it . . . by the way, I saw DS Stanley earlier. He said he'd upset you over a criminal record check . . . Pearl somebody, was it?'

'I'm thinking of letting out a room in my flat to Pearl, but the fact is Stanley was snooping round, saw her details and checked her out . . .' Jane said, still annoyed about it.

'For what it's worth, he was just concerned for your safety. I told you about sleepers, didn't I?'

'You said they're members of the IRA who appear to be ordinary members of society until they're needed?' she said, concentrating on the road.

'A sleeper for the IRA is someone whose background and demeanour enable them to go unnoticed in England, so that they can better help the IRA in their bombing campaign. When they're needed, they're contacted. No big drinkers, and they need to know when to keep their mouths shut and stay as anonymous as possible. Never assume anyone you come into contact with is who they say they are.'

Dexter directed Jane down back streets, from Trafalgar Square along Floral Street until they arrived at Covent Garden. The street was still cordoned off and the tube station was out of service. Police cars and vans were scattered outside the station entrance, with forensic officers still searching and gathering the rubble and debris left after the bomb. They had already cleared the rubble outside the station itself, as it was imperative to get it reopened and for daily life to resume.

Jane accompanied Dexter through the crime-scene barrier, and followed him into the wrecked ticket area of the station. A few officers acknowledged Dexter, who held up his ID as he guided Jane towards the top of the staircase that lead to the platform below, stepping over potholes and mounds of rubble.

'I want you to walk me through exactly where you were positioned from the moment you came upstairs.'

Jane turned to face the ticket barriers, her back to the stairs.

'I had just walked up from the platform. There was a woman behind me with a pushchair . . . she was carrying her baby and finding it difficult to manage them both. I was about halfway up when I offered to carry the pushchair. We both reached the top, and I handed back the pushchair, and she put the baby inside.' Jane turned away from him, recalling the young mother's face covered with a sheet in the emergency ward. She was almost in tears.

'I saw the nurses with the baby . . . the poor woman died from her injuries . . .'

Dexter dug his hands deep into his trouser pockets. 'Don't go there, Jane. Let's just keep going through your movements.'

She nodded. 'I was holding my ID up to the ticket collector, who was standing at the far side of the entry from the stairs. It was very crowded, with passengers getting off from the Underground and climbing up the stairs, and then more passengers going down to get to the platform . . . so it was really thronging with people, because it was rush hour. They were just innocent people going about their daily lives . . .'

Dexter gripped Jane's arm tightly. 'Just focus on why we are here, Jane.' He gestured for her to continue.

She moved about four steps towards the station exit, with the ticket office on her right.

'Then I heard Daphne Millbank calling out, "You left your bag!" She was pointing to a rucksack. I followed her gaze and caught sight of a man wearing a hooded winter coat, walking away with his head down. He was moving quickly towards the station exit.

Jane paced out exactly how she had followed the man toward the exit.

'By now I'd become concerned, so I began to run and called out "Police", but he didn't stop. As I got close enough to make a grab at his arm, he turned and swiped my hand away, I stumbled backwards and he ran on.'

Dexter held his hand up. 'So, he kept on running straight ahead, no turning or crossing the road?'

'No, he just kept running . . . So I went back to the ticket office to warn everyone. I was worried about the way he'd behaved, and the rucksack he'd left behind.'

'Walk me through what happened next,' Dexter said gently. He could see that Jane was becoming even more tense. Together they re-entered the station. Jane explained how she'd been hemmed in with people trying to get out and others pushing their way towards the ticket barriers.

'I saw the mother and child ahead of me, then I saw the ticket collector pick up the bag. Daphne Millbank had already started to walk out and was beside the wall when the bomb exploded. I was saved because a big man moved directly in front of me . . . if it wasn't for him I would have been . . . Dear God, I have no idea who he was! I owe him my life, and I don't even know if he made it. After the explosion, the thick cloud of smoke and debris made it impossible to see clearly.'

Jane recalled the screams and pandemonium as the terrified passengers tried to get out, the injured lying on the ground. She described again the whine of the bomb in her ears as she spotted the overturned pushchair, the sight of the mother shielding her child, Daphne Millbank's missing leg . . .

Dexter nodded and gently patted her shoulder. 'Just need you for a short while longer . . . come on outside with me.'

They left the station and Dexter held her elbow as they walked along the pavement a few yards. Up ahead there were two Bomb Squad detectives with a SOCO dusting a red phone box for prints. The door was propped open with a large piece of concrete that must have been blown loose by the blast.

Dexter indicated to Jane to wait, as he ducked beneath the cordon that marked off the phone box. There was a lengthy conversation between him and the officers, and Jane saw Dexter nodding and looking at the amount of fingerprint dusting that had been taken. He then walked slowly back to Jane.

'I've just been told we have a witness who has described a female using this phone box at the time of the bombing. She was aged twenty to thirty, wearing a headscarf that hid her face, but she was in there for some considerable time. They're dusting for prints but it's doubtful they'll be much good as it's a public phone box, so God knows how many people have used it. But they've got a good high-heeled imprint and scuff marks . . . although, again, it'll be a stroke of luck if it pans out.'

'You think a woman planned this explosion?'

'We don't know for sure. The witness had been waiting to make a call to her husband, and there was a woman inside the phone box. She gave us a reasonable description but she never saw her face as she was wearing a very expensive headscarf . . . it looked like it could have been Hermès, with dogs like red setters printed on it. She said it was tied under the woman's chin in a knot, just like the Royals wear them. I'm pretty sure the bomb was a radio-controlled device and the woman in the headscarf might have been an accomplice. She might have been attempting the coded call to the newspaper when the panic-stricken bomber pressed the button, or maybe she had the detonator . . . we just don't know.'

'Did your witness see them together?'

'Not exactly . . . she was walking away from the phone box to find another one, but recalled seeing a man with the woman, running across the road shortly before the bomb exploded. It's even possible three people were involved at the scene.'

'Three people?' Jane sounded surprised.

'Sometimes they will use a lookout as well while the bomb is planted.'

Jane sighed. She had been right when she described the man having his hands free, so maybe he hadn't been carrying the detonator? On the other hand, it could have been in his pocket . . .

They returned to the underground station and although all items of interest had already been removed to the Woolwich lab, she watched Dexter make a lengthy inspection of the damage. When he was satisfied, he announced he would return to the lab to see if there had been any developments.

'Why don't you go home?' he suggested to Jane, checking his watch. 'You've had a pretty traumatic time going over what had happened. I'll speak to Church about Daphne, and pick you up in the morning and let you know how it went.

'You free for dinner tonight?' he added.

'I'm not, actually. I need to call this girl about moving in. But thanks for the invitation.'

'Rain check again. You look after yourself.' He grinned.

Jane watched Dexter stride off. She would have liked to spend more time with him but Lawrence's warnings had made her wary of his intentions. It would be better if she kept him at a distance.

It was late afternoon by the time Jane got home. The plain-clothes SPG protection officers gave her a nod as she approached her flat and let herself in. She rang Pearl and confirmed that she would like her to move in if she still wanted to.

Pearl sounded relieved as she thanked Jane. 'I've been on tenterhooks all day.'

'Just one thing I meant to ask you Pearl . . . do you smoke? I really don't like the smell of cigarettes.'

'Oh no, I don't smoke.'

'That's good. So when do you want to move in?'

'Well, a friend said he could help me move my few things, so would it be possible to come over this evening after I finish work?'

Jane hesitated. It was sooner than she had expected. 'Who is your friend?' she asked cautiously.

'Eric? Oh – he's a friend from work,' said Pearl.

Jane felt she couldn't ask any more questions, so said that would be fine. She hung up, and then rang in to check in with DCI Church. He was as concerned for her welfare as everyone else seemed to be, and Jane had difficulty biting back a scathing comment or two as they spoke. She tried to turn the subject away from herself by asking about Regina Hernandez, but as before, he warned her to leave the investigation to Vice.

She had just replaced the receiver when the doorbell rang. It was Pearl, so she pressed the buzzer to release the main front door. Pearl had said she only had a few belongings so Jane couldn't believe how many cardboard boxes were being carried up the stairs by a rather scruffy-looking man with bad acne. He was heaving for breath by the time he reached the top floor. Pearl herself lugged up two heavy suitcases.

Jane took the boxes and carried them into the spare room, whilst Pearl opened the two large suitcases on the bed. Jane didn't like to mention that they would leave scuff marks on the thick white cotton bedcover, and she put the boxes down on the floor. Pearl had thrown her coat onto the floor, and was still wearing her green beret, and a shapeless woollen dress.

'Gosh, you've got rather a lot of things.'

'Not really . . . those are full of my shoes and books, and Eric is bringing up the heavier ones with the TV and radio and my typewriter.'

'I see,' Jane said, pursing her lips. Where on earth was Pearl going to put everything in the tiny bedroom? There was only one small fitted wardrobe and a dressing table. Eric staggered to the top of the stairs again, sweating and red-faced.

'Right, this is it . . . that's everything,' he gasped, as Pearl hurried out and handed him a pound note.

'Thank you, Eric, you've been wonderful. I'll see you at work tomorrow.'

Eric quickly pocketed the pound note and headed down the stairs to make his escape.

Jane stood in the hall, aghast at the large boxes.

'This box is for the fridge,' Pearl said. 'Just some fresh salad and fruit, and then I've got a few tins of soups and some dishes . . .'

Pearl carried the box and placed it onto the kitchen counter. She then lifted the box containing the TV and staggered into the bedroom. Jane carried the next box, with the old-fashioned typewriter, which was equally heavy.

'Er . . . look, I'll leave you to unpack. Maybe we can have a cup of tea when you're ready. Although I honestly don't know where you're going to put everything. I really didn't expect you to have so much.'

'I'll sort it, don't worry. I'm used to squeezing into small spaces. One of the boxes is just coat hangers, and when I've unpacked everything I'll flatten all the boxes and they can be stored, or thrown out . . . Do you have a loft?'

Jane knew there was one in the hall, as she had seen a small rope attached to a hatch door with a plastic handle, but she hadn't used it. She fetched a kitchen stool and climbed up to open it. It took over an hour for Pearl to empty the contents of the boxes and flatten them. She handed up the suitcases and boxes to Jane to stack in the small loft, which was thankfully empty. Pearl's bedroom now had books stacked along the floor, with her typewriter on top of the chest of drawers. Balanced beside it was the portable TV set with an aerial on top.

Pearl breezed into the kitchen, spinning her beret around on her finger like a wheel.

'Phew! I'm almost unloaded, but I'm gasping for a cuppa. I've brought my own as I usually only drink herbal tea. Where can I put all my goodies? I only eat fresh food as I am a vegetarian, and I don't like too much tinned food as it's full of dreadful ingredients . . .'

Jane opened the fridge, and Pearl began emptying her grocery box onto the shelves, taking more space than Jane had allocated. Then she stacked her vitamins, herbal teas and tins of various beans in the cupboards.

'Would you like a sandwich?' Jane asked, trying to remain pleasant.

'No, thank you, I don't eat wheat. But I would love a cup of camomile tea. Then, if it's all right with you, I'd love to have a bath as I'm so hot and sweaty after all those boxes. Then perhaps we can sit down and sort out the rent and deposit?'

Jane closed her eyes, trying to keep calm. Already the prospect of Pearl as a flatmate was not the perfect arrangement that she had hoped it would be.

CHAPTER TEN

Jane's alarm woke her at seven. It was the first time since the explosion that she had slept soundly and she went out into the kitchen to make herself a cup of coffee, then returned to her bedroom. There was no sound from Pearl's bedroom, so Jane went into the bathroom to use the toilet and brush her teeth. She went back to her bedroom to get dressed, then brushed her hair and applied a little make-up.

She was ready to leave just after quarter to eight, and there was still no sound of movement from Pearl's bedroom. Jane hesitated outside the door, wondering if she should knock and let Pearl know that she was leaving. Having a flatmate was taking some getting used to. Suddenly there was the shrill ring of a loud alarm clock bell, followed by a screech.

'Fuckin' hell!' Pearl came hurtling out of the bedroom. 'My God, I should have been up half an hour ago! I must have set the wrong time on my alarm clock!'

'I'm just leaving for Woolwich,' Jane said, opening the front door.

'What?'

'I have to be at the lab early this morning.'

'Could I borrow your hairdryer? I keep meaning to get myself one.'

Jane hurried back to her bedroom and took her hairdryer out from her wardrobe.

'Just leave it in the kitchen, will you?' she said as she closed the bedroom door.

'Right, yes . . . OK . . . See you tonight then. That bloody alarm bell gives me heart failure when it goes off.'

As Jane closed the front door, Pearl was thumping around the kitchen fixing her breakfast. Jane heard the fridge door being slammed shut and crockery and cutlery clanking as drawers were opened and shut. As she went down the stairs she began to feel a little bit unsure of whether flat-sharing with Pearl was going to be a positive experience. She hoped Pearl would leave the kitchen in a better state than she had the bathroom.

As agreed the previous evening, DS Dexter drew up in front of Jane's block, in an unmarked CID car, at exactly eight o'clock. He leaned over and opened the passenger door for Jane to get in.

'Morning,' he said, tetchily.

'Morning!' Jane replied, wondering if she'd done something to upset him.

As Dexter drove through Regent's Park he said nothing. Jane broke the ice by asking about what she thought might be bothering him.

'Did you speak with Crowley about me showing Daphne Millbank the artist's sketch.'

'Yes, last night. He was really pissed off . . . we had a bit of a slanging match, but he calmed down after I told him that showing Daphne the artist's sketch was unavoidable.'

Jane looked concerned. 'What did you tell him?'

'That Daphne had seen the artist's sketch in the paper and told you it didn't look like the man she saw with the rucksack. You then, quite rightly, showed her the sketch to see if she changed her mind, but she didn't . . . So he now thinks it was all above board and not your fault.'

'Thanks, but you didn't need to lie for me.'

'It's more like I bent the truth a little. Crowley is under immense pressure. He knows what he did was wrong, not that he'd ever admit it. He was hoping that the sketch would lead to the discovery and arrest of the IRA man in the surveillance photo. He bent the truth hoping the end would justify the means.'

'I understand what you're saying, but it's still left me in an awkward and vulnerable position.'

'I know, but my advice would be to let it go. If we get the man Crowley's after, then he may lead us to the whole ASU, and vice versa if we get the man Daphne described. Do you think you actually saw the same suspect as Daphne?'

'I'm not 100 per cent sure, but it makes sense that I did . . . Then again maybe it's like you said . . . there was another man acting as lookout who caught my eye and he was the one I chased.'

'It's possible, Jane, but don't beat yourself up about it, we'll get the bastards responsible.'

Dexter headed towards St John's Wood, before driving towards Belsize Park and Hampstead.

'I thought we were going to Woolwich?' said Jane. 'Where are we going?'

'Daphne's place in Hampstead. I've got a couple of guys checking it over to make sure it's secure. If the IRA have got wind she exists they might have been to her house . . . I'm also having an alarm put in that's linked to the Central Control Room at Scotland Yard.'

Dexter eventually turned off into an area with expensive large houses, many of which had been divided into flats with gardens that overlooked Hampstead Ponds. It was clearly an affluent area and Dexter slowed down as he drove along Nesbitt Avenue. He parked the car and waited for Jane to get out before locking it and striding ahead of her towards number 16.

The glass-panelled front door had a row of doorbells next to it. Dexter pressed the ground-floor bell, which had 'D. Millbank' neatly printed on the nameplate. The door was opened by a plain-clothes officer in his mid-thirties. He had red hair and was wearing jeans and a loose jacket over a T-shirt.

'Anything of interest, Johnny?' Dexter asked.

'Not yet, Al. We got in with a set of skeleton keys, did a clean sweep of the entry hall, back door and French windows . . . there's no sign of any forced entry.'

Dexter and Jane followed Johnny into the house. The wide, mosaic-tiled floor was well swept and there was a polished mahogany table in the centre for the occupants' mail and deliveries. The door of Daphne Millbank's ground-floor flat was wide open. Dexter stopped to have a long, concentrated look around the entire door frame before he seemed satisfied that it had been checked out.

In comparison to Dexter, Johnny seemed easy-going. He was deferential towards the sergeant, who kept up a quiet conversation. The décor inside Daphne's flat appeared almost to be stuck in a time warp of the forties. The decorations were faded, and the curtains and furniture equally so. The old-fashioned kitchen was painted in a dull green and contained old appliances, but everywhere was spotlessly clean.

The sitting room had two large French windows overlooking an untended garden with a tall hedge that needed cutting back and an old rickety gate that led straight onto the Heath. Old plant pots lined the fence, all containing bedraggled and dead plants, and a rusted watering can lay on its side next to a rolled-up hosepipe attached to an outside tap.

Jane followed the two men as they walked around outside, listening to their conversation. Dexter was asking exactly how long it would take to fit the alarm. Johnny was giving him details of the areas that needed wiring and said they should finish it today, by late afternoon. When they went back inside the flat they inspected the dining room and study, which was lined with framed black-and-white photographs. There was one of Daphne on her wedding day, and numerous large photographs of her in ornate ballgowns, as well as one of her in uniform as a Wren.

'She was very beautiful,' Jane said quietly.

Dexter nodded and walked around the room. Jane told him that Daphne needed some reading glasses and Dexter told her it was OK to have a look round for some. She opened a drawer in the old desk and took out a few pairs of glasses.

'Her husband was a pilot,' Jane said, looking at a photograph of a handsome man in a flying jacket.

Neither of the men seemed interested so Jane continued to look at the other photographs lining the walls, as well as the many silver-framed photographs that covered every available surface. Many of them were of handsome young men in evening suits, and there were some of Daphne in full riding kit, as if about to go on a hunt. She was always smiling, and although there were a few more recent photographs, most of them appeared to be of her past. In one of the oldest shots she was a very young woman, wearing a full white evening gown with a diamond necklace and elaborate tiara.

'She was a debutante,' Jane said softly, as she took an envelope from the desk and put three pairs of glasses into it. 'Now I've got Daphne some glasses we could get an artist's impression of the suspect she saw,' she added.

Dexter was quick to reply. 'Crowley's got it in hand. He visited her last night. After yesterday, I'd leave it to him.'

Jane nodded in agreement, put the envelope into her handbag and stood waiting patiently as Dexter and Johnny discussed the security of the building.

'We may be lucky and it won't be leaked about her being able to ID the suspect . . . but it's better to be safe than sorry. When the time comes for her to return I want it all rechecked,' Dexter told Johnny.

All three of them jumped as a loud voice boomed out, 'What the hell is going on here?'

Dexter was the first out into the hall, and was confronted by a white-haired elderly man using a walking frame. He was smartly dressed, wearing a blazer and flannel trousers, with an RAF tie. His snow-white hair was cut short and he had a small white moustache.

Dexter hastily showed his ID and asked who the old man was, but had to wait whilst his ID was scrutinised.

'I'm Raymond Brocklesby, an old friend of Mrs Millbank. I was very concerned to see the front door left wide open, and then to discover strangers wandering around her home. Where is Daphne? Has something happened to her? Is she sick? Has she been run over?'

Dexter put on the charm and asked Mr Brocklesby to join him in the sitting room. Despite his infirmity, he moved quickly towards the room.

'I've not heard from her for days. We always have a game of bridge, regular as clockwork. Has something happened to her?'

Dexter waited for him to sit down before he gently explained that Daphne had been in an accident, and that she was in a critical condition. He took down Mr Brocklesby's address and phone number, which he obtained from a laminated mobility card that the old boy took out of his wallet. Dexter said that they would inform him as soon as she could have visitors, explaining that they were visiting Daphne's flat as a matter of course because they had been told she had no immediate family.

'That's right. She never had children. Her husband died in the war; he was a bomber pilot . . . brilliant chap. Daphne is my sister-in-law, from my first wife, so we're not actually related by blood, but we're very close. As I said, we play a hand of bridge on a regular basis.'

'I see there have been no newspaper or milk deliveries?'

'No, she likes to walk to the local newsagents and prefers to get her own milk. She says it's better not to give any burglars a hint when she's not at home . . . she travels a lot, you know. I've been worried sick because she usually tells me when she's off on one of her jaunts, and I've been calling and calling.'

Jane liked the fact that Dexter was patient with Mr Brocklesby, and that he reassured him that he would most certainly be in touch when Mrs Millbank was allowed visitors. Eventually Mr Brocklesby stood up to make his way to the front door, pausing outside the sitting room.

'She was one of the most beautiful women I've ever met. Such a great sport, and so full of energy, and her cocktails are lethal! She could tango like no other woman, and despite being short of money she always dressed like a queen. But she would never marry again, although she certainly had plenty of opportunities . . . the men flocked around her. I hope I'll be able to see her soon. We go back a long way.'

Jane thought of the small figure of Daphne in the hospital bed, her leg missing. Dexter was clearly eager for him to leave but Mr Brocklesby seemed drawn to the photographs lining the walls.

'She goes into the West End two or three times a week, to visit the art galleries and theatres. She always keeps abreast of the latest artists and knows all the latest plays, films, and actors . . . but I'm not that mobile so I rarely accompany her.'

'Why don't you see Mr Brocklesby out, Jane?' Dexter said.

Jane escorted Mr Brocklesby down the hall, and into the main hallway of the building.

'You seem to care for Mrs Millbank a great deal,' she said.

'I adore her and always have. So many of our friends have passed on . . . I've buried two wives. I now live in what they call "sheltered accommodation", so it took me a while to get over here.'

They walked out of the main front door and Mr Brocklesby became short of breath, leaning heavily on his walking frame.

'She is coming home, isn't she? Only it seems strange to have police officers in her flat. She is a very private woman, you know. When will I be able to see her?'

'Soon I hope. We have your contact numbers, and I'll pass on your good wishes to Mrs Millbank. I'm sure she will be keen to see you when she has recovered.'

Jane felt badly about not being able to give him more details, and even worse about the fact that she doubted Daphne would be able to cope alone with her injuries and return to living in her flat, but for her safety Jane didn't dare divulge any more.

Mr Brocklesby shook Jane's hand and thanked her as he made his way towards his mobility car. It took a while for him to get his walking frame inside before he drove off.

Dexter came outside to watch the pale blue car drive away. 'Nice chap. Pity to have to lie to him, but it's basic security until we know how useful she is going to be.'

'I don't think she'll be able to cope coming back home . . . she'll be in a wheelchair.'

'From what Brocklesby said about her, I think Daphne will find a way of managing. As soon as I know she's allowed to have visitors I'll make sure he gets driven there to see her.'

'So you do have a heart.' Jane smiled, pleased to see Dexter's mood had lifted.

He cocked his head to one side and smiled. 'You bet I have . . . I'm just not a morning person, especially after a row with Crowley. Give me a couple of minutes as I need to call into the station to double-check our walking-frame chap.'

Crowley listened at the other end of the phone as Dexter told him the old lady's flat had been given a clean sweep.

'Is Tennison with you?' he asked.

'Yes. Can you notify the armed officer at the hospital to allow her to visit? She's got some reading glasses for Daphne, and it's a good thing to keep her on friendly terms with our witness. Don't worry, she won't be discussing the bomber's description with her.'

'Good. Seems you're on friendly terms with Tennison?' Crowley asked, mockingly.

'I'm looking out for her, as requested.'

'Not got into her knickers yet?' Dexter glanced over to Jane to make sure she was out of earshot.

'For Christ's sake, leave it out, Crowley!'

As they drove back towards St Thomas' Hospital, Dexter was affable and Jane was enjoying his company. He told her Crowley said it was OK for her to take the glasses to Daphne and changed the subject.

'So, how's the new flatmate? Has she moved in yet?'

'Yes, last night . . . She had so much stuff, even though when I asked if she had a lot of belongings she said she had very few. I don't know how it's all going to fit in. Also, she's a vegetarian and has endless tins of pulses and bottles of vitamins.'

'Just never stand downwind of a veggie!'

Jane laughed. 'Thanks for that advice. I'm sure it will all work out.'

Dexter told her the lab scientists had begun to piece together the type of bomb used, as well as the detonator distance. The team had agreed that it felt as though this was the calm before the storm. Without any arrests or suspects under surveillance the IRA might be waiting for the next opportunity to create terror on the streets of London.

At the hospital Jane showed her ID at the reception desk and made her way up to see Daphne, who had been moved to another private room away from the fire escape, for further security measures. As Jane walked along the corridor, Michael, the charge nurse, saw her.

'I wondered when you'd be back!' he said with a smile. 'I'd very much like to see you away from this environment. Are you free tonight, maybe for a drink or something to eat?'

'That would be lovely, but I'm not sure what time I'll be off duty. I could call you when I get back to where I'm working, and then we could arrange to meet up?' Jane said, pleased.

'Great! Now, let me give you an update on our patient. She's making strong headway. We're slightly concerned about the healing process, and she might need further surgery as in this kind of amputation there can be a risk of gangrene . . . the surgeons were checking it out earlier this morning. If the wound doesn't heal then she'll have to undergo another operation to amputate the remaining part of her thigh.'

'Oh God, I hope not.'

'She's remarkably relaxed about it, but we've been administering more morphine for the pain. She does ask for me to constantly increase the level . . . says she likes the feeling of floating, especially at night . . . she says she has wonderful dreams! We've got to be very careful as patients can often have an adverse reaction to drugs. I am obviously aware of the importance of keeping her stable, but you'll see that she has regressed slightly and isn't eating as well as we would like her to. We do still have concerns about her.'

Michael led Jane down the main ward and through the double doors to the private section. The armed officer was sitting outside her room and promptly stood up when Jane approached. He had already been given her name to allow access, so Jane signed the record sheet, giving her time of arrival, then entered the room.

Daphne was still shrouded with a cage covering her from the waist down, which was draped in a white sheet. She was lying flat with one pillow behind her head. Her face was pinched and she seemed smaller and frailer. The lids of her eyes, which were closed, had a faint purple colour, and her white hair looked as if it needed to be washed, and the greasy strands were combed back from her forehead.

Jane pulled up a chair and took out the envelope containing the spectacles. She pulled out the three pairs of glasses and put them on the bedside cabinet. Daphne's arms looked painfully thin, with awful black bruises from the cannulas. Nobbled veins stood out from the wrinkled loose skin, and her tiny hands were the size of a child's.

Jane was expecting to have to wait a while for Daphne to wake up, but after only a few minutes she began to stir and murmur, and Jane leaned closer to hear.

'You smell nice,' Daphne said. She opened her eyes and turned her head to look at Jane. 'You get used to having so many different people coming and going and they all smell of hospitals . . . you know, that Dettol smell. You smell fresh.'

'I brought you some reading glasses.' Jane said, with a smile.

'Oh good . . . Can you ask them to buy me a decent paper? I only get given the *Sun*, and some awful women's magazine full of teenagers' broken hearts. Do you think you could just press the button and move me slightly higher dear? I can't reach the control thingy.'

Jane bent down and saw the control pedal attached to the steel bed frame. She gently pressed the pedal and the front of the bed raised slightly, elevating Daphne's head, but not putting her in a sitting position.

'That's better. I'm supposed to lie flat, then sometimes they lift my legs, or should I say leg, a bit higher. Anyway, it's frightfully uncomfortable.'

'I've been told that you're not eating much?'

'Are you surprised? The food here is terrible, and by the time they've raised me high enough to eat it, it's stone cold. And they keep giving me this plastic baby mug with a lip to drink my tea . . . it's disgusting. I've complained to Michael and he said he's going to see if he can get me a decent china cup, and maybe some cheese and biscuits. He's a nice-looking young man.'

'Yes, he is . . . I like him. In fact, we might be going for a drink together later.'

'Charge nurse seems a strange occupation for a strapping chap . . . not that he's my type. Mind you, I could never have been a nurse. They have to empty bedpans and wash patients down, you know . . . but he's very pleasant.'

'Don't put me off him, Daphne!'

'I'll tell you who I'd like to have dinner with . . . that tall, attractive blond policeman. He reminds me of Steve McQueen. He's got lovely blue eyes, although he could do with sharpening up his clothes, but I'd have that sorted pretty quickly!'

'Do you mean DS Dexter? He's been here to see you?' Jane asked, wondering why Dexter hadn't mentioned it to her.

'Yes, last night . . . we had a good laugh. He does ask a lot of questions though, and I get tired repeating myself. I don't like that other man, Crowley . . . can't stand him. When he comes I just close my eyes and pretend I've nodded off. I would have thought they could just ask you to repeat what I said? They just keep wanting statement after statement, and I start to get confused.'

'They shouldn't tire you out so much,' Jane said.

'Well, I can't really read much, as I don't have my glasses.'

Jane showed Daphne the three pairs of glasses she had brought in, and Daphne frowned.

'These are my old glasses . . . where did you get them from?'

'I went to your flat.'

'You had no right to do that without my permission! I'm not mentally ill, you know. All you had to do was ask, and I could have organised for my friend to be there.'

'Sorry, Daphne. I wanted you to have your glasses as soon as possible so we could get a detailed artist's impression of the suspect you saw, and because you said you had no family I just thought you would appreciate someone getting them for you.'

'Well, I don't approve at all.' Daphne sniffed. 'The pair with the tortoiseshell frames are the best ones, and they're also very light.'

'Whilst I was there, your friend Raymond Brocklesby called by. He was concerned about not hearing from you. I explained that you were in hospital, but didn't give him any details. I just said that there had been an accident, and that when you were allowed visitors I would arrange for him to see you.'

'Well dear, you seem to be taking a lot of responsibility on your shoulders. Surely if I wanted Raymond to see me I could contact him myself? He is a dear man, and I know he's not that mobile so it must have taken him some time to make the journey to my flat from his home.'

'Daphne, we are really only concerned for your welfare and recovery. As you must now be aware, you are a very important witness to the IRA bomb explosion, and until we catch the perpetrators your safety is imperative.'

'I understand that, dear. I could pick him out in an identity parade. But I do find this invasion into my private life unacceptable. I don't want strangers in my home. I don't want you, or anyone else, telling my friends when they can or can't see me.'

'If you would like to give me a list of friends you'd like to visit you, I can arrange that.'

'Most of them are in the grave, apart from Raymond, who has wandering hands. As soon I'm able, I'll be out of this place. I'm not afraid . . . I've never been afraid and I don't intend to live the rest of my life being fearful. Now, I would like you to leave . . . and please ask Michael to bring me a copy of *The Times*.'

Jane was astonished at Daphne's strength of will. Far from regressing in her recovery, it appeared to be the contrary. Michael was busy attending to another patient, so she left a message for him.

As Jane was walking along the corridor towards the stairwell down to main hospital exit she bumped into a young woman passing her.

'I'm so sorry . . .' she said to Jane, then she stopped and turned. 'Good heavens! It's Jane Tennison, isn't it?'

Jane was nonplussed for a moment and then recognised the woman as Natalie Wilde, who had been a trainee with her at Hendon Police College. Natalie was taller than Jane, with short, curly, blonde hair, and she was wearing a fawn raincoat over a dark, tailored suit.

'We were at Hendon together, don't you remember? I was the one who had to drop out because I couldn't swim well enough.'

'Of course I do! It's Natalie, isn't it?'

'Yes! What're you doing here?'

'Just visiting a sick colleague,' Jane said, keen not to give any details about who she was seeing.

'I'm visiting a friend on the maternity ward who's just had a baby. She was rushed in yesterday after her waters broke. I used to share a flat with her, before she got married.'

'Is she all right?'

'Yes, she's fine . . . Anyway, you're not in uniform . . . are you no longer in the Met?'

'I am, actually: plain-clothes detective.'

'No!'

'Yes . . . I've been in the CID for just short of a year and a half. What about you?'

Natalie flipped open her raincoat to show she was wearing a name tag.

'I work for NatWest. It's rather tedious, but the pay is good. Do you have time for a coffee, so we can talk about old times? I'd love to know what all my old Hendon classmates are up to.'

Jane hesitated, then decided that perhaps she should go straight back to work. She opened her bag and took out her notebook.

'Here's my phone number . . . I should be back about seven tonight, so call me and we can fix a date to go out, or you could come over to me.'

'Great, I'll do that. I should get back to work anyway. Whereabouts are you stationed?'

Jane didn't mention that she was temporarily working at Woolwich, and instead said that she was with a squad at Vine Street. They walked out of the hospital together, and Natalie gave Jane a hug.

'It's so good to bump into you . . . I've often thought of contacting you. We had some good laughs at Hendon, and I was so depressed when I didn't make it. But time goes on, and I lost contact with everyone from Hendon. Let's have a good catchup when we meet.'

Natalie hailed a taxi and Jane headed for Waterloo East station. They had not been all that close at training school, but they had liked each other. Natalie was an open, friendly recruit who had tried her hardest to become a fully-fledged probationary WPC. She was intelligent, but had been dismissed over an incident in the swimming exercise sessions. All recruits had to be accomplished swimmers, and they were all tested and timed doing lengths. There was also an exercise that involved either diving or jumping from the top board of the swimming pool. Natalie had not done well in the swimming timings, and had also stopped mid-length as she had a fear of water. When the instructor had told everyone to climb to the top board Natalie had refused and had shouted at the instructor, before breaking down in tears and admitting that she was frightened of heights. By the next morning her locker and been cleared and Natalie had gone. She had not even been given time to say goodbye to any of the other recruits.

Jane worked out that it must have been October 1972 when she had last seen Natalie, who looked very different now. They would certainly have a lot to catch up on, and Jane was looking forward to meeting up with her.

The journey back to the Royal Arsenal was quicker than Jane had expected. Arriving at the explosives lab Jane was told by the MOD police officer on guard that DS Lawrence had requested that she report to him at the chemistry section. She thanked him and went straight to the lab where Lawrence greeted her in a tone that gave away his excitement.

'We've managed to reconstruct most of the Covent Garden bomb from the bits found in the debris. It was detonated by high-frequency waveband, using a 27-megahertz radio signal.'

'Do you mean the detonator was a radio that you listen to?'

Lawrence laughed. 'No, it was a transmitter switch from a remote-control toy car. It's powered by a small HP7 battery and can be easily concealed in the palm of your hand, or a handbag or purse . . . you press the switch, it sends a radio signal to the receiver, which triggers the bomb detonator lodged in the explosives.'

'Does that prove I was in no way responsible for the bomb going off?

'You weren't responsible, Jane. Whoever had the detonator was.'

'So, it had to have been detonated remotely by the man I chased or an accomplice?'

'One or the other.'

Relieved, Jane asked if DCI Crowley and DS Dexter had been informed about the results.

'Of course they have. I'm on my way over to the explosives range where they're testing out a new explosives protection suit and jammer.'

'Can I come with you?'

Lawrence looked uncertain. 'Only approved personnel are allowed on the testing range.' He saw the disappointment on her face and added, 'But it's fine if you stick with me.'

They walked towards a large area of waste land where there was a small reinforced bomb shelter. 'That's called a "splinter-proof",' he explained, 'it's capable of withstanding bomb fragments.'

As they approached, Jane could see a figure about two hundred feet away wearing a bulky green bomb suit and head protector. She was certain it must be Dexter, standing beside a rucksack like the one she had seen at Covent Garden. Suddenly a red light on the shelter came on and a klaxon sounded.

'Oh shit . . . looks like they're about to live test the jammer!' Lawrence grabbed Jane and pulled her towards a wall of sandbags nearby.

'What's a jammer?' she asked, ducking down with him behind the sandbags.

'It's an electronic counter measure . . . a device for blocking the 27-megahertz signals on the toy car transmitter . . .'

Suddenly there was a large explosion, causing Lawrence and Jane to crouch down even further. Jane peered over the sandbags as a mushroom of sand, dust and debris spiralled upwards. She could see Dexter flying through the air, then hitting the ground and lying completely motionless. She let out a scream of panic and started to run towards the prostrate body.

'Bollocks! It didn't work,' Dexter shouted, as he walked out of the shelter and threw the jammer on the ground. He looked at Jane and saw her shock.

'What's up with you?' he asked.

'The explosion . . . I thought . . . I thought you'd been hurt by the bomb . . . I thought you were dead!'

To Jane's amazement, Dexter started laughing, as Crowley and the head scientist walked out from the splinter-proof.

'You all right, Tennison?' Crowley asked.

Dexter turned to Crowley. 'She thinks I'm dead, Guv . . . Do you reckon the mannequin in the bomb suit felt much pain?'

'There's no need to be sarcastic, Dexter, not after what Jane went through at Covent Garden,' Lawrence said. 'She was concerned for your safety, that's all. I'm sorry, Jane. I should have explained that there would be a mannequin in the bomb suit.'

Dexter was quick to turn on the charm. 'I'm flattered by your concern, Jane, but believe me, I'm not stupid enough to test a bomb suit on live explosives . . . even in a controlled situation.'

Crowley, totally unaware of the tension between Lawrence and Dexter, interjected. 'On a positive note, I'd say that, with a bit of adjustment, we can get the jammer to work.'

Dexter nodded. 'Besides, the Covent Garden bomb was crude and amateurish . . . a schoolboy chemistry student could build that piece of crap.'

'I wouldn't underestimate the IRA. They're well-trained and quick to develop new technology. They know we will piece the bomb together from the debris, so the next one may well have a different remote mechanism,' Lawrence retorted.

Dexter looked complacent. He knew that was possible and said that he was about to do some stopwatch-timed practice on disarming different types of mock bombs, with both radio-controlled and time-delay detonators.

Lawrence, irritated by Dexter's blasé attitude, turned to Jane. 'Do you want to come back to the lab?'

'I apologise for my overreaction, but if you don't mind I'd like to stay and watch Dexter at work . . . if that's all right?'

'That's fine by me.' Dexter said, with a smile that irritated Lawrence even more.

As Lawrence walked off Crowley brought out another replica rucksack from the shelter, handed it to Dexter and took a stopwatch out of his coat pocket.

'I'll blow the whistle and start the stopwatch when you give me the signal. Then, after eight minutes, I'll sound the klaxon to simulate detonation.'

'Make it five. I like to minimise the danger, so the quicker I'm in and out, the better. They don't call me Felix for nothing.' He laughed.

Seeing Jane looking puzzled, Crowley explained that Felix was Latin for 'lucky'.

'I thought Felix was a cat's name.'

'Cats, like Dexter, have an innate ability of always landing on their feet.'

Dexter invited Jane to stand beside him and watch as he disarmed a bomb. She looked nervously at Crowley. 'Are we going to wear protective suits?'

'No, we aren't using real explosives. But to make the exercise more difficult, Dexter here doesn't know what type of bomb mechanism is inside the rucksack.

'It's standard procedure to talk through the disarming of the bomb,' Crowley added. He picked up a small military radio and tucked it into Dexter's back pocket before clipping the mic to his shirt collar. 'Normally the bomb disposal officer wears a tape recorder, but in a mock situation we use a radio to communicate, and record the exercise on tape.'

Dexter tapped the radio in his pocket. 'Life is irreplaceable . . . but in a real situation if I was blown up and killed, the recording would give other bomb-disposal officers an insight into what went wrong. An expo was killed recently and the tape was invaluable. We learn from our mistakes.'

Dexter picked up the rucksack and Jane followed him over to the practice area. As they walked he explained that the first rule of bomb disposal was to assess the improvised explosive device, or IED, to minimise the chance of accidental ignition when disarming it. He would then either cut the circuit or interrupt it by cutting out a section of detonation cord. Finally, he would remove the detonator and main charge by hand.

Jane was impressed. 'How many bombs have you defused?'

'Hundreds, maybe, but to be honest I've lost count. Most of them were when I was working in Northern Ireland with the Army. I had to attend suspected or live devices, and the aftermath of explosions, almost every day.'

'You must have seen some horrible sights.'

'Yes, and lost colleagues. But you have to put it out of your mind to do the job. If you can't detach yourself, you could make a mistake that leads to your own death.'

As they passed the mannequin she was amazed to see that the bomb suit was intact. A large burn mark ran like a bruise over both jacket and trousers. Fragments of metal peppered the dummy. Dexter knelt over the mannequin and prodded the chest.

'The bomb suit stops fragmentation injuries, but the explosive force from larger bombs doesn't care about the suit. Either the explosive force hits you without it and you haemorrhage and die, or it hits the suit and the suit hits you and you haemorrhage and die.'

Jane was amazed at how matter-of-fact and unemotional Dexter was. Both of the mannequin's hands had been blown off.

'Don't you wear protective gloves?'

'No, they're too bulky and make it nigh on impossible to hold the tools properly.

'I made this tool kit up myself,' he said, unfolding his toolkit. 'Medical items, like scalpels, are best – high quality. I've also got pliers of various sizes, wire cutters, screwdrivers and spanners. Everything is non-magnetic so they won't cause a spark, which could detonate the bomb. Mind you, if you're lucky and it's a combustible-type IED, then simply pulling the fuse from the device and separating the detonator to render it safe takes seconds.'

'What's the worst type of bomb to deal with?' Jane asked.

'Bloody car bombs. The vehicles are usually booby trapped so even getting to the bomb is a major problem. It's worse still if it's radio-controlled, as the bastard bomber could be nearby. He waits for you to approach the car and triggers the bomb.'

'Would you two fucking get on with it?' Crowley shouted over the radio.

Dexter turned to Jane. 'No more questions now . . . I need to concentrate.'

He placed the rucksack by the sandbags before raising his hand in the air to indicate to Crowley that he was ready, then the klaxon sounded.

Kneeling beside the rucksack, Dexter carefully opened the flap, and very slowly removed a large wooden cigar box. He held it at eye level and, using a magnifying glass, checked around the rim of the lid. Next, he took a thin paper clip from his toolkit, which he unravelled, then eased it into the rim of the box, slowly moving it along the edges. As he did so he gave a continual commentary over the radio.

'I'm checking for any anti-handling wires that may be connected to the lid to set the bomb off on opening it. I'm satisfied there's no such device attached.'

Dexter placed the box on the ground and Jane watched as he carefully opened the lid. She could see some Eveready batteries and an alarm clock with wires attached leading to a small metal rod which was protruding from a round white lump of what looked like bread dough. She suddenly felt nervous and took a couple of paces backwards.

'Don't worry, it's only a lump of Play-Doh. It's rigged so the only thing that will happen if I screw up is a small pop and a puff of smoke from the detonator.'

Dexter continued to describe in detail what he had in front of him over the radio, using terminology and phrases that Jane didn't understand. Under the circumstances, she thought it best not to ask. Dexter picked up a pair of wire clippers and moved his hand towards one of the wires on the alarm clock. He was about to snip it when he stopped, put the clippers down and lifted the box. He picked up the paper clip and, using it as a measuring stick, held it against the cigar box, both outside and inside.

'Thought you had me there, didn't you, Crowley? But I've seen this type of device when I was in Northern Ireland. The box is deeper on the inside than it appears ... so that means the bomb mechanism is resting on a false bottom and the wires I can see are probably part of a collapsing circuit.'

Dexter slowly removed the false bottom. Attached to the under-side were more wires and another battery. He looked at Jane.

'It's a form of booby trap. If I'd cut the wire attached to the alarm clock, the power would have been relayed to the concealed circuit, and BOOM.'

Dexter took out another paper clip from his kit, connected it to two wires, then removed the detonator.

'Job done,' he said into the radio. 'How long did it take to disarm the bomb, Crowley?'

'Well done . . . three and a half minutes.'

Dexter and Jane walked back to the shelter as the head scientist and Crowley started clapping and congratulating him. He shook his head.

'I could, and should, have done it in three minutes . . . Right, let's get to work in the lab on another jammer.'

Jane watched the three men walk away. Dexter's composed professionalism had impressed her. When she returned to the lab, she found Lawrence standing by a table with one of the scientists. Pieced together like a jigsaw and laid out on a white sheet were lots of pieces of torn and burnt grey cloth material, bits of brown leather and the piece of strap and buckle which Jane had found when sifting through the debris of bin eight. The two shapes formed the back and front of the rucksack she had seen the ticket guard holding when the bomb went off, she was sure of it. Lawrence smiled and, with a gloved hand, picked up a half inch square scrap of material.

'Looks like you were spot on about the colour of the rucksack. We even found a bit of the label with "Karri—" on it. It's a positive lead. We now know the bag was a Karrimor Joe Brown. The preliminary Griess test on the rucksack cloth samples was positive; as was the more sensitive TLC test.'

'TLC?' Jane was lost when it came to forensic terminology.

'Thin layer chromatography. That was positive for nitrates . . . we can conclude that the bomb at Covent Garden was nitroglycerine based and contained between 4–6 pounds of explosive.'

Jane remembered what she'd learnt about fibres from the Carol Ann Collins murder investigation at Hackney.

'So, if the suspect still has the jacket he was wearing there may be fibre traces from the rucksack all over the back of it.'

'Exactly. We found some black fibres on parts of the rucksack that probably came from the same jacket.'

'Did you find any more bomb shards?' she asked.

Lawrence nodded. 'Yes, quite a few pieces – but they're still reconstructing it in the other lab. Things are beginning to move in a positive direction now, Jane.'

Jane was less enthusiastic when Lawrence told her that she would have to spend the rest of the day in the dusty hangar, sifting through debris from the bomb site. This time, though, she didn't mind getting dirty. Now more than ever she realised how important it was to find the evidence left behind by the IRA Active Service Unit – evidence that might lead them to the killers.

CHAPTER ELEVEN

Jane returned home just before seven that evening. Pearl was already there and the TV was switched on in her bedroom. Jane called out that she was back and went into the kitchen. It was immaculate, which pleased her. She was about to put the kettle on for a cup of tea when the phone rang. It was Dexter.

'Do you fancy fish and chips?' he asked. 'I can be at your place in half an hour, and I know a restaurant in Ladbroke Grove that serves the best in London.'

Jane didn't hesitate and said she would be outside her flat in three quarters of an hour. She needed time to shower and change, and doubted he had been truthful about being such a short distance away. After seeing Dexter at work on the testing site she had to admit to finding him even more attractive, despite the warnings she'd been given.

Jane went into the bathroom. The shower unit was attached to the bath taps, and there was a small, plastic curtained rail around the bath. She turned on the shower and hurried into her bedroom to decide what to wear. The *Coronation Street* theme tune echoed from the spare bedroom, but Pearl had not appeared. Just as Jane was hurrying back to the bathroom, naked but carrying a towelling robe, Pearl's door opened.

'Oh, sorry! I was just going to make myself some supper.'

Jane quickly wrapped the robe around herself. 'I'm going out, so I'm just about to have a quick shower ... but I shouldn't be too late.'

'There were a couple of calls for you earlier. A guy called Church, who said he'd ring back later, and one from someone called Natalie. She said it was nothing urgent, but I left the number in the kitchen.'

'Thank you ... I didn't see your note.'

'I thought that call might have been her calling you back. You're obviously very popular.'

'Oh, it was just work ...' Jane said, going into the bathroom. Whilst she stood under the shower she couldn't help smiling. When she came out, she found Pearl in the kitchen, chopping up vegetables.

'Could I have my hairdryer back?'

'Sorry, I put it on your dressing table.'

Jane didn't like the fact that Pearl had gone into her bedroom, but didn't say anything. As she closed her door behind her, she decided that she would get a lock for it.

Jane dried her hair and pulled on a T-shirt and a pair of fawn trousers. She used a magnifying mirror on her dressing table to quickly apply some foundation, mascara and eyeshadow, finishing with a light lipstick. She put a matching fawn jacket around her shoulders. After checking herself in the mirror, she walked out into the hallway and closed her bedroom door behind her.

Pearl was sitting on one of the kitchen stools, drinking a glass of a greenish liquid. There was a strong smell of cabbage permeating the hall. She glanced at Jane as she passed the doorway.

'You look very nice.'

'Thank you ... Is that cabbage I can smell?'

'Yes, I'm making a soup with lentils, onions, spinach, carrots ... and cabbage. I usually make a big pot so I can have it when I get home. It becomes thicker the longer I keep on boiling it up.'

Jane was tight-lipped as she went out. The cabbage smell lingered all the way down the stairs, and the thought that Pearl would be boiling it up every night made her feel sick.

Dexter was as good as his word, and Jane only waited a few minutes before he drew up in a silver Porsche. He leaned over to push open the passenger door.

'A Porsche – I'm impressed!' Jane said, as she bent down to get inside.

'It's my pride and joy. Used to belong to my father. I keep it garaged at a pal's place, and he keeps it tuned up for me.'

The engine roared as they pulled out, but then he slowed to drive down Melcombe Street, past Balcombe Street and Marylebone Station, before turning right towards Ladbroke Grove. Dexter was wearing pale blue jeans and a leather jacket, and Jane smiled to herself as she remembered Daphne's description of him looking like Steve McQueen. He was quite similar, although Dexter was much taller. He parked a few yards from a fish and chip shop that had a line of people waiting to be served.

'I told you this was the best in London . . . they get customers from all over.'

Dexter was very much the gentleman and moved around the car from his side to open the passenger door for Jane. He held out his hand to help her out, locked the car, then took her by the elbow to join the queue of waiting customers. Jane was unsure how to react. She hadn't expected to be eating her dinner from a newspaper, and there didn't appear to be any dining tables inside. Before they reached the counter, Dexter told Jane to look at the blackboard for the fresh fish of the day, or to choose from the lit-up menus above the counter.

'I'll have cod and chips, please,' she said to him.

'D'you want mushy peas, and salt and vinegar?'

'Yes, please.'

Dexter ordered the same and their portions were dished up in cardboard take-out cartons with plastic forks, then wrapped in newspaper. Jane was still unsure where they were going to be eating, as she followed him back to the car. Dexter unlocked the passenger door, and because he was holding the fish and chips she opened it and got back into the car.

Dexter then opened the boot, put their dinner inside and got in to the driver's seat.

'Right, we'll eat at my place . . . I've got a nice bottle of Chablis in the fridge, and if I put my foot down the food will still be hot.'

'Do you live near here?' Jane asked.

'Not far . . . just off Kilburn High Street.'

He leant forward and switched on the cassette player, his choice of Mozart surprising Jane. The journey was longer than he had implied, and they drove past her parents' block of flats before turning off the Edgware Road and reaching Kilburn High Street. Dexter turned left into a wide street of four-storey Victorian houses. He parked, jumped out and retrieved the fish and chips from the boot, whilst Jane pushed open her door.

'Out you come!' he said, holding out his hand towards her. She clasped onto it and heaved herself up from the low-slung Porsche. Dexter locked the car and waited for her as she straightened her jacket, then gestured for her to follow him up wide stone steps to the front door. It was not exactly run-down, but the property had obviously seen better days. There was a row of bells by the front door. Dexter swung his set of keys around to unlock it and on pushing it open he gestured for her to walk ahead, kicking the door shut behind them both.

'Keep going . . . up to the first floor.'

Jane climbed up the wide staircase, which would have been light and airy in daylight, as it was overlooked by big windows. A dark stair runner held down by old brass clips, and the stone steps either side, were rather grubby. She arrived at a wide corridor with a fitted grey carpet and whitewashed walls. There were two doors, both of which were painted a similar shade of grey to the carpet.

'Number 2,' Dexter said, selecting another door key.

Jane stood to one side as he opened it, and he let her go in ahead of him as he banged the door closed with his hip.

The floor in the hallway was stripped pinewood.

'The kitchen is straight ahead of you,' he said, gesturing with his head.

Jane was taken aback by the large kitchen, which was full of modern steel equipment. There was a double-door fridge-freezer, and a large six-ring cooker. The counters were granite, and the floor was covered in dark grey lino tiles, whilst the sinks and taps were more suited to a restaurant than a flat. There was a small utility room with a washing machine and dryer. Everything had been designed in a very modern style.

Dexter put the food down on the counter and unwrapped it, switching on the oven and putting the fish and chips into a large white oven dish.

'Keep them nice and hot . . . I hate soggy chips. If you open the fridge there's a bottle of uncorked wine. I'll be back in a minute.'

Jane was completely surprised by his dexterity in the kitchen. She hesitated in front of the big fridge-freezer, then found the wine bottle and placed it on the counter, then she opened a few cupboards to look for some wine glasses. Jane was eager to keep occupied as she was feeling ill at ease, even more so as in every cupboard she opened she found neatly stacked white plates, cups, saucers, cereal bowls, milk jugs, and a sugar bowl. But she couldn't find any glasses.

Dexter appeared at the door holding two fluted wine glasses. 'The cutlery is in the top drawer. If you take these through, I'll bring in the fish and chips.'

Jane opened the drawer and took out two sets of knives and forks, then Dexter handed her the glasses and she walked down the stripped pinewood floor in the hallway. The main room again took her by surprise. It was huge, with high ceilings, two white sofas, and what looked like a very expensive woven rug lying between them, with a clear glass coffee table on top of it. The large windows had stripped pine shutters that matched the bare wooden floorboards.

There was a modern, long, white dresser with silver handles for the nine drawers. Two decorative bowls sat on top of it, one containing bunches of keys and the other containing packs of Marlborough cigarettes and Henri Wintermans Café Crème Cigars, along with several boxes of matches.

There was a rack of records and an expensive-looking stereo system, with two speakers positioned on the wall above it. The dining table was glass-topped pine, with six matching chairs and was positioned in front of a floor to ceiling window. Jane laid the two sets of cutlery out, along with the wine glasses, and took her jacket off to place around the back of one of the chairs. There were no paintings but on the far wall there were some black-and-white framed photographs. Oddly there were three white oblong canvasses with large black dates painted on two and the third was empty. Jane moved closer to look at the photographs. One was of a mangled car and printed beneath it SILVER PORSCHE 550 SPYDER SPORTS CAR 1955 JAMES DEAN'. Another photograph was of Dexter wearing a ski suit, carrying a set of skis with another older man, laughing.

'Dinner's served!' Dexter said, carrying in a tray made up of the fish and chips on white plates, a large tomato ketchup bottle, and the wine. He had two mats and napkins and deftly flicked them down onto the table.

'Sit down, and mind out . . . the plates are hot.' He quickly put one plate on each of the mats.

Jane sat down as Dexter poured the wine, then sat at the end of the table.

'Cheers!' he said, lifting his glass.

She was trying hard to think what to say. She felt so out of her depth and uncomfortable, but he was completely relaxed. He proffered the ketchup and she shook her head, so he poured a large dollop on the side of his plate and started to eat.

'You have an amazing flat,' she said.

'Thanks. How's your new flatmate getting along?'

'Pearl? She's fine. She was at home when I left, watching *Coronation Street*. To be honest, I don't know if it'll work out. We seem quite different now she's moved in.'

'You were wise to have her checked out first . . . you have to take precautions and you did the right thing. I hope you also make a note of any odd phone calls, and look out for anyone loitering near your flat . . .'

'I do . . . and I appreciate DCI Church is also looking out for me. I even checked with Pearl's previous landlady and Madame Tussauds, where she works. There was no connection to any Irish background and her family come from Southport . . .'

'So, she works at Madame Tussauds?'

'Yes, she does the guided tours.'

'You know there was an IRA bomb there in 1974, but a coded warning was sent and they managed to evacuate the premises just before it exploded.'

Jane looked shocked, 'Oh, my God, I had forgotten about that! She never mentioned it.'

'It's easy to get a bit blasé, we have so many bomb scares in London nowadays.'

Jane ate sparingly. She was nervous and was still trying to make polite conversation.

'In comparison to your place, my flat would probably fit into one room! How many bedrooms have you got?'

'Just one. I had two, but knocked them together. It's not what I would call guest-friendly . . . well, not for my mates anyway.' He smiled. 'By the way, I had Daphne's friend, Raymond Brocklesby, checked out. He's quite a character . . . been married twice and inherited a fortune when he was in his thirties. He's also a highly-decorated war hero, but he's now living in sheltered accommodation as he has Parkinson's. He's wealthy enough to have bought his own mobility car and have it adapted to his specifications. He's got quite a lengthy paragraph in *Who's Who*.

Jane was beginning to relax now they were on a subject that she could interact with him on.

'When I told Daphne we had met him, she wasn't at all happy we'd been in her flat. She said we should have asked her permission to collect her reading glasses.'

'We were just being cautious . . . but I think we've kept her well under wraps so far.'

'She mentioned both you and Crowley spent time with her last night? I thought it was just Crowley.'

Dexter nodded, and poured more tomato ketchup onto his plate. 'Sorry, I thought I said it was both of us. It was after I had the row with him about you and the artist's sketch. Crowley wanted to pop in and explain what was happening. She was rather high on morphine, but she's exceptionally intelligent and, considering what she's been through, she's amazing.'

'Did she give you a description of the man she saw?'

'Yes. Like she told you, it was different from the artist's impression. Daphne took great delight in pointing that out to Crowley.'

'What did he say?'

'He told her it was possible there were two IRA men working together at the tube station . . . she saw one and you the other. Anyway, she agreed to an artist's impression being made of the man she saw. Crowley's organising it.'

'So Crowley's still saying that the man in the artist's impression is the Covent Garden bomber? Even though Daphne and I have both said it isn't?'

'Well, either way, it doesn't matter now. Crowley can't issue a press release saying the artist's impression was wrong and that the Covent Garden team could have been two men and a woman. Whoever the bastards are, they could still be around London, feeling confident that we haven't identified them. IRA members don't fit a single defined stereotype; they come to London under the guise of looking for work, rent flats to live in and store nitro-glycerine and other equipment in a bedroom. What we also need to try and trace is the contact he made in the telephone box . . . all we know is that she was a woman with a fancy headscarf, but we can't even be sure she had anything to do with it as we only have one witness who came forward.'

'So the witness definitely didn't see the face of the woman in the phone box? And she didn't see our suspect approach her?'

'No. The phone-box witness only saw the headscarf with Red Setters on it and the leather gloves she was wearing. Typical woman, she can describe the Hermès scarf and remember the gloves, but she can't give any useful information after that . . . no description of her face or height.' He stopped to take a sip of wine, then continued, 'Can you take me through what you saw again . . . maybe something has jogged your mind since we were at Covent Garden?'

'Being a typical woman, I haven't recalled anything that I haven't said already.'

'I'm not having a go, Jane, it's just that traumatic things we see or experience are put to the back of our mind. They're in there somewhere and all I want to do is help you remember. So far, Daphne was the only one who saw him leave the bag by the ticket booth and the only one who can identify him when he's arrested.'

'If I'd seen his face I would have immediately told DCI Crowley or you. It all happened very quickly . . . a minute maybe, before that big man moved in front of me and the bomb exploded . . . He saved my life, whether he knew it or not. There is nothing more I can add to what I have already said repeatedly. If there was, believe me, you would be the first person I'd tell.'

Jane had only eaten half of her fish and chips but Dexter had wolfed down everything on his plate. He said nothing as he wiped his mouth with his napkin. She tried to think up something else to say, and turned to the three oblong canvases.

'I'm interested in those dates . . . what do they mean?'

He looked over at them. 'The first one, 22 November 1963 . . . you should know that?'

Jane shrugged.

'It's the date JFK was assassinated.'

'Oh.'

'The other one, 5 August 1962, is when Marilyn Monroe died.'

'Oh, really? And the blank one?'

'Well, that could be mine.' He laughed.

'I don't think that's funny . . . it's sort of tempting fate.'

'I do that for a living. They're just people that I admire. Well, I admire JFK, and Marilyn is my perfect woman . . . sexy, that great blonde curly hair, and she was a lot brighter than anyone ever gave her credit for. "If you can make a woman laugh you can make her do anything." She said that.'

Jane flushed, and sipped her wine as Dexter drained his glass and poured himself another.

'James Dean's Porsche was stolen from an exhibition and never recovered . . . some ghoulish fan has to have it hidden somewhere, but that picture was taken at the scene when he crashed it and was found mangled. It's my dream car . . . a big step up from my 1965 911 Carrera.'

He got up to take her plate and stacked it on top of his. 'Right, I can offer you coffee or cheese? I might have some ice cream.'

'I'm fine, thank you. Let me help you.'

'No, stay put, I won't be a moment.'

'Actually, could I use the bathroom?'

'Sure, first door on the left in the hall and through the bedroom.'

The bedroom was as immaculate as the rest of the flat. A bright Mexican rug with a fringe was thrown across the huge double bed. Beside the white fitted wardrobes, a section of low shelves held an electric typewriter and stacks of A4 paper, in front of which stood a leather chair. Next to the bed was a small steel table with a silver

Anglepoise lamp, an empty ashtray and a large alarm clock. There were no mirrors or ornaments, and the room was devoid of pictures and photographs. The en-suite bathroom was tiled from floor to ceiling in white. There was a separate shower in a glass booth, next to a free-standing claw foot bath, and a washbasin set in white marble. Above the basin was a large, mirror-fronted cabinet.

Jane eased the cabinet door open. An array of shampoos, deodorants, shaving equipment and aftershave faced her. Oddly there was also a large bottle of Dior perfume. The toilet was set back in an alcove with a bidet next to it. Jane washed her hands and dried them on the pristine white hand towel that was hanging on a heated rail beside thick white bath towels. On the back of the bathroom door were two towelling bathrobes. The smaller one had the belt tied around it, as if it was from a hotel, but the larger one was open and left loose.

Jane went back into the main room to find Dexter lounging on one of the sofas, smoking a cigarette and dangling his glass of wine. He had refilled her glass, which was now on the glass coffee table opposite the other sofa.

'This place is incredible. Have you lived here a long time?'

'No, only about six months. It took a year of refurbishment before I moved in. It was a dump when I bought it.'

Jane nodded and smiled. She would have liked to ask how he could afford it on his salary. He must have a wealthy family.

'Did you design everything, to get it the way you wanted?'

'Yes and no. I hate clutter and small spaces, so I got an architect to draw up the plans, and a girlfriend helped furnish it and buy some of the stuff. She used to live in Mexico, so this carpet was a housewarming gift, and I brought back the throw in my bedroom from Acapulco.'

Jane sipped her wine. 'Do you still see her?'

'Occasionally, when she's in town. What about you?'

'Me?'

'Yes, what about you?'

'Well, there's not a lot to tell you really . . . I was a probationary officer at Hackney, then I moved to Bow Street Station . . .'

'I didn't mean your career, I meant what about your personal life?'

'Oh, I've sort of concentrated on my career. I have a sister, Pam, and my parents live in Maida Vale.'

'So, no relationship?'

'Not at the moment.'

It felt as if he was interrogating her and it made her uncomfortable – even more so when he eased himself off the sofa. She thought for a moment he was going to come and sit beside her, but instead he walked to the table and picked up her jacket.

'I should run you home. I've got an early start in the morning, unless you've changed your mind about wanting a coffee?'

Jane sprang up. 'No, really . . . I should be getting off. It's been a really nice evening, and very kind of you.'

Dexter moved behind her and held out her jacket. As she slipped her arms through the sleeves, he gently eased her hair away from under the collar, softly touching her neck. He smiled.

'You have lovely skin, Detective Tennison.'

She blushed at the compliment. Her heart was beating rapidly as she picked up her handbag. Taking her hand, Dexter led her out into the hall.

As they drove back to her flat, Jane wished she could think of something to say. Dexter chatted away, saying that next time he would attempt to cook for her instead of buying fish and chips. Before she knew it, they had pulled up in front of her building and Dexter had switched off the engine. He casually rested his arm along the back of her seat.

'Goodnight. I'll probably see you at the lab some time.'

Jane smiled and moved to open the door but Dexter used his free arm to reach across her and open it. She now had both his arms around her, and he kissed her cheek as the door swung open. Then he climbed out and went around to the passenger door to help her out.

'Goodnight, and thank you again.' She hesitated. 'Perhaps I could cook dinner for you one evening.'

'That would be nice . . . I'll look forward to it.'

As Dexter revved up the engine and drove off, Jane sighed. Considering that she couldn't cook, had never entertained anyone for dinner, and lived in a tiny flat that stank of Pearl's cabbage soup, it could be a very embarrassing evening.

Jane waved to the SPG officers opposite, and walked slowly up the stairs. At least the awful smell of cabbage had faded. She unlocked her front door and dropped her key down on the small table by the telephone. A note was on top of the receiver: *Natalie called again*. Jane picked up the note and walked into her bedroom. She took off her jacket and tossed it onto her bed, wishing that she'd worn something less boring. It was old-fashioned and the matching trousers were now creased. She unzipped them and kicked them off. She looked at herself in the mirror and decided that on her first weekend off she would ask Pam to cut her hair and put some highlights in it.

Still feeling disgruntled, she took off her make-up, brushed her teeth and went to bed. She closed her eyes and, unable to sleep straightaway, thought about the evening. She was disappointed at herself for being so overwhelmed. She had never met anyone like Alan Dexter, or been entertained in such an elegant and tasteful flat. She was also surprised at how attractive she found him. She felt as if she had behaved like a besotted teenager, and was now even more confused. Why had he been so attentive? Perhaps he was monitoring her, to try to find out if there was anything more she could add to her statement? She dismissed the thought. She was being paranoid. Dexter had no need to go to such lengths to get her to repeat everything she knew about the Covent Garden bomb. Increasingly restless, Jane couldn't stop thinking about the way he had touched her neck, and then kissed her. She wondered what it would be like to lie next to him in his big double bed and feel that gentle touch over her entire body. Eventually, she drifted off to sleep.

Jane was woken by the deafening sound of Pearl's alarm clock in the next bedroom. It sounded as if she was lying next to Big Ben. By the time she had wrapped a robe around herself and gone into the kitchen Pearl was sitting eating her bowl of muesli, with a glass of awful-looking green liquid.

'Morning! Your friend Natalie called again. She's quite persistent, isn't she?'

'I saw your message . . . We were friends at training school. She left the police and we lost contact until recently. I expect she just wants to catch up. How come you're up so early?'

'I thought I might have a jog in the park before I go into work.'

'Oh, that's nice.' Jane put the kettle on and got out the tin of instant coffee, spooning two heaps into a mug.

'Did you have a nice time last night?'

'Yes, I did.'

'You know,' Pearl said as Jane filled her mug, 'that stuff is full of preservatives . . . and you shouldn't use sweeteners. They're not good for you either.'

'I know. I couldn't face that seaweed thing you're drinking, not first thing in the morning.'

'You get used to it . . . and it gives me so much energy.'

Jane made no reply and walked back to her bedroom. It was six thirty and she decided she'd have another half an hour in bed. She heard Pearl leaving and felt irritated that she was out jogging as she knew that she should do some exercise herself, but all she could think of was going out to buy some new clothes and making a hair appointment for the weekend.

It was just after eight when a sweating, panting, Pearl returned and went into the bathroom to run a bath. Jane had fortunately already dressed and was ready to leave for work when the phone rang.

'Hi, is that Jane?'

'Yes, who's this?'

'It's Natalie . . . I'm sorry if I've called too early but I have to go to work and wanted to catch you. I rang last night and someone else answered, but I was worried they might not have passed on the message.'

'I'm sorry, I was out and didn't get back until late. I was going to call you later.'

'Well, perhaps we can we meet up? Are you free this evening?'

'Yes, I should be home around seven.'

'Why don't we meet up at eight? I can come to you, or you could come over to my place?'

Pearl banged out of the steam-filled bathroom and Jane covered the phone.

'Are you home this evening, Pearl?'

'Yes . . . be here about six.'

Jane nodded and uncovered the mouthpiece to speak to Natalie. 'Why don't I come to you . . . whereabouts do you live?'

'My flat's in Belsize Park, but I work in Marble Arch. I finish work at five. Where do you live?'

'I'm near Baker Street.'

'Well, I can come over to you if it'll be more convenient. Do you know somewhere we can eat?'

Jane hesitated. She hadn't had time to explore the area and wasn't sure where to suggest. 'Er . . . there's an Italian restaurant not far from the underground station . . . It's called Fratelli's. I haven't actually tried it, but it looks OK.'

'Why don't we meet up there then?'

Natalie was being very persistent. Jane felt she couldn't get out of it.

'All right, eight this evening, then?'

'Great! I'm really looking forward to seeing you, and chatting about old times.'

Jane replaced the receiver. She'd planned to have an early night, but it would be rude not to go for dinner with Natalie, especially as she hadn't returned her calls, and Natalie was so keen to catch up with her. Pearl came out of the bathroom, a towel wrapped around her wet hair.

'I couldn't borrow your hairdryer again, could I? By the way, Fratelli's is a nice restaurant and very reasonable. I've often eaten there, as they do a special lunch price.'

Jane fetched her hairdryer and handed it to Pearl.

'Do you mind just leaving it in the kitchen? I'm sorry but I don't really like you going into my bedroom.'

Pearl shrugged. 'Fine by me. Thanks, and I'll see you later.'

Jane fetched her coat and handbag. She was feeling irritated and slammed out of the flat to walk to Baker Street.

As usual it was a lengthy journey across London to Woolwich, but Jane's initial irritability gradually subsided as she joined two junior trainee scientists and a female clerical officer in the canteen. They were having a conversation about all the scientists and officers, giving them marks out of ten for sexual attractiveness. Jane felt rather annoyed by their discussion, but took an interest when they started talking about Dexter. He was rated as a ten plus.

A very skinny, petite girl with incredibly thick hair was eating a bowl of rice pudding, wafting her spoon around.

'I think he's gorgeous . . . very sexy . . . but there's something sort of detached about him. I was told he gets any female he wants. He's very wealthy . . . his older brother was killed in a skiing accident so when his father died he inherited a fortune. His ex-girlfriend – who he lived with in Mexico – is the daughter of some famous artist. And he's a bit of a rarity: he's the only serving police officer who is also part of the bomb disposal unit. I was told he was in the Royal Army

Ordinance Corps as an explosives officer and was initially trained by the now head of the Met's bomb disposal unit. Dexter was exceptional at what he did during army service and received gallantry awards for bomb disposal. That's why he's shit hot here . . . after a few years' service he was transferred to the Bomb Squad thanks to his knowledge of disarming explosives. He can disarm me any day!' She laughed.

Jane couldn't resist asking, 'Have you been out with him?'

'Chance'd be a fine thing! Although I think he's got quite a lot of baggage . . . but that doesn't make him any the less attractive. Mind you, I couldn't go out with someone who does a dangerous job like his . . . I heard someone in the lab say Dexter has a death wish.'

One of the other girls, who had been eating throughout the entire conversation, looked up. 'I had a one night stand with him,' she said. 'I'd do it again, but when that Mexican woman is in town he just drops you . . . so I'm going to drop his mark to a seven.' She laughed as she glanced at Jane. 'Crowley got a minus four!'

Jane said nothing as the skinny girl pushed the remains of her rice pudding around the bowl and asked if anyone wanted a tea or coffee. None of them had seen Dexter walking up to stand behind them. He rested his hand on Jane's shoulder.

'Hello, Jane. So what's this about Crowley being a minus four?'

There was an embarrassing pause. Jane had to bite her bottom lip hard to stop giggling, as the other girls flushed and jumped to their feet.

'Oh, nothing,' the skinny girl said. 'Er . . . we're going to get coffee. Do you want one?'

'No, thanks, I'm just looking for Lawrence but he doesn't seem to be here.'

Jane was left alone with Dexter, and he sat down next to her. She could see the other girls at the coffee counter whispering, then turning to look towards their table.

'I didn't think you were the giggling type. What's so funny?'

'They were marking all the men here out of ten, for sexual attraction.'

'Really? So, tell me, how many points did they allocate to me?'

'You did very well . . . you started with a ten but then dropped to a seven. I was just listening in, not taking part.'

'What score would you give me?'

It was Jane's turn to blush. She shrugged and Dexter leaned in closer.

'Go on, tell me.'

'I'd say you were easily a ten . . . but then, I'm biased. You bought me fish and chips.'

He stood up, smiling, and pushed the chair beneath the table. Then he leaned in and kissed her cheek.

'Thank you, DC Tennison, that's really made my day.'

Dexter walked off and, rather than get into any further conversation with the two girls, Jane took her crockery and cutlery to the wash bowl provided for everyone to deposit their used dishes. She didn't escape as the girls caught up with her as she was stacking her tray.

'How much did he overhear?' the skinny girl asked nervously.

'Just the bit about Crowley . . . I told him it was a joke.'

'Oh.'

They looked at each other as Jane started to walk off, because they had seen Dexter kissing her cheek.

'Another one bites the dust . . .'

Jane turned and glared at them.

'If you are referring to me, I resent that remark. We are working together, nothing more. You should grow up and stop gossip-mongering.'

They watched her heading out of the canteen and nudged each other.

'Well, I'd say the lady doth protest too much! We need to be careful what we say around her . . . she's obviously smitten.'

Jane banged through the doors of the canteen and bumped into DS Lawrence. He threw up his hands.

'It's bloody unbelievable, that guy needs someone to straighten him out!'

'Who are you talking about?'

'Bloody Dexter, he thrives on risk-taking and thinks he's indestructible. He's nabbed a disarming device I'd left in the lab to test.'

'He was in the canteen a minute ago . . .'

'I'll go find him. We are all on tenterhooks and he's playing silly buggers with untested equipment. If you ask me he has a death wish.'

'You know, maybe he lives life to the full because he knows each day could be his last, and every time there is a warning call from the IRA he could be killed disarming one of their bombs.'

'I doubt it,' whispered Lawrence. 'His best pal, who went in ahead of him to assess the bomb at Selfridges, was killed when it exploded. Dexter's got some guardian angel sitting on his shoulder.'

'I hope so,' Jane said quietly, then asked Lawrence what he wanted her to do for the day.

'The victims' clothing needs bagging and tagging . . . if you don't mind doing that. Everything's hanging up in the drying room down the corridor.' He pointed to a room on the left.

Jane knew that much of the clothing was heavily bloodstained. It wasn't a job she relished doing, but she was determined to show willing. Paul handed her the key and she unlocked the door. There were no windows in the drying room; it was in total darkness and felt like an eerie sauna. Jane switched on the neon strip lighting, which flickered for a few seconds before illuminating the room. She inhaled deeply at the sight of the torn and tattered bloodstained clothing hanging from washing lines strung up around the room. Her eyes instantly caught sight of a bloodstained Babygro, and for a moment she was back at Covent Garden, hearing the child's muffled cries. She relived carrying the pushchair up the stairs, then less than a minute later turning the seriously injured mother over. The sight of the baby beneath its mother, covered in blood, and the weight of the baby in her arms.

Jane unpegged the Babygro from the washing line. She held it tightly in her hands and the good smell it made was like sweet pancakes and a cup of warm milk. The musty smell of dry blood then came through and the grit from the explosion rubbed against her hands. It was wretchedly sad. The child would never know its mother.

CHAPTER TWELVE

Jane walked into the Italian restaurant and asked for a table for two. She'd arranged to meet Natalie at eight and had arrived a bit early to ensure she could get in. The tables were covered in red-and-white checked tablecloths, and in the centre of each was an empty Chianti bottle with a candle stuck into the top. A long counter displayed breads and sweet pastries, together with a vast display of cheeses, on the other side of which a dark-haired man was busy cutting wafer-thin slices of cured ham.

Jane opened the menu. There was a lunch menu on one side, then the dinner menu and specials were on a thick laminated page on the other side. It was exactly eight when Natalie walked in. Seeing Jane sitting at the side of the room, she waved and walked over to join her. She tossed a stylish thick, wool jacket over the back of her chair, and tucked her soft leather clutch bag under the table as she sat down.

'It's not very posh,' Jane said.

'It's fine . . . I love Italian food. Have you decided what you want to order?' Natalie said as she took off her gloves and placed them on the table.

Jane noticed the checked lining. 'I like your gloves,' she said. 'Are they Burberry?'

'Yes. Christmas present from an old flame. I never spend that much money on gloves.'

'I think I might have the tomato and basil soup, followed by spaghetti bolognese . . . unless you're not having a starter?'

As Natalie looked over the menu Jane admired her pale denim shirt, tight jeans and cowboy boots. Jane thought to herself that as well as getting Pam to cut her hair she'd do some clothes shopping.

'I'll have the minestrone, and then the chicken with garlic and mashed potatoes . . . or maybe the cannelloni.' Natalie turned to attract the waitress's attention.

'Is the cannelloni freshly made on the premises?'

'Yes, we make all the pasta dishes here . . . my father is the chef.' The waitress nodded to the dark-haired man behind the counter.

They ordered their food and a bottle of Pinot Noir. Natalie smiled at Jane.

'Isn't this nice? On my way here I was trying to calculate just how long it's been . . . you don't look all that different.'

'I remember you used to have very long hair.'

'Oh God, yes! I had this terrible perm and it went like a frizzy mop, so I had it cut really short, you know that sort of pixie cut . . . but it didn't really suit me, so I've let it grow a bit.'

'I was thinking of getting my sister to cut mine, and give me some highlights . . . I've not really taken that much interest in my hair-style, and always used to put it in a pleat under my police hat. But it *was* a relief when I came out of uniform. Those policewomen's hats are not very flattering, and the uniform was continually having to be brushed down and dry cleaned, shirts starched, tie in place . . .'

'And those black stockings and awful police-issue shoes,' agreed Natalie. 'But you know, I was really heartbroken when I was kicked out of Hendon. Truthfully, I don't think I would have made the grade, though. Where were you posted to when you came out?'

'Hackney . . . one of the toughest areas. Didn't really have too much time to think about it as I was thrown into the deep end. There was only one other uniformed WPC there.'

Jane was relieved when the waitress came to the table and uncorked the wine, as she didn't want to get into a discussion about Kath Morgan's death. Natalie took a small sip of the wine to taste it and nodded in approval.

'This isn't too heavy . . . light and not too fruity.'

The waitress filled their glasses and placed the bottle in the centre of the table. Jane sipped the wine and nodded.

'Mmm, it is very nice. So, what did you do after you left Hendon?'

'I did a course in accountancy. I worked in a couple of firms at a low level, but it was so boring . . . and, you know, it takes ages to qualify as a fully-fledged accountant. Then I applied for a job on a cruise liner.' She laughed. 'I thought it would be a cheap way of seeing the world . . . but, my God, they worked my socks off. I saw the West Indies, and the Bahamas and the Virgin Isles, but nothing ever prepares you for the pettiness of the crews. And most of the guests on board treat you like a glorified waitress and cleaner.'

At this point their starters arrived. Two more customers came in and were seated as another couple left. The restaurant was still only a quarter full. As they ate Jane gave a brief outline of how she had moved from Hackney to Bow Street and succeeded in qualifying for CID.

'CID . . . wow! That's terrific! Do you deal with murder enquiries?'

'I have done. But there's a lot of discrimination in the Met. You learn to deal with it.'

'How do you mean?'

'Well, women often get sidelined, or given incredibly boring enquiries . . . even on murder cases you end up doing tedious paper-work. I remember when I was a probationer it felt like I was nothing more than wallpaper. Only useful for making teas and coffees. It's better now I'm a detective, but it's still there.'

'It's the same at the bank. Some of the clerks and bank managers I've had to deal with would make your hair stand on end . . . so rigid, and obsessive timekeepers. God forbid that you should make the smallest error . . . all hell breaks loose.'

'So, do you live with someone? Are you married?' Jane asked.

'I have lived with a few men, and when I was on the cruise ships I was quite naughty . . . but I haven't found the right one yet. What about you?'

'There's nobody, really. I've just rented out the spare room in my flat.'

Jane went on to describe Pearl Radcliff and her vegetarian diet, and relayed the story about asking her if she had many belongings – 'and now the spare bedroom looks like a book depository,' she finished. Natalie swapped stories of previous girls she had shared with, making Jane laugh when she told her about one girl who had so many boyfriends coming and going, and that eventually she had found out she was a complete nymphomaniac.

'Her name was Françoise, and she came from a very upper-class family . . . I think they owned vineyards in the South of France because she always had loads of money. She made model airplanes, and would spend hours gluing and using thin wires to hang them from her bedroom ceiling. I asked her if she was interested in flying and she said they represented her lovers! Anyway, one time she brought back this handsome chap and kept on saying that he was the one . . . then she made this small helicopter and pinned it up! So, he was gone and eventually I had to ask her to leave.'

By the time their main course arrived they had drunk almost the entire bottle of wine. Natalie was very complimentary about her cannelloni, explaining how difficult it was to roll the light pastry around the meat and make the rich tomato sauce.

'I love cooking, and I have to say that I'm not too bad . . . I even did a Cordon Bleu cookery course, because I really like experimenting and trying out new dishes. Do you like Indian food?'

Jane shrugged, saying that she was embarrassed at how hopeless she was in the kitchen. 'When I'm at work, or was living in the section house, I always ate in the canteen. My mother's a good cook . . . did it all when I lived at home . . . you know, big roast dinners on a Sunday. I can just about boil or scramble an egg with some bacon. I've never tried anything fancy . . . there are blokes at work who know more about cooking than me.'

'Well, I am going to change that, Jane Tennison! I'm going to give you a beginner's course in some basic culinary dishes. What are you doing this weekend?'

'Well, I've planned to see my sister tomorrow . . .'

'Why don't you come over on Sunday? I'll do a grocery shop tomorrow and we can cook lunch together.'

Natalie was wonderful company and Jane realised that she had never had a close girlfriend. She felt so at ease with her, and readily accepted her offer of a cooking lesson.

By the time they both had coffee and a delicious sweet honey pastry each, they had agreed to meet on Sunday. Natalie wrote down her address in Belsize Park and insisted that Jane come by early so she could start the cookery lesson.

'It's just a garden flat in the basement, so don't be too excited. I'm going to insist I pay for our dinner tonight, and you can pay the next time we eat out. But I'm hoping you'll be able to invite me to your place to meet your vegetarian Pearl, and then cook for me.'

They were the last customers to leave the restaurant, and the closed sign was flipped over on the main door. As they headed out into the street towards Baker Street station, they paused at the traffic lights.

'This is where I head back to Melcombe Street,' Jane said.

'I had a great evening. See you Sunday,' Natalie replied. She gave Jane a hug and kissed her on the cheek before hurrying across the road.

Jane was just turning away when a highly polished black Jaguar pulled up at the red traffic light. Jane wouldn't have noticed the vehicle and its occupants, but for the face in the passenger window. Jane instantly recognised Regina Hernandez, the young girl she had rescued on her first day with the Dip Squad. Regina looked like a startled fawn. As the lights turned to green, Jane, hardly believing what she was doing, flagged down a cab.

'Can you follow that black Jaguar?'

'Lost your boyfriend, have yer?' The cab driver smirked as Jane got in.

'I'm a police officer.'

'Right, luv, doing an Agatha Christie, are you? I'll follow it.'

From the back seat, Jane watched as the Jaguar drove along Regent Street, crossing straight over Oxford Circus they passed the London Palladium Theatre's billboards and then Liberty, taking a right at Brook Street. The cab driver half turned to Jane, 'Do you know where your friends are going, luv?'

'No, I don't.' Jane said, wondering if the driver of the Jaguar suspected he was being followed or was unfamiliar with the area.

'Well, I hope they're not doing a sightseeing tour! That looks like a courtesy car.'

'Just keep following, please.' Part of Jane was uncertain she had even recognised Regina. As they approached Grosvenor Square and headed into the traffic in Park Lane, they were directly behind the Jaguar and when it stopped abruptly outside the Playboy Club, the cab driver almost drove into the back of it.

'Did you see that? No indication he was stopping!'

Jane already had her wallet open. Ahead, she saw a man in a shiny suit get out and open the passenger door. Dressed in a plunging top, tight-fitting sequined mini skirt, high-heeled silver sandals and a white fox fur wrap, the fifteen-year-old Hernandez girl did not look her age.

'Could you wait for me?'

'No, luv, I can't park out here. Just pay me off. It's four pounds.'

Jane thrust a five-pound note at the driver just as the Jaguar pulled away from the pavement. The Playboy Club's black gleaming door opened as Jane ran towards Regina. That was the moment she saw that the man ushering the frightened girl in front of him was Regina's uncle, Andres Hernandez. The club door closed and the doorman barred the entrance.

'I need to speak to that girl.'

'Members only,' the bouncer replied without looking at Jane.

'You don't understand . . . it is very important that I speak to that young girl. She's underage.'

'You got a membership card, luv?'

'No, but –'

'Then you ain't getting in.'

Jane got out her warrant card, 'I'm a detective with the Metropolitan Police.'

'So are quite a few people in there . . . and a lot more senior than you, sweetheart. Shall I go disturb a commander and get him to come and have a word with you, or would you like to toddle off and get a warrant?'

It was pointless to argue with the doorman. She suspected he was right: there were probably a few senior police officers in the club and they wouldn't take kindly to being disturbed by the likes of a detective constable. Deciding to give up, she headed home.

Jane woke up early the following morning and walked to the nearest laundrette, which was on Edgware Road. She couldn't wash bed linen in the flat as there was only a small washing machine and no tumble dryer. As she waited for the dryer to finish she was haunted by Regina's scared face as she was pulled into the club. She hurried home and was glad to see that Pearl had already left to visit her parents in Southport. She called DCI Church. He wasn't in his office, but she spoke to Stanley, who seemed almost to live in the squalid office.

'There's something going on, Stanley. Last night I was in Baker Street and I saw this very polished black Jaguar . . . It might be a courtesy car the Playboy Club provide for its clients.'

'So?'

'She was sitting in the back seat.'

'Who are you talking about?'

'Regina Hernandez.'

'What?'

'I haven't finished yet, Stanley. The man who took her into the Playboy Club was that Andres Hernandez who they say was her uncle. I was told that she was being looked after! Stanley, she is only fifteen and was dressed like a hooker and I'm certain that the club management would be wary of allowing an underage girl into the premises. She's too young to even be allowed to drink, never mind go into a casino.'

'Did you make a note of the Jag's licence plate?'

'Yes, I did.' Jane repeated it. 'The taxi driver suggested it might be a courtesy car.'

'Where does the taxi driver fit into this?'

'I told you, when I saw Regina in the car, I hailed a taxi and followed it from Baker Street.'

'Right, I'll pass this on to the Vice Squad and just before you hang up, Jane, do you mind if I give you a little word of advice? I wouldn't try to claim your cab fare on expenses. You were told this was no longer connected to us and you don't want to piss DCI Church off.'

'Thank you for the warning,' Jane said shortly.

Feeling dispirited after her conversation with Stanley, Jane drove to her parents' flat in Maida Vale. It was just after one when she arrived, and they were delighted to see her. They made such a fuss of her that she felt guilty for not having been to see them before. Her father didn't speak about the events at Covent Garden, but did say that DCI Church had been to visit them again and left contact numbers in case they had any enquiries.

'Mr Church said they were all taking good care of you,' her father said when her mother went out of the room. 'He was considerate and supportive, and explained the situation. Mum and I are proud of you, Jane, but I'd rather hear it from you . . . Are you coping?'

'Yes, on the whole, but there are moments when it's hard to focus. Please don't tell Mum . . .'

'You know I won't, Jane.'

'I had to bag and tag the victims' clothing the other day. There was a mother who was killed at the scene, but her baby survived. I had to bag the mother's torn, bloodstained clothes and the child's Babygro, which had the mother's blood on it . . . I found it really upsetting.'

Mr Tennison hugged his daughter. 'Your job is really harrowing at times . . . you are very brave and I admire you . . . so does your mother, but sometimes she's not much good at showing it.'

Her mother was cooking a leg of lamb with all the trimmings. Jane offered to help but as usual her mother refused, as she hated anyone getting under her feet in the kitchen.

'Does Pam know how to cook, Mum?'

'Good heavens, no! Poor Tony gets more takeaways than he ever has a good cooked meal. Why do you ask?'

'I've lived off canteen food for too long. Now I've got a place of my own I'd like to fend for myself on something more substantial than eggs and bacon.'

Mrs Tennison laughed. 'I was self-taught, dear. Practice is what makes a good cook. Mind you, I burnt a few things and used the wrong ingredients to start with. I'll give you some of my cookery books to take with you. The Fanny Craddock one is good – you know, the woman who's always on TV, with the monocled husband? They're a good double act, a bit like me and your dad.'

They didn't eat lunch until after two, then sat watching TV whilst Mrs Tennison told Jane that they had booked a two-week cruise. Jane was astonished, even more so when they said they were going to Norway. She could hardly believe they were being such adventurists. They talked about her new flatmate and Mrs Tennison was relieved that Jane was no longer living on her own. Her father was also relieved that the rent was being paid in, and Jane was repaying his deposit loan towards her mortgage.

It was five thirty when Jane left and drove to the salon, hoping that Pam might be able to cut her hair and do some highlight streaks. Pam was obviously tired after a long and busy day but she made Jane a cup of coffee whilst she finished her last client. By the time Jane was in the chair, it was after six. Pam put on a rubber cap, and pulled strands of Jane's hair through the small holes before she layered the bleach, using square-cut sections of tin foil. It had to be left on for twenty minutes so Pam pulled up a stool and sat beside Jane.

'I'm still not pregnant . . . but it's not for lack of trying!' She gave a soft laugh, but Jane could tell she was not happy.

'Maybe if you didn't worry so much?'

'But I can't help it . . . we want a baby more than anything. Every month I take a test, and it's so depressing when it's negative.'

Eventually Pam washed Jane's hair and cut two inches off before blow-drying it with a large bristle brush into a short pageboy style. She refused to charge her, but Jane insisted that she take ten pounds. She wasn't sure about the way Pam had styled her hair, and it looked much blonder, but she thought that after she had played around with it, it would look more to her satisfaction.

Jane decided to have an early night, and was looking forward to seeing Natalie again in the morning. She was glad that she had seen her parents and Pam, and felt more relaxed after all the security precautions and pressure she had been under. She didn't get home until after eight, parking her car a short distance from her flat and getting the usual nod from the plain-clothes officers on watch as she opened the front door. Crowley, for all his tough, blustering manner, had kept his word when he'd told her father he intended to maintain the protection until the ASU members were arrested.

At eleven o'clock the following morning, Jane drove to Natalie's via St John's Wood and into Belsize Avenue. She managed to park close to number 44 and walked up to the large, imposing, four-storey house, then descended the steps to the basement.

Natalie opened the front door almost immediately after Jane pressed the doorbell. She was barefooted and wearing an apron over her jeans and T-shirt.

'Hi there! You found me . . . come on in.'

Jane wished she'd bought a bunch of flowers, but it hadn't occurred to her. Natalie seemed so pleased to see her, helping her off with her coat and hanging it on a hook in the narrow hallway.

'It's small, but it's all my own.' Natalie said, as she drew Jane into a lovely living room with French windows overlooking steps up to a walled garden.

The living room was full, with bright, fabric-covered chairs and a two-seater sofa by a low pine coffee table. There was a fireplace with wooden logs and a coal bucket beside it. The walls were lined with bookshelves and there was a cabinet filled with pottery, coloured glass miniatures and rows of wine glasses. There were some rather amateurish oil paintings, and stacks of magazines. It was a warm and cosy room. Natalie had lit some scented candles and the glow and smell made the room feel welcoming.

Natalie opened the French windows and stepped outside. Stone steps led up to a flourishing plant bed and there was a bench and wooden table. Numerous pot plants were placed around, containing herbs and bulbs, but a lot of the flowering plants were no longer in season. On the table there were empty bottles of wine holding melted candles, and the paved area had moss growing between the cracks. A large oak tree dominated the end of the garden and shaded most of the patio.

'I eat out here when the weather's good, but come on back to my favourite place . . . the kitchen.'

'How long have you lived here?' Jane asked, as she followed Natalie back inside.

'Five years. It needs quite a lot doing to it, and as it's a basement it gets a bit on the damp side. But I love lighting a fire in the winter, and it's cosy, which is important to me. I bought most of the furniture second-hand from charity shops.'

They went into the narrow hall and Natalie pointed to a closed door.

'That's my bedroom. I have my mother's old quilt, and my desk and a portable typewriter, but it needs some more wardrobe space. I'll get it sorted one day.'

She had expected the basement flat to be dark, but when Jane followed Natalie into the kitchen it was surprisingly light.

'This is the best part. The previous occupant went to great lengths to modernise the kitchen and put in the big window.'

Jane was impressed. The kitchen was painted a bright blue, with a fridge-freezer, large cooker with an extractor hood, and a wide sink with wooden draining boards. There was a painted old-fashioned wide-legged table, with four hard-backed painted chairs with bright cushions on the seats. Tall glass-fronted cabinets were filled with crockery, and wide drawers beneath with cooking equipment.

'Every available inch has been used for storage. I have a washing machine and dryer tucked in the little recess, so it's very compact. But as I love cooking I spend most of my time in here.'

'I think it's lovely . . . it has a sort of country cottage feel.'

'Yes, exactly . . . you'd never think we were in the basement. I bought it because of the little garden. At one time it must have been three times the size but the properties backing onto it have the rest. I was going to get a cat, but I just never got around to it . . . like all the redecorating I keep on meaning to do!'

Natalie had fetched two mugs and put the kettle on. As she showed off the kitchen, she brewed up some fresh coffee in a small percolator and opened a tin to take out a packet of biscuits, placing them down on the table.

'Sit down . . . We'll have a cup of coffee and then I can talk you through what you would like to cook for our lunch. I bought a variety of ingredients for you to choose from, but I think we won't get too extravagant to begin with, and stick to something basic. I've got chicken, liver, bacon and some fresh minced beef to maybe make spaghetti bolognese. It depends what you'd like to start off with.'

'I'm speechless . . . this is so kind of you! Let's make spaghetti bolognese as I really love it, but I wouldn't know where to begin . . .'

'Well, we'll make the sauce first. I've got all the tomatoes, onions and garlic, and then we've got some fresh pasta.'

Natalie poured them both a coffee, placed milk and sugar on the table and sat opposite Jane. She delved into her pocket and took out a packet of cigarettes.

'Hope you don't mind? Do you smoke?'

'No, I don't . . . but please go ahead.'

Natalie took out a long, thin, white-tipped cigarette.

'I want to give up so I started on these, but I've got so used to them. They're menthol . . . "Snow-fresh Filter Kool" . . . it's sort of like smoking a polo mint.'

She lit up and fetched an ashtray as Jane poured some milk into her coffee and ate a custard cream. Natalie drank her coffee black, and laughed as she added three sugars.

'I've got a terrible sweet tooth . . . this is very strong Colombian coffee, so I try to limit myself to just a few cups a day.'

'Do you live here all by yourself?' Jane asked.

'Well, most of the time. My last relationship went on for a couple of years . . . he was very easy-going but this is a tiny flat and even though he only stayed at weekends I was often pleased to have the place back to myself on Mondays.'

'I was at dinner with a friend the other night, and I've never seen such a sophisticated flat. It was a sort of ultra-modern design and was very unexpected. I thought we were going to a restaurant, but after picking up fish and chips he drove us to his flat. I honestly don't think I've ever felt so inadequate, because he was so capable, and . . .' She giggled.

'Why were you feeling inadequate?'

'Oh, it was just so sophisticated and I'd worn this awful suit, fawn trousers with a safari jacket.' Jane drained her cup of coffee and continued, 'I don't know what made me wear it . . . I felt so old-fashioned, and couldn't think of anything interesting to say.'

'You aren't old-fashioned at all . . . I like what you've had done to your hair. What does this friend do?'

'He's one of the officers, not in the same team, but sort of working alongside me in the Dip Squad.'

'Dip Squad? What on earth is that?'

Jane stood up abruptly and screeched as her coffee cup turned over. Natalie immediately reached for a napkin as Jane deftly put her hand into Natalie's handbag, which was on the arm of the dining chair, and took out her wallet and held it up between two fingers.

'You see, I just got your wallet because I distracted you with my coffee cup. There was no coffee in it.'

There was a beat of an unpleasant moment as Natalie snatched her wallet back. 'You shouldn't have done that.'

'I was just dipping you to explain how pickpockets work. I'm sorry if I've offended you.'

Natalie's face relaxed. 'Oh no, you haven't! This Dip Squad sounds outrageous. So, tell me, what work does this designer house bloke do?'

'He's a DS on the Bomb Squad and he's got quite a bad reputation when it comes to women. But it's been extraordinary lately . . . I've gone from having nobody showing the slightest interest in me, to a date with him. And I think my DCI is sort of interested as well. And there's also a lovely man called Michael Mitchell, who's a charge nurse at St Thomas' Hospital, where I met you.'

Natalie rinsed their coffee mugs and began to open cupboards and take out all the ingredients required to make the bolognese sauce.

'Well, you can now invite any one of them over to your flat to have dinner. My mother always used to say that the best way to a man's heart is through his stomach.'

Natalie handed Jane an apron, then got out a large chopping board and a sharp knife. Jane watched as Natalie peeled and sliced the onion into fine sections. She showed Jane how to squash and chop garlic cloves and let her have a go at it herself. Natalie got a large pan, poured in some olive oil, turned on the gas and scraped in the garlic and onions from the chopping board. She handed Jane a wooden spoon, told her to keep the gas low and keep stirring until the onions were see-through.

Jane was enjoying herself as Natalie put in the minced meat, then when it was brown she let Jane add some diced tomatoes, herbs and tomato puree, then after giving it a good stir they left it to simmer. Natalie uncorked a bottle of red wine while Jane was stirring the bolognese.

'I've bought freshly made pasta, which will only take about five minutes. You need to test if it is cooked through, but it should be what the Italians call "*al dente*" . . . slightly firm on the bite.'

Natalie lit another cigarette whilst Jane kept on stirring the sauce, then put the pasta into the boiling water.

'So, now you know how to make spaghetti bolognese! You should serve it in a bowl with some grated parmesan cheese on top and garlic bread which should be crispy, not soggy, when it comes out of the oven.'

They both sat at the table with a glass of wine. A large ceramic bowl contained the finished spaghetti bolognese, with two serving spoons beside it. The garlic bread was laid out on a large warmed plate, and looked and smelled delicious.

'*Bon appétit!*' Natalie said, as they clinked glasses. Jane enjoyed everything, and was surprised at how simple it had been to prepare.

'Thanks, Natalie, I really appreciate you showing me how to cook this . . . it's not as difficult as I thought it would be.'

'Next lesson will be a roast chicken with stuffing. But I think you've now learnt enough to entertain your male suitors. So, tell me, which one's your favourite and what does he look like?'

'He's a detective sergeant, tall, blonde, blue-eyed and drives a Porsche. I don't think he's that interested in me, but he might . . .' Jane already felt that she had said too much.

Natalie leaned forwards across the table. 'Did you sleep with him?'

'No!'

'What about the other two . . . the nurse from the hospital?'

'Good heavens, no! I shouldn't really even be talking about them.'

'Why not? What about the DCI . . . is he sexy?'

Jane felt a trifle uncomfortable.

'He's very attractive. There's a big black-tie event coming up in the CID, and he asked if . . . well, sort of suggested he accompany me.'

'Is he married? Are any of them married?'

'No.'

'Well, that's a relief. I had a long scene with a married man and I swore I would never, ever, be dumb enough to do it again. You know, I got the same old story that he was going to leave his wife, but he never did. I don't think he had any intention of leaving her, but I was very hurt. So, this black-tie do . . . have you decided what you're going to wear?'

'No, I haven't given it a thought . . . but it's full evening gowns so it'll have to be a long dress.'

'I tell you what you should do . . . I'll give you the address of a special place on the King's Road where you can hire a dress. Some of them are really spectacular and it'll cost less than forking out for something you might only wear once . . . Where is the ball being held?'

'I'm not sure. To be honest I'm not even certain of the exact date, but it's a formal dinner and I believe it's a very popular night with all the CID officers and their wives.'

Natalie lit another cigarette, and started to clear the plates.

'Let me help you,' Jane said, jumping up. 'If you could give me the address for that dress hire place I'd be grateful. I've decided my entire wardrobe needs an overhaul, and I am going to chuck out that terrible safari suit.'

'Just remember that you shouldn't dress to please a man, you should do it for yourself. If you think you look good and you feel confident then whatever they think is immaterial . . . so sayeth my dear departed mother, who once . . .'

Natalie started to laugh, as Jane ran the hot water into the sink to begin washing the dishes.

'She once said to me, in a very confidential manner, that if I wanted to know what kind of a body a man had . . .' She giggled again, and Jane couldn't help joining in.

'I was gobsmacked because I couldn't think of what she was going to come out with! But she whispered to me that I should go swimming with him, as you can tell what kind of body he has in a pair of swimming trunks! And do you know how often I've thought about that when I've been having sex, wishing I'd done a test run in a swimming pool!'

They both laughed, as the dishes were washed and put away, and by the time the kitchen was cleared it was after six. Natalie wanted Jane to stay but Jane didn't want to outstay her welcome. When they said their farewells, Natalie gave her a big bear hug and a kiss, as they promised to meet up again for another cooking lesson.

As Jane drove home she suddenly remembered that Natalie hadn't given her the contact details for the dress hire company, and decided she would ring her when she got back to her flat, but there was no answer when she called. She had enjoyed herself, and liked having someone to confide in. She did wonder whether perhaps she had said too much about her work, but then dismissed it. So that she didn't forget exactly how to make spaghetti bolognese in the future, she wrote down all the ingredients and cooking instructions. Sitting in her tiny kitchen she doubted she could invite anyone for dinner, as they would have to perch on the kitchen stools. Then there was Pearl to consider, unless it was a weekend when she was away visiting her parents.

As if on cue Jane heard the main front door bang shut, and then heavy footsteps on the stairs before the key turned in the door. Pearl slammed the door shut behind her, causing Jane to wince as she appeared in the kitchen doorway. Pearl pulled off her green beret, shook her hair and dumped her overnight bag down on the floor. She sighed.

'I had a big row with my mother, so I got the earlier train back.' Pearl was about to go into her bedroom, when Jane noticed that she had two books tucked under her arm.

'More books? You must be an avid reader.'

'Yes, well it's part of my job, or at least I feel it's necessary. We sometimes have private parties who rent out the museum, and then I give a tour and they ask me a lot of questions. I like to know the background on all the exhibits. We even have sort of scenes from crimes, murders like Dr Crippen, and Lizzie Borden the axe-killer. I'm always asked for details, which is why I do the research. I like the murderers in our collection; it's fascinating how and why they kill people. I'm always the one asked to give the private tours because most of the other employees have no idea who half the people are . . . and I get extra money.'

'Oh, that's very innovative of you.' Jane said, and then she smiled. 'Do you have a Marilyn Monroe waxwork there?'

'Oh yes, of course.'

'I believe she had lots of witty remarks recorded . . .'

'She did . . . My favourite is: "I don't mind living in a man's world, as long as I can be a woman in it."'

'Oh . . .' Jane was impressed. She had been going to try and catch Pearl out by repeating what Dexter had told her.

'Did you have a nice weekend?' Pearl asked.

'Yes, I did . . . I had a cooking lesson.'

'Oh, cooking . . . that's what started the argument with my mother. She infuriated me. I have told her repeatedly that I am a vegetarian and she says that she knows – and then she decided to roast a duck for Sunday lunch. I reminded her that I didn't eat meat and she got into a real temper saying that duck wasn't meat, it was a bird . . . then it just escalated into a big argument as to whether or not ducks and chickens were acceptable for vegetarians. I said: "Mother, they are fowl and therefore, meat", and the next minute there was drama and tears . . . so I had enough and left.'

'Would you like a cup of your green tea?'

'No, thank you. I'm tired out and have an early start in the morning. Oh, how was dinner at Fratelli's?'

'It was very nice.'

'I often have their veggie lunch . . . but most days I like to go into the Planetarium. My friend Eric works there so I get in free. Do you believe in star signs?'

'I've never really thought about it to be honest . . .'

'Well, I do . . . I'm an Aries, and when you look at the formation of the planets and realise that we are such a small speck, it's very meaningful. When I go back to work with all those wax figures of famous and historical people, I sometimes feel as if I am the keeper of their souls.'

'Really?' asked Jane, trying to keep up as Pearl skipped from one subject to another. But Pearl seemed to have run out of steam.

'Do you mind if I have a bath?'

'No, go ahead . . . I'm going to have an early night.'

Pearl picked up her bag, and went into her bedroom. Jane waited for the door to bang shut, but this time Pearl closed it quietly. Jane washed her coffee cup and cleaned the kitchen before turning off the lights and going into her bedroom. She heard the bathwater running and as she got into bed she could hear Pearl singing, not too loudly but with a sweet voice. Jane recognised the song as 'The

Age of Aquarius' from the musical *Hair*. She closed her eyes. Pearl was such a different creature to her she found it hard to relax with her, unlike Natalie, who she felt was already a friend. Pearl thought of heartless murderers like Dr Crippen as entertainment for visitors to Madame Tussauds, whereas Jane knew that real killers left behind horror and heartbreak.

CHAPTER THIRTEEN

On Monday morning at the explosives lab Jane was told to finish bagging and tagging the victims' clothes and then get to work on the items of personal property that had been recovered, checking them against victims' statements. There was a large table covered with items of jewellery, wallets and purses, dropped by victims or torn from their clothing by the explosion. She didn't find it as traumatic as the first time she handled the bloodstained clothing. She realised she was becoming desensitised to the situation, thanks, perhaps, to Dexter's advice to put the worst of it out of her thoughts.

As Jane sat taking her break in the canteen she was hoping to see Dexter, but he didn't come in. Just as she was finishing her lunch, however, Crowley approached her table.

'We've had some worrying news about Mrs Millbank. She was taken down for more surgery this morning. I want you to go over there and see how she's doing.'

'Is it her leg?'

'Yes, there's been a complication. It's gangrene, so she'll need more taken off, which, given her age, could be touch and go.'

Jane felt awful and agreed to go straight to the hospital.

'Keep me updated . . . Bring her some grapes . . . you know, look out for her.'

'Yes, sir.'

Before going in to see Daphne, Jane waited to have a word with Michael, the charge nurse. He looked tired as he approached, but then broke into a wide smile when he caught sight of Jane. His mood became sombre again when she asked for an update on Daphne's condition.

'Well, she's out of surgery. Her antibiotics have been increased, and so far, she has come through. It was another major operation to remove the infected tissue and thigh bone. All we can do now is hope for the best.'

'Can I see her?'

'Of course, but she won't be very responsive. She's heavily sedated and on a morphine drip.'

Jane headed towards the private section. She showed her ID and filled in her name, rank and time of visit on the visitors' sheet before going in to see Daphne.

The blinds were still pulled down and the room felt cold and clinical. Daphne's fragile figure was still surrounded by drips and medication. A sheeted cage had been erected over her from the waist down, and Daphne's upper body was covered by a thick, white blanket drawn up to her chin. What little Jane could see of Daphne's arms were covered by tubes and drips, and her tiny bird-like hands were horribly marked by dark black bruises from endless injections. As Daphne had said to Jane, 'I feel like I'm a pincushion, dear . . .'

Jane pulled a hard-back chair closer to the bed and sat down, hoping that Daphne would wake up so that she could hear her lovely, gutsy voice. But there was just the shallow sound of her breathing and the hiss of the ventilator. Jane sat with her for an hour, watching the nurses come in and out to check her blood pressure. Daphne's eyes didn't open.

Jane met Michael on her way out of the ward, and as he was on a break they went to the canteen for a coffee and a pastry. Michael told her that they were short-staffed, still catching up with work after the explosion; they had taken in a lot of seriously injured patients the week before. Jane tried to lighten his mood by asking if he liked spaghetti bolognese.

'Only, I wanted to ask if you'd like to have dinner at my place this week,' she explained. 'And it's the only thing I can cook.'

He gave her a winning smile. 'I love it! I'm free on Wednesday night . . . actually, I'm pretty free for the rest of the week if dinner is on the cards!'

Jane smiled. 'Why not Wednesday . . . say about seven thirty? Let me give you my address.'

Jane was about to leave the hospital when Michael's name was called out on the Tannoy system, asking him to return to the ward immediately. He went to the nearest internal phone and spoke to someone briefly before he gestured to Jane.

'Daphne's awake and demanding potted shrimps.'

'So it's OK to see her?'

'Sure. We can go up together.'

'Oh . . . I'm going to get her some grapes from the hospital shop.'

'Fine. I'll see you up there.'

The shop on the ground floor didn't have any grapes, just a few rather bedraggled-looking bunches of flowers and endless rows of chocolates, biscuits and magazines. Jane bought a copy of *The Times* and a packet of peppermint creams.

As Jane went through the security process again, Michael was called to tend to another patient. He left Daphne's room and gave Jane the thumbs up.

'Daphne is a remarkable woman, but she's annoyed I didn't bring her those potted shrimps!'

'It's a bit late in the day for anything fresh from the fishmongers,' Jane said, smiling.

'I'll ask the kitchens to make her a light meal, although I doubt she really wants to eat anything right now. The good news is that she's breathing on her own.'

Jane waited for Michael to walk down the corridor before she eased open Daphne's door and went into the room. Daphne's lower half was still under the cage but she had been given another pillow to raise her head. She was still attached to various drips and tubes, but she looked wide awake.

'Hello, Daphne, it's Jane Tennison.'

'Hello, dear . . . What a to-do. They've had me in surgery again. It's down to bloody incompetent doctors if you ask me . . . they should have done a better job the first time around. Now I'm full of morphine, which makes me dippy in the head.'

Jane sat down beside her. 'You don't sound dippy to me, Daphne . . . You are an amazing woman, you know?'

'I'd really like to have a radio to listen to, instead of having to hear those thumping footsteps up and down the corridor. And I've asked that nice male nurse to bring me a drop of gin . . . I told him that if he couldn't get me potted shrimps then he can bloody well get me a gin and tonic!'

'I'll bring you a pot of shrimps tomorrow, Daphne, I promise. And if I can, I'll sneak you in a little hip flask of gin.'

'That's awfully nice of you, dear . . . Are you a nurse here?'

'No, Daphne . . . I'm Jane Tennison, remember? I'm a detective.'

'I was a Wren, you know. The uniform suited me but I hated wearing the hat. I need to see Heather as well . . . I love her so much, and she must be getting anxious.'

'Is she a friend?'

'Who?'

'Heather?'

'No, silly, she's my Scottie. I walk her every day, and I think I'd better get up now . . .'

Daphne started pulling at her drips and pushing the cage away from her bed. Jane hurried out to the corridor and yelled for a nurse, as a loud crash came from the room. Two nurses hurried in and eventually managed to get Daphne settled, but she was shouting and had become abusive. One of the nurses told Jane to leave the room and as she went outside Michael was running down the corridor towards her.

'She tried to get up . . . she was becoming hysterical and talking about a Scottie dog. I don't think she has one though?'

'That'll be the morphine talking. I'll call you later and give you an update, all right?'

'Thank you.' Jane waited for a while outside Daphne's room before she left the hospital. Daphne's behaviour had disturbed her. Considering her frail condition, the strength and determination she had shown in trying to get out of bed was astonishing.

Jane went back to the Woolwich lab and reported what had happened. It was not until she had returned home in the evening that she received a call from Michael with an update. Although Daphne had quietened down after being sedated and was still breathing on her own, she was in a poorly but stable condition. Michael said he was looking forward to dinner on Wednesday, but explained that he couldn't talk any longer as he was still doing his rounds.

Pearl was cooking something that made the flat smell like a soup kitchen. She was wearing an old terry towelling robe and had applied a cucumber face pack, making her look like an alien. Jane retreated into her bedroom and was sitting on her bed when Pearl knocked on her door.

'Sorry, I forgot to mention it . . . when I got in that woman Natalie rang again. She's at home and asked if you could give her a ring . . . something about a frock.'

'Thank you. Have you finished in the kitchen?'

'Yes, all clear. Do help yourself to some soup . . . it's lentil, potato and chickpea.'

'Thank you, but I ate in the canteen at work. Oh, there's something else . . . I'm having a friend over for supper on Wednesday at seven thirty, so I'd appreciate it if you could give me some space in the kitchen.'

'Fine by me, I'll be very unobtrusive. I might see if I can go out to the cinema with Eric.'

Jane waited until she heard Pearl's bedroom door shut before she went out into the hall to ring Natalie.

'Hi there, it's Jane. You rang earlier?'

'Yes, I did. It's about the hire place for your big do. The woman who runs it is quite protective of her clients as she buys from all the debs, so you'd have to go to her home in Chelsea. I think it would be a good idea if we meet up for a coffee beforehand, so I can introduce you to her. It's always good to have someone else's opinion when you're choosing the dress that'll make you the belle of the ball!'

'Oh, that's kind of you, but I'm working over at Woolwich this week.'

'She doesn't keep to shop hours, so why don't we meet up after work and I can organise for her to meet you in the evening . . . say, Wednesday?'

'I can't on Wednesday. I have a dinner date.'

'Oh, I say! Which one of the suitors is that with?'

Jane laughed. 'It's the charge nurse . . . and guess what I'm cooking? Bolognese.'

Natalie laughed. 'What about tomorrow night?'

'Yes, why not. Where shall we meet?'

'There's a coffee bar on the corner of Sloane Square, by the Royal Court Theatre. I can be there whenever it suits you . . . at the bank we get off quite early.'

'How about six thirty?'

'Terrific, see you then. I look forward to it.'

Jane smiled as she replaced the handset, and took her notebook into the kitchen. She pulled out a stool and sat down at the counter, making a list of ingredients she would need to buy for Wednesday. Although Pearl had left the counters wiped down, the top of the cooker was dirty and needed cleaning, and the pedal bin was full of wrappers and mounds of potato peelings. There was a large pan on the stove containing thick, congealed soup. Pearl had made enough to last her for days.

Jane emptied the bin, irritated that Pearl hadn't done so. She had to take the rubbish bag all the way down the stairs to the front door. By the time she had deposited it into a bin allocated for all the flats she was even angrier, and went back upstairs to have it out with her.

Jane knocked on Pearl's bedroom door and waited. When there was no reply she opened the door and looked in. The room was very untidy and there seemed to be even more piles of books than she remembered.

'Pearl? *Pearl*?'

'I'm in the bathroom, taking off my face mask,' Pearl shouted.

Jane stood outside the closed bathroom door. 'Pearl, when you fill the pedal bin in the kitchen could you empty it and take it down to the bins outside? I've just done it, but in future could you try to keep it clean as otherwise it starts to smell awful.'

'OK, I didn't know where the rubbish went . . . sorry.' The bathroom door swung open and Pearl stood in the doorway holding the kettle.

'Do you need to use the bathroom? Only I'm giving myself a steam-cleansing treatment . . . the face mask draws all the dirt out of the pores.'

'No, you carry on.'

'I can get bad acne you see, so I have to really take care of my skin. I pour very hot water onto the flannel, then cover my face.'

'Well, I'm sure you know what you're doing . . .'

'You should try it . . . removes blackheads better than anything.'

Jane gave Pearl a condescending smile as she walked back to her own room and closed the door. *Too much information* . . . she thought, hoping Pearl's facecloth was not left hung over the basin next to hers.

The following morning, as Jane was getting dressed for work, DCI Church rang.

'Just checking in to see how things are going at Woolwich.'

'It's quite a schlepp there and back, but it's OK. I had a fascinating day last week watching Dexter disarm a bomb.'

'What, a real one?'

'No, just a fake one, but when I saw the dummy being blown up I thought it was him.'

'One of these days that risk-taker *is* going to blow himself up. Use your time there to your best advantage – it's good experience . . . Then we'll have you back on the Dip Squad. In the meantime, we're just allocating names to the tables for the Good Friday event. You are coming, aren't you?'

'Yes.'

'Good, and will you want a ticket for anyone else?'

Jane could tell from Church's tone he was being inquisitive. She thought about Dexter, then Michael.

'No, just one ticket.'

'Right, well in that case you can come as my guest.'

'Thank you, but I insist on paying for my own ticket.'

'Fair enough. For obvious reasons we'll be getting taxis there and back, but I'll need to get there earlier as I'm doing the seating plan.'

'Where exactly is it?'

'St Ermin's Hotel in Caxton Street, just opposite Scotland Yard. The invitation is for 7 p.m. prompt, so I'll arrange for you to be picked up by Stanley and Blondie from home.'

'I can easily get a taxi straight there.'

'Up to you. It's black-tie, by the way.'

Jane laughed softly. 'Yes, I know . . . you've told me. And long frocks . . . in fact, I'm sorting mine out this evening after work.'

'Maybe we could have a catch-up drink on Wednesday evening?'

'Actually, I'm having dinner with someone on Wednesday . . . in fact, I'm cooking.'

'It's not Dexter, is it?'

'No, sir . . . it's the charge nurse from the hospital.'

'Oh, right. I read the report saying that the old lady's had a bit of a setback.'

'Her name's Daphne . . . Daphne Millbank . . . I think it's more than a setback, but I'll know more when I've talked to Michael.'

'Michael?'

'He's the charge nurse.'

'Ah, right, I see. Just keep in mind that we do need you to be wary at all times. And make sure we know where you are and who you're with.'

'Yes, sir. I'll make out a report for the office diary so it can be updated every day.'

'Good girl . . . well, that's it for now.'

'Can I ask, sir, would it be possible for me to take a day's leave today? I've got housework to catch up on and shopping. And I'd like to look at some evening dresses for the do on Good Friday.'

'A woman's work is never done, eh? I can't see it being a problem. Take it as a yes. I'll inform Crowley and the lab you won't be in today.'

Jane replaced the receiver with a soft smile. She found his concern for her very endearing, and noticed how quick he was to ask if it was Dexter who was her dinner guest. She felt excited about meeting up with Natalie to choose her dress and was looking forward to the Good Friday event.

DCI Church perched on the edge of Stanley's desk, swinging one leg.

'You know, I don't think Tennison has really taken on board this situation regarding the Covent Garden suspect. If Daphne Millbank dies, which she was bloody close to the other night, it will leave the bomb squad completely reliant on Jane. As it is, we've all been seconded to Crowley's lot to help find the ASU and Tennison is the only other witness to have actually seen the bomber.'

'Yeah, but just his profile, unlike our Daphne, who's had the balls to say she'd come to an identification parade and is certain she would be able to pick out the scumbag.'

'But right now we don't bloody well have anyone ... The four suspects from the Balcombe Street siege are waiting to go on trial and are refusing to give up anyone who could be connected.'

'Is Dexter knocking her off?'

'What?'

'I heard you mention his name on the phone to her just now.'

'I dunno. Crowley did ask him to keep an eye on her.'

'Well, it's all gone very quiet.'

Church nodded. He and Stanley both knew that in reality it was too quiet. It was then that Church noticed the memo left on his desk. He drew the single piece of typed paper towards him.

'What's this?'

'Tennison reckons she saw the Hernandez girl getting out of a Jag with none other than Uncle Andres. They were headed into the Playboy Club.'

'Are you serious?'

'Yeah. She got the reg plate. It's a top-end car service. They supply chauffeurs, drivers, you name it.'

'Did you pass this on to the Vice Squad?'

'Yes, of course I did. That's why I didn't bother you with it.'

Church snapped. 'I'm not *bothered*, Stanley, but I should've been informed. How is this Andres still out on the streets?'

'All I've been told, Guv, is that he is a problem. He is a very wealthy guy. He lawyered up the girl and her brother, and the other scrote, as well as himself. And there's some connection to a diplomat. That's all I know.'

Jane spent the day resting and watching TV after she had tidied her flat and washed her dirty clothes. She felt relaxed and refreshed when she went to the coffee bar to meet Natalie. She had only been sitting in the coffee bar for a few moments when Natalie arrived and waved across the room to her.

'Hi there! Have you been waiting long?'

'No, I've only just got here. I haven't even ordered yet.'

Natalie drew out a chair opposite Jane as a waitress came to their table.

'I'll just have a cappuccino, please. What about you, Jane?'

'Same for me ... and a toasted ham and cheese sandwich, please.' Jane smiled as the waitress walked away. 'I haven't eaten since lunch. I just need to double-check that I haven't forgotten any ingredients for the dinner tomorrow.' Opening her handbag, she took out her list of groceries for the dinner with Michael. 'When I get home I'll make the sauce, and I'll cook the spaghetti fresh tomorrow.'

Natalie lit one of her Kool cigarettes, pulling the ashtray closer to her side of the table. 'Just remember to add some wine to the sauce before you heat it up ... It always tastes much better when it's had time to marinade overnight.'

Their order was brought to the table. Natalie shared Jane's toasted sandwich with her, then checked her watch and said that they should get going as she had made an appointment for seven thirty.

Jane insisted on paying, then they left the café and made the short walk to a grand four-storey house in Sloane Avenue.

'So, when is the event? You might need to have some alterations made,' Natalie said, as they climbed up the stone steps to ring the doorbell.

'It's on Good Friday, at St Ermin's Hotel.'

'Ooh, impressive!' The intercom phone buzzed and Natalie spoke into it. 'It's Natalie Wilde and Jane Tennison.'

The front door opened with a loud click sound and an aristocratic voice instructed them to go straight downstairs.

'It's in the basement flat, but there's nothing dark and dingy around here,' explained Natalie. 'This is a very exclusive area . . . the flats above are huge.'

They entered a thickly carpeted main hallway, where an ornate, gilt-framed mirror hung above a three-legged mahogany table. Circulars and unopened mail were neatly laid out in piles for the various flats in the building. They walked past the wide, red-carpeted staircase and the elegant front door of the ground-floor flat, passing through the open door to the basement flat. At the bottom of a narrow staircase they found an elegant white-haired woman waiting for them. She was wearing a flamboyant kaftan, with a chunky amber necklace and matching earrings. She was well made-up, with deep red lipstick.

'Long time no see, Natalie. Do come in. I'm Isabelle Hunt.' She held out a manicured hand to Jane, which was adorned with a lot of diamond and gold rings.

'Jane Tennison.'

'Lovely to meet you. Do please come on through. As you can see, I have quite a selection . . . I'd say you are probably a size ten to twelve so you'll find quite a lot that will fit you. I've just got a very special velvet and satin Valentino in . . . but I'll let you have a good sort through everything to see what you like.'

Mrs Hunt went to the end of the corridor where there was a door covered with framed photographs of her younger self, wearing elegant gowns. There were also numerous photographs of other women, with 'Thank you' scrawled across them from, Jane supposed, her clients. They were mostly wearing beautiful ballgowns, but a few were in wedding dresses.

She opened the door and gestured for them both to walk through ahead of her. The velvet curtains were drawn but she flicked a light switch on. The vast room was lit with high-powered bulbs from tasteful wall sconces, and from the centre of the ceiling hung a large crystal chandelier. There were five racks of dresses running the entire length of the room. Some were not covered by plastic sheets but hung on covered hangers and attached to them were cards with the sizes, and prices for hire or purchase.

'Is it a special occasion? I like to make sure that my clients don't over- or underdress, if you know what I mean.'

'It's a black-tie dinner dance,' Jane said, looking along one of the racks.

'Well, I always think if you're sitting down you shouldn't have anything that shows too much cleavage, or has a tight bodice. I would select something like an empire-line gown . . . always suitable for dining. If you're hiring we have rules about food stains. You'd be surprised how many dresses are returned with wine spilt down them, or with hems that have been trailing in mud. We add the cost of dry cleaning to the price, as all the gowns are professionally cleaned by an excellent valet service. The sizes are clearly shown at the end of each rail, and get bigger towards the end. I have a selection of designer labels on rail four – Valentino, Ossie Clarke, YSL, Mary Quant, Balmain, Chanel, and so on. The cheaper range is from some of the major department stores, but asually none of them have ever been worn more than once before. The debutante season brings in a lot of younger styles, and obviously all the hunt balls. I even have clients coming over from Ireland . . . but I don't advertise, it's all word of mouth.'

Jane nodded and smiled. She took a quick glance at some of the prices and knew they were way out of her budget. It shocked her to see that most of them were between £150 and £200 and one even had a price tag of £250, but it was a very beautiful sequinned satin gown with a long train.

'There's a changing room with full-length mirrors. Now, shoes . . . I do have a selection but they're mostly either dyed to match a gown, or I have them for when you try something on so that you can see what it's like with high heels.' Mrs Hunt moved back towards the door. 'I'll leave you both to it . . . just call me when you're ready.'

As Mrs Hunt closed the door, Jane let out a sigh. 'My God, Natalie! They're all far too expensive, even just to hire out!'

'Don't worry, we've not got to the end rail yet.'

They began sorting through various styles. Natalie kept on selecting dresses and taking them off the rail, whilst Jane constantly checked the price tag to make sure it wasn't too much. They had eventually pulled out seven possible dresses and Jane took them all into the curtained dressing area to start trying them on.

Jane stripped down to her bra and knickers, then found a pair of high-heeled silver strap shoes to start trying on one gown after another. She quickly discarded the dresses she didn't like, until she tried on a pale blue chiffon with a fitted bodice and wide layered skirt. She drew the dressing-room curtain aside and stepped out.

Natalie screwed up her face.

'Oh, no . . . I think it's a bit old-fashioned, Jane . . . and it's loose over your waist and too high over your boobs! I've got some other dresses I've picked out that I think are gorgeous.'

After almost an hour of trying dresses on, Jane still hadn't found one that she liked, or that Natalie approved of, and she was beginning to feel tired.

'Oh, Jane, look at this one . . . it's just gorgeous! It's Chanel . . . look at the beautiful bodice, and the tiny buttons and bootlace straps. It's your size, and the skirt has wonderful frilled layers of lace and silk.'

'How much is it?'

'One hundred and fifty . . . It's worth it. You'll look stunning . . . please try it on. And if you do your hair up in a chignon . . .'

Jane sighed and went back into the dressing-room area, taking off a Mary Quant dress that was far too tight across her chest. She stepped into the Chanel gown and drew it up, putting her arms through the tiny satin straps. She needed Natalie to do the buttons up at the back of the bodice and by the time they had all been fastened she still hadn't had a look at herself in the mirror. In truth, she felt unsure about wearing black.

'Oh my God – it's perfect!' Natalie exclaimed, clapping her hands and hovering behind Jane as she stood in front of the full-length mirror. 'Maybe you need a push-up bra . . . but honestly, it fits like a dream and shows off your lovely shoulders.'

Jane chewed her lips, turning backwards and forwards in front of the mirror. It was a perfect fit and the tight velvet bodice showed off her breasts and small waist. The layered frilly skirt was just the right length and moved beautifully as she swayed and turned. She thought she could wear a small pearl necklace, which she knew her mother treasured.

'All right . . . I think this is the one. I'll need Pearl to help me into it with all the buttons.'

It was a further three quarters of an hour before the dress was finally wrapped carefully in tissue paper and packed into a large box. Mrs Hunt had given her a receipt for the dress to be hired out for two weeks, and suggested that she bought a small wrap or bolero jacket to go over it. She made it clear that the dress had to be returned on the date on the receipt, but she always liked her customers to have the dress for a while before the occasion so that they had time to accessorise.

'It's not until Good Friday,' Jane said, hesitant about the cost of hiring it for two weeks.

'So, you can spend time deciding, and can get used to wearing it. I have to say, you looked quite stunning.'

Mrs Hunt didn't mention that the Chanel dress Jane had chosen was such a low price because the fragile frilly hem had been repaired a few times and the bodice had been stained under the armpits.

Jane and Natalie walked into Sloane Square together, and Natalie suggested that they could go and have dinner somewhere. Jane declined saying that she felt tired and needed to go to the late-night grocery shop to get all the ingredients for the dinner with Michael.

'Why don't you come over at the weekend and I can give you another cookery lesson?' Natalie asked. 'I enjoy cooking, but never really bother when it's just for me.'

'I'd love to, but let me get back to you . . . I need to check the duty rota, and I also want to go and see my parents.'

'OK, just call me when you know. Listen, you made the right decision with the dress . . . you're going to knock them sideways.'

By the time Jane had bought all the groceries she needed, and had carried those and the large cardboard box containing the dress up the stairs to her flat, she felt exhausted. She left the box on her bedroom floor, not even unpacking the dress before she went into the kitchen.

Pearl was sitting on one of the stools, eating pasta and reading a thick paperback volume of *War and Peace*.

'Hi, there. What was in that big box?'

'My dress for the Good Friday dinner.'

'Would you like a bowl of my pesto, onion and pasta mix? There's plenty left.'

'I'm going to make the bolognese sauce for my dinner tomorrow, then have a long bath. But thanks anyway.'

'I'll leave you to it then, and finish this in my room . . . Not the book, my pasta!' She laughed as she carried the bowl out to her bedroom.

Jane made the sauce and ate a spoonful just as a taster. It was delicious. She cleared up the kitchen and made a mental note to buy the wine when she came home from work the next day. It was nearly eight and she decided to have a bath before trying some of Pearl's pasta mix as she was still hungry.

While the bath was filling, she took out the dress and hung it in her wardrobe. She would need to get a strapless bra, a pair of shoes, and some sort of wrap. She was just turning off the taps when the phone rang. It was DCI Crowley.

'We've had information from the Intelligence Services in Northern Ireland that the ASU is possibly holed up at an address in Kentish Town. I'm putting a raid team together and I want you to be there to see if you recognise the man you saw at Covent Garden.'

'Tonight? Right now?'

'Yes, right now, Tennison. Get yourself to the CID office at Kentish Town nick ASAP for a briefing.'

Jane replaced the receiver. 'I don't believe it.'

She turned and saw Pearl standing in the hallway.

'Is it all right if I have a bath?' Pearl asked quickly. 'Only I've been waiting because I thought you were having one.'

'I've just run one, but now I've got to go to Kentish Town on a search.'

'Ooh, anything interesting?'

'I hope so, I really hope so.'

Jane was no sooner out of her flat door when Pearl came out of the bathroom naked. She was just about to pick up the phone and make a call when it rang. She jumped, hesitating before she answered.

'Hi – it's Natalie. Is Jane there?'

'No, she just got called out to Kentish Town. Do you want to leave a message?'

'It was just about her outfit for the dinner dance. I'll call again tomorrow.'

Pearl replaced the receiver. A couple of seconds later she picked it up again and dialled a number.

CHAPTER FOURTEEN

As Jane entered the CID office, she saw DCI Church with about twelve plain-clothes officers, who were all male. Through a window she spotted Crowley in a separate office, having a conversation with Dexter and DS Lawrence.

Church was standing beside a table with guns, bullets and shoulder holsters laid out on it, some of which he was handing to the detectives from the Dip and Bomb Squads. There was a tense atmosphere and everyone had a solemn look on their face as they signed for their .38 revolvers and loaded them.

'You an authorised shot, Tennison?' Church asked, his eyes scrunched tight as if anticipating danger ahead.

'No, sir,' she replied, beginning to feel nervous about the whole situation, but not wanting to show it.

'Stanley's got some pickaxe handles in his car if you want one,' a detective said in earnest.

Jane felt a tap on her shoulder, and turned to see Stanley.

'A lump of wood will be about as much use as a glass hammer if the raid turns into *Gunfight at the OK Corral.*'

Jane shook her head and frowned. 'I could have guessed you'd be the one to make light of a serious situation, Stanley.'

'Only trying to make you relax, luv. Besides, anyone who's not carrying a shooter won't be called into the premises until it's secure. You'll be well away from the action.'

Stanley's comment didn't bother Jane. The truth was that she'd happily stay at a safe distance when the raid was carried out.

Crowley and Lawrence walked into the CID office followed by Dexter, who was carrying an A1 Plain Paper Flipchart, which he placed on an easel. Crowley clapped his hands to get everyone's attention.

'Right, you lot,' Crowley said. 'Listen up, and listen well. As you are all aware, it was not that long ago that a police officer was shot and killed in London during a stop-and-search incident with a man who turned out to be a member of the IRA. I cannot emphasise enough how dangerous this operation is. The ASU that we are about to take out will undoubtedly be armed with handguns and explosives so the last thing I want are any fuck-ups by us.'

Crowley nodded at Dexter, who turned over the blank cover of the flipchart to reveal a detailed street map of the address that was about to be raided: 61 Caversham Road, NW5. Crowley pointed to the map.

'The Intelligence Services informant has proved to be a reliable source in the past. Our targets are holed up in a two-bedroom ground-floor flat in a row of three-storey terraced Victorian buildings. Unfortunately, the information only came in earlier this evening so we haven't been able to do a full daytime recce to evaluate the surrounding area, or any comings and goings from the target address.'

One of the officers raised his hand and Crowley nodded for him to speak.

'Do we know anything about the occupants of the other two flats in the building?'

'Luckily, we do. One of my squad located the landlord and is bringing him over as we speak, with a set of keys for the whole premises. The top-floor flat is currently unoccupied, and a young Jamaican couple with a baby have recently moved into the middle flat. The landlord says that an Irishman, who said he was a delivery van driver, started renting the ground-floor flat about a month ago. When the landlord visited a couple of weeks ago there were two other men in the ground-floor flat, but they didn't speak to him. On a positive note, the description of one of them fits the artist's impression we released to the press.'

Dexter interjected, 'Generally, we've found that IRA bomb makers live alone, but as it's a two-bedroom flat, I wouldn't be surprised if more than one ASU operative is staying there. Maybe if they're there together to plan a big explosion we'll strike lucky and get all of the bastards.'

Crowley turned over to the next sheet on the flipchart, which showed more detail of the surrounding area. Number 61 was next to a builders' yard, which in turn led directly onto the overground railway line running through the nearby Kentish Town station.

'As you can see, they have a good escape line via the yard and onto the train tracks. The last thing I want is to be chasing armed suspects on live rails, or facing a moving train head-on . . .' He flipped over to another page showing the details of each team.

'Stanley, you and a team of three others will go to 107 Gainsford Street, behind the target address. Via those premises you can gain entry to the garden of 61 Caversham to cut off their escape route. If they do come out through the back, then let us know over the radio right away as we don't want to get caught in any crossfire. Understood?'

Stanley nodded and grinned, as if almost relishing the thought of a shootout. Crowley then explained that his team would be 'Gold', Stanley's would be 'Silver' and the third team would be 'Bronze'. Only two people in each team would have a radio, to avoid too much airwave chatter. Crowley said that DCI Church and three other members of the Bomb Squad would be in his lead team and the rest would continue to cover the outside as backup, if needed.

'Isn't DS Dexter in the main team?' one of the Dip Squad officers asked.

'As much as Dexter likes to be in the thick of it he won't be much use to us if he gets shot at the outset . . . unless anyone else here feels they're capable of disarming a bloody bomb!'

Everyone could see Crowley was on edge and not in the mood for what he perceived to be silly questions. Stanley raised his hand, causing everyone to glare at him in expectation of an inane remark or question that would further annoy Crowley.

'What about getting the young couple out?' Stanley asked.

'Good point, Stanley. Once we go through the main door and are in position to force entry to the target flat, one of my team, accompanied by WDC Tennison, will go up to their flat and remain with them until the premises are secure and they can be safely evacuated . . . You OK with that, Tennison?'

'Yes, sir,' Jane replied, wondering apprehensively how much damage might be caused to the flat above if a bomb went off. She thought of her mother and the state she'd be in if she was listening in on the briefing. The thought made her smile and she knew that her nervousness was caused by adrenaline.

Crowley explained that once the suspects were arrested and the premises secure no one was to touch anything in the flat. Dexter would then search for any explosive devices, or bomb making parts, and Lawrence would deal with the forensic aspects of the search.

The duty sergeant entered the room with a box full of radios for everyone. He spoke with DCI Crowley, who didn't look pleased as he picked up a radio and talked into it.

'Oscar Papa One from Gold, receiving, over.' The radio hissed and there was no reply. Impatiently, Crowley repeated his call to the officers watching the suspect's address.

'Oscar Papa One, receiving . . . go ahead . . . over,' came the reply.

'I've just spoken to the duty sergeant . . . is the situation still the same? Gold over . . .' Crowley asked.

'Yes . . . nothing further to report . . . over . . .'

'Keep me updated.'

Crowley banged the radio down on the table.

'This could be a long night, gents . . . I had two of my officers enter the second-floor flat at 59 Caversham with listening devices while we were grouping up here. At present the lights are on at 61 but they can't detect any movement. It looks like we sit and wait in obo vans and unmarked cars for now, in the surrounding streets.'

There was an air of despondency in the room.

'It'll be just our luck if the ASU's out planting a bomb,' one of the Bomb Squad officers said.

'It's a possibility,' agreed Crowley. 'We'll know soon enough if they have, it'll be all over the radios.'

'How long do you intend to wait, Guv?' Dexter asked, knowing that Crowley was in an awkward position. If a bomb did go off the ASU might not return to the premises, and might get out of town.

Crowley was silent, apparently thinking about his next move. Instead of replying, he walked over to Jane. 'Tennison,' he said. 'A word with you in private.'

Church followed them out into the adjoining office.

Crowley looked at him. 'I want a private conversation with Tennison.'

Church shook his head. 'Not when she's one of my officers. Her safety is my responsibility . . . if you want her to stay, I stay as well.'

Crowley didn't have much option other than to agree.

'I was thinking that Tennison could go up to the first-floor flat alone and speak with the Jamaican couple . . . find out what they know about the recent movements at the suspect's flat. She's young, like them, and doesn't stick out as old bill like the rest of us. Anyone watching would think she was just a friend, visiting.'

Church looked apprehensive. 'And what if it all goes pear-shaped? You seem to forget that when she saw the suspect at Covent Garden, he also saw her. You've had a surveillance team protecting her and now, just to satisfy your own ambition, you're willing to risk her life? No. It's not on. We sit and wait, or go straight in. Those are the only viable options, and you know it.'

'This is not about me, Church, it's about arresting a bunch of murderers. The people in the flat above may be able to tell us more.'

Jane was fed up with the two of them bickering. 'I'll do it. I've got a scarf in my bag and a different coat from the one I wore at Covent Garden. I can tie up my hair, and take off my make-up so I look older . . . and keep my head down.'

Church was adamant that it was too risky but Jane stood her ground.

Crowley said he would have her fitted up with a covert radio and asked if she knew how to work one.

'Yes, sir, I do.'

'Right, let's get this show on the road . . .' Crowley said, rubbing his hands together.

Within half an hour everyone was in position on the nearby streets. Stanley's Silver team had gained entry to the builders' yard from the rear of the opposite premises and were hidden, ready to go when the order was given. Jane had done everything she could to make herself unrecognisable and Dexter, ever the charmer, said she still looked attractive even without make-up. She tested the covert radio before getting out of the obo van and walking slowly down Caversham Street towards the block of flats. The light rain had given a yellow sheen to the pavement. She was wearing her sensible Cuban-heeled shoes and found her own footsteps sounded loud to her.

Crowley gave her the landlord's keys so she could just let herself in through the front door and go straight up to the first-floor flat.

Jane felt nervous, particularly when someone walked towards, or passed, her. She kept her head down and didn't make eye contact in case the person was the IRA bomber she had seen. Her heart was pounding as she moved up the worn narrow flagstone path and stepped up to a dirty, sodden doormat. There were two empty milk bottles on the doorstep. The front door had peeling paint with four mottled glass panes. She opened the front door, then placed the key under the mat for Crowley. As she carefully walked up the threadbare, carpeted stairs, some of them creaked. There was a yellowing plastic lampshade around a low wattage bulb hanging from what had once been an elegant ceiling rose. Outside flat 2 she got her warrant card out and knocked on the door. It was eventually opened by a young, attractive Jamaican woman in a nightdress. Jane held up her warrant card and put her finger to her mouth to indicate to the woman to be quiet. To Jane's relief she remained silent and let her in. Jane then introduced herself and the woman looked distressed, speaking in a strong West Indian accent.

'We done nuttin' wrong! We only just come here from Jamaica . . . you can check me passport and visa . . . and me husband's . . . he got a job in de baker's.'

Jane gave her a reassuring smile. 'It's OK . . . there's nothing for you to worry about. It's the downstairs flat I'm interested in, and anything you or your husband can tell me about the residents.'

'Me husband's not here at de moment. He's still out lookin' for de cat. But he should be back soon.'

Crowley sat impatiently in the obo van with Church, Dexter, Lawrence, and the rest of the Gold team.

'She's taking her bloody time. She should have radioed in by now.'

Lawrence was quick to defend Jane. 'Give her a chance. She's only been gone a few minutes. If any of us were in her shoes we wouldn't be in a rush.'

The radio hissed. Everyone sat upright waiting for Jane's update, but the call was from the officers inside the neighbouring flat.

'Oscar Papa One to Gold . . . we just heard movement in target premises . . . over.'

'You sure?' Crowley asked.

'Yes, certain . . . someone just dropped a glass and we heard it shatter.'

Crowley spoke over the radio. 'Silver team go, go, go to rear of target and notify when secure . . . we'll drive down closer then go in when you're in position.'

Dexter said he and Lawrence would wait outside on the street while they made the arrests and secured the scene. It took only seconds for Stanley's team to climb the garden fence and radio Crowley that they were in position. Crowley and his team were out of the obo van in an instant, crouching down like panthers stalking prey as they moved up the steps, guns held ready.

Crowley retrieved the key from under the mat and quietly opened the front door. He and Church took up position in the hallway either side of the ground-floor flat door. A detective with a large metal rammer stood in front of the door and Crowley raised his hand to give a countdown of three using his fingers and silently mouthing the number 'one' as he did so.

'No! Don't do it!' Jane screamed as loudly as she could from the top of the stairs. Everyone froze for a split second, apart from the officer with the rammer, who raised it backwards. Again Jane screamed as she ran down the stairs.

'STOP! It might be booby-trapped. They've left already!'

Crowley raised his palm in the nick of time to stop the officer ramming the door open. Dexter and Lawrence, who had heard Jane's screams, came running in. Jane's voice was trembling as she spoke.

'The woman upstairs said she was looking out of the window a quarter of an hour ago, and saw three men leaving the premises. She recognised the Irishman who occupied the ground-floor flat. They were carrying a suitcase, holdall and rucksacks and got into a black cab. It looks like they've moved out.'

There was a unanimous groan.

'All of you shut it! And back off. I need to check the door for a booby trap. Stand back, stand right back!' shouted Dexter. Using a crowbar he forced open the front window to access the premises and it wasn't long before he opened the front door. He was holding a scruffy-looking cat in his arms and stroking it.

'Doors not rigged to explode . . . Place is empty, apart from this little bugger, who, it would seem, is the culprit that knocked a glass off the table.'

'Oh t'ank you, sir! You find Bob Marley!' the Jamaican woman said, as she walked down the stairs. 'He must ha got in d'ere when de men leave.'

Dexter handed her the cat. 'He very nearly used up one of his nine lives, luv.'

Crowley looked furious, but the absurdity of the moment was not lost on the others, who started to laugh. Dexter congratulated Jane on her quick action and said that if the door had been rigged she would have saved a lot of lives.

Crowley wasn't impressed. 'The Commander is going to be livid, and I'm the one who's got to tell him the suspects moved out before we even got here. He said he wanted to know the result right away so I'm going back to the Yard to call him.'

Crowley told everyone to stand down over the radio and asked Dexter to check the rest of the premises with Lawrence for explosives before they carried out a full search.

'Could I assist with the search of the flat, sir?' Jane asked.

'No, I don't want too many people in there, just the two experts.'

'I could take a statement from the Jamaican couple . . .'

Crowley was on edge. 'Their statement is far too important for someone with your lack of experience to take. Just go home, Tennison!'

As Crowley stomped off, Lawrence saw Jane's crestfallen face. 'Listen, you can help me with the exhibits. Is that all right with you, Dexter?'

'Fine by me so long as Crowley doesn't find out.'

Jane gave a small smile of thanks to Lawrence as he radioed in to Kentish Town and asked them to call the Control room at Scotland Yard to make a request for at least four night-duty SOCOs to attend the scene and carry out a fingerprint search.

The flat had a small living room, kitchen and two small bedrooms. In one of the bedrooms the bed had been placed upright against the wall to make room for a large work table, on which there were a number of small pieces of cut wire and globules of burnt solder wire. All the cupboards and drawers were empty and it was clear to Lawrence that the suspects had used cleaning cloths to remove fingerprint traces. Lawrence took out his camera and started photographing the bedroom and the work table.

'They may not have been as smart as they think about cleaning up their fingerprints . . . any idea why?' he asked Jane, testing her crime scene abilities.

She paused. 'If they've taken the time to remove them, it could mean they have a criminal record and could be identified by fingerprints.'

'Yes, but there's something else. Sometimes we miss what we can't see.'

Lawrence pointed to the table.

'That table must have been carried in here as it wouldn't fit if the bed was in its normal place . . . so . . .' He paused and Jane twigged where he was going.

'You lift a table with your hands on the underside and leave fingerprints that you can't see.'

'Exactly . . . and likewise with the bed and chair. You heard of a mechanical fit?'

Jane nodded. 'Yes, on the forensic module during my CID course. The tutor tore a piece of paper into six pieces and put it back together like a jigsaw. Because each part came from the same paper each bit was a unique mechanical fit and therefore considered conclusive evidence that all the pieces were of the same origin.'

'You've got a good memory.'

'I only did the course two months ago, so it's still fresh in my mind.'

'Nevertheless, you obviously paid attention and that will stand you in good stead as a detective. See the bits of cut wire on the table? If we can trace the wire cutters that were used to a suspect's possession, then that is another possible mechanical fit.'

Jane was confused. 'How?'

Lawrence explained, 'Often wire cutters and similar implements wear over time and unique nicks or marks are created on the cutting edge. When they are used to cut wire the striation mark from the edge of the cutting implement is transferred to the wire.

'We then do test cuts with the suspect's pliers and compare the test wires against those on the table here. If there is a match with the cutting marks ... bingo! We have evidence that the same cutters were used.'

Jane watched, fascinated, as Lawrence took a small glass bowl out of his forensic kit, together with some small bottles of liquid. He placed the bowl on top of his kit bag and pulled on a pair of rubber gloves.

'I'm going to do what is called a Griess test for traces of explosives.'

Jane watched as he rubbed a piece of white filter paper on an area of the table, then placed it in the glass bowl.

'The test involves taking a sample with the filter paper then sodium hydroxide is added to the bowl followed by the Griess reagent ... if the paper turns pink within ten seconds, this indicates the presence of nitrites.'

Jane was rather lost with the terminology of the procedure but was engrossed with what Lawrence was doing. When one of the filter papers turned pink within three seconds she knew that Lawrence had got a positive result. He grinned, but appeared quite calm.

Jane, in contrast, was excited. 'Is it nitroglycerine?'

'It's only a preliminary test ... the explosives lab will carry out the more sensitive thin layer chromatography on further samples from the table top ... But for my money you can be 99 per cent sure it's nitro.'

Lawrence handed Jane some rubber gloves and small exhibits bags and asked her to help him bag and list each bit of wire. Dexter called out from the kitchen, asking Lawrence if he could have a word with him.

'You found something?' Lawrence asked, as he entered the kitchen.

'There's more wire in the bin, along with the remnants of a remote-control car and the shell of an alarm clock . . . If they had planned to move on then I'd expect a more thorough clean up.'

'I agree. The attempt at cleaning off fingerprints looks rushed . . . and I got a positive for nitro on the work table.'

Lawrence looked around the kitchen and noticed a large cooking pot on the stove with some stew in it. He picked up a soup spoon and dipped it into the pot.

Dexter looked shocked, 'You're not actually going to eat that shit, are you?'

Lawrence moved the spoon up to his mouth, making Dexter cringe, then with a cheeky grin stopped and dipped his finger in the spoonful of stew.

'It's still lukewarm. If they were planning on moving out tonight then why not eat this first?'

'The bastards must have been tipped off. They knew we were coming!' Dexter punched a kitchen cabinet with his fist.

Lawrence spoke calmly. 'Well, it can't be anyone on the raid. None of us knew where we were going until Church briefed us.'

'My bet's on a leak within the Intelligence Services. Keep this between us. I'll go back to the Yard and tell Church.'

'Rather you than me. I'll finish up here with Tennison. The SOCOs can work through the night on the fingerprinting and I'll arrange for uniform to guard the premises until everything's been examined.'

'How long will it take to get results if you find any prints?'

'A week or two.'

'What? Why so bloody long?'

'Because the suspects are probably all paddies, and if they have a criminal record their fingerprints will be held with either the RUC or Garda Síochána fingerprint bureaus. We have to search them manually here first, then send them over to Ireland and that takes time.'

'And time's something we haven't got. I can feel it my blood . . . the IRA are planning something big in London.'

Jane arrived at the lab expecting to be given some menial tasks or asked to type up reports. She perked up when Lawrence told her that she could help him with the items recovered from the flat in Kentish Town.

'They're running further tests on the samples I took from the table tops. So far it's looking pretty positive that it's nitroglycerine but the final chromatography result takes a while, and they'll need to do a second test to be sure.'

'It's all very intricate and time-consuming work,' Jane remarked.

'It has to be. We can't afford to get it wrong, especially when it comes to a trial. Defence scientists will be allowed to examine everything and check our reports. If they can find the slightest error, they will be on it like a rash. They'll allege our tests weren't carried out properly or that there was contamination to try to discredit us.'

'I was in court on a case once where that happened over the signing of a confession statement. The defence alleged that the defendant had been tricked into signing a doctored page of the notes admitting the crime.'

Lawrence looked surprised and Jane realised he thought the allegation was against her.

'It wasn't me they were accusing; it was the DI I was working with, though I did get a hard time when I gave evidence. I was accused of being part of the "fit-up".'

'So what happened?'

'The confession evidence was ruled inadmissible by the judge. Luckily there was other evidence and the jury convicted.'

'Well, take my advice, Jane: fixing or tampering with evidence or forensic results is never worth it. You could lose your job, pension, and even end up in prison. Gather the evidence and present your case with honesty and integrity, then let the jury make the final decision. Even then, you'll lose some cases, but it's all part of learning on the job. You move on to the next case.'

Jane liked working with Lawrence. When it came to honesty, he was above reproach, and as usual she was learning so much from him. Now Lawrence showed her two bits of different coloured wire under a double-microscope, which he told her was called a comparison microscope. He pointed out how the striation marks on each were identical, which meant the same cutters had been used on each wire.

Jane helped Lawrence for the rest of the day, dealing with the bits of wire and piecing wires together. Apart from the time she'd watched Dexter disarm the fake bomb, it was the best experience she'd had at the lab so far.

Jane got home just after six, having stopped off to pick up a bottle of Saint-Nicolas-de-Bourgueil red wine on her way. She quickly changed into jeans and a T-shirt, then poured a cup of the wine over her pre-prepared sauce, ready to heat it up. She filled a pan with water to boil for the pasta. As she was laying out the cutlery and plates for dinner, Pearl appeared in the doorway to say that she was going to have a drink with her friend Eric, so Jane would have the flat to herself.

By seven fifteen, Jane felt confident that everything was ready. She applied some fresh makeup, combed her hair loose, and sprayed on her favourite perfume, Diorissimo by Dior. Just as she was coming out of the bathroom the doorbell rang. Jane pressed the intercom to open the main front door, and went out onto her landing to wait for Michael. Unlike most of her other visitors, he wasn't gasping for breath and moved quickly up the stairs carrying a bottle of wine and a bunch of flowers.

'Perfect timing!' Jane said, as she ushered Michael into the flat.

'These are for you,' he said, handing her the flowers. He was wearing a tweed jacket with leather-patched elbows, over a polo-neck sweater and jeans.

'Thank you. I'm sorry, I don't have a dining table so we're eating in the kitchen. I've got a bottle open so come on through.'

Jane poured two glasses of wine and drew out the kitchen stools.

'Cheers,' Michael said, clinking his glass against hers. 'I wasn't sure what to wear, so I went for the casual look.'

Jane smiled, turning on the gas ring to heat up the sauce. 'I should have got some salad . . . but I have some garlic bread which I'll pop in the oven when everything is almost ready.'

'Smells delicious.'

'Do you cook?' Jane asked.

'Yes and no. To be honest I mostly eat in the canteen, and lately I've been on such long shifts that I'm completely exhausted by the time I get home.'

They chatted about how long she had been in the flat, as she busied herself at the cooker.

'Do you live here on your own?'

'No, I have a flatmate but she's out for the evening. It's obviously not really the sort of flat for entertaining, but it's the first place I've owned.'

Jane made Michael laugh as she recounted her parents' first visit when they were heaving for breath by the time they got to the top of the stairs, and then said they thought it was too small.

They drank more wine as the sauce began to simmer, but the water for the pasta was taking ages.

'Maybe switch the pans over to different rings . . .' Michael suggested, and got up to lift the water pan as she moved the sauce onto a lower small ring. She had turned on the oven ready to put in the garlic bread, and the heat in the kitchen was becoming uncomfortable.

'I'll open a window,' he said. He squeezed past her to lean over the sink and opened the kitchen window a fraction. 'There you go . . . that's better.'

Jane was relieved when the water finally boiled and she gently lowered in the spaghetti, waiting for it to bend and soften in the pan. Michael perched on his stool as she peered into the pan. She was unsure exactly how long it was going to take to cook, and didn't know when to put the bread in.

The front door banged open and Pearl walked in holding a carrier bag.

'Sorry, Jane, Eric's got a migraine. I won't get in anybody's way, but if I could just have a minute to peel some carrots for my tub of hummus . . .'

Jane felt like throttling Pearl, but introduced her to Michael as she hung up her coat and squeezed past Jane to get to the sink with her bag of carrots.

'I'm not cooking them . . . I just need to peel them so that I can dip them into my hummus.'

'I think the pasta is ready,' Jane said tersely.

'You know the best way to tell? Take out a piece of it and throw it up onto the ceiling. If it sticks, it's cooked!' Pearl laughed, and began scraping her carrots.

Just as Jane was about to take the pan off the stove and drain the spaghetti, the phone rang. Michael volunteered to look after the pasta while Jane went into the hall to answer the phone.

'Hello?' she said angrily.

'Jane dear, it's Edith. I've not heard a peep out of you for so long, I was worried.'

'I'm fine, thank you, Edith. In fact, I'm just about to serve dinner.'

'Well, I won't keep you. I just wanted to give you an update on my mother . . .'

Jane rolled her eyes up to the ceiling as Edith went into a lengthy description of her mother's latest escape antics. In the kitchen Jane could hear Pearl laughing and Michael joining in. She was obviously throwing spaghetti up at the ceiling.

'You see . . . perfectly cooked! Here, let me help you drain it. Pop a knob of butter in it, as it tastes much better. Why don't you stir the sauce, as it's bubbling? So, what do you do? Are you a detective like Jane?'

'No, I'm a charge nurse at St Thomas'.'

'Oh, a male nurse . . . that's a new one on me. How do you know Jane?'

'Through a patient we're looking after. Do you remember the bomb at Covent Garden?'

'Oh God, yes I do. I have to tell you that I was a bit worried when I first came here. You know Melcombe Street is very close to that awful siege in Balcombe Street? I work at Madame Tussauds, just around the corner from there. It was so dreadful because it went on for days . . . all the streets around here were cordoned off during the siege, but I never mentioned it to Jane. Have you put the garlic bread in yet? It needs to be wrapped in tin foil.'

Jane had heard enough and interrupted Edith mid-flow.

'Edith, I really have to go. I'm sorry about your mother but I have to serve dinner, as I have a guest waiting.'

'Oh, I'm sorry, dear . . . I'll call back another time.'

Just as Jane replaced the receiver the phone rang again. She was so frustrated she snatched it up. 'Hello?'

'It's Daddy, darling . . . I'm just checking in as we haven't heard from you for a while.'

'I'm sorry, Daddy, could I call you back?'

'I just wanted to see if you're coming over for Saturday lunch? As you know we'll be leaving for Harwich on Sunday for our cruise and your mother and I wanted to see you before we went.'

Jane heard Michael offering Pearl a glass of wine and quickly told her father that she would be there for lunch on Saturday, then hung up.

Pearl had a small plastic tray with a plate of peeled carrots, a pot of hummus and a glass of wine.

'I think we've sort of got it all ready for you,' she said, smiling at Michael.

'Thank you,' Jane said curtly.

'Nice to meet you, Michael. And if you ever want a free ticket for Madame Tussauds, just ask for me.'

Michael was standing by the stove with the pasta in a large bowl and a serving bowl of the sauce with a ladle.

'Just got to get the garlic bread out and we're ready to go,' he said.

'Please sit down and let me serve it. I'm sorry, that was a friend from my old station and she's very hard to get off the phone. Her mother has dementia and goes walkabout . . . Then my dad called. My parents are going away on a cruise on Sunday . . . Amazing really, as they hardly ever take holidays.'

Jane retrieved the rather charred garlic bread from the oven, then served the spaghetti and bolognese sauce in soup bowls. She took out some grated Parmesan cheese from the fridge as Michael poured himself another glass of wine and topped Jane's glass up.

'This is so good,' he said, winding the spaghetti around his fork, against a spoon.

Jane was delighted when he had a second bowlful, and afterwards she laid out a cheese platter with biscuits. Michael rinsed their dirty dishes in the sink and noticed Pearl's carrot peelings lying on a brown paper bag to one side, which he placed in the bin as well.

'You're well-trained,' Jane said, smiling. She started to make some coffee.

'Yep, there's nothing worse than having to wash up a stack of dirty dishes.'

They finished the bottle of wine with the cheese and biscuits, then both had some coffee. Irritated by the sound of Pearl's TV, Jane knocked on her door.

'Pearl, can you turn the volume down please? It's too loud.'

Michael joined her in the hall, carrying their cups of coffee. He obviously presumed there was a lounge area somewhere and Jane, feeling rather embarrassed, explained that there was no place to sit comfortably, other than her bedroom.

'You're welcome to sit there if you don't mind. I don't have a TV, as I can hear Pearl's every night!'

Jane opened her bedroom door. She had placed scatter cushions over her bedspread so that it didn't appear like an invitation to get too cosy. Michael sat down on her bed and put his coffee on her bedside table. Jane sat down beside him.

'My parents said I should have got a bigger place as there's no sitting room ... I'm beginning to think they're right, but I really need the rent from Pearl.'

'I live in a bedsit, but it's actually very spacious,' he said. 'It's in one of those huge Victorian houses that have been split into flats. I've got a small cupboard as a kitchen, and I share the bathroom with two other guys on my floor. I'm saving up to buy my own place, but for now it suits me. And, like you, I don't do much entertaining.'

'You noticed!' she said, feeling totally at ease beside him. Michael put his arm around her and drew her closer.

'So, tell me all about you ... because on our next date I'd like to take you out to dinner and a movie.'

'I'd like that. I haven't been to the cinema for ages. I'd hate to go by myself, and as I am often on night duty there's not that much opportunity. I go to my parents as much as possible at the weekend, and –'

Michael tipped her chin up and leaned close. It wasn't a lingering kiss, just a light touch of his lips against hers. Jane was about to move closer towards him when the phone rang again.

'I'm not going to answer it,' she said, enjoying the feel of being curled up next to him with his arm around her shoulders.

The phone continued ringing and Jane was about to get up when she heard Pearl come out of her room.

'I'll get it!' she called.

The next moment she knocked on Jane's door. 'It's for Michael.'

He jumped to his feet. 'I'm so sorry . . . I had to leave a number where I could be contacted if there was an emergency. We're short-staffed, and I'm on call.'

Michael went out into the hallway and spoke briefly to the caller before he returned, looking worried.

'It's the hospital. Daphne Millbank's fading fast. Her organs are shutting down.'

Pearl went into the kitchen to put her plate into the sink. She considered washing it up, but then couldn't be bothered.

In her haste to leave with Michael, Jane had left her bedroom door open. Pearl looked inside and noticed the coffee cups left on the floor. She pushed the door open wider and went into the room. She had a nose around, pretending to herself that she was looking for the hairdryer. She peered into the large box that had contained Jane's dress and neatly reclosed the lid. Then she opened some drawers and checked inside them before looking in the wardrobe. The dress was hanging in the middle with space either side of it, made by pushing the other clothes along the rail. Pearl took the dress out and admired it, reading the Chanel label before she read the tag attached to the dress. It had the price, date of hire and date of return. Pearl replaced the dress and flicked through Jane's other clothes before she closed the wardrobe door, stepping back over the coffee cups on the floor as she left the room.

Jane sat in the brightly lit reception area, impatient to know how Daphne was doing. When they arrived at St Thomas' Michael had rushed off to find the night duty doctor. The large reception area was eerily silent, with just one administrator manning the desk.

There was the continual sound of ambulances going back and forth to the A & E department, where there would be a lot more action than here in the private section.

It was just after ten when Michael walked through the double doors. He was now wearing his uniform and Jane could tell by his expression that it was bad news. He came and sat beside her and took her hand.

'She didn't make it. I'm sorry, Jane. She was such a fighter, but she started having difficulty breathing and then complications set in . . . it was hopeless.'

Jane blinked back tears and asked if she would be allowed to see Daphne. Michael hesitated, then agreed to take her up to the ward. He walked ahead of her down the private corridor where the armed guard was still standing at the door. He looked bewildered, confused about what he should do.

'Only the nurses and doctors have been allowed entry . . . no one else has been here,' he said, shuffling his feet.

Ignoring him, Michael opened the door to Daphne's room and ushered Jane inside. The cage that had been protecting her amputation was no longer over the bed. Daphne lay with just a sheet covering her tiny body, her arms tucked underneath it. Without all the paraphernalia that had surrounded her she seemed even more vulnerable and fragile. Jane moved closer to the bed. She could see that Daphne's hair had been combed away from her face, and her mouth and closed eyes were sunken.

'She would have liked to have her teeth in . . .' Jane said quietly.

Michael opened the box, and, moving Jane aside, he put in Daphne's precious white false teeth.

'That's better,' Jane said. After a moment, she turned to Michael. 'It *was* natural causes? I mean, there was nothing suspicious, was there?'

He shook his head. Jane knew that Michael could not really have any notion of the significance of Daphne Millbank's death. And she didn't want him to know. She forced herself to sound calm as she asked if she could use a phone.

'There's one in the nurse's bay,' Michael said.

He waited as she called Scotland Yard and asked the duty sergeant to inform DCI Crowley that Daphne Millbank was dead.

'All done?' he asked softly as she replaced the receiver.

'Yes,' she whispered, 'all done.'

'Would you like me to call you a cab?'

'No, thank you, I think I need to walk for a while.'

He gently took her arm to escort her out of the hospital. 'I'd come with you but I have to stay.'

'I understand. I really just need to walk for a while.'

'I'll call you.'

Jane took off walking briskly across Westminster Bridge. By now, it was nearly eleven and cold, with a sharp wind from the river. She knew she should have phoned for police transport to take her home, but she wanted to be alone and she couldn't believe she was in any real danger. Her mind was churning: she had now become the only witness. One moment she felt almost panic-stricken but then she quickened her pace again, feeling angry at the waste of lives the bomb had caused. She passed the Houses of Parliament, Big Ben's clock face looming in the moonlight as she pulled her jacket tightly around her. As she headed towards Westminster tube station she could see the bars were across the entrance: it was closed. She had no option but to keep walking towards the bus stop and hoped the next night bus wouldn't be too long.

Fifteen minutes later she was thankful to see the brightly-lit red double-decker bus heading towards her stop. There were few passengers travelling so late. She took a lower-level window seat, opening her purse to show the bus conductor her warrant card.

The bus seemed to take forever heading across Trafalgar Square, round Nelson's Column, and left into Charing Cross Road. Late as it was, the streets were thronging with people, mostly young. All the theatres along Charing Cross Road were closed, shows over. As they passed Oxford Street she glanced at her wristwatch. Midnight. It felt as if she was never going to get home.

The bus stopped next to Foyles on Charing Cross Road and Jane was surprised as to how many passengers were getting on. Two drunk young men began to argue with the bus conductor. That was when Jane saw Regina on the corner of Manette Street. The bus was just about to move off when Jane hurried down the aisle and jumped down from the platform. Jane was familiar with the area from a previous case involving a search for a prostitute, and knew she was heading into the red-light district. This is where she had checked out all the strip clubs and porn shops. She saw Regina turning right off the narrow dark road into Greek Street. Greek Street was packed with small lit-up cafés and restaurants and way up ahead of her she could see Regina pushing and shoving aside anyone in her way. She was wearing a cheap white PVC jacket, mini skirt and very high platform boots. Jane was shocked as she watched her approach a car and lean in, but she swiftly moved away. Five minutes later she approached another man and did the same thing. Jane had seen enough. She strode towards Regina, grabbed her by her arm and pushed her against the wall.

'What do you think you are doing?'

The driver from the last car, in a red Cortina, swore at Jane and told her to mind her own fucking business. Still gripping Regina's arm tightly, Jane turned to the driver. 'I'm a detective with the Metropolitan Police. This girl is underage. Do you want to be arrested with her?'

He drove off fast. Jane now grabbed Regina's other arm, pinning her up against the wall. She didn't struggle and Jane only needed one look at her face to see she was out of her head.

'Do you know who I am? Do you remember me?'

Regina nodded. 'I know you.'

'Where is your brother?'

'He go home.'

'We tried to help you. I want to help you now.'

'You no help me, you give me right back to him.'

Jane was so intent on Regina she didn't see the Cortina reversing and stopping directly behind her. The driver got out and was moving close to Jane. Regina punched her, causing her to stumble back into the man. To Jane's stunned amazement DS Stanley appeared just as Regina vanished down an alley between the buildings.

'Get in the car, Tennison,' Stanley snapped, opening the passenger door.

She didn't have much choice. He pushed her roughly from behind into the back seat of the car. He got in beside her, slamming the door. They drove off fast.

'We just lost Regina Hernandez,' Stanley said into the radio. 'She's in Greek Street. Could be heading towards you.'

The driver did a U-turn in Old Compton Street, speeding back to the north end of Greek Street in time for Jane to see other under-cover Vice Squad officers herding girls out of a club. Jane recognised some of the girls from the passports they'd found in the Shepherd's Bush raid.

Stanley gave her a dismissive look. 'Stay in the car, Tennison. You've got a lot of explaining to do. Vice were just bringing the girl in and you screwed it up.'

'Oh my God, Stanley . . . I am so sorry.'

'What the hell are you doing out at this time of night in the red-light district?'

'I was on a bus coming back from the hospital. Daphne Millbank died. And I saw Regina in the street.'

Stanley stared out of the window as the Vice Squad officers led two more girls from the club. He knew the old lady's death was going to cause bigger problems for Jane.

'Listen, you take a taxi home. I'll do what I can to iron this situation out. The plus side is that your information about Hernandez and the Playboy Club meant that Vice Squad were able to dig up his contacts. They busted two of his seedy businesses tonight, bringing in the Dip Squad to assist.'

'Regina said that we didn't protect her. We sent her back to her uncle.'

'Yeah well, we weren't to know, luv. Turns out he's got contacts at the Colombian Embassy. We've got him now, thanks to Regina. Let's hope we find her before one of Andres' henchmen does.'

CHAPTER FIFTEEN

After a fitful night's sleep, Jane got dressed for work. She was in a bad mood and very irritated when she saw Pearl had left dirty dishes in the sink.

'You left all your carrot peelings by the sink,' she snapped, 'and your used plates.'

'Well, how could I clear up when it was full of your bolognese mess?' Pearl replied equally shortly. 'But don't get bad-tempered . . . if we do it together it'll be done before I have to go to work.'

'I have to go to work as well!' Jane retorted.

Together they washed and dried the dishes, and Pearl wiped over the counters. She then threw the dishcloth towards the sink.

'Right, all done and dusted. I've got to put some make-up on, then I'm off . . . if that's all right with you?'

Jane rinsed out the dishcloth that Pearl had thrown over to the sink.

'Thank you . . . I'm sorry I was so bad-tempered. I was late getting home last night, and I couldn't sleep.'

'How was the patient?' Pearl asked, hovering in the kitchen doorway.

'She died. It was very sad . . . she was a wonderful old lady.'

'What did she die of?'

'She was badly injured in the Covent Garden explosion.'

'Oh, I'm sorry . . . Michael did tell me, now I think of it. I liked him. And he's very attractive.'

Pearl went back into her bedroom, as Jane glanced over the now clean kitchen. She washed her hands in the bathroom and ran a comb through her hair before going into her bedroom to get dressed. She opened her wardrobe to take out a clean shirt, and then pursed her lips. She knew that last night she had carefully pushed back the hangers either side of the Chanel dress, as she wanted to let the creases drop from the frilly skirt. The dress was now squashed back alongside her other clothes.

Jane banged open her bedroom door catching Pearl just about to leave.

'You were in my room again! You can't deny it because you moved my clothes in the wardrobe.'

'Oh yeah . . . I needed the hairdryer. I was just looking in the wardrobe for it, sorry. But that dress is just gorgeous. Bye for now . . .'

Pearl hurried out, leaving Jane to stew in her anger. She quickly got into her work clothes and was just about to leave when the doorbell rang. She didn't press the entry buzzer as she thought it might be the postman, so she hurried down to the main front door.

'Morning, Tennison.' DCI Church was standing on the pavement. She looked at him with trepidation, certain he was there because of the fiasco the previous night.

'I wasn't expecting you, sir.'

'So it would seem. And you didn't check who it was before you opened the door. Now Daphne's passed away you need to be more aware of –'

'I saw you approaching out the window and was on my way out anyway,' Jane lied to appease him. She'd had enough of being lectured about her safety.

'Right, well, it's always best to double-check. I'm here to take you over to Scotland Yard to meet Crowley. I would have called but, as it's still early, I thought I might catch you before you left.'

'Why does Crowley want to see me?' Jane asked.

'He wants you to look at some more mugshots, surveillance photographs and artist's impressions of suspected IRA members. He's hoping you might recognise the man you saw at Covent Garden.'

As they walked to his car she could feel the blood rushing to her head, certain she was in trouble. He opened the passenger door and

Jane climbed in. The door was still sticking and he had to slam it hard before he walked around to the driving side.

'You all right?' he asked, starting up the engine.

'Yes, I'm fine. My flatmate is just winding me up and I'm rather sad about Daphne. I was at the hospital last night. Is that why you're here?'

'In a way. How was your evening?'

'Not that great, I was having dinner with that charge nurse I mentioned, Michael Mitchell, when he got a call about Daphne. I was a bit worried that he had given my number out, but he said he was on call if there was an emergency, so he had to give his contact details.'

'It's good to be wary and careful. He should have checked if it was OK with you.'

Church drove in silence for a while, then gave Jane a sidelong glance.

'So, it's not working out all that well with the flatmate?'

Jane sighed, staring out of the window. 'Not really. She did at least help me with the washing-up this morning, but then I found out she'd been in my bedroom again. I specifically asked her not to go in there, but I know she's been looking through my wardrobe. She's very nosey and is always asking questions.'

'What sort of questions?'

'Just being generally nosey about everything. I'm going to get a lock put on my bedroom door.'

'She was vetted, wasn't she?'

Jane turned to him in surprise. 'Yes. She works at Madame Tussauds.'

'Do you know what a "sleeper" is?'

Jane straightened her back. 'Yes, I do. It was explained to me. Pearl doesn't concern me in that way ... I mean, she isn't doing anything suspicious.'

She'd started to hope Stanley hadn't told Church about her mistake with Regina the previous night.

'But you just said she asks a lot of questions, and that she goes in and out of your bedroom. You need to start thinking whether she might have an ulterior motive. I'm sure she doesn't, but just be vigilant. You didn't tell anyone about the raid, did you?'

'No, I didn't know anything about the target address until the briefing at the station. Why are you asking?'

'Crowley thinks the ASU may have been tipped off just before we got there.'

Jane was distraught. 'What! Are you suggesting it was me?'

'No, not at all, Crowley thinks the Intelligence Services have a leak. Look, all I'm saying is you need to be careful . . . we all do.'

Jane chewed at her lip and stared out of the window again. She began to wonder if she had inadvertently mentioned anything to Pearl after Crowley's call. Could Pearl's interest in her work, and what was in her bedroom wardrobe, add up to more than just nosiness? Pearl had asked Michael if he was a detective, and she'd asked about the hospital. Why had Pearl come back early when she knew Jane was cooking dinner? Had she innocently given more details to Pearl than she'd realised?

'Here we are,' Church said, showing his warrant card to the PC guarding the entrance to the underground car park at Scotland Yard.

Church had not given any indication that the reason he had shown up to collect Jane was that Crowley was concerned about her vulnerability. He was aware that the news about Daphne Millbank's death and role as a vital witness might be leaked to the press and yet again reflect badly on the investigation. To minimise the risk of this an announcement had been organised and a statement would be made that a further victim of the Covent Garden explosion had died from their injuries.

The day after the raid Crowley had been to Brixton prison where he interviewed the four Balcombe Street IRA men who, as Category A prisoners, were segregated whilst awaiting trial. Crowley hoped they would give him names of the men connected to the recent

IRA activity in London. Three of the men all insisted that the Bomb Squad had fabricated confessions and convicted the wrong men for the Guildford and Woolwich pub bombings. One prisoner had given Crowley names for two men who were part of the ASU in London, but it turned out they were already in a Northern Irish prison and could not have taken part in either the Guildford or Covent Garden bombings. It infuriated Crowley that the Balcombe Street men were playing games with him and wasting time.

Jane accompanied DCI Church to Crowley's office. He was as abrupt as usual and gestured for her to take one of the two chairs in front of his desk.

Jane sat with her hands folded in her lap, watching as Crowley laid out a series of photographs face down in front of her.

'I know you're adamant that the artist's impression released to the press was not your recollection of the suspect. Nor did it match the deceased Daphne Millbank's description.' Crowley leant back in his large desk chair. 'I want you to look closely at the photographs in front of you. Some are surveillance photos, others are of men who have been arrested on suspicion of being sympathisers with, or members of, the IRA – not convicted or currently in prison. Take your time, and try as best as you can to recall the moment you tried to stop the suspect at Covent Garden.'

Jane leant forward to the edge of the desk, turning over one black-and-white photograph after another. She took her time, studying each one in turn.

'No, I'm sorry. None of these men look familiar.' She tapped the surveillance photograph of the man Crowley suspected with her index finger. 'I'm sure this wasn't the man I tried to stop at Covent Garden.'

'I don't want to undermine your confidence, Jane, but I believe this man was involved in the bombing at Covent Garden, maybe even as an accomplice. The landlord of the Kentish Town flat stated it was this man he saw when he visited the premises two weeks ago.'

Jane glanced at DCI Church in the hope of getting some response, but he was studying the row of mugshots and surveillance pictures.

'Would you be prepared to attend an identity parade?'

'Yes, of course I would. But even if the man I saw was on it I can't be sure I'd pick him out.'

'We can get the men on a parade to turn sideways,' Church added.

Crowley leaned across his desk, gathered up the photographs and stacked them like a pack of cards.

'I'm not sure you're aware how much we're depending on you, Tennison. We have very little evidence to assist us in tracing the woman seen in the phone box. We've issued a press release asking for anyone with information to come forward, but we still only have one witness claiming to have seen her, so it seems unlikely we'll be able to trace her.'

There was a knock on the door and a uniformed officer asked if DCI Church could take an important call from a member of his Dip Squad.

Church placed his chair back against the wall and glanced at Jane as he walked past her. She seemed anxious and was twisting her hands in her lap. Crowley would have to put more pressure on her. He went into an adjoining office to take the call.

'Guv, it's Stanley . . . Something's cropped up that you need to be aware of.'

Church sat on the edge of a desk and listened as Stanley spoke.

'Listen, we have a problem. The uniformed duty sergeant at Paddington Green Police Station just rang the office. His uniformed lads just arrested Tennison's flatmate, Pearl Radcliff, and she's being held for questioning. She gave WDC Tennison's address and her name to vouch for her. When they asked her where Tennison worked she said in Woolwich at a lab, but thought it was a bit "hush-hush". Paddington's duty sergeant checked with police records who told them Tennison was attached to our squad –'

'What's Radcliff been nicked for?'

'He wouldn't tell me, just said to inform you as Tennison's boss . . . and they want access to her flat.'

'Tennison's here with me . . . I'll speak with the duty sergeant for more information and inform Crowley.'

He was just about to replace the receiver, but Stanley hadn't finished. 'I think Tennison's a liability, Guv.'

'What?'

Stanley gave DCI Church the details of Tennison's interaction with the Vice Squad raid. Church listened without interruption as Stanley made it clear that Jane's actions had placed the operation, and Regina, in jeopardy.

'I can't believe I'm hearing this. I told Tennison not to get involved and she blatantly disobeyed me!'

'I think, Guv, she was maybe in a very emotional state, having just left St Thomas' Hospital after Daphne Millbank's death. But now, with the Radcliff situation as well, I felt that you should know.'

'Thanks, Stanley.' Church hung up, then called the duty sergeant at Paddington and after a brief conversation went back to Crowley's office.

Jane was looking through a fresh selection of surveillance shots.

'I'd like to speak with you alone,' Church said to Crowley.

'Jane, go and get a coffee while I speak with DCI Church,' said Crowley.

'Meet me outside reception in ten minutes,' Church said sharply to Jane.

She gathered up her things and left the room, puzzled as to why she was being dismissed so abruptly. As soon as she left the room Church told Crowley about his conversation with Stanley regarding Pearl Radcliff.

'For fuck's sake, who is this Pearl woman and how much does she know about our investigation?'

'She's been living with Tennison for a few days. She's been arrested for shoplifting. I told the duty sergeant at Paddington to hold her for questioning by your team. It gets worse, though. Last night Tennison managed to screw up a big job the Vice Squad took over from us.'

'She's a bloody loose cannon!' Crowley exclaimed. 'What on earth does she think she's playing at?'

'Paddington want to search her address. They suspect Radcliff may have more stolen gear there. I told them not to force entry and I'll take Tennison there now to let them in.'

'Well, give her a good grilling on the way. I want to know everything she's said to this Pearl from the moment she met her . . . chapter and verse!'

'That was already my intention,' Church said and left the room.

Carrying her plastic cup of coffee, Jane went down to the Scotland Yard reception area to wait for DCI Church. When he arrived, he was abrupt and told her to follow him. As they were driving away in his battered car, Jane, her hands cupped tightly around her coffee, asked anxiously, 'Is this to do with last night and my interaction with Regina Hernandez?'

Church frowned. 'Why don't you tell me about that?'

'Last night, heading home from the hospital after Daphne Millbank's death, I was on the bus when I saw Regina Hernandez. She was ducking and diving like a tart and it really upset me because we were supposed to protect her. So I got off the bus to approach her and I inadvertently interrupted a Vice Squad officer taking her into custody.'

Church closed his eyes for a brief moment. Jane had a terrible sinking feeling in her stomach. She had been warned not to get on the wrong side of DCI Church and she knew she was on it.

He gripped the steering wheel so tightly his knuckles went white.

'I warned you to keep your nose out of the Hernandez situation, Tennison. Not once, but twice! I told you the Vice Squad were now handling the case. I don't care if you have some emotional compassionate attachment to this young girl but she is now missing and the Vice Squad don't know where she is. If Andres Hernandez discovers she agreed to testify against him we could find her body in a dumpster. If that happens, it'll be on your head!'

Jane could feel her eyes brimming with tears.

'Please don't waste my time answering – and I assure you your tears will not help you in any way. If there wasn't a more pressing issue to deal with right now, I would have you back in uniform directing fucking traffic.

'Oh, and you may wonder why we're driving back to your place. Your flatmate has been arrested . . . she gave your name and address to vouch for her.'

'What?' Jane was so shocked that she spilt some of her coffee over her skirt.

'I had no choice but to tell Crowley about this. She also knew you currently worked in Woolwich and said it was "hush-hush".'

'Oh, my God – how? What has she been arrested for?'

'She was caught nicking a book from Smith's in the High Street.'

'A book? Is this a joke? I mean, I know she's always coming home with books but surely it must have been a mistake? She probably just forgot to pay for it . . . I mean, it must have just been an oversight.'

'Well, we'll see. You were uptight this morning about her snooping in your bedroom, and always asking you questions . . . Did you tell her you worked at Woolwich?'

'I may have . . .' she replied, trying to catch her breath as Church concentrated on manoeuvring through the traffic, swearing at the congestion.

'The local uniforms are waiting to gain entry to your flat for a search. I've given instructions to keep Radcliff in custody. Crowley will want to interview her in case the investigation's been compromised.'

By the time they drew up outside Jane's flat her nerves were in shreds. Two uniformed officers were waiting and as soon as Jane joined them they headed up to the top floor. Jane unlocked her front door and Church told her to sit in the kitchen whilst they searched Pearl's bedroom.

Jane tipped her cold coffee down the sink and took a wet cloth to wipe down her skirt. Church stood in the doorway.

'She's got a room full of books. Half of them have been nicked from libraries, they're knee-deep in there. Are you telling me that you weren't suspicious? I mean, they're stacked all around her bed in every available space.'

'I knew she was always bringing books home, but I didn't think she was stealing them.'

'Well, the one she was caught nicking was the Guinness Book of Records. After what we've found, she might make it into the next one!'

Jane sat in the kitchen whilst the officers carried out books to the hallway, ready for them to be taken away as evidence. Church said he was going to Paddington to see Crowley and Stanley was coming over to sit with her. The uniforms had made a thorough search of Pearl's room and found nothing else incriminating, but they also wanted to look in Jane's bedroom and the loft.

Jane felt humiliated. She offered to make tea, but everyone declined. A uniformed officer brought in some flat cardboard boxes to assemble and fill with books. Stanley arrived about an hour later. He was his usual scruffy self and said very little to Jane as he assisted the uniformed officers in separating the library books from others that might have been stolen from elsewhere. After another hour, the boxes were carried out to a paddy wagon to be taken to the property store at Paddington. Stanley came back to sit in the kitchen and have a cup of tea with Jane.

'Right, the guv wants her belongings moved out of here by tonight. Crowley's interviewing her just now. She'll be held in custody until the theft charges are sorted, then taken to a magistrate's court first thing in the morning. That should give you time to pack up all her gear. She'll probably be granted bail, so she can return to collect it. Church has suggested that I should be here to make sure she leaves.'

'But where will she go?'

'That's not your problem, sweetheart. You're a detective constable in the Met, and there could be repercussions about her lodging here with you.'

'Should I call her work and explain something about her not turning up?'

'Again, luv, that's not your problem. We just need to get her out of here, then it's done and dusted.'

Stanley left. Feeling even worse, Jane went into Pearl's bedroom. She found her suitcases and placed them on the bed, and started packing clothes. They were soon too full to close, so she began filling up rubbish bags, and placing them in the hall. In the drawer of the bedside table she found bundles of letters and cards, many with New Zealand stamps. She wrapped the TV in one of Pearl's blankets and then filled a carrier bag with all her toiletries in the bathroom.

The hallway was quickly filled with Pearl's belongings, and Jane took out the vacuum and began to go over the dirty, food-stained carpet. Jane stripped the bed and bundled the sheets and pillow cases into yet another plastic bag for her to take to the launderette. She polished and dusted every surface. By six o'clock the empty room was devoid of any connection to Pearl Radcliff.

The doorbell rang at eight and Jane looked out of the window to see who it was before she buzzed DCI Church up to the top floor. He gave her a glum smile when he saw the cluttered hallway.

'Radcliff's been given a hard time by Crowley, but to be honest, I don't think there is anything you need to be concerned about. She'll spend a night in the cells and at about midday tomorrow she'll be brought here to remove all her stuff.'

'I never even thought not to mention to Pearl that I was going to Woolwich. I feel so stupid . . .' Jane said.

'Don't. These things happen. You could actually say we got lucky because if she hadn't been caught red-handed you might have been arrested along with her, for dishonest handling of a ton of nicked library books.' He grinned.

'What did DCI Crowley say about it?'

Church shrugged and tried to make light of it. 'He's not exactly happy, but he's calmed down a bit. Understandably, he wants Pearl out of your flat ASAP.' The truth was that he had hit the roof, snapping that DC Tennison must be a bloody idiot not to have been suspicious.

Church stood awkwardly in the small hallway. He could see how upset Jane was.

'Are you ready for the Good Friday do, then?' he said, changing the subject.

'Yes, I've got my dress.' she said, rather lamely.

'Well, it's only a week to go. The tickets are sold out, so it should be a big bash. There'll be cocktails before we sit down, and there's a great menu. Then there'll be a few speeches, and onto the dance floor with the band.'

Jane felt tearful as she nodded her head. Church reached over and took her hand.

'Listen, don't beat yourself up . . . these things happen. After tomorrow, you'll be clear of her, and Stanley will be here to make sure she picks up everything. I suggest you just go to work as usual . . . Stanley will get her front-door key and lock up afterwards.'

'Thank you.'

Church let go of her hand.

'I may have come on a bit heavy this morning but the reality is, Jane, you have to learn to not allow your emotions to override your professionalism. Regina Hernandez is a sad case but you'll find there will be many more like her. There is not an officer in the Met who doesn't have the faces of victims haunting them. It's quite possible the Vice Squad will find her and this time endeavour to protect her. I'm not going to hold this against you. You have a lot on your shoulders with the situation here in your flat and with Crowley putting pressure on you.

'You've been reassigned so you're not at the explosives lab anymore,' he added. 'As from tomorrow, Crowley wants you working in the Bomb Squad office at the Yard. He didn't give a reason but I guess it's so he can keep a closer eye on you. You've had a long day. Get some shuteye and put this all behind you.'

Church waved his hand and she burst into tears as he shut the door behind him.

CHAPTER SIXTEEN

Jane left earlier than usual for work on the Friday, not just to get out of the flat, but also to see what she would be working on. In some ways it came as no surprise that she had been assigned to the clerical office, typing and filing reports. She felt as if it was Crowley's way of punishing her over the Pearl incident and just hoped that DCI Church had not made him fully aware of her indiscretions.

Jane missed the lab and working with Paul Lawrence. She knew if she was with him she could speak in confidence, that he would be understanding and give her sound advice on what to do. The day was labourious and she was given nothing of sensitive interest to type up, it was all reports about new office equipment and expenditure. She knew that word of an officers' indiscretions travelled fast on the police grapevine and it made her feel uneasy. Every time someone walked into the room to put something on her desk she felt as if they were looking at her with disdain because of Pearl's arrest.

Although she couldn't wait for the day to end, part of her was dreading going home. When she finally got back to the flat, it was silent. All of Pearl's belongings had been taken. Jane made an omelette and a cup of tea and sat at the kitchen counter trying to work out how she was going to be able to afford living there alone. The phone interrupted her thoughts. It was Natalie.

'Natalie, I meant to call you . . . I'm sorry. I've been sort of up against it at work, and I've had a situation here at the flat that you just would not believe.'

Jane found it good to talk about Pearl. Natalie was understanding, and sympathised about how dreadful it must have been for Jane to find out she was a thief.

'I sort of feel sorry for her. But at least I now have the flat to myself.'

'Oh, I know exactly how you feel. I love being here on my own. How did dinner go?'

'It was good, but then we had to go to the hospital as there was an emergency and Michael was on call.'

'Oh dear, I hope it wasn't serious.'

'It was, unfortunately. Do you remember when we first met up again I'd been to see one of the victims of the Covent Garden explosion? She was such a wonderful lady, but she didn't make it. . . . it was very sad.'

'Poor you. What with that and the Pearl situation you must be totally stressed out.'

'To be honest, I am. But I'll get myself together.'

'Well, the reason I was calling was that I got into rather a panic as I remembered you needed a shawl or a little bolero of some kind, and I wondered if I was too late . . . is the dinner tonight?'

'No, it's next Friday . . . Good Friday. I do need something, though, and I still haven't got any shoes.'

'What about coming over tomorrow to try this little jacket I've got? I think it will look really nice . . . it's got a few sequins around the edge, with capped sleeves.'

'I can't tomorrow as I'm going to my parents'. What about Sunday morning?'

Natalie said that was perfect and suggested Jane came over after ten as she was going out jogging first thing with some colleagues from the bank.

'Tell you what, I can show you the best stuffing for a roast chicken, and maybe we can have lunch together.'

'I'll look forward to it. Thank you for calling.'

Natalie laughed. 'I've noticed your most overused words are "thank you"!'

'It shows you what a nice, well-brought-up girl I am! See you tomorrow.'

The following morning, Jane decided to buy a pair of evening shoes. She walked from Baker Street to Oxford Street; London's main shopping area was heaving with people and Jane spent over an hour window-shopping before she saw a pair of high-heeled slingbacks in the window of a Saxone shoe shop. She was uncertain about them and tried on a few different styles before putting the slingbacks on again and walking up and down the shop to stand in front of a full-length mirror.

'I think they're very flattering to your legs.' the salesgirl said, with hardly any interest.

'I'm going to be wearing a long dress.'

'Oh well, most important is they're comfortable. They're a good price.'

'You don't think they're too high?' Jane asked, as she took them off.

'No, they show off your ankles. Unless you want to go for flatties, like the ones you're wearing?'

'No, I'll take these,' Jane said, slipping her feet into her old, comfortable shoes.

After walking home and putting the box with her new shoes into her wardrobe, Jane collected her car and drove to Maida Vale. She had taken her bag of dirty laundry to do at some point in the evening. It was already almost midday as she rang the doorbell before using her key to open the front door.

'It's me,' she called out, shutting the front door behind her. In the hallway were two large suitcases with name tags, ready for their Norwegian cruise. Her mother hurried down the corridor her arms open wide.

'Jane! Give me a big hug and a kiss.'

Jane sometimes forgot how attractive her mother was when she did her hair and make-up. She had had her hair coloured and permed, and was wearing a pale blue, round-necked sweater with a dark-blue pleated skirt.

'Daddy's just gone to get a bottle of rosé, and I made a steak pie last night, which I've got in the oven. I'm just going to make some gravy, and we'll have mashed potatoes and green beans. Then we've got your favourite ice cream, vanilla and chocolate.'

'That sounds delicious, Mum. Is Pam coming?'

'Good heavens, no! She'll be working until six in the salon and then she'll want to check all her packing as Tony is useless.'

'They're going with you?' Jane asked, surprised.

'Yes, Daddy's treat. They were a bit miffed about the money he'd loaned you for the flat, so this is a sort of peace deal.'

'Well, that'll be nice, and good company.'

'I am so excited . . . I've never been on a cruise before. It's been difficult to know what to wear as we have to dress for dinner every night, and then be prepared for very cold weather, and they have lots of games and entertainment indoors and out on the deck.'

Jane walked into the kitchen and pulled out a stool.

'I was wondering if I could borrow that little pearl necklace you've got, with the small drop earrings?'

'Oh dear, I've packed it. If only you'd let me know sooner . . . although it is rather lovely and I need some jewellery to wear on board the *Bolette*. That's the ship we're going on. It was only launched a couple of years ago.'

'Never mind.'

'Are you going somewhere nice?'

'Yes, it's a dinner dance for all the CID officers, at St Ermin's Hotel.'

'Oh well, if there's anything that I'm not taking you're welcome to try it on. Have you asked Pam?'

'No, don't worry . . . I'll find something.'

Mrs Tennison busied herself setting the table and mashing the potatoes, whilst Jane sat on a kitchen stool watching. Her father returned from the local off-licence and they opened the chilled bottle of wine. They talked about the forthcoming trip to Norway and their excitement was endearing. She enjoyed being with them and didn't spoil the mood by telling them about the situation with Pearl. She told them instead about meeting Natalie and how they had become close friends, but the conversation mostly returned to the cruise. As soon as her mother had prepared the veg and gravy she handed Jane the brochures for her to look at.

'Fred Olsen is supposed to be a really good company. They do all sorts of trips but your father and I have always wanted to visit Oslo, and the fords look so beautiful.'

Mr Tennison smiled, and winked at Jane. 'They're pronounced fee-ords dear . . .'

Jane flicked through the brochure, thinking how much she would hate being cooped up on a ship for any length of time. She couldn't imagine anything worse than dressing up every night to have dinner with a table of complete strangers. It had taken her long enough to find a dress to wear for her one night out at the Good Friday event, let alone two weeks of dinners. However, she was happy that they were so excited about the cruise and made an effort to sound enthusiastic.

'It does look lovely, Mum . . . I'm sure you'll all have a great time. Oh look, they do painting classes, and flower arranging as well . . .'

'Oh, I'm not sure we'll have time for any of that, dear. We'll be too busy visiting the fords . . . I mean, fee-ords. Do you know, there's even a hair salon on board? Pam will be so impressed. She does like to keep up to date and make sure she's got all the latest hair styling techniques . . .'

Jane smiled and nodded, aware of just how competitive her sister was. Mr Tennison leant over and handed Jane a sheet of paper on which he had written, neatly and precisely, their cruise itinerary.

'Just in case you need to get in touch with us in an emergency. You can call Fred Olsen's office in London, and then they can send a telegram out to the ship. But let's hope you won't have any more emergencies for a while. You've been caught up in too many dangerous situations recently. Please be careful. Your mother and I do worry about you.'

Jane could tell that Mrs Tennison was starting to get anxious, so she quickly changed the subject.

'I'm just going to get some things from my bedroom.'

Although it had previously been kept just as if she was still living at home, her bedroom was now full of boxes and there were bags all over her bed. She didn't mind, but she was hoping her mother had not cleared out her underwear drawer. The drawer was almost empty as she had taken most of her things with her when she had moved to her flat. The remaining items were neatly folded and Jane searched through looking for the strapless bra she had used when she had been Pam's bridesmaid. She found it at the back of the drawer and popped it into her bag to take home.

After helping her mother wash the dishes and clear the kitchen Jane sat down with her father, who was sitting in a wingback chair with his feet up on a stool.

He asked her how everything was at work. As usual Jane didn't go into any details, but hinted that she was eager to leave Woolwich and return to the Dip Squad. She was just explaining exactly what the Dip Squad was when her mother interrupted, carrying a velvet-covered jewellery box.

'Have a little hunt through here, dear, and see if there's anything that takes your fancy.'

Jane sorted through various beads and chains in the main section, then looked through the top layer, which had compartments for rings and earrings. Everything she picked out her mother had an explanation of when she had been given it, and when she had worn it. Just as she'd decided there was nothing suitable, she found a thin gold chain with a small teardrop pearl attached.

'I like this, Mummy.'

'Daddy gave me that when your brother was born.'

'Oh.' Jane's mother never spoke about the son she'd lost. Jane didn't know what to say.

'It's an eighteen-carat gold chain, and the pearl is real.'

'It's beautiful.'

'You can borrow it, if you like.'

'No, really . . . I think it's too precious.'

'So are you,' her father interrupted, and Jane found herself near to tears as he got up from his chair and carefully placed the chain around Jane's neck.

Jane looked at her mother's uncertain expression, but then Mrs Tennison took the jewellery box and closed the lid.

'Well, you'll always know when you wear it how much it means to me, because I've hardly ever worn it. It reminds me too much of holding him in my arms as a newborn baby. He would reach out to try to grab the pearl and I was always afraid the chain would break. Instead it was my heart . . .'

Mrs Tennison walked out with the jewellery box and her father put his arm around Jane's shoulder.

'She wants you to have it. I know she was going to give it to Pam for her baby, but when she miscarried it didn't seem right.'

'I'll take good care of it.'

'I'm sure you will. Who knows, maybe this cruise will give Tony and Pam a break and she'll get pregnant again. That'd be icing on the cake.'

They had tea together and it was just after seven when Jane felt it was time to leave. Her parents were keen to get their clothes set out for their journey to Harwich in the morning. She hugged them goodbye, wished them a happy holiday and promised yet again that she'd be careful.

Jane stripped off her clothes and grabbed her robe before realising that she didn't need to worry about bumping into Pearl on the way to the bathroom. She liked the fact she could walk round stark naked in her flat and not worry about anybody else being there. She looked at her reflection in the long wardrobe mirror, wearing just high heels, and momentarily found herself laughing. The tiny thin gold necklace, with the perfect teardrop pearl, hung down just above the curve of her breasts. She touched it lightly with her fingers, and thought of the gift from her father to her mother on the birth of her beloved little brother, who was now dead. She carefully undid the clasp and cupped it in the palm of her hand.

So many times she had wished she could be more honest and open with her parents, and be able to tell them truthfully how she was feeling and what she was going through. Over the years she had begun to understand the depth of their grief and she never wanted to subject them to any more pain regarding her chosen career. She hadn't made a conscious decision to keep her fears and tribulations from her parents. The caring, loving side of Jane had made her always want to protect them, as if she was the parent and they were her children.

CHAPTER SEVENTEEN

Jane had a light breakfast that Sunday morning, then drove to Natalie's flat. She had bought the Sunday newspapers and had picked up the bottle of wine that Michael had given her when he had come to dinner.

Natalie had already prepared the potatoes and vegetables for their lunch, which were waiting in pans on the stove. The small chicken lay on a board and Natalie insisted on showing Jane how to make the sausage meat, herbs and lightly fried onions into stuffing to put inside it.

'This is always a good stuffing because the sausage meat keeps the chicken moist. And I always use a few strips of bacon to cover the wings and breast . . . it stops them burning.'

Jane sipped her glass of wine and nodded in approval as she watched Natalie transfer the chicken to a roasting tin and put it in the oven. Then Natalie went on to explain that the best roast potatoes were made by boiling them up first until they were fluffy round the edges. She then said that the trick was to 'score' them all over with a fork, then place them in a very hot baking tray with good olive oil drizzled over the top. 'They come out really crispy on the outside, but lovely and soft in the centre.'

Jane nodded again as she sipped some more wine.

'Right, got that . . . For my next dinner guest I'll serve chicken . . .'

They went into the cosy lounge and Natalie asked for a blow-by-blow account of everything that had gone on with Pearl. She roared with laughter about the stolen books and Jane almost joined in, but did feel some compassion for poor Pearl.

'So, you're now living alone, just like me.' Natalie lit a cigarette and poured them both another glass of wine.

'Yes. It'll be a strain financially but I'm already enjoying the privacy. I just hope Pearl won't be too traumatised by her arrest, and that she finds somewhere else to live.'

'So, tell me all about Michael . . .'

Jane told Natalie that he had seemed to really enjoy the spaghetti, and had even had two servings, but then he had received the emergency call so they had to leave, just as they were getting to know each other better.

'What happened at the hospital?'

'It was awful, because . . .' Jane hesitated.

'You can tell me, Jane. What happened?'

'We had a very important patient and sadly she didn't make it. She died from the injuries she suffered during the explosion at Covent Garden.'

'Really? Why was she so important?'

'She was a witness, so without her . . . This is very confidential and I shouldn't really even be discussing it . . .'

'Let's change the subject. Tell me, did Michael make a pass at you?'

'Sort of. He's really very nice . . . in fact, this is the wine he brought round when he came, but I'd already opened a bottle.'

They continued chatting, glancing through the Sunday papers as they talked. Natalie went in and out of the kitchen to oversee the cooking, and eventually they sat down to have lunch. Natalie carved the golden-brown chicken with the crispy bacon attached to the skin.

'These roast potatoes are absolutely delicious,' Jane said. The gravy had been made from the juices in the roasting tin, and was thick and very tasty.

Natalie had produced an apple pie but they were both too full to eat it straightaway, so they decided to wait for a while.

'I know, why don't I show you my wrap and bolero? You can try them on and see which one you'd like to borrow to go with that amazing dress!'

They went into Natalie's bedroom and she opened the wardrobe door and took out a velvet bolero. It had a tiny row of sequins decorating the edge of the sleeves and the hem.

Jane took off her jacket and unbuttoned her shirt as she wouldn't be wearing anything but the velvet bodice with the tiny straps. She felt unself-conscious as she slipped the bolero over her bra.

'I love it . . . it's perfect!'

'I think so too . . . but I've got a lovely nice pink shawl as well, which is a good length to wrap around and toss over your shoulder.'

Natalie opened a drawer in her chest of drawers and rooted around, pulling out a long, delicate, shawl.

'See – it's gorgeous, isn't it?'

'Oh yes . . .' Jane wrapped it around the velvet bolero and stood in front of the full-length mirror inside the wardrobe door. She couldn't decide between the two, and kept on putting it on and off as she looked at herself in the mirror.

The oven timer suddenly went off and Natalie yelped.

'Oh, that's the apple pie done! I'll make some custard whilst you decide. Personally, I like the bolero and I think it'll look absolutely perfect with that Chanel dress.'

Jane took off the shawl and held it in one hand as she studied herself in the bolero again. She knew Natalie was right and carefully folded the shawl to put it back. As she went towards the open drawer she noticed a Hermès label. Realising it was a scarf, Jane gently pulled the corner of it out from beneath the pile of other scarfs it was under. It was clearly expensive and had a distinctive pattern of red horses' heads and gold horseshoes. An icy chill spread through her veins and she took a deep breath. Her heart was pounding as she remembered the description their witness had given, of the woman seen in the phone box outside Covent Garden when the explosion had happened.

Jane swallowed and pushed the Hermès scarf back underneath the other scarves, then placed the shawl on top and closed the drawer. She was shaking as she took off the bolero and put her shirt and jacket on. Many women wore Hermès scarves, she reminded herself, trying to dismiss it as a coincidence. She wanted to have another look at the scarf and was about to open the drawer when Natalie came into the room.

'Have you decided?' Natalie asked, holding a jug of custard in her hand.

'Yes, it's the bolero.'

'Good. Now, come and have some pie. It's ready on the table, and I've made the custard.'

Jane picked up the bolero and followed her into the lounge where they had eaten at her small, drop-leaf dining table.

'Gosh, I don't know if I can manage anything else . . . I'm so full.'

'Don't be silly! Sit down and have another glass of wine.'

Jane sat quietly opposite Natalie, watching as she sliced the apple pie and proffered the custard jug.

'Just a really small piece for me, honestly . . .'

Natalie gave her a thin slice and took a larger piece for herself.

'I didn't make the pie, but it's from a fabulous deli on Hampstead High Street.'

Jane thought back over her time with Natalie. The coincidence of bumping into her at the hospital, her repeated calls to the flat, her determination to meet up after not seeing each other for years. But here was Natalie cooking dinner for her, offering her apple pie, surely there was nothing sinister going on? But as she struggled to eat a small mouthful of pie, doubts niggled away.

'It's delicious . . . tastes just like it was home-made.'

Her head was spinning as she tried to think of a way she could leave. She was feeling sick to her stomach.

'Would you like some coffee?' Natalie asked, pushing her half-eaten dessert away. She lit a cigarette. 'Or perhaps we could have a walk on Hampstead Heath, then maybe have coffee when we come back?'

'Actually, I really need to call my parents just to double-check everything's OK. They're leaving for Harwich this afternoon to go on their cruise. Can I use your phone?'

'Sure. Let me start clearing up the kitchen and then we can set off. Hampstead Heath and Parliament Hill's not far from here, and sometimes there are a few shops open on a Sunday.'

Jane watched as Natalie stacked the dirty dishes and carried them out to the kitchen. She quickly crossed over to the phone and dialled, knowing that her parents would have already left.

'Hello, Daddy,' she said to the dialling tone. 'It's Jane. Just checking everything's all right before you leave?'

Natalie was in the kitchen when Jane returned.

'I'm so sorry, but I need to go. One of the locks on my mother's suitcase has broken and they can't close it. I'm going to have to pick up one of mine and drive it over there now. They're in a real flap and they'll miss the ship if I don't go.'

'Oh, no . . .' said Natalie. 'I was hoping we could have a lovely evening together, and go to a nice pub.'

'Well, let me see how I get on. I can always come back afterwards.'

Natalie held up the bolero as Jane headed towards the front door. 'Take this with you, just in case you can't get back . . . It's Good Friday at the end of this week.'

'Right . . . Gosh, sorry. My parents can be rather needy sometimes, but I'd hate them to miss their cruise . . .'

'Don't worry. Just call me if you can make it back afterwards.'

Jane hurried out to her car and climbed inside. She sat in the driver's seat for a few minutes, telling herself that she was being an idiot and was probably just being paranoid after the Pearl situation. She started the engine and drove home, worried that she had drunk too much wine to be driving. By the time she arrived at her flat she was a nervous wreck.

Letting herself in Jane tried to work out whether she had been jumping to ridiculous conclusions about the Hermès scarf she'd seen at Natalie's. She lay on her bed and closed her eyes, trying to recall exactly what was in the statement she had read from the witness. Something was nagging her. The scarf that the woman in the phone box had been wearing had been described as possibly Hermès style, with red setter dogs on it, which was obviously different from the one in Natalie's drawer, which had horses' heads and horseshoes. But perhaps the witness had been mistaken? When she'd first seen it in Natalie's drawer, she'd thought for a moment the pattern had been dogs – that's why she'd pulled it out.

Jane thought through all of her interactions with Natalie. She wavered constantly between refusing to believe that any connection could be possible, to questioning all their conversations. Eventually she decided that perhaps she needed to talk to DCI Church.

Jane rang the Dip Squad but Church wasn't available; however, Stanley would be in later that afternoon and he would know where Church could be contacted. Jane replaced the receiver and, almost as if she were on automatic pilot, went back out to her car. Desperately trying to remember the exact address, she drove to Kilburn.

Jane passed Dexter's road twice before she recognised it. She drove down it slowly until she found his building. She told herself that if Dexter was not in she would just go back home and call Stanley again. Maybe by then she would have come to the conclusion that she was just being paranoid.

Her stomach was churning as she rang the bell for Flat 2. There were no names listed, but she remembered that he lived on the second floor. She rang the bell three times and was just about to turn away when the main front door opened.

Dexter was barefooted, wearing only a pair of tracksuit bottoms. 'Jane!'

'Sorry to disturb you . . . I just needed to talk something over with someone, and DCI Church wasn't available. If I'm interrupting you I can –'

'No, come in.'

Jane followed him up the stairs and along the landing to his flat, where the door had been left wide open.

'I was just going to have a shower, but sit down. Do you need a drink? You look a bit shaken.'

'I am rather shaken, actually . . . no, I don't want a drink. I just need some advice. I might just be adding two and two to get five, or whatever the saying is.'

Dexter sat opposite her on one of his big comfortable sofas, as Jane sat perched on the edge of the other sofa, clasping and unclasping her hands.

'So, what's the problem? I heard about your flatmate being arrested . . .'

'It's not about her . . . It's about someone else I befriended, and . . . er . . .'

Jane stuttered her way through the story of how she had met up with Natalie again years after they had been at the training academy together, and that Natalie had failed the course and was now working in a bank.

Dexter held up his hand.

'Do you want to get to the reason you're here, Jane?'

'Her name is Natalie Wilde.'

'That's a good Irish name.'

'What?'

'Oscar Wilde . . . Sorry, I didn't mean to interrupt.'

Jane took a deep breath and explained that she had seen the headscarf with the Hermès label and the horses' heads in Natalie's drawer, and that she wondered if it could possibly be the same scarf that had been described by the woman who gave a statement, regarding the suspect in the phone box at the time of the Covent Garden explosion.

Dexter smiled.

'Well, I'd say it's a long shot . . . unless she happens to smoke Kool cigarettes as well!'

'*What*?' Jane's face completely drained of colour.

'We believe that the female suspect connected to the bomber smoked a brand of menthol cigarettes called "Kool" . . . We recovered two stubs from the phone box, with lipstick on them. According to the witness the suspect was smoking and was also wearing leather gloves.' Dexter laughed. 'Incredible really . . . she was able to describe a headscarf and gloves, but not her bloody face!'

Jane felt as though she was suffocating, and swallowed hard as Dexter stood up. It was clear that she was very distressed.

'Natalie Wilde smokes menthol cigarettes, and I've seen the packet . . . they're called "Kool" . . .'

'Jesus *Christ*!'

Dexter walked over to the drinks cabinet and poured two glasses of whisky before returning to sit down next to Jane.

'Here you go . . . drink this. You look like you're going to faint.'

Jane's hand was shaking as she took the glass and gulped from it. Tears began to stream down her face.

'Listen, sweetheart,' said Dexter. 'I want you to take your time and give me a blow-by-blow account of how you met this woman. Start from the beginning and take me right up to the point you found the scarf. You didn't take it, did you?'

'No. I made an excuse and left her flat. I said I was going to my parents' and that I would call to say if I could get back to see her later. She wanted to go out to a pub this evening.'

Dexter went into the bedroom and came out with a notepad and pencil, which he put down on the coffee table in front her.

'I'm going to have a quick shower, and put some clothes on. You just calm down and sip your whisky, then we'll talk everything through . . . all right?' Dexter hesitated, then rubbed his head.

'You know, just in case you may have made her suspicious, why don't you give her a quick call now and say you got held up at your parents'? Make some excuse.'

Jane nodded, and Dexter gave her a gentle, affectionate, pat on her head. He went into his bathroom and shut the door, letting out a long, deep, sigh.

'Jesus Christ Almighty . . .' he said quietly under his breath, as he turned on the shower. He was so stunned by Jane's revelation that he forgot to take off his tracksuit bottoms and swore as the jets of water soaked them.

Jane had to really talk herself into making the phone call, but it was easier without Dexter there. She dialled the number and waited as the phone rang a couple of times before Natalie picked it up.

'Hello, it's me . . . Jane. I'm just ringing to say thank you so much for lunch, and for the bolero . . . it's perfect. I'm sorry not have been able to get back to you earlier, but I had quite a time sorting out my parents' luggage.'

'I tried to call you at your flat,' Natalie said, and Jane had to think fast.

'I'm still at their flat. I didn't realise how much I'd had to drink, and got really worried that I might be stopped . . . and being a police officer it would have been really embarrassing. So, I'm going to sleep here and go back home in the morning.'

'OK, well, let's talk during the week. Thanks for calling.'

Jane replaced the receiver, and went to sit back down on the sofa. Confident that Natalie had believed her, she began to make bullet points to describe everything about her interaction with Natalie.

By the time Dexter had showered and returned to sit next to her, she was much calmer. She found his closeness unnerving. He was wearing a loose T-shirt with white tracksuit bottoms, and he smelt of soap and shampoo. Dexter glanced over her notes then, as if he sensed that his closeness was making her feel uncomfortable, he stood up and poured some more whisky into their glasses. This time he added ice cubes.

'Did you phone her?'

'Yes . . . I said I was staying over at my parents'.'

'Good. So, DC Tennison, let's crack this. You need to go step by step. Then we'll either need to take this to HQ in the morning, or we go with the possibility it's all down to conjecture and coincidence.' He paused. 'That said, we've never released the information regarding the brand of the two cigarette stubs we recovered from the phone box . . . Let's go from the first time you met Natalie Wilde, up until this afternoon.'

Jane concentrated as she recounted how she had met Natalie at the hospital shortly after the bombing. She could recall exactly what they had said and that they had talked about being at Hendon training college. She described their first dinner at Fratelli's restaurant and the later cooking lesson at Natalie's flat in Belsize Park. Dexter listened intently and only interjected with reassurance, encouraging Jane to expand and give details about how long Natalie had said she had lived at her flat, and what the furnishing was like. When Jane admitted she had given the names of the officers she was working alongside, Dexter gave no hint of disapproval. But as she spoke more about the things she had discussed with Natalie, Jane felt increasingly alarmed.

After nearly two hours Jane had finished talking and Dexter had been brought up to date with everything to do with Natalie. He had made copious notes and had topped up their drinks again. Jane felt completely drained and was ashamed at how much she had divulged to Natalie, albeit innocently. Only that afternoon she had even told Natalie about their key witness, Daphne Millbank, dying.

'I didn't give her Daphne's name, but I did say she was an important witness.'

Dexter stood up and drained his glass.

'That might actually be advantageous. If she is who we think she is, and feeds the information to her ASU cohorts, then they will be feeling confident.'

Jane stood up and suddenly felt very dizzy and sick.

'I'm so sorry but I think I'm going to be –' She started retching and Dexter grabbed her by her arms and hurried her through his bedroom into the bathroom. Jane didn't quite make it close enough to the toilet bowl before she threw up into her hands and all over herself, falling to her knees to continue vomiting into the toilet bowl. She emptied her stomach of the lunch, the wine and the whisky, until she was heaving up bile. Her head felt like it was going to explode as she tried to stand back up on her feet.

'You sure it's all out of you?' Dexter said, holding a towel out towards her.

'Yes. I just feel dizzy.'

Dexter ran some water into the sink and rinsed out a cloth for Jane to wipe her face. He then suggested that she might want to have a shower, as her clothes were covered in sick. Jane leant on the edge of the sink as he turned on the shower.

'Get undressed and wash yourself down . . . I'll leave you something clean to wear afterwards. If you need me, just yell. I'll be right outside.'

'Thank you . . . I'm so sorry,' she whispered.

Jane took off her soiled shirt and put it in a basin of warm water to soak. Her skirt was even more stained, and she felt so faint that she left it on the floor as she removed her underwear to get into the shower. She used the 'soap on a rope' to wash, then shampooed her hair from a bottle in the shower tray. She was beginning to feel less dizzy, and stepped out of the shower to find a thick white bath towel on the heater and a smaller towel to wrap around her wet hair. When she was dry, she put on the oversized James Dean T-shirt that Dexter had left on the radiator for her. As she pulled on her knickers there was a knock on the door.

'You all right in there?'

'Yes, I'm just coming out . . .' she called. She spent another few minutes checking around the edge of the toilet and using the brush from the stand beside it to make sure it was clean. She took a deep breath and walked out.

Jane went through the bedroom and into the drawing room, where Dexter was sorting through his copious notes whilst eating a sandwich.

'There's a glass of iced tonic water on the table . . . always good to have after you've thrown up.'

'I'm so sorry. It was the whisky, on top of the wine I had at lunch.'

'No need to apologise. You've had a lot to deal with.'

Jane sipped the iced tonic water, and then remembered that her soiled shirt was still in the washbasin and, feeling very embarrassed, asked Dexter if she could have some washing powder so that she could rinse it out.

'Forget it. Sit down. I'll sort it for you.'

'No, really, I insist. I can hang it up to dry, or just take it home in a plastic bag.'

'Do you know what time it is?'

She had no idea. She had left her watch in the bathroom.

'Tennison, it's after midnight. I'm going to get a blanket and kip down here on the sofa . . . You can have my bed. You're in no fit state to drive.'

'No, I'll go home. I've got my car outside.'

'Just do as you're told . . . come on.' Dexter took her hand and drew her into the bedroom. He threw back the duvet and gestured for her to get into the big double bed.

'My hair's still wet.'

He shook his head and went over to the bedside table. He took out a hairdryer from the drawer and plugged it into the socket next to the bed.

'OK, dry your hair while I clean up in the bathroom.'

Jane stood in front of the bedroom mirror and, not having a brush, she ran her hands through her hair as she dried it. Dexter spent quite a while in the bathroom and she heard the toilet flushing a couple of times before he came out carrying her soiled skirt and her wet shirt.

'I'm going to put this on the boiler so it'll be dry by the morning.'

He came back into the bedroom just as she was about to climb into his bed.

'I don't know what to say . . .' she said softly.

'I think you've said more than enough for one night. You should really try to get some sleep. Tomorrow will be quite a day.'

'Do you think this is going to put my career in jeopardy? You know . . . if I've been disclosing information that I shouldn't have?'

He sat down beside her. 'At the moment it's just a lot of conjecture and suspicion. But you've been upfront about it all with me. Obviously, it will all have to be checked out; you might be wrong. On the other hand, if you are right and Natalie Wilde is a sleeper, then this is a big lead. Let's face it, right now, with no Daphne Millbank, we are nowhere near identifying the Covent Garden bomber.'

'Will Crowley investigate?'

'I would think so. You're going to have to be prepared for a lot of questions, and it's a slow process. His team won't want her tipped off that she's being investigated and she'll more than likely be under immediate surveillance. They'll have to be careful because her contacts could be close.'

He reached out and traced her face with his hand. Whether he instigated the kiss or Jane did, when his lips touched hers she didn't hold back and the next moment he moved onto the bed to lie beside her. She didn't want to let him go, even when he leaned up on his elbow and looked uncertainly into her face.

'You sure about this?'

'Yes, don't go . . . please.'

He cradled her in his arm and she buried her face in his neck, kissing him until he slowly drew up the James Dean T-shirt to kiss her breasts. He made love to her gently at first but then they became more passionate together and Dexter's obvious sexual experience resulted in explosive orgasms that made her feel as if she was flying. Eventually they lay still together. Dexter drew Jane close to him and she rested her head again in the crook of his shoulder.

'Well, that was unexpected . . . but very nice,' he said, softly kissing the top of her head.

'Tell me about you,' she said.

'I already have . . . There's not much more than what you already know.'

'What does it feel like when you have to defuse a bomb?'

'Well, that part you get used to . . . it's what you've been trained to do. The worst is always what we call the "long walk" . . . when you have to slowly approach the bomb . . . that's when your heart beats faster. You don't know if it's been booby-trapped or whether it's going to explode in your face before you get to it . . . that's always the worst part. I suppose it must be a bit like the bridegroom waiting at the altar, unsure if the bride's going to turn up!'

'It's the bride who has to do the long walk, not the groom,' Jane replied, but Dexter was silent.

She put her hand on his chest and felt the steady rhythm of his breathing, knowing that he was asleep. She didn't want to move and all the tension and paranoia she had felt that afternoon and evening evaporated. She was safe, cushioned by Dexter's warmth, and she quickly fell into a deep, dreamless sleep.

Dexter had already showered and dressed by the time she woke up. He sat next to her on the edge of the bed, waking her with a start. She smiled and closed her eyes again.

'There's coffee brewing . . . Your shirt's dry, but your skirt stinks. If I were you I'd make a quick detour to your flat to get some clean clothes, then drive to Scotland Yard. You did say you had your car here?'

'Yes . . .' She opened her eyes again. 'Are you leaving?'

'Yeah. I want to get to Crowley and set up the meeting, then go over everything before you get there.'

Jane sat up, still feeling rather disorientated. 'What time is it?'

'Six thirty. Just shut the front door after you when you leave. I'll see you at Crowley's office about nine.'

Dexter was gone before Jane had time to say anything. She was disappointed at his hasty exit, but forced herself to do exactly what he had asked of her. She dressed in her less-than-fragrant clothes, and then drank half a cup of coffee before leaving his flat. Jane took Dexter's James Dean T-shirt with her so that she could wash and return it, but she also liked having something of his. As the T-shirt lay on the passenger seat beside her it was a reminder, not only of their lengthy discussion about Natalie Wilde, but also of their passionate lovemaking. All Jane could think about was being safely wrapped in his arms again, but as she got closer to home she began to feel very nervous. She knew that the meeting with Crowley was going to be one of the most difficult experiences she had faced.

Jane dressed in clean clothes and was ready to leave when the phone rang. She hoped it might be Dexter, but it was DCI Church.

'Jane, it's Church. I know you tried to reach me through the station last night, but when I called you back there was no reply.'

'I'm sorry. I just needed to talk something through with you . . .'

'I know, Dexter's already told me. I'll collect you in about fifteen minutes and drive you to HQ. We're setting up a big meeting in Crowley's office and I just thought you might need some support. It's important that you handle yourself well. We'll all be looking out for you, Jane, so just stay calm . . . and check that it's me before you come down to your front door, all right?'

'Yes, thank you . . . I'll be ready and waiting, sir.'

Jane replaced the receiver, and looked at her watch. It was still only eight thirty and DCI Church's call, instead of reassuring her, had made her stomach churn. She had only had a few gulps of coffee at Dexter's flat earlier, and after being sick the night before she was worried that she might not be able to focus on an empty stomach. She quickly made herself two slices of plain toast and swallowed down a couple of aspirins with a glass of milk. She went into the bathroom and cleaned her teeth, checking her clean, pressed, white shirt and black slimline pencil skirt to make sure they were in order. By the time she had put on her jacket and picked up her handbag and briefcase, the doorbell rang.

Jane peered through her bedroom window and saw DCI Church standing beside his car. She took a deep breath and walked out into the hallway, locking her front door and heading down the stairs. She opened the main front door and Church turned to give her a warm smile, waiting as she closed the door behind her.

'OK, let's go . . .' he said, as she climbed into the passenger seat beside him.

Church started the engine and gave her a sidelong glance.

'You OK?'

'Yes. I'm fine, thank you.'

'Dexter took care of you, did he?'

She blushed and hated the fact that she wasn't able to disguise it. She stared ahead.

'Yes, he did.'

'It's not going to be easy this morning. Just answer everything clearly, and don't think you have to make any excuses. We just need to know the facts. Don't embroider anything, just tell it straight down the line.'

'I will.'

'Don't let Crowley unnerve you. All you have to realise is that he'll be keen to establish whether or not we might have a breakthrough in Natalie Wilde. So be confident about your suspicions, and don't worry that you may have fucked up.'

Jane couldn't help laughing, and shook her head. 'You certainly know how to make a girl feel reassured! I'm really worried that this might have damaged my future career.'

'No way. If you're proved right this could be your ticket to the Flying Squad,' he said, smiling encouragingly.

'I'm just very concerned after the Pearl situation, and now this . . .'

He tapped her arm. 'Listen, Crowley's position on the Bomb Squad is in jeopardy unless he gets results. Your mistakes could reflect badly on him, but if Natalie leads us to the ASU and arrests are made, cock-ups can be overlooked.'

Jane tried to relax, which was exactly what DCI Church had intended.

What he didn't add was that she was going to be under enormous pressure about having unwittingly disclosed information that could have placed officers at risk. Jane's career in the CID could very well be over – and if this was yet another example of her unprofessionalism he would aid Crowley in kicking her out.

CHAPTER EIGHTEEN

Arriving at Scotland Yard Jane left Church and went straight to DCI Crowley's office. He invited her to take a seat and walked over to a trolley with a hot water urn on it and five or six dirty cups alongside a few clean ones.

'Water's a bit tepid but is instant coffee all right for you? All the tea's gone now.'

'Yes, thank you . . . milk and no sugar, please.' She realised from his remark and the dirty cups that he must have had an earlier meeting. It had probably been about her cock-up.

Crowley poured a coffee, placed it on the table in front of her, then sat down at his desk before opening a notebook and picking up his pen.

'Right, WDC Tennison . . . let's go over everything from the moment you met Natalie Wilde in the hospital. This time really concentrate on everything she said or asked.'

'I told DS Dexter everything. Has he not spoken with you?'

'Yes, and I made notes.' He tapped the book with his pen. 'But under the circumstances you may have been hesitant with Dexter about exactly how much information Wilde was able to get from you . . . so I want to go over everything again in fine detail.'

Jane wondered what he meant by 'under the circumstances'. Was he implying he knew she had spent the night at Dexter's flat, or simply the fact she had been distraught about the whole situation? Crowley opened a packet of Player's cigarettes. He lit one, then offered the pack to Jane, who shook her head.

'I don't smoke, sir.'

Again, Jane recounted meeting Natalie at the hospital. She explained that it had taken a moment for her to recognise Natalie from their Hendon days. Jane spoke slowly, trying to remember each time she had met Natalie, the conversations they had had and any probing questions she had asked. Then something struck Jane as unusual.

'There is something about the first time we met at the hospital, but I'm not sure if it's relevant.'

'I'll be the judge of that, Tennison . . . so come on, spit it out.'

'At the hospital, Natalie said she was visiting a friend who'd just had a baby, but she wasn't carrying any flowers, chocolates or any kind of gift. She didn't even say if it was a boy or girl.'

Crowley was taking notes as Jane spoke. 'Good. Anything else strange about that first meeting with her?'

Jane thought about what she'd learned on the Dip Squad. 'I remember she bumped into me on the same floor that Daphne was on and asked me what I was doing at the hospital . . . but the maternity ward is on the ground floor. She distracted me by bumping into me so that I didn't notice she wasn't in the right place.'

'If she'd seen the paper then she'd know you had been at Covent Garden . . . so the bump was probably a deliberate ploy. Anything else?'

'Yes, she said she was interested in finding out what all our old Hendon classmates were doing now.'

'What's strange about that?'

'She's never once asked me about them since then. She was more interested in me and what I was doing, but I just didn't see it as suspicious at the time.'

Crowley moved on and asked Jane when she next saw Natalie.

'It was at an Italian restaurant called Fratelli's.'

'Did you drink much?'

'A couple of glasses of wine . . . Why?'

'Alcohol loosens the tongue, Tennison. Did you say anything about Daphne Millbank or the phone-box witness?'

Jane was upset by his remark. 'I wasn't drunk, sir, it was a friendly meal together and I never discussed my work at all.'

Crowley asked her about the next meeting with Natalie. Jane told him it was at Natalie's flat in Belsize Park and she had said she rented it, but the bank gave her a housing allowance.

'I'd gone there because Natalie said she'd give me a cooking lesson.'

'Makes a change from cooking up bombs, I suppose,' Crowley said flippantly.

Jane felt his remark was uncalled for, but kept her head down as she recounted their discussions about her relationship with Michael, the charge nurse, and DS Dexter and DCI Church.

'So you gave her the names and ranks of officers you were working with?'

'No,' said Jane, embarassed. 'I don't think so. It was just a flippant conversation about who I found attractive . . .'

Crowley tapped the table with his pen, and shook his head. 'So, inadvertently, or any way you like to describe it, you were giving away confidential details and discussing officers involved in a major investigation.'

Jane nodded, her head down, as Crowley looked at his notebook and continued, 'She then encouraged you to accompany her to find a dress at a hire company she knew.'

'Yes. When I got home I remembered that she hadn't given me the address, but when I called her she wasn't at home. She called me later the next day to suggest we meet up in a café in Sloane Square before going to the dress-hire venue together. So, the following evening, after I finished work, I met her.'

'Did she know what you were hiring a dress for?'

'Yes, the Good Friday Ball . . .' As she spoke Jane realised the importance of what she'd given away to Natalie.

'And did you tell her the location of the ball?'

Jane couldn't speak, she felt so ashamed, just nodded, but was surprised Crowley didn't shout at her.

'Did she ever come to your address?'

'No . . . There was one possible Irish connection, which at the time I didn't register. Some of the clients who hired dresses were debutantes, and during the hunting season some clients would even come from Ireland for the hunt balls.'

'Did Wilde tell you she had been in Ireland?'

'No, she didn't. But I presumed she must have hired a dress from Mrs Hunt at some point as she seemed to know her quite well.'

'Did it never occur to you that Natalie was being over helpful . . . especially as you hadn't seen her since being at Hendon in 1972?'

'No, sir.'

'Well, it's clear to me that she may have had you over big time. She weaselled her way back into your life and slowly tapped you for information. As a result you may not only have put yourself at risk, but your colleagues and the public. We don't know for certain yet if Natalie is part of an IRA ASU, but from what you have just told me I'd say it's highly probable.'

Jane felt awful; there was nothing she could say, She knew he was right. She had messed up terribly and was now terrified her career in the police could be over. As Crowley continued to question Jane her head began to throb. She told him about the next meeting, their lunch yesterday, which she realised had again been instigated by Natalie. She remembered with a lurch in her stomach that they'd talked – over yet more wine – about her dinner date with Michael, and about the emergency call from the hospital regarding Daphne Millbank. She could not look at Crowley as she admitted she'd told Natalie that an important patient had died and that Natalie had seemed interested in this news.

'Did this not trigger your suspicions about her?'

'Not directly . . . it was only when I was left alone in her bedroom that I accidentally came across the scarf.'

'Does she know you've seen it?'

'No. I made an excuse to leave when I remembered the description the witness who saw the woman in the phone box had given.

Although I knew about the headscarf, I didn't know that two Kool cigarette stubs had been found in the phone box until DS Dexter told me. Natalie smokes that brand.'

'Yes, yes . . . we've already discussed that. I'm concerned that she may have been aware of what you found.'

'No, she wasn't. I said when I left that I would hopefully be back later. I told her that my parents were leaving for Harwich to embark on a cruise and I had to help them.'

'How did you explain about your parents?'

'I pretended to make a phone call to them whilst she was in the kitchen.'

Crowley nodded as she told him again the events of the previous evening, and about the phone call she'd made from Dexter's flat.

'What did you tell her?'

'That I was staying over at my parents' flat because I had drunk too much wine and I didn't want to drive all the way back to Belsize Park.'

Crowley lit another cigarette and inhaled deeply.

'I'm sorry if this seems to be pedantic of me, but I need you to go over everything you've told me again. You've admitted that you were drinking on virtually every occasion you met with Natalie Wilde. As a result, you divulged information about the officers investigating the Covent Garden bombing, and you gave her details that would allow her to conclude that our star witness was deceased.'

Jane was close to tears, but Crowley got up and stood behind her.

'Tennison, listen to me. You're still inexperienced and Natalie Wilde, if she is a sleeper, will undoubtedly have been coached. I can't condone or make excuses for your unprofessional conduct . . . It might have severe repercussions for your future with the CID. That said . . .'

He rested both of his hands on her shoulders and they felt like dead weights.

'If we find evidence that Natalie Wilde was involved in, or detonated the Covent Garden bomb, she could lead us to the IRA unit
she is working with. Your reacquaintance with Natalie could be
our first major step towards finding the bomber and ASU. On the
other hand, it might just be a wild goose chase. If that's the case,
there's nothing for you to worry about.'

Crowley squeezed her shoulders, then returned to his seat. Jane
was not comforted by his encouragement because he had hinted
at repercussions and if things fell apart she was certain he would
make her the scapegoat and put her back in uniform.

There was a knock on the door. DCI Church entered and said
they were ready in the conference room. Jane remained seated
as Crowley picked up his notebook and pen and started to walk
towards the door.

'Shall I wait here until your meeting's over, sir?'

'No, Tennison, you're very much a part of it. Come along. And
don't look so worried . . . I'll be doing the talking.'

Jane was glad to have DCI Church with her, but as they entered
the conference room she felt overwhelmed with nerves. There were
several men sitting around an oval table, and they all fell silent as
she walked in. Crowley guided her towards a vacant chair and drew
it out as he gestured towards Dexter.

'You obviously know DS Alan Dexter and DS Lawrence from
forensics . . . Next to him is Commander Gregson, head of the
Bomb Squad, a representative from the Intelligence services, Mr
Quick from the Home Office, and Chief Superintendent Jones from
Special Branch.'

Jane could hardly take in the introductions, but kept nodding
politely. Only DS Lawrence acknowledged her with a small smile.
Church sat in a chair further round the table and Crowley sat next
to Jane.

'Right, let's get moving on this . . .' Crowley said and gestured to
Jane with the palm of his hand. 'This is WDC Tennison, who came

forward with information that may be important to our investigation concerning the Covent Garden bombing and the IRA Active Service Unit responsible. So, let me make it clear that this entire discussion is, and must remain, highly confidential, until we are ready to take an agreed and appropriate course of action. I assume DS Dexter has already briefed you concerning Natalie Wilde and her association with WDC Tennison?' He paused while everyone in the room nodded.

'It's possible Wilde is an IRA sleeper and deliberately rekindled her friendship with Tennison to surreptitiously gain information about our investigation. She may also be the woman seen in the telephone box close to Covent Garden just before the bomb exploded. If she is, then she could lead us directly, not only to the bomber, but to the whole ASU. We need to check out her background and movements to be certain. If she is a sleeper she will be wary of anything untoward. One slip-up could leave us with nothing. Let me reiterate, we have to move with extreme caution . . . With that in mind, I have put together a plan of action.'

Crowley removed some sheets of paper from a file marked 'Highly Confidential' and handed them out to everyone in the room apart from Jane. She glanced discreetly towards Dexter but he was lighting up one of his cigars. The intelligence officer sitting next to her asked if he could get her a coffee and indicated that there were some doughnuts on the trolley if she was hungry. He refilled his own cup as Crowley began to go through the notes he had handed out.

'First on the agenda is to get a surveillance photograph of our suspect . . .'

Jane nervously raised her hand. 'You could contact training school, sir . . . they may still have her photo from when she joined the police.'

There were a few nods of approval at her suggestion but Crowley dismissed it.

'We need an up-to-date photograph. To that end I will be using DCI Church's Dip Squad, who are highly skilled in surveillance operations. Detectives on the Bomb Squad will compile a full intelligence docket on Wilde's background, covering family history, current and previous employment and places of residence. Special Branch and the Intelligence services will liaise with their counterparts in Northern Ireland to see if Wilde has connections over there.'

The Commander asked if they knew where Wilde was currently living as her exact address didn't appear on the action plan.

'Tennison has been to the flat and will draw up a layout of the premises after the meeting,' Crowley remarked in an attempt to deflect the question and was about to continue when Jane spoke up.

'It's a small basement flat in a four-storey block, sir. She's lived there for five years. There's one bedroom, kitchen, garden and . . .'

The Commander frowned. 'I'm not interested in the layout right now . . . What's the street and number?'

'It's in Belsize Avenue, number forty-four, the basement.'

Crowley moved on to the discovery of the scarf.

'We will be asking Hermès about the different scarf designs they sell, and getting some brochures and photographs to show our phone-box witness so she can pick out the one she saw the woman wearing.'

The Commander nodded his approval at this idea and Crowley asked Lawrence to give a forensic update.

'As expected, we recovered a large number of prints from the public phone box which were submitted to Fingerprint Bureau here at the Yard. Twenty officers from FB One, Two and Three have been working on them day and night . . . even the Senior Fingerprint Officers have been helping. We've had several hits but only to small-time criminals, and none with any IRA or Irish connections. Some of the prints are still unidentified and may belong to people without a criminal record.'

Dexter added, 'I did a CRO check on the name Natalie Wilde and she's never been arrested. Also, the witness did say the woman in the phone box was wearing gloves.'

Lawrence looked at Dexter, 'Well, when Wilde is arrested her prints can be taken for comparison against the outstanding marks, or we could do a covert entry to her flat to seize something we can examine for her prints.'

Crowley shook his head, 'That's a bit risky just now, I'd rather do some surveillance on the premises first.'

Lawrence nodded. 'If she puts a dustbin out we could try to get a discarded envelope or something from the contents. Also, if she took a glove off to put a coin in the box we might get a result. On a previous investigation with WDC Tennison we examined the coins from a call box and discovered the print of a woman who was later charged with murder. But sadly, without anything to match what we do have, it's likely to be a waste of time.'

Jane raised her arm and everyone turned to look at her.

'What about the two "Kool" menthol cigarette butts that were discovered in the phone box?'

'I know you told DS Dexter Miss Wilde smokes the same brand, but that is not really incriminating evidence.'

'I just thought that opening a cigarette pack, and taking out a cigarette is quite cumbersome if you are wearing gloves . . . I was wondering whether it was possible that she may have taken off a glove to light a cigarette?'

Lawrence interjected. 'As everyone probably knows, fingerprints are left due to sweat, oil and grease on the hands. Heat from a cigarette usually destroys those marks, but it was a good point, Jane, and worth a try.'

Crowley snapped, eager to get on. 'This operation has to be totally covert . . . if Wilde gets so much as a sniff we're on to her we could lose our only hope of tracing the bombers.'

Jane held up her hand again and he glared at her impatiently.

'Then what about the training school at Hendon?' she asked. 'Sir . . . all officers have their fingerprints taken the day they join.'

It was so simple that they had all overlooked it. Dexter gave a slow handclap which annoyed Crowley, but he instructed Lawrence to get onto it immediately.

'I don't need to remind you all that it's imperative we tread carefully so we don't spook our target. Take it slowly and make sure that all enquiries are tight and secure. WDC Tennison had a concerned interest in Daphne Millbank, and rekindled a friendship with someone who had been at Hendon with her. In her naivety, she believed Natalie Wilde to be a good and honest person.'

Jane felt her cheeks flush and was embarrassed by Crowley's reference to her 'naivety', which had made everyone glance in her direction, apart from the man from the Home Office, who did not seem all that keen on Crowley.

'She may have been duped, DCI Crowley,' Mr Quick said, 'but to her credit she did come forward to you with her suspicions. If it wasn't for WDC Tennison then we wouldn't be sitting here now.'

'And that is why I am taking her concerns seriously, Mr Quick. We know from experience how IRA sleepers operate and we need to work on the premise that Natalie Wilde deliberately set out to befriend Jane as a source of information. Thank you all for coming in at such short notice and now that we have the full picture we can get started.'

The room filled with the sound of scraping chairs as everyone stood up. Jane remained seated, her heart pounding as everyone else left the room.

Two hours later the team had acquired a Hermès catalogue of all the scarf designs that depicted animals. They were sold at Harrods, Liberty and from the Hermès store in Bond Street. Jane sat in Crowley's office leafing through the catalogue, but found it off-putting that he kept leaning over her shoulder asking if she'd 'seen the scarf yet'. She was determined to take her time and eventually held up the page showing the identical scarf she had seen at Natalie Wilde's home. Crowley instructed one of his officers to show the catalogue to the witness who had seen the woman in the phone box, hoping she'd pick the same scarf as Jane.

When the officer left the room, Crowley sat in front of Jane and leaned forward. 'Just a while longer and you'll be free to go. I didn't mention it earlier in our private meeting or in the conference room, but I believe you gave Natalie Wilde the date and venue for the Good Friday bash?'

'Yes, sir, but it was only in passing. You don't think . . .'

'Who knows, Tennison? Anything is possible if she's really part of an IRA cell. Be assured I will take precautions. Our priority right now is that to get her to lead us to the bastards who killed innocent people at Covent Garden.'

DCI Church found Jane in the canteen, morosely contemplating a plate of inedible cottage pie and a glass of milk.

'Well, the story Natalie told you about working at NatWest was true, at least.' He glanced at his notebook. 'Head office says she's been employed by them for four years and resides at 44 Belsize Avenue. She's worked in two of their London branches and sounds, to all intents and purposes, like a diligent and trustworthy employee.'

'Perhaps she fooled everyone there as well,' Jane said quietly in an effort to show she was not the only person Natalie deceived.

'Seems so, but unlike you, Jane . . . they're not detectives. Crowley has suggested you get off home, so I can run you back there when you've finished your lunch.'

'I have . . . I'm not hungry.'

'Gimme ten minutes. I have to make a couple of phone calls, then I'll see you outside reception.'

Jane took her plate and scraped the cottage pie into the rubbish bin. She returned to the table to clear her still full milk glass when

Dexter walked in. He walked over to the coffee and tea section and gestured to her to see if she wanted anything. Jane shook her head.

She sat down and waited for him to join her with his coffee. Dexter nodded towards her untouched glass of milk.

'That for your hangover?'

'I don't have one. But I could do with another drink. I think Crowley would like to see me back in uniform directing traffic.'

'I doubt that . . . If it wasn't for you we'd not have much going for us.'

'What did you tell the people in the conference room before I came in?'

'Not much, really, kept it simple, recounted what you told me and that you may have been used by Natalie Wilde. I also told them you informed me and Crowley as soon as you became suspicious of her.'

'Thanks. Crowley didn't tell them much of the detail of my private conversation with him.'

'That's because he's worried about how he'll come out of it all. When a junior officer screws up it often reflects on their superior, so he wouldn't want to have said too much. After all, he was the one who decided you should work under his supervision.'

'They checked out that she worked at the NatWest, and she does . . . so maybe I'm wrong about her.'

'Yeah, but that's part of a "sleeper's" agenda, to look totally legitimate and blend in with society, so as not to raise any flags. If you're right about Natalie, and the evidence *is* there, then we'll all come up smelling of roses . . . it's just the way it works round here, so don't beat yourself up about it.'

'Crowley really put me through it . . . I must say, you were pretty fast off the mark telling him everything I told you.'

'What did you expect?'

'Maybe to give me some space when I got here? But it felt like an interrogation. He made me repeat everything again and again.

He said that "under the circumstances" I might not have told you everything . . . What did he mean by that?'

'I dunno. I didn't tell him you spent the night in my bed, if that's what you're implying.' Dexter sounded evasive.

That whole day, she realised, he hadn't shown the slightest sign of affection towards her – not even when he'd woken her up. She wasn't convinced and couldn't look at him. It felt as if their night together had never occurred.

'I have to go,' she said. 'DCI Church is taking me home.'

'OK . . . you'll obviously be kept informed about any developments, if not from me then I'm sure Jimmy will take care of you.'

Jane stood up and picked up her handbag from beside her chair.

'Are you all right about last night?' he asked, quietly.

'Yes . . . I'll get your T-shirt washed and back to you.'

'Keep it. Jane, are you –'

'I'd better go down to reception,' she interrupted, unable to look at him. 'I suppose I'll see you when I see you.'

'You know where I am if you need me.'

'Yes, I do . . . bye for now.'

Jane walked away feeling deeply depressed and humiliated. It was obvious she was nothing more to Dexter than a one-night stand.

Dexter finished his coffee and lit a cigar. He knew he should have been more caring towards her but he didn't want to encourage something between them. Although he had to admit the sex had been good.

Mrs Eileen Douglas lived in a pleasant second-floor flat in Aldwych, furnished with good antiques and some ornate oil paintings. A widow in her late fifties, articulate and with an aristocratic accent, she had obviously, at one time, been more affluent, judging by the contents of the flat.

She had begun to get used to the sight of police officers in her home since the bombing at Covent Garden. Even though she'd given a full statement about what she had seen, they always seemed to be back with more questions. Still, she was always very accommodating when the officers arrived at her flat, explaining again that she didn't have her own telephone, and that she'd wanted to use the phone box to ask a friend to meet her in Covent Garden.

This time one of the policemen handed her a Hermès catalogue and asked her to find the scarf she'd seen. She sat in a large wing-backed chair, turning over one glossy page after another. She peered at the officers over her half-moon glasses.

'Well, now I do feel really rather stupid. I was so certain the scarf had a pattern with red setters because I knew someone who had a pair of them. Such a lovely red-brown colour . . . but I see that I was wrong. I do apologise, but this is the scarf here. You see the similarity of the colours? But they're horses, not dogs. I distinctly recall that golden colour around which I thought was some kind of ribbon, but of course they're horseshoes. Oh – and I remembered another thing about the leather gloves the woman in the phone box wore . . . I think they may have been Burberry as I recall they were turned slightly over at the wrist revealing the Burberry check . . . but I'm not certain.'

Eileen had picked out the same scarf as Jane. By the time the information reached Crowley, Jane had already left the Yard.

On the journey back to her flat Jane had been quiet, and Church hadn't attempted to make conversation. It was not until they were parked that he stopped her from getting out of the car.

'You are to remain at home until we contact you. But I don't want you thinking that this whole situation is going to be detrimental to your career. So, don't think –'

'Don't think what?' Jane snapped, interrupting him.

Church was taken aback by her tone. She was about to get out of the car when she turned angrily to him.

'I suppose it will be common knowledge by now that DS Dexter shagged me, and it will be round the whole Yard. I don't believe "nothing detrimental" will happen . . . I know my career is screwed, in the literal sense. "Stay at home, you've done enough damage, Tennison".'

'You're wrong.'

'You think I'm stupid? Well, obviously I am with regard to bloody Natalie Wilde, never mind the Regina Hernandez situation. How do you think I'm feeling about it, DCI Church? Or have you brought me back home for a one-night stand as well?' Jane was becoming hysterical. Church grabbed her shoulder hard and shook her.

'Shut it! I mean it, Jane. You need to be careful about making any judgements. We're all protecting you. If we do get a result and can prove that Natalie Wilde is the connection it will be because of you and your suspicions. You recognised the scarf and were wise enough not to confront her. No one, and I mean not one officer, is not looking out for you . . . that includes me. Any sexual encounter you had with DS Dexter is not public knowledge, and I can guarantee it will remain private.'

Jane bowed her head.

'I'm sorry I shook you . . . You heard Crowley at the meeting, he's gathering a big team of officers and using some of the Dip Squad to assist. All this is entirely down to your information. We did have a static observation on your flat, but from now on it will be round-the-clock protection. You are of vital importance, Jane. You need to stay in your flat and wait for us to contact you.'

Church patted her awkwardly on the shoulder. She apologised, and then got out of the car. Church waited until she was inside the main front door and gave a quick wave of acknowledgement to the two SPG men on duty outside her building before driving off. Given her present state, he made no mention that they had already been inside and double-checked that her flat was safe.

CHAPTER NINETEEN

By mid-morning Stanley had arranged a suitable observation point in a second-floor flat opposite Natalie Wilde's home. The owner, a professional photographer, had agreed to allow his flat to be used as he was travelling to the Bahamas to shoot a commercial. He was inquisitive about why the police wanted to use his flat, and Stanley told him there had been a spate of daylight robberies in the street and he would be compensated for the use of his flat and calls made on his telephone. The owner told Stanley he would be back in a week and left.

An observation point, also manned by Dip Squad officers, had been set up opposite the NatWest branch where Natalie worked. Stanley used the landline to call the team and give them the address and phone number of his observation point. He asked one of them to make enquiries with the letting agent about when Natalie Wilde moved in and how long the lease was for. He had not made enquiries with any of the neighbours living either side of Natalie's rented flat, or in the flats above the basement, in case this alerted Natalie to their surveillance. It was also possible that Natalie's contacts could be living close by.

A short while later Stanley received a call from the office about Wilde's flat. He was informed that it was fully furnished and had only been rented in the past two months, for a six-month period, with the option to extend the lease. As Wilde had not made any contact regarding the extension of the lease it was possible it might become vacant. It would seem Natalie had lied to Jane about how long she had lived in and rented the premises.

DCI Church rang Jane to let her know that the observation on Natalie was up and running and she was currently at work.

'She lied to you about how long she's lived in that flat,' he added. 'And the phone-box witness has identified the same Hermès scarf that you did. Says she was mistaken about it being dogs on it. She also mentioned the suspect might have been wearing designer gloves and we wondered if you had seen –'

'Were they Burberry?' asked Jane. 'At Fratelli's, Natalie had a pair of Burberry gloves . . . she said a boyfriend gave them to her at Christmas.'

'Yes, that corroborates our other witness's description. The gloves and scarf are now crucial evidence, Jane, and you are a witness to the fact even if Natalie throws them away before we get to her. Things are moving along fast now. Are you all right?'

'Yes, I'm fine . . . But being at home with nothing to do is hardly making the time pass.'

'Just sit tight and keep calm. I will update you if and when there are any further developments. We're taking it slowly in case she gets wind that we're onto her.'

Jane replaced the receiver and went over to the ironing board. She slowly ironed Dexter's clean T-shirt and folded it neatly, feeling mixed emotions about everything that had happened. She had really liked Natalie and enjoyed her company. She'd thought she'd at last found someone she could talk to and share her feelings with. She felt bad about poor Pearl and her stolen books, but it looked as if Natalie had stolen Jane's trust. It hurt her deeply that she could have been taken in by someone so easily. She was now beginning to hate Natalie for all the lies and, above all, for the terrible devastation and loss of life caused by the bomb at Covent Garden.

Stanley was with a colleague at the window watching Natalie's flat for visitors when, at one o'clock, he received a call from the other OP that Wilde had left the bank and travelled to North London, stopping at a supermarket. It didn't look like she was planning on returning to the office. Although she had left work early, the trip to the shops suggested she would return home. A short while later she got out of a taxi, carrying a bag full of groceries, and went into her flat.

There was a light knock on the door as DS Maynard waited to be let in to relieve the officer who was with Stanley. Maynard removed his duffel coat and put down a black holdall. He sat down in the easy chair by the window. There was a small telescope set up, along-side a camera. Stanley's roll-up cigarette stubs were piled high in an ashtray next to a dirty cup and saucer. Maynard pulled out a flask of tea and some sandwiches from his holdall, which he shared with Stanley. As they both settled down to watch Natalie's flat, the phone rang with the information that Natalie had gone home sick from work. She'd said she had flu, and that she wouldn't be in tomorrow.

Hours later, Natalie was still indoors, no one had visited her and it seemed she wasn't going out. Stanley had fallen asleep in the armchair and was snoring. Maynard nudged him and suggested he get off home for some kip. Stanley said he'd sleep in the flat-owner's bedroom and told Maynard to wake him if anything happened, but Natalie remained in her flat all night.

The following morning Blondie Dunston arrived to take over the surveillance from Maynard.

'It's quarter to nine so it doesn't look like she's going to work,' Maynard said, putting on his duffel coat.

Blondie suddenly clocked Natalie leaving her flat. 'Target's on the move, Sarge.'

'Shit. Stanley's in the bedroom, go and wake him. I'll stick with Natalie and call him on the radio with my location. You stay here and keep eyeball on Wilde's flat.' Maynard grabbed a covert radio and left.

Natalie walked to Hampstead underground station and bought a morning paper from the news-stand. Maynard stayed a short dis-tance behind her and radioed his location so Stanley could join him. Stanley was already out of the flat and quickly caught up with

Maynard. They agreed that it was best for them to split up but keep in radio contact, in case she saw them together and sussed they were Old Bill. Stanley said he'd follow Natalie first for a while and then call in Maynard to take over so as not to blow their cover.

Stanley had Natalie in sight as she boarded the southbound Northern Line. He kept his distance and got on the carriage behind the one she was in. Maynard was in the carriage behind Stanley. The train was busy as it was still the rush hour, but Stanley was able to position himself so he could see Natalie through the adjoining carriage window. She was looking around and he wondered if she was aware she was being followed. As the train stopped at Tottenham Court Road, Natalie jumped off at the last second, just before the doors closed. Stanley was quick to react and just managed to get off himself. He breathed a sigh of relief when she didn't turn round and see him. Perhaps she was just being surveillance conscious and wasn't aware she was being followed.

Stanley looked for Maynard, but he hadn't got off the train in time.

Stanley followed Natalie out of the station into Oxford Street. Shoppers and commuters thronged the street, and Natalie weaved in and out of his sight as she walked westwards. She's well-trained, he thought to himself, but she didn't look back, which made him think she was carrying out a standard IRA anti-surveillance routine rather than actively trying to lose a tail. He radioed Blondie and said he needed backup.

Just then, Stanley's radio crackled into life. Maynard had just surfaced at Leicester Square.

'Target's heading on foot towards Oxford Circus,' Stanley told him. 'Get a cab.'

Maynard hailed a cab. When he got to Oxford Circus, he spotted Natalie on the other side of the street. He paid off the cab and took over the tail from Stanley, following her as she continued down Oxford Street.

'She's outside Selfridges. Have you got eyeball?' he radioed to Stanley.

'Not yet . . . I'll make contact as soon as I see her.' Stanley picked up his pace as Maynard came back on the radio.

'She's gone into Selfridges.'

Stanley's stomach sank as he radioed back. 'Shit. The IRA planted a bomb there last August, in the south-east corner . . . Don't lose her, Maynard!'

On that occasion, the IRA had given a coded call to the press, the store had been evacuated and the bomb diffused by Dexter. Now, both officers were becoming very tense. There were large crowds of shoppers milling around. If their target was planting a bomb, they needed to contact the store's security services – but first they needed to find Natalie. Stanley eased past the wandering shoppers, but there were so many different departments . . . He was still on the ground floor, passing the make-up and perfume counters, when he caught sight of Natalie's reflection in one of the mirrors. She was moving fast.

'Target eyeballed . . . she's heading towards the south-west corner exit.'

Stanley picked up his pace, shoving shoppers aside, and ran out to the street. Maynard joined him and they looked around, desperately trying to sight Natalie. They breathed a sigh of relief when Blondie's voice came over the radio saying he had eyeball on Natalie and she was heading down into Marble Arch underground station. They sprinted across the road, weaving in and out of the traffic, then down the stairs and escalator, splitting up to check both the east-and west bound platforms, but Natalie was gone. They had lost her. All three of them were gasping and Stanley had to bend over to catch his breath.

'Christ! Do you think she planted a fuckin' bomb?' Blondie asked.

Maynard shook his head. 'No, I didn't lose sight of her in Selfridges. She was only carrying a shoulder bag and it never moved from her shoulder. If she didn't know she was being tailed, she certainly made it tough for us to follow her.'

Stanley banged his fist against the underground map on the wall. 'Fuck knows where she might get off or where she's going. Crowley's going to be livid when he finds out we lost her!'

It had been another long day for Jane. She'd cleared out the fridge and, with the day stretching ahead of her and still unable to leave the flat, she'd made a list of groceries that she'd have to ask one of the officers to get for her. The highlight of the morning had been finding one of Pearl's herbal teabags at the back of a drawer. It was mid-afternoon and she was busy cleaning the bath when the phone rang, making her jump. It was Church.

'Have you eaten?' he asked.

'No, I don't actually have anything in the flat and it's a bit early for supper.'

'I'll come around at six with fish and chips,' he said and put the phone down.

He could have at least asked what I wanted, she thought. She hoped he didn't want to go over everything that had happened again as she was sick of repeating herself. She finished the housework and put two plates in the oven to warm. She thought about the fish and chips that Dexter had bought for their first dinner. Was DCI Church going to go to the same well-known fish and chip shop in Ladbroke Grove?

At six on the dot the doorbell rang. Jane checked through the bedroom window that it was Church, and let him in. Unlike most of her visitors, Church demonstrated his fitness by moving up the stairs two or three at a time, carrying his newspaper-wrapped parcel of chips.

'I've got the plates warming,' Jane said, showing him into the kitchen.

'Never mind plates. Always eat fish and chips out of the news-paper.' He plonked the paper down on the kitchen counter and started eating.

'First,' he went on, 'the bad news ... and it's not about you, for a change. Natalie went sick from work. Stanley and Maynard tailed and lost her in Oxford Street after she'd been into Selfridges. Thankfully she didn't plant a bomb, but she could have been doing a recce, looking for a suitable target.'

'If she knows she's being watched then she'll have told the ASU. They'll all do a runner and we'll never find them.'

'Stanley was pretty sure she didn't know she was being followed, plus she did a grocery shop the previous evening. Our guys are still watching her flat, but she hasn't returned home yet ... In fact, we don't know where she is. My guess is the ASU is planning some-thing big and she's gone to meet up with them ... thus her use of counter-surveillance tactics.'

'How did Crowley take it?'

'Do you really need to ask or want to know? The good news is we have more information about Natalie Wilde. She's of Irish Catholic descent and moved to England from Belfast with her parents when she was six years old. It was a time when sectarian tensions were rising thanks to widespread discrimination and resentment. Her father managed his own small business and they were financially secure, although by no means wealthy. She is their only daughter and was well-educated at an established grammar school.'

Jane made a pot of tea. 'Why did she become a sleeper for the IRA?'

'In May 1964 her father returned to Belfast for his eldest brother's funeral. There was a gun battle between the UVF and the army, and he was killed in the crossfire. It isn't clear if the shooter was UVF or a British soldier. Natalie was only sixteen at the time and the loss of her father was undoubtedly traumatic. Not long after that, her mother committed suicide . . . it would seem those two incidents in her life were the catalyst and turning point . . .'

'So she must have already been recruited as a sleeper when she joined the Met?'

Church nodded and continued to eat the remainder of his fish and chips at an incredibly fast rate. Jane found them rather greasy and soggy.

Jane was shocked at the thought. 'It's frightening. If she hadn't caused a scene and been kicked out of Hendon, she could have by now made detective . . .'

'Yep, and the inside information she could have given the IRA would be immense. We can only surmise that she became involved thanks to her cousin, who we now know to be an active member of the IRA, and it may have been as far back as her father's death that she became a sleeper. She had all those jobs she told you about before she joined as a trainee at the bank – have you got any sugar?'

Jane got off the stool and found the sugar. Church added three spoonfuls to his tea before continuing.

'Natalie was a cashier at the bank – that's a very useful position for an underground organisation. She could be used by the ASU to pass communications whilst her contact was cashing cheques, for example. But as yet we have not seen anything subversive or suspicious at the bank.'

Jane sighed. 'She may have told the truth about working at the bank, but I suspect what she told me about working on a cruise ship and her cordon bleu course was all lies.'

'Probably.' Church crumpled up the greasy newspaper that had contained his fish and chips. 'I want you at the Yard in the morning for an 11 a.m. briefing in the main conference hall. Go to Crowley's office first at half ten, OK?'

Jane nodded. 'What's it about, sir?'

'You'll find out when you get there ... Nothing to worry about. See you in the morning.' He finished his tea and left.

Crowley seemed to be in a permanent bad mood these days. As Jane sat on the edge of the chair in front of his desk, forcing herself to maintain eye contact, she tried to forget that she was usually the cause of it.

'I believe DCI Church informed you of his squad's fuck-up yesterday,' he said sharply.

'Yes, sir. Have they found Natalie yet?'

'No, they haven't ... but we'd all better pray they do – and soon!'

'Yes, sir.'

'We ran some checks at St Thomas' hospital regarding births on the day you say Natalie Wilde was there. We spoke with the four women who had a baby and not one of them knew her. There were two on the previous day but ditto, and the staff couldn't recall anyone visiting the maternity ward who fitted Natalie's description.'

He opened a thick file on his desk. 'These are surveillance photographs of people passing her flat and during her time at the bank the day she went sick. We have not had any recognition from our team, but they photographed everyone entering and leaving the bank ... Have a look through them and see if you recognise anyone.'

Jane looked through the stack of photographs but eventually shook her head and said she did not know or recognise anyone.

'Do you have enough evidence to arrest her?'

'If I knew where she bloody well was, then yes ... but what we don't want to do is tip off her contacts. If we find her we could grab her off the street, or even at her flat, but that might jeopardise our tracking down who she's working with. So, we're waiting in the hope we find her or she returns to her flat.'

Crowley lit a cigarette, stood up and, checking his watch, gestured for Jane to accompany him. 'Come on, time to go.'

Jane was surprised at just how many officers were attached to the surveillance operation as various uniformed, plain-clothes and undercover officers began filtering into the conference hall. On the small, raised podium, there was a large noticeboard covered with all the surveillance photographs taken outside the Belsize Park flat and the bank, which Jane had already seen. There were also numerous shots of the dress hire property, and the hospital reception. A lot of work had been done to cover Natalie's every move. As Jane tried to slip into a seat at the back of the room Crowley called out loudly to her.

'DC Tennison, please come up to the podium.'

Jane flushed as she stepped up to sit beside him.

'Right, everyone: an update on the Natalie Wilde case. Her whereabouts are at present unknown, but we are actively looking for her. We still need to discuss whether or not we arrest her when she's found in the hope she'll tell us the identities of the men responsible for the atrocity at Covent Garden . . . or whether to keep up surveillance in the hope she will lead us to them.'

Jane listened as various officers discussed the two options, and which was best for the investigation. Some wanted to know why they hadn't broken into the basement flat to see if they could find any incriminating evidence, or any connection to their bomber. Crowley said it was too risky as the neighbours might see something and tell Wilde.

The doors opened and DS Lawrence walked in. He was holding an envelope, and went straight up to the podium to hand it to Crowley.

'We've got a match . . . Wilde must have taken a glove off to put money in the coin box when attempting to make a coded call to the press. We found prints from an index finger and part of the right palm on the coin box . . . it matches Natalie Wilde's prints from Hendon, but, of course, we can't date a fingerprint and say it got there on the day of the explosion.'

Crowley was elated. Although the print could be classed as circumstantial evidence, it was still evidence of Natalie Wilde's connection to the bombing at Covent Garden.

'Right. You lot get out there and find Natalie Wilde. When you do, contact me and I'll make the decision as to arresting or tailing her.'

'Was Natalie's phone tapped?' Jane asked, as Church drove her home.

Church shook his head. 'Problem with phone taps is that they cause a slight click and delay on picking up the receiver. She'd be trained to look out for that and wouldn't use her landline if she heard it.'

Jane opened the passenger door, hesitating. 'Do you want a coffee?'

'You know, I would . . . thank you.'

Jane filled the kettle as Church made a call to Maynard, who was at the Observation Point opposite Natalie's basement flat.

'Any show?' he asked.

'Not yet, Guv, it's all very quiet.'

'OK . . . I'll get you relieved in a couple of hours.'

Church was about to walk back into the kitchen when he saw the ironing board left up outside Jane's bedroom. Neatly folded on top of it was a man's T-shirt. He unfolded it and saw the faded design of James Dean wearing a cowboy hat. He knew where he had seen it before, and it was Alan Dexter's. He checked his watch and went back into the kitchen.

'She's still not shown up at her flat.'

Jane handed him a mug of coffee. 'It's only instant I'm afraid.'

'I don't mind . . . But I wouldn't mind a slice of toast if you've got some bread?'

'Of course . . . how about cheese on toast?'

'Love it, thank you.'

'Do you think Natalie was tipped off?'

'I don't know. She might have just been a lot better at sussing us out and became wary enough to do a runner. I know my team have been cautious . . . maybe that caused them to lose her at Oxford Circus.' He sipped his coffee.

Jane lightly toasted two slices of bread, then put cheese on top. Placing them under the grill she watched the cheese begin to bubble before using a fork to place them both onto a plate. She opened the fridge to take out a bottle of tomato ketchup and held it up.

'I've also got HP or Lea & Perrins if you'd prefer it?'

'Yes, please, L & P.'

Jane put the bottle down on the counter and was about to sit next to Church when the phone rang. Jane went out into the hall and picked up the receiver.

'Hello?'

'Hi there.'

Jane almost dropped the phone and moved closer to the kitchen.

'Natalie! I was going to call you.'

Church jumped off his stool and turned on the tape recorder they had installed and connected to Jane's phone. He took a pen out of his pocket, then gestured for Jane to keep talking as he opened his notebook.

'I've been back and forth to Woolwich and have only just got home. I feel bad about not calling to thank you for Sunday. I had a terrible hangover . . . I didn't realise how much I had been drinking.'

Church wrote on his note pad: SEE HER TONIGHT?

Jane nodded. 'I haven't eaten dinner yet. How about us meeting up and having something at Fratelli's?'

'What, tonight?' Natalie asked

'Yes . . . it was good there. Or you can choose somewhere else.'

'I can't, Jane. I've only just got home myself. We had a lengthy session after the bank closed because there were some discrepancies in the accounting department. I can't tell you . . . one slip up and all hell breaks loose.'

Jane had broken out in a sweat. She took the pen and wrote N SAYS SHE'S AT HOME. Both of them knew she wasn't, and Jane also knew she was lying about having been at the bank. It was unnerving that Natalie could lie so easily.

Church held up another note: GET HER TO MEET YOU.

Jane was now lying every bit as much as Natalie was, and she was finding Church's closeness unnerving. She waved her hand at him to move away.

'So, are you all ready for the big dinner dance?' Natalie asked.

'Just about, but I wonder . . . could I ask you a big favour regarding tomorrow night?'

'Ask away.'

'You know Pearl has left? I mean, she's not living with me anymore. So, I really don't know how I'm going to do my dress up tomorrow, as I was banking on her helping me.'

'Oh God, yes . . . all those little buttons,' Natalie said.

'It'll be impossible for me to do it up by myself. Besides, I'd really like you to give me your opinion about accessorising with your jacket, and whether I should wear my hair up or down.'

'What time will you be getting ready? I have to go to work, but I suppose I could come over to you straight afterwards?'

'Oh, that would be fantastic! If you could be here for about 5.30 p.m., or before . . . whatever suits you. You've never seen my flat and I'd love to show it to you and see what you think of it.'

'What time does your dinner start?'

'It's not until 7.30, but there's drinks beforehand.'

Church finished his cheese on toast as he listened to Jane giving Natalie her address. He was astonished to hear her laughing.

'No, no! Not Balcombe Street! That was where the siege happened – it's *Mel*combe Street . . . the first turning on the left if you're coming from Baker Street underground. It's not far from Fratelli's.'

Jane replaced the receiver and felt her legs turn to jelly.

'She's agreed to come here tomorrow about 5.30 to help me get dressed for the dinner dance.'

Church cocked his head to one side.

'At first I couldn't fathom out what the hell you were talking about – Pearl and the dress . . . Then when you laughed and mentioned the siege . . . I'm really impressed.' He took out a lighter and flicked it open to light his cigarette. 'It'll be perfect. She's hiding out, but it looks like she doesn't know she was under surveillance and her shenanigans yesterday were to see if she was. Our boys may have lost her but they didn't blow their cover.'

Jane sat back on the kitchen stool and sipped her coffee. 'I'm dreading her coming here. The thought of her being in my flat makes me feel sick . . . but the other side of me knows she has to turn up if she's to be arrested.'

'She's coming to you because she has to be certain that you haven't got any suspicions about her. We'll be onto her as soon as she comes out of the underground station . . . with the evidence piled up against her, she's looking at twenty-five years. She'll talk . . . they always do.'

Jane swallowed and nodded at Church's packet of cigarettes. 'Do you mind if I have one?'

He took the packet and opened it. Jane hesitated before taking a cigarette out and placing it between her lips. She leaned forwards and before he could pick up his lighter she had it in her hand. She held it for a moment, then used her thumb to flick it open and light the flame, inhaling the smoke and flicking the lighter closed again. Her eyes suddenly filled with tears and Church gently touched her cheek.

'No need for tears, Jane . . . you did good. I'm proud of the way you handled that phone call.'

She blew out the smoke, which tasted rancid on her tongue, then turned away.

'The tears are not about that . . . I was just remembering something . . . someone else.'

The memory of DCI Bradfield was still so strong in her mind. She knew he would have been proud of her. Church reminded her of the man she had loved, who had died so tragically.

'Listen, Jane, I'm going to have to get to the Yard to set things up for tomorrow and give old Crowley the good news. If there are any further developments, call me. I can come back later tonight and stay with you if you want.'

She knew that what he had suggested was not going to happen, even if she wanted it to. She inhaled another deep lungful of smoke, but it still tasted awful so she slowly stubbed the cigarette out in the saucer he had used.

'That's really nice of you, but to be honest I'm exhausted. It's been a long day and I need to get organised for tomorrow. If there's any news just call me and let me know if I have to see Crowley again.'

Church leaned over and kissed her cheek. He seemed embarrassed and kept his arm around her shoulders as she walked with him to her front door. He gestured towards the ironing board.

'That T-shirt . . . I know who it belongs to. I've seen him wearing it.'

Jane moved away from him a fraction.

'Oh, that . . . I had to borrow it. When I went to see Dexter, very embarrassingly I was sick over myself. So, he gave me that to change into, to get home.'

Church gave her a sardonic smile and dropped his arm from around her shoulders.

'Take care with him, Jane. He's an amazing guy . . . but takes terrifying risks . . . He's also got a bad reputation over his relationships with women.'

'Thanks for the warning,' she said, with a weak smile. She shut the flat door behind him and locked it as he went down the stairs.

Returning to the kitchen, she washed up the dishes, then picked up the packet of cigarettes that Church had left on the counter. She shook out another one and lit it from the gas ring on the cooker. She inhaled and this time it didn't taste as bad. Holding the cigarette between her lips she tucked Dexter's T-shirt under her arm, not caring that she was creasing her careful ironing. Still smoking, she collapsed the ironing board and stashed it away in the hall cupboard, then went into her bedroom. She slowly unfolded Dexter's T-shirt and held it to her as she closed her eyes.

'Don't hurt me,' she said, softly.

CHAPTER TWENTY

It was Good Friday, the day of the dinner dance. Natalie Wilde had still not returned to her basement flat, nor did she go to work at the bank as she had called in sick. Without any knowledge of where she was, Crowley gave the go ahead for two officers to force entry into her basement flat accompanied by forensic expert DS Lawrence. Crowley requested that Jane Tennison accompany Lawrence to the flat so, after being collected in an unmarked police vehicle, Jane was taken to 44 Belsize Park Avenue to join the forensic team.

After being given the all-clear from the bomb disposal expert, who had checked the door frames for possible booby traps, Jane and Lawrence made their way down the steps to the front door. It was easy to open the simple Yale lock with a skeleton key. Lawrence pushed the door but it wouldn't open fully as something was behind it. The smell that greeted them made it clear that bags of rubbish had been left to rot in the hallway.

'Take those back to the lab for sorting,' Lawrence told one of his team who had now joined them.

As one officer removed the bags the two other officers moved silently round the flat, searching the entire basement. There were numerous empty drawers in the main room, and in the kitchen there were more rubbish bags containing half-opened tins and used food cartons, as well as many empty wine bottles.

'God, this place is a mess. Was it like this when you were here, Jane?' Lawrence asked.

'No – it was neat and tidy. It looks as if other people have been here since I was. The furnishing and the pictures on the walls are the same, but it's all a façade now that we know who Natalie really is.' Seeing it like this, empty and neglected, Jane wondered how she'd been fooled.

She crossed to a bookcase filled with Penguin paperbacks and took one down. The browning book smelt musty. Jane and Lawrence went into the bedroom where a few items had been left in the dressing table-drawers.

'This is where you found the scarf, isn't it?' Lawrence asked.

'Yes. It was with all her underwear, in that drawer there.' She indicated the bottom drawer.

'Well, it's not there now,' he said, rummaging around.

Jane checked the wardrobe. Inside was an old coat, a rain jacket, two blouses, and a pair of shoes that were down at the heel and had a hole in the sole.

'I don't think they belong to her.' Jane glanced at the scuffed shoes and then looked over to the double bed. 'She told me it was her mother's quilt,' she said.

Lawrence lifted it up. Underneath it there were sheets and pillow cases, all in need of a wash and smelling of mildew. 'She must have moved most of her stuff out before Stanley set up the observation over the road,' he said.

'Church said when they last saw Natalie enter her flat she was carrying a bag of groceries?'

'All part of the front to appear normal in the eyes of others. She's a skilled operative, Jane ... I doubt any one of us on this investigation would have rumbled her cover.'

In the waste bin they found the unopened groceries and tins of food that Natalie must have bought on the day she'd left work early. Some used candles were also in the bin. Jane bent down and took one out, sniffing it. Lily of the Valley. She held it up.

'Natalie must have lit scented candles to cover the smell of mildew when I came here. Plus, she was always cooking when I was here.'

Lawrence nodded. 'You never know ... Besides her prints we might find some other useful ones here that match to known IRA members.'

He did several spot tests for nitroglycerine but all proved negative and he said he thought it was unlikely that the premises had
been used for bomb-making.

They opened the French windows onto the small garden;
moss-covered stone steps led to a garden table and two benches.
Overshadowed by a huge tree with enormous branches, it felt
dank and cold.

'I keep on making excuses for my naivety . . . Why didn't I pick
it up? She lied to me about everything, even telling me she had
picnics out here.'

Lawrence shrugged. He was surprised that the usually observant
Jane hadn't detected the underlying state of the flat. But instead he
said, 'Don't beat yourself up about this, Jane. You didn't have any
reason to doubt her.'

Jane looked around, picturing the flat as it had been when she'd
last visited. Now all she could see was lies.

Back in the lab, Lawrence set up three trestle tables covered in plastic sheeting before each rubbish bag they'd brought from Natalie's
was tipped out on them. The stench of rotting food filled the lab.
Lawrence wore a mask as he plucked out a chicken carcass that was
crawling with maggots. Using a wooden spatula, he picked his way
through the mound of potato peelings and apple pie crust. It was
a tedious and distasteful process. He set aside the empty food cans
for fingerprinting, but it was not until he reached the damp, stink-
ing, newspapers that many of the items had been wrapped in that
he came across something of interest.

The newspapers had been flattened out, and the dates were
noted in the blurred wet print. One of the headlines from the
Evening Standard was COVENT GARDEN BOMB HORROR. Lawrence had to be careful as the sodden paper was falling apart, but
the front page had a picture of Jane Tennison standing by an
ambulance. Using a magnifying glass and leaning closer to the

blurred picture, Lawrence could see a very faint red ring drawn around Jane Tennison's face, and her name underlined. Sifting further through the bin he found a cutting of the press release with the artist's impression of the suspect and the interview with Jane.

DCI Crowley sat in his office with DCI Church discussing the investigation.

'Natalie Wilde must have recognised Tennison from the press conference or bomb scene photographs in the paper,' Church suggested.

'Yes, and no doubt the rest of the ASU were rubbing their hands with glee once they realised Wilde knew Tennison from Hendon training college.'

'It's lucky then, that she couldn't swim otherwise she might have been Commissioner by now,' Church said, trying to make light of the situation, but Crowley wasn't amused.

'Don't even go there. The press will have a field day when it comes out, which it will if we arrest her and she stands trial. Every one of us will be made to look fools, thanks to Tennison.'

'She's young and inexperienced. She wasn't to know who and what Wilde really was. I'm not pointing any fingers, but the reality is that we all put Jane in this situation with Natalie. Jane was adamant that she could not identify the bomber, but the press release and artist's impression marked her out as our only witness who saw him.'

'Whatever I did or didn't do was for the sake of the investigation and arresting those IRA bastards before they killed and maimed more innocent people. Tennison divulged confidential information to a fuckin' IRA sleeper and now they are one jump ahead of us!'

'So, why the phone call from Natalie last night?' Church asked quietly.

Crowley pursed his lips, not answering. Church leaned forward, patting his pocket for a cigarette pack.

'She's coming out of hiding. It doesn't make sense, unless she's not going to turn up tonight. Why lie about working late at the bank and being at her flat when she'd already gone to ground? Stanley's one of my best guys, and he is adamant that she was not aware of being tailed. The way she acted was like a pro, making sure she was safe. I mean, Jesus Christ, for one second Stanley thought there was going to be another bomb explosion at Selfridges.'

'But she didn't have a bomb so there wasn't,' Crowley said. He pulled out a pack of Marlboro from his jacket pocket and tossed them over his desk to Church. 'Listen, we've had talks about what could be on the agenda . . . We know that Natalie Wilde is aware of the time and place of tonight's dinner, but we've got high security at the hotel so it's still going ahead. The Yard's detective squads have had a dinner dance on Good Friday for years and I'm not letting the IRA stop this one.'

'I know that! But why did she call Jane?' Church snapped.

Crowley leaned back in his desk chair and counted off the points on his fingers. 'One, she was making sure the venue was still the same. Two, she's checking we had no knowledge, or evidence, of her connection to the bomber. Three –'

'Three, she takes Tennison out, removing our key witness, and we never catch the bomber. Then another bloody bomb goes off and we're to blame.'

'I was coming to that. I think she's going to turn up. We need a wire on Tennison to record everything Wilde says as evidence against her.'

Church said angrily, 'Wilde is going there to help Jane with her dress . . . how on earth is she going to conceal a bloody wire? Have you not considered her safety at all?'

'Of course I have . . . OK – the wire won't work, but we can hide listening devices in the flat instead.'

'Even then Natalie might stumble across a listening device. Armed officers should arrest her on the pavement before she gets into Tennison's block of flats.'

'That's a fair point,' Crowley conceded. 'Safer all round.'

Together they began to select officers to be in position outside Baker Street underground station so they could arrest Wilde on the street. As an extra precaution, they would have two men in the surveillance position opposite Jane's flat. 'And we should place Stanley inside the flat with her as additional protection,' Church added. Crowley agreed.

By the time DCI Church had left Scotland Yard he was confident that Crowley had set a watertight trap for Natalie Wilde. He drove to Melcombe Street to update Jane. When he arrived it was after two o'clock. She was in her dressing gown with her hair in rollers, and had been waiting for him. He spoke calmly as he explained what the plan was: just as he'd promised, Natalie would be arrested before she even got to Jane's flat.

'All you have to do is sit tight and wait. You'll be given a blow-by-blow account over the surveillance radio. Just keep that close by and then you and Stanley will get to the venue by taxi when it's all clear.' He smiled. 'Save the first waltz for me?'

As Church left, Jane seemed surprisingly relaxed, saying that she would start getting herself ready for the evening.

'Stanley will have to do up all the little buttons on my dress,' she joked, 'that part was true, you know, I can't do the dress up by myself.'

After Church had gone, Jane smoked the last cigarette in the pack he had left behind the day before. Holding her other hand up, she saw that it was shaking. She inhaled a deep lungful of smoke, stubbed out the cigarette and went into the bathroom.

Jane spent a long time applying her make-up. She used more foundation than usual, with a damp sponge to smooth the pale ivory liquid down her neck and over her cleavage. She darkened her eyebrows, and outlined her eyelashes and lids in brown eyeshadow and liner before finishing with black mascara. The pale lipstick was enhanced with a little dab of Vaseline, making her lips look shiny as she pouted in front of the mirror.

She jumped as the phone rang, then went into the hall and tentatively picked up the receiver.

It was Michael, asking if she was free for dinner that night. She told him she had a work function, and that she'd call tomorrow to arrange a date over the weekend. She would have liked to have told Michael everything was far from fine, but she couldn't. She checked her bedside clock and saw that it was after five, so she began taking out her rollers. She brushed her hair loose and was about to pin it up, but decided against it as it looked lovely down. She put on her best underwear and the strapless bra, which reminded her of the awful bridesmaid's dress she'd worn for her sister's wedding. Her mother had followed her round, constantly trying to pull up the dress, worried about Jane showing too much cleavage, which had attracted even more attention.

Jane had hung the Chanel gown up on her wardrobe door so that the creases in the spiral silk and lace frills of the skirt would drop out. She took the gown off the hanger and stepped into it. There was no way she was going to be able to do up all the buttons herself. Stanley really would have to help her when he arrived.

Crowley had four teams of undercover officers at Baker Street station, on the platforms and outside in the street. Also in position was a surveillance van with a driver, and two officers inside. They had all been issued with recent surveillance photos of Natalie Wilde, taken when she had brought the groceries back to her flat before vanishing. Their orders were to arrest her on sight and get her into the van to be driven to Scotland Yard for an immediate interview with DCI Crowley.

Two more officers were on duty across the road from Tennison's flat, just in case their target somehow managed to avoid arrest. All officers were in radio contact and by four fifteen everyone was in position. Crowley remained at the Yard with DCI Church, waiting for the outcome. Both men had brought in their evening suits and shirts for the dinner dance that night.

At four twenty Tennison's doorbell rang. She looked through the window and saw that it was Stanley, although she had to look twice as he was wearing a purple velvet dinner suit with a frilled shirt and a velvet bow tie. His usually greasy hair was tied back in a ponytail. She buzzed him in and opened her front door as he headed up the stairs.

'You look very smart,' Jane said, as he joined her.

'Thank you ... The suit belongs to my brother-in-law, and my wife had it altered to fit me – trousers shortened and the waistcoat made to measure. The shirt's mine, and the cufflinks were my dad's.'

He displayed one of the large gold and onyx cufflinks, then looked up.

'What?' he said. 'You don't like them?'

'I just find that I don't really like you.'

'Ah, well ... it takes all sorts.'

'I trusted you, Stanley. The other night, with the Vice Squad, you said that you would do what you could to look out for me with DCI Church.'

Stanley made a hissing sound through his teeth.

'Yeah, I know what I said. Can we go and sit down in the kitchen for a minute?'

Jane reluctantly followed him. He poured some water into the kettle and switched it on, then fetched a box of teabags from the cupboard and a bottle of milk from the fridge.

'You're making yourself at home ...'

'I'll tell you what I'm doing, Jane, I'm trying to relax enough to talk to you seriously. I want you to understand why I had to inform DCI Jimmy Church of the screw-up with the Vice Squad. D'you take sugar?'

Jane perched on the stool beside him. 'No, I don't.'

'I need to go further back, Jane . . . Maybe you don't know this, but your old boss at Bow Street Station kind of twisted Jimmy's arm to bring you in . . . I know you have ambitions, farcical as they may be, to get into the Sweeney, but Jimmy agreed to take you on in the Dip Squad because we might be able to use a female officer.'

Jane didn't interrupt as the kettle boiled and Stanley made the tea.

'So, first thing . . . After, I admit, a brief training, we have WDC Tennison working on the Underground. We had a major suspect, a man already wanted for assault and handling stolen property – Andres Hernandez.'

Jane said nothing. Stanley could hardly look at her.

'First day up, Tennison, you almost get pushed under a bloody train, we lose our main suspect, but we bag Miguel Hernandez and the yob in the big leather coat. I have to give it to you that the poor joker who had his wallet lifted gave you a description of Regina Hernandez.'

Jane nodded. 'I know that, Stanley. Until then, nobody on the team knew there was a girl involved. It was only when we were questioning Miguel – when I spoke to him in Spanish, remember? – that he admitted that Regina was his sister.'

Stanley poured the tea. 'Yes, yes, yes . . . we know that. Through Miguel we get access to the rundown flat they were living in –'

'– and you arrest Andres Hernandez,' Jane interjected.

'Yes, yes . . . And we take Regina, who was being sexually abused . . .'

'She was being RAPED!' Jane exclaimed. 'She was fifteen years old and terrified! I had to take her to be examined –'

'Shut up, and listen to me! As a consequence of raiding the Portobello flat we discovered fourteen passports belonging to underage girls from Colombia.'

Stanley pointed his finger at Jane.

'At this time we were instructed, by the guv, that we were no longer running with this case and that we were handing it over to the Vice Squad . . . Do you recall him saying that?'

Jane shrugged. 'Yes, I do. But we were told that Regina would most likely not go to trial and that someone at the Embassy would arrange for a safe place for her to stay.'

Stanley raised his hand. 'Please – just let me take this in order!'

Jane turned away and sipped her tea.

'The next thing we have is WDC Tennison on the front page of the tabloids, involved in the horror of the bomb blast at Covent Garden underground station. Whether you were or were not aware of photographers being there is another matter . . . What is important, obviously even more so because of what's going down today, is that you are possibly a vital witness to the bomber. Have you followed everything so far, Jane?'

'Yes,' Jane said resentfully. 'I am following you perfectly well, Stanley. I'm just not sure why you feel it is necessary for you to go into all this detail?'

'Because you bloody *need* to know the details . . . The next thing is that you take it upon yourself to follow Regina Hernandez, who you spot as a passenger in a car that we later discover is a courtesy vehicle for the Playboy Club in Park Lane.'

Stanley went on to say that he was aware that this information had been passed on to the Vice Squad and they immediately acted on it. The reality was that they were already focusing on Andres Hernandez.

'After that you were told, again, that the Vice Squad were handling the situation and that it was not the Dip Squad's territory.'

'She was wearing a mini skirt, stiletto shoes, and her breasts were hanging out of a skimpy top! We were supposed to be protecting her, Stanley!' Jane felt her anger rising.

'Shut up! Your little fifteen-year-old isn't as naive as you think she is. She was brought in for questioning and agreed to lead the Vice Squad to two further establishments that this Andres bastard runs – one in Beak Street and the other in Greek Street. On the night they've organised a raid, our innocent little Regina goes walkabout . . . so, as they need her to give evidence against Andres Hernandez, they go out looking for her. WDC Tennison, in the middle of the red-light district with no backup, attempts a street arrest of Regina Hernandez, completely unaware that the guy who had stopped to talk to her was Vice Squad. And Regina, our witness, runs off – vanishes.'

Jane felt her cheeks flush.

Stanley rolled a cigarette. 'I know what I said to you, Jane . . . but you had yet again ignored orders and if DCI Church found out you would have been in dire trouble – so my intention was to dig you out of the shit. However, the following morning, I discover that your flatmate has been arrested. What the fuck do you expect me to do? When I was told, I thought you were a bloody liability! NOW it turns out that your friend from training school is a wrong 'un and the major suspect!'

'You arsehole, Stanley!' Jane was really angry now. 'How dare you suggest I was in some way complicit with what happened? Tell me, can you honestly say, hand on heart, that Natalie Wilde wouldn't have fooled you?'

'That's irrelevant,' snapped Stanley. 'What's relevant is that if, via Natalie Wilde, the Bomb Squad can identify the bomber, you'll be hanging on to your career by your fingernails – but at least you might still have one.'

He took out the radio from his pocket and spoke into it. 'This is OP Juliet Tango to control, testing . . . over.' The transmitter crackled.

'Receiving you, Juliet Tango . . . loud and clear . . . control over.'

'Juliet Tango, premises safe and secure, over.' Stanley shook his head at the radio. 'Piece of crap . . . it's one from the Dip Squad's office. They keep promising we'll get new ones.'

He suddenly looked properly at Jane for the first time since he had arrived. 'My God, that's a bit low at the front, isn't it?'

'I need you to do up all the little buttons at the back.'

'Well, I have to say, Tennison, you've got a good pair . . . just keep them under wraps.' He smirked and checked his watch. 'It's coming up to five o'clock – fingers crossed.'

He sat on a stool as Jane went into her bedroom to collect her evening bag. Inside it she had put her warrant card, lipstick, comb, some folded bank notes, keys and a handkerchief. She needed time alone to digest everything that Stanley had said. What she had not told him was that she knew what it felt like to get on the wrong side of DCI Church. When Church had reprimanded her and told her that they still had not traced Regina Hernandez, he had said that if Regina was subsequently found dead it would be on her head.

Jane heard another radio communication come through. Stanley called out from the kitchen to say that so far all was quiet and that there had been no sign of Natalie yet. She could hear him slurping his tea as she looked at her bedside clock. It was now five past five.

She looked up to see Stanley standing in her bedroom doorway holding a mug of tea.

'Time's ticking . . . She said five to you, didn't she? It's after that now?'

'I said five thirty, and she said she would be here earlier as she would come straight from working at the bank.'

'Well, we know that's a lie as she's not been back to the bank, or to her flat.'

Jane was almost ready for Stanley to do up the buttons on her dress, but the radio transmitter suddenly crackled in the kitchen and he went to find out what the update was.

'Still no sight of the target,' he called back to Jane. He finished his tea, washed up the mug and left it on the draining board. When he tried to make contact via the radio again, he just got bad static and no reception.

Jane was becoming nervous. She went out into the hall.

'She's not coming. I don't think she ever intended to.'

'Then why the phone call? Stay positive,' said Stanley. 'She might just be taking her time.'

'It's five thirty.'

'I know . . . we all know.' He came over to stand behind her. 'Now, let me do your buttons up.'

Just then, the doorbell rang. Jane ran into her bedroom and looked down to the main front door. A large truck was double parked across the road outside the dry cleaners, blocking the undercover officers' view to her flat. Jane could see Natalie standing below, and spotted the soft top of a blue Triumph Herald driving away from the pavement, passing the parked truck as the driver returned to move it. Jane turned to Stanley, trying not to sound panic-stricken.

'It's her! It's Natalie . . . she's here. There's a truck blocking the undercover SPG officers' view. I don't think they've seen her!'

'Let her in. I'll radio for backup.'

Jane buzzed the front door open and Natalie stepped inside just as the truck moved away. They heard her hurrying up the stairs as Stanley desperately tried to make radio contact, but there was no pickup signal. If Stanley was seen, Natalie would be tipped off – and there was no way he could head down the stairs now. She might be armed.

'Go into the spare bedroom,' she hissed at him. 'The wardrobe's empty – you can hide in there.'

Stanley hesitated, but Jane pushed him towards the room.

'She'll want to look around. She's never been here before. I'll keep her talking and take her into my bedroom, then you call for backup.'

Stanley hurried into the spare bedroom just as Natalie knocked on Jane's flat door.

'Hi, there . . . it's me!' she called out.

With a quick glance to check that Stanley was inside the wardrobe, Jane opened the front door.

Natalie jokingly heaved for breath and laughed. She was carrying a large leather and canvas shoulder bag.

'My God, those stairs must keep you fit!'

'They do! Come on in.'

Jane ushered Natalie inside and closed the door.

'Well, this is it. Just down the hall here is the kitchen—'

'Let me get my breath back. You sound like a desperate estate agent!'

'Sorry . . .' Jane forced herself to slow down. 'It's just that you were a bit late and I have to get ready. Would you like a coffee?'

'No, thanks. It's very nice and compact . . .' Natalie said, looking around the kitchen.

'The bathroom is in here,' Jane pushed open the bathroom door.

'Nice tiles – and you've got a shower as well.'

Jane gestured to her bedroom. 'My bedroom's in there. I'm so glad you made it. As you can see, I can't possibly do these buttons up . . .'

'You look terrific, though. What's in that room?'

'Oh, that's just my small spare bedroom. The one Pearl had. I'm thinking of making it into a dining and TV room.'

Natalie took a step into the spare bedroom and took a good look round. The single bed was piled high with boxes.

'Yes, I think that's a good idea . . . It's a bit small but you could get a sort of folding table.'

'That's exactly what I was thinking. I'd get rid of the single bed and maybe buy a two-seater sofa.'

Jane's heart was pounding. She was terrified that Natalie would be able to hear Stanley calling for backup on the radio. In fact, he was crouched down inside the wardrobe, with his back pressed against the door.

Natalie turned and smiled.

'You've got it made, haven't you? Right, let me do your dress up.'

They walked back into Jane's bedroom and Natalie went over to the bed to pick up the bolero jacket.

'This will look really lovely with your dress . . . it's fabulous, and it was a real bargain.'

Jane left her bedroom door slightly ajar. As Natalie placed her bag on the bed Jane turned her back towards her so that she could begin doing up the buttons.

'Gosh, they really are tricky. They're so small, and some of the buttonholes are really tight.'

Natalie did one button up after another, pulling the velvet top tightly together. In the spare bedroom next door Stanley was still crouched down in the wardrobe, unable to make radio contact. He slowly eased open the wardrobe door and stepped out, moving cautiously into the hall and standing outside Jane's bedroom door to listen.

'You're going to have quite a cleavage, but it makes you look very sexy,' Natalie said.

'Did you come on the Underground?' Jane asked. She was finding it hard to maintain her composure.

'No, I got a lift from a friend. We're meeting up later for dinner, and we might go to Fratelli's – you know, where we had our first dinner together?'

Natalie fastened the last two buttons of her dress and stepped back.

'You're shaking! Don't tell me you're nervous about tonight? You look gorgeous . . . Anyway, I'd say that, after what you've been through recently, nothing should make you anxious. Do you ever worry about the consequences?'

'What consequences?'

'Well, according to what it said in the newspapers about that bombing at Covent Garden, you saw him, didn't you? I mean, could you recognise him?'

Now, Jane realised exactly why Natalie was there. 'No,' she said. 'I told you, the witness who could have identified him sadly died in hospital. Now, what about my hair?'

'Oh, well . . . I don't think you need to put it up in a chignon. It looks lovely loose.'

Stanley overheard the relaxed conversation and moved silently to the front door, easing it open. He began to hurry down the stairs.

Natalie ran her fingers through Jane's hair and shook it out to make it looser.

'I like it the way it is. You've done your make-up beautifully. What about earrings?'

'Oh, I've got a necklace . . . it's in the box on the bedside table.'

Natalie opened the little leather box and took out the gold chain with the small teardrop pearl.

'Oh, this is lovely! Turn around and let me put it on for you. The clasp is tiny.'

Jane turned her back to Natalie and waited while she carefully hung the necklace chain around her neck and did up the clasp.

'There – let me see. Oh, it's really sweet.'

'It was given to me by my mother.'

Halfway down the stairs, Stanley's radio chattered into life, and the transmitter bleeped loudly. He froze and looked back at Jane's flat door. He had left it wide open.

Natalie turned towards the bedroom door.

'What was that?'

'Oh, it might have been the bell on the cooker? I haven't got used to the timer yet and I keep on setting it by mistake.'

Natalie stood still, listening. She suddenly seemed very wary. She crossed over to the bed to pick up her handbag.

'I have to go.'

'Oh, just wait – let me try your jacket on to see what it looks like.'

Jane put on the velvet bolero just as Natalie pulled open the bedroom door and saw that the flat door was wide open. She turned back to Jane.

'Yes, that looks good,' she said mechanically. She put her arm through the shoulder strap of her handbag, but Jane stepped forward and snatched it.

'What are you doing?' Natalie exclaimed.

'Isn't it more what *you're* doing? I don't know how you can live with yourself!'

Natalie's face twisted as she tried to pull her handbag away from Jane. There was a moment when they were both tugging to hold on to it, but then Jane yanked hard and stepped backwards, almost losing her balance as she held on. Natalie threw a hard punch, which Jane dodged by stepping sideways, but Natalie made contact with her shoulder. Jane hurled the handbag aside and all the contents tumbled out onto the carpet. Using all her training Jane went for Natalie's right arm, pulling it back and up almost out of the socket before bending it behind her back and then twisted her hand towards her wrist.

'You murdered a young mother and injured God knows how many others – for what?'

Natalie was bent over in agony, but she didn't scream or call out as she was forced to lie on the ground. She stopped struggling.

'The British Army murdered my father,' she snarled. 'I hate you, and all that you stand for! Tonight you'll see what we're capable of!'

Jane was leaning over, still putting pressure on Natalie's arm but Natalie had such strength and venom that she seemed completely numb to the pain. In a flash, she turned and caught hold of Jane's necklace with her free hand. The next moment she had pulled Jane down and was twisting the necklace like a garrotte, choking her until Jane could hardly breathe.

Just then Stanley hurtled into the bedroom and grabbed Natalie by her hair, stamping with all his force on her back to make her release Jane. Pressing her face into the ground with his foot, he dragged her arms behind her back. Natalie screamed in agony, her face twisting with rage as she realised she was helpless. By the time the two other officers Stanley had called in rushed into the flat, it was over.

Stanley cuffed Natalie and dragged her to her feet.

She spat in his face. 'You bastards! You're all fucking bastards who'll rot in hell.'

Stanley handed her to the uniformed officers 'Get that bitch out of here . . . take her to the Yard, radio ahead for DCI Crowley to meet you.' He helped Jane to her feet.

Natalie kicked and swore, but it was pointless. Together the two uniformed officers hauled her out into the hall, and dragged her down the stairs screaming at the top of her voice.

Stanley yelled at them to wait as he picked up the contents of Natalie's handbag and stuffed them back inside. He looked up at Jane as he picked up a small .22 Ruger pistol.

'I know why she came here,' said Jane. 'She was asking about me being able to identify the bomber.'

'I think the bitch would have used this on you. Let me take this out to the guys.'

Left alone Jane took a few deep breaths, then went over to the mirror. She had a vivid red welt around her throat and, touching her neck, she realised that her mother's pearl necklace was missing. She began to search the room getting down on her hands and knees to pat the carpet where she had been forced down by Natalie.

Stanley walked back into the bedroom holding his radio and swearing.

'This is dead as a fucking dodo . . . the guys called in to Crowley to pull in all officers still around Baker Street underground station with their thumbs up their arses.'

Jane was close to tears as she searched for the necklace. Stanley knelt beside her.

'Hey . . . come on, it's over. You were brilliant. Let's get you up . . . I don't know about you, but I need a drink.'

'No, it's my mother's necklace. Natalie tore it from my throat and I can't find it!'

'All right, all right . . . let me help you. What does it look like?'

'It's a teardrop pearl on a thin gold chain.'

Stanley patted the carpet with the flat of his hand, lifting the bedspread from around her bed. He peered under the bed, then sat back on his heels.

'I've found it!' Jane exclaimed, standing up and holding the broken chain between her fingers.

Stanley looked up at her. 'I've found something too.' In his hand he held a radio-controlled detonator. 'Either Natalie was going to set a bomb off or hand this detonator over to someone else. Without this, there's no bang.'

'Can you make it safe?'

'No, but Dexter can and he'll be at the hotel.'

Jane's voice shook. 'Oh, my God! Natalie said: "Tonight you'll see what we're capable of" . . . there could be a spare detonator for a bomb . . . Crowley and Dexter were using more than one when I watched them on the explosives range.'

'Pull yourself together!' Stanley almost lost his cool as he tried his radio again to contact Crowley.

'DS Stanley to Crowley, are you receiving? Over.' There was a hissing noise but no reply. 'God damn this bloody cheap piece of shit!' Stanley swore at the dead radio.

'Use my phone.'

Stanley picked up the receiver, but Crowley's number was continually engaged.

'Come on, come on, Crowley . . . put the phone down!' Stanley shouted becoming more and more impatient as he tried to redial with no success. He slammed the phone down.

'We need to get to the hotel right now.' He quickly ushered Jane ahead of him. 'Go on! Get moving! We can't wait for a patrol car.'

Jane moved as quickly as she could down the stairs, which was not easy in evening wear. Stanley stepped on the back of her dress, and Jane stopped dead as the frill around the bottom of her skirt came loose. She bent down to look at the damage.

'Never mind your effing dress Jane ... move it! Come on, hurry up!'

Holding the loose frill in her hand, Jane hurried out into the street. At first she thought Stanley was hailing a cab as he stepped into the middle of the road holding his warrant card. He raised his hand to stop an approaching old Ford Anglia, which braked sharply. The driver swore loudly and was even more shocked when Stanley suddenly opened the door and pulled him out.

'DS Stanley, Met CID. I'm sorry, but I have to commandeer this vehicle for a police emergency ... Get in, Tennison.'

The young driver was so shocked he didn't say a word as Stanley clunked the car into first gear, put his foot down hard on the accelerator, and drove off at high speed.

Stanley weaved expertly through the traffic. When they reached Caxton Street he turned into the large concourse in front of the hotel. The car park was already quite full, and a uniformed PC was directing the new arrivals into empty spaces. Outside the hotel a queue of officers and their guests in evening suits and dresses waited to have their names and warrant cards checked by uniformed officers who were standing at the top of the entrance stairs. Stanley pulled up in the concourse and jumped out of the vehicle. Jane followed more slowly, hampered by her dress. As she got out of the car, torn frill in one hand and warrant card in the other, a voice called out:

'Tell him to come back and park that car properly!'

She looked up to see the uniformed PC directing a driver to reverse into a parking space beside a blue Triumph Herald. Suddenly she experienced a nightmare flash of recognition. It replayed rapidly before her eyes: the moment she had run after the bomber at Covent

Garden, how she had called out to him, reached for the sleeve of his coat, how he had half turned towards her and shoved her roughly away. She was in complete shock and couldn't call out or move. She was frozen.

'Jane . . . *Jane!*'

Dexter had grabbed her by the shoulders and was shaking her. She heard his voice as if waking from a nightmare.

'You look fabulous! Let's ask Stanley to set up the champagne.' He took her by the elbow to escort her into the hotel, but she was stuck to the spot.

'Are you all right?' he asked, concerned.

Jane turned away from the uniformed PC and slowly nodded her head. She tried to speak but there was no sound.

Dexter had been told that they had arrested Natalie Wilde inside Jane's flat and found a detonator. Assuming she was suffering from delayed shock, he put his arms around her.

'Everything is going to be all right, I've taken the battery out of the detonator, so it's disarmed. And the whole place was swept for explosives this afternoon. Come on, let me take you inside and get you something to drink . . .'

Jane leant against him and took more deep breaths as he tried to move her, but she held on to him tightly.

'The bomber . . . Covent Garden . . . I recognise him. He's here. Don't turn around . . . he's the uniformed PC directing cars into the parking bays.'

Dexter tensed, then moved closer to her as if embracing her. His lips were close to her ear as he turned a fraction. He could now get a better view of the officer, who was assisting a driver to park at the far end of the bays, in almost the last space left.

Dexter gave her a reassuring smile. 'Because Natalie was aware of the big do, Crowley's had uniform and police dogs go over the hotel with a fine-tooth comb . . . It's safe, nothing was found, and there's a heavy uniform presence inside and outside the hotel.'

Jane tensed up again. 'But I recognise him . . . I recognise him!'

'All right, all right . . . just stay calm . . . I'll ask the duty inspector in charge of security about the PC dealing with parking.'

Jane nodded as Dexter took her by the arm and, to the annoyance of the queuing officers, led her straight into the hotel. Dexter got her safely through security and told her to find Stanley and wait for him in the saloon bar, while he spoke with the Duty Inspector. Dexter showed his warrant card to the inspector who was holding a clipboard.

'The officer directing the parking . . . do you know him?'

'What's his shoulder number?' the inspector interrupted.

'I don't know.'

The inspector flicked through the paper attached to his clipboard. 'Uniforms have been drafted in from various stations so I don't know them all personally. Let's see now . . . parking duties . . .' He ran his finger down the list of names, numbers and allocated duties. 'Ah here we go . . . PC 332. A. Crane from Cannon Row directing parking . . . Does he need help?'

'No, I was just checking he was on the list.'

Dexter was relieved. Jane must have been imagining things.

Back in the saloon bar the drinks were flowing. Everyone was in evening dress, black ties and full-length dresses. Jane had to hold up her ripped skirt as she searched for Stanley, but he was nowhere to be seen. She eventually caught sight of Blondie Dunston from the Dip Squad, and grabbed his arm, causing him to almost drop his glass of champagne.

'My God, Tennison, you look terrific! But what's the matter?'

'I urgently need to speak to DS Stanley . . . where is he?'

'Went off to call Crowley . . . By the way, this is Alison, Stanley's wife – and that's my girlfriend.' Blondie pointed at a glamorous redhead who was busy talking to Maynard.

Jane turned to Alison, a pretty girl, wearing a thick decorative band in her hair.

'It's lovely to meet you,' Jane said, 'but I'm really looking for your husband . . .'

'You all right, Jane? What's happened to your skirt? You need a surgeon to stitch it up?' Maynard joked.

'Where did Stanley go? Please – I really need to speak to him.'

Maynard shrugged and gestured to the wide staircase beside the dining room. 'Probably the police security room. It's somewhere on the first-floor corridor.'

Jane pushed her way through the growing throng, who were all intent on kicking the evening off at the free bar. She ran up the stairs and down the red-carpeted corridor, shouting at the top of her voice.

'Stanley . . . STANLEY!'

Stanley appeared at the door of one of the rooms.

'You have to come downstairs, NOW! Dexter's waiting . . . The bomber from Covent Garden . . . I've just seen him . . .' Jane was gasping for breath.

'*What?*'

'He's directing the parking! He's wearing a police uniform.'

'Jesus Christ! Are you serious?'

'Yes . . . YES! Come on, Stanley, PLEASE!'

Stanley followed Jane back down the corridor. As she approached the top of the stairs she tripped and had to tear off the now trailing frill from her dress, almost falling head-first down the stairs in the process. Stanley grabbed her arm and they barged through the crowd.

Dexter was in the gents, at the urinal, when a uniformed PC walked in and stood next to him. It took a couple of seconds before Dexter noticed that the officer having a piss next to him had the number 332 on his shoulders.

'Are you PC Crane?' Dexter asked as he zipped up his fly.

'Yes.'

'I thought you were on parking duties?'

'I was, but another officer said he'd been posted to it so I let him take over.'

'Go and find the duty inspector and bring him to the reception right now.'

'No need to get uptight!' said the PC. 'I haven't disobeyed an order . . . just swapped roles, that's all.'

'Well, this is *my* order: find the inspector *now* and tell him it's an EMERGENCY!' Dexter barked, making the officer jump and pee on his own boots.

Dexter hurried back to the foyer and looked out of a window from a safe distance. He could see the car park was full and a queue of vehicles was now blocking the entrance and lined up in Caxton Street. He looked for the uniformed officer Jane had recognised as the Covent Garden bomber, but couldn't see him. He turned, heart beating fast, as Jane and Stanley approached,

'You were right, Jane,' he said urgently. 'The officer out front isn't the PC assigned to car parking. It could be nothing – but he could be our man posing as a police officer.'

'Shit,' Stanley gasped.

The duty inspector appeared. Dexter pointed from the foyer window where they could now see the suspect standing between two parked cars.

'That PC out there, standing on the left . . . did you tell him to take over parking duties?'

'No, never seen him before . . . what's his shoulder number?'

'I don't think he has one. We suspect he may have planted a bomb on the premises.'

The inspector looked offended. 'We've searched this place top to bottom, sniffer dogs 'n' all and it's clean . . . there's no bomb in here!'

'Well, check again, but make it discreet,' Dexter ordered. 'I don't want a mass panic on our hands. Look for a rucksack or holdall hidden in or near the ballroom.' He turned to Jane. 'Are you sure you recognise him?'

'Yes, I caught his profile and it just came back to me. Like you said it would. It's him. I know it is.' Jane was relieved that she had been right, but fearful of what would happen if he had succeeded in planting a bomb.

Dexter took a deep breath. How devious the IRA were to dress one of their own as a police officer to blend in with all that was going on at the hotel. It was audacious but so simple and it would have fooled them all but for Tennison's flash of recognition.

'Let me go and get Maynard and the lads out of the bar.' Stanley suggested.

Dexter shook his head. 'We've wasted enough time. I'll walk past him while you approach from the left, then I'll turn on your shout and we take him out together.'

Dexter took off his jacket and threw it at Jane. 'Hang on to this for me.'

The suspect was now walking out from between the parked cars towards the exit onto Caxton Street. He had to move to one side as there were two vehicles attempting to look for a free parking space. Stanley and Dexter looked at each other: they had to reach their target before he got to the street. They moved quickly, but the suspect stopped and instinctively looked over his shoulder. Dexter and Stanley froze instantly, not wanting to give themselves away. It was no more than a fraction of a second, but the suspect started to run.

Dexter and Stanley were ten feet behind and closing as the suspect ran up Caxton Street and right into Buckingham Gate where all three of them narrowly missed being hit by passing vehicles. As the suspect crossed the road and ran left into Castle Lane, he threw something into the basement area of a row of terraced flats. Neither of them stopped, but Stanley was flagging as the suspect turned left into a narrow dustbin-lined alleyway which, to their relief, turned out to be a dead end. They thought they had him trapped, but the building along one side of the alley was the rear of a four-storey office complex with a fire escape leading up to the top floor at the far end. The suspect ran up the fire escape two steps at a time and, reaching the top, hesitated as he looked down to see Dexter and Stanley moving up below him. He kicked at the fire-escape door but it didn't budge, so he pulled himself up onto the narrow safety rail and crouched down like a monkey.

'Shit ... he's going to jump onto the opposite roof!' Dexter shouted running up the fire escape. As he reached the top, he lunged forward, attempting to grab the suspect's leg, but it was too late. The man sprang forward through the air, his arms outstretched as he just managed to grab hold of the parapet edge and, with his legs dangling, pulled himself up onto the roof. Dexter now climbed onto the safety rail behind him.

Stanley, still labouring up the fire escape, called out, 'That's nearly ten feet across and twenty-five down! Don't risk it, Dex. We can get backup and surround the area.'

Stanley had hardly finished his warning when Dexter took off through the air in pursuit. Stanley shut his eyes, expecting to hear a sickening thud, but when he opened them again he saw Dexter dangling from the parapet by one hand. Then, in a swinging motion, Dexter managed to get his other hand on the roof and pull himself up. He was gasping for air, but once safe he seemed to find a new surge of energy and set off along the roof in pursuit of the suspect, feet slipping on the tiles as he went.

Realising the suspect was probably doubling back, Stanley decided to get back down to the ground and track them along Castle Lane and Buckingham Gate. Due to the narrow lane and angle Stanley couldn't see them, but from the loose tiles that broke free and crashed down near him, he knew he was heading in the right direction. He prayed that a tile didn't hit him on the head. By the side entrance of Westminster Chapel Evangelical Church,

Stanley could hear people singing 'All Things Bright and Beautiful'. A poster on the church wall showed a steeple-shaped graph, coloured lines indicating how much money had been raised for restoration of the church roof. Judging from the number of loose tiles falling, they'd need a lot more money . . .

Up on the roof, Dexter was getting closer to the target who had climbed even higher. As he tried to keep his balance he looked across the roof and could see the suspect crouched down on his haunches, ready to make another terrifying leap. Dexter slid down the steep roof slowly for fear of slipping over the edge if he went too fast, shouting to the suspect to give up.

Stanley heard the shout. Looking upwards, he could just make out Dexter approaching the suspect high up on the rooftop opposite. He watched as the man made the insane leap, and screamed out to Dexter not to jump, but it was too late. Suddenly there was an almighty crashing sound as the roof gave way. The last verse of the song rang out from inside the Church: 'How Great is God Almighty, Who has made all things well', followed by hysterical screams.

Fearing the worst, Stanley ran inside. Lying on the altar in a pool of blood, his head cut to shreds from the sharp-edged tiles, was the suspect. The church choir huddled together by the pulpit, some of them crying. Stanley was desperately scanning the area for Dexter's body when he heard a voice from above and looked up. Peering through a big hole in the roof was Dexter.

'Do us a favour and call the fire brigade . . . I don't fancy going back the way I came to get down.'

The vicar, a small balding man, was rigid with shock.

'Officer . . .' he stammered. 'There is a roof edge that we had reinforced and if your c–c–c–colleague follows it round to the left he'll find a bell tower with a d–d–d–door where he can let himself in.'

Stanley looked up. 'Did you get that, Dex?'

By the time Dexter was down from the roof several uniformed officers were at the scene, dealing with the small but distraught group of people who had been rehearsing for the Easter Service. A uniformed officer approached Dexter and handed him his radio.

'The duty inspector wants to speak to you, sir.'

Dexter spoke into the radio. 'Go ahead, DS Dexter receiving . . . over.'

'We found a radio-controlled bomb in a rucksack. It was left with the hotel reception staff by the suspect PC after the first search.'

'Jesus Christ, I'll be right there.'

'No, no, it's OK . . . The device has been successfully defused by one of your colleagues.'

'Did you evacuate the hotel?'

'No. Everything is now secure and there was no need for an evacuation.'

'Yes, but where's the bloody bomb now?'

'It's been taken back to the explosives lab for further examination and fingerprinting.'

'Have you informed DCI Crowley?' Dexter asked.

'Yes, and after consultation with the Bomb Squad Commander it's been decided that the ball's going ahead . . . they'll be summoning all the guests for dinner in fifteen minutes.'

Dexter handed the radio back to the PC. 'What a wanker . . .' he remarked, and the PC nodded.

Stanley tapped Dexter on the shoulder. 'I'm sure the suspect threw something away in the basement area of the flats in Castle Lane.'

'How big was it?' Dexter asked Stanley.

'I didn't get a good look . . . it wasn't big, but it kind of jangled . . .'

'You know what it could be? A backup radio transmitter for the rucksack bomb. We'd better instruct a couple of uniformed officers to go and search the area.'

They didn't have to wait long before two SOCOs arrived to bag the body and have it removed to Westminster mortuary. Dexter had searched the pockets, but he had found nothing more than a wallet with a few one and five pound notes in it. He turned to one of the SOCO officers.

'Can you do me a favour and get me a dead set of fingerprints? I'll get someone to take them straight over to the Yard's fingerprint bureau so we can check them against the prints we found at the Kentish town flat and criminal records.'

The young PC gestured to Dexter.

'Excuse me, sir – DCI Crowley wants to see you and DS Stanley in his office now . . .'

Stanley raised his eyes to the vaulted ceiling.

'Oh, shit! My wife's going to file for divorce if I miss this dinner with her . . .'

CHAPTER TWENTY-ONE

Dexter and Stanley stood the other side of the two-way window looking into the interrogation room. Outside the room was a uniformed officer. Inside, Crowley, like the two of them, was wearing evening dress with a large black velvet bow tie. It was odd to see him dressed so formally opposite Natalie. Two uniformed officers stood at either end of the room and DCI Church sat beside Crowley making notes.

This was the first time that Dexter and Stanley had seen Natalie Wilde. She was wearing a police issue overall and was looking remarkably unruffled.

'Well, she's no Maureen O'Hara, is she?' Stanley commented.

'Who?' Dexter looked at him.

'You know, the red-headed Irish movie star . . . Natalie just looks pretty ordinary.'

'That's the whole point, Stanley. She just fits into everyday life. Just a cashier in a bank.'

They watched for a while longer. Crowley was repeating the same questions over and over again. Natalie kept saying 'No comment' to everything she was asked.

Dexter spoke to the officer outside the door. 'Can you get DCI Crowley out for us?'

'She's a nasty little bitch . . .' Crowley said to them as he emerged from the interrogation room.

'Well, maybe she'll react when you tell her that her partner's dead,' said Stanley. 'We found the rucksack planted at the hotel, and when he tried to make his escape he fell through a church roof and split his head open. He's a goner.'

'It's a shame I won't be able to question him about the ASU safe house and other IRA members . . .' Crowley loosened his bow tie. 'But if he's anything like that bitch he probably wouldn't tell me anything. You two did a great job tonight . . . not to mention risking your own lives.' He took a ten-pound note out of his pocket and handed it to Dexter. 'Go and enjoy your evening – you deserve a stiff drink on me. I'll join you after I've finished questioning her and then I'll have her taken to Paddington.'

Dexter slipped the note into his pocket. 'Thanks. I'll have a large Scotch waiting for you, and Church as well.'

As Crowley re-entered the interrogation room, Natalie pointedly turned her face away from him.

'Well, Miss Wilde . . . we found the bomb in the rucksack at the hotel. Seems your intention to harm as many of our officers as possible has failed.' He leaned across the table but Natalie didn't react.

'And your partner, attempting to escape arrest, had an unfortunate fatal accident . . .'

This was the only time Natalie showed what lay beneath her controlled demeanour. She sprang forward and spat at Crowley, directly in his face. It took every ounce of control for him not to slap her for her smirking arrogance. She was pure evil.

Dexter and Stanley returned to the hotel just as pudding was being served. Stanley had lost his bow tie and a cufflink, and Dexter's white evening shirt had dark stains all over it and the caps of his shiny shoes were badly scuffed.

'It's all over!' Stanley raised his hands in the air.

Jane still had Dexter's evening jacket and was waiting anxiously in the empty bar.

'Didn't you go in for dinner?' Dexter asked.

'No . . . I couldn't eat a thing . . . I was too worried.' She handed him his jacket. 'Is it really all over?'

'Yeah . . . we got him, but we won't be getting anything out of him. The madman fell through a church roof and broke his neck on the altar.'

Stanley smiled. 'They were singing "All Things Bright and Beautiful" and literally on the words "How great is God Almighty" the suspect fell through the roof . . . His face was smashed to pieces, and –'

Dexter held up his hand. 'That's enough, Stanley.'

Jane moved closer to Dexter. 'What about Natalie?'

'Crowley's been interrogating her . . . he said she's a hard nut to crack.'

'Did she say anything about me?' Jane asked, anxiously.

'Not as far as I know.'

Despite their air of bravado, Dexter and Stanley ordered stiff drinks. They were on their second Scotch when Crowley and Church both joined them. Dexter pointed to the bar where their drinks were waiting for them. Crowley raised his glass.

'I'd like to propose a toast to Dexter and Stanley for their brave and unselfish actions . . . Mind you, the Commissioner may be a bit miffed if he has to donate a couple of grand to the Westminster Chapel roof fund.'

They all laughed and raised their glasses. They could hear the noise coming from the busy banqueting room, which was buzzing with chatter, laughter and the clinking of glasses and crockery. Everyone was in a good mood, all getting along and having a laugh at each other's expense.

'Come on, you lot . . . if we don't get in there we won't get anything to eat,' Dexter said. He was about to go into the banqueting room when the duty inspector walked in.

'We searched the whole of Castle Lane and the basement flat areas as best we could, using torches. I sealed the area off for a daylight search, but so far this is all we've found. It's a Triumph car fob and key.' He placed the item on the bar.

Dexter sighed. 'Yes, I can see that, but it's hardly likely to detonate a bomb . . . so, if you don't mind, I'd like to go and eat.'

The duty inspector picked the key up and was about to walk off when Jane spoke up.

'Excuse me, but I think there's something else that could be important.'

The inspector stopped and Crowley turned to her as she looked towards Dexter, who was busy lighting a cigar.

'Out with it . . .' Crowley demanded.

'Seeing the key fob reminded me of something . . . When Natalie rang my doorbell I looked out of the window . . .'

They all looked at her impatiently

'The reason your teams didn't pick her up at Baker Street station was –'

'Yes, yes?'

'She came by car. I saw the roof, a soft top . . . I'm sure it was a blue Triumph Herald. I mean, I can't be positive, but I think I saw a blue soft-top car parked in the hotel concourse.'

Jane now had everyone's attention. Crowley shrugged.

'Probably coincidence. I mean, we disarmed the rucksack bomb and found the transmitter Natalie had, so . . .'

Dexter interrupted him banging his hand on the bar and turned to the inspector.

'There's something not right here . . . did the expo say how big the rucksack bomb was?'

The inspector nodded. 'Yes, about a pound or two of TNT.'

Dexter picked up the car key. 'He never had a detonator for the rucksack because Natalie failed to deliver it. He's running for his life and chucks these away because he didn't want us to find them or a connection to the car . . .'

Everyone's attention was now on Dexter.

'OK – this is the possibility: the rucksack could have been a primary device intended to cause some damage and mass panic.'

Church was very tense. 'If it had gone off it would have killed or maimed any of the receptionists standing near it.'

'That's not the point, a small explosion may kill one or two, but it makes everyone else retreat away from it and run straight into the path of a much bigger secondary device!'

Crowley grasped the enormity of Dexter's point. 'If the rucksack went off while we were in here, then everyone would have run out the front of the hotel into the concourse parking area.'

'Exactly . . . so I need to examine that Triumph right now.' Dexter shook the key in his hand.

The duty inspector braced himself. 'Shouldn't we take it to a safer place to examine?'

Dexter glared at him. 'What's your name?'

'Inspector Brian Curtis.'

'Well, Inspector Curtis, you let an IRA terrorist plant a bomb and then do parking duties! So excuse me if I don't listen to your opinion this time.'

Although it was Jane who had given them the heads-up about the car, no one was paying her any attention. The men grouped together to discuss what to do. Inspector Curtis said that he would start organising the evacuation of the building.

Crowley interjected. 'I am the DCI from the Bomb Squad. It's too dangerous to evacuate. People will be seriously injured if a car bomb goes off.'

Dexter agreed and said that as the banqueting hall was at the back of the hotel it was the safest place to be at the present time. Looking a bit put-upon, Curtis said he'd do his best to keep everyone in situ without causing alarm.

Dexter stubbed out his cigar, took off his jacket and once again handed it to Jane. She saw him exchange a glance with Stanley, who nodded back. They headed towards the hotel reception entrance, followed by Crowley and Jane.

The rows of parked cars in the hotel concourse were illuminated by the lights from the hotel, and there were three lamps positioned on the brick wall of the private marked-out areas. The pale blue two-seater Triumph Herald was instantly noticeable due to its age; it was not in good condition and parked right by the hotel entrance. Surveying the now full parking area Jane could see why Dexter was concerned the reaction to a smaller device would make everyone run into the path of another bigger bomb.

Crowley calmly told the reception staff to make their way up to the banqueting room and asked one of the porters to get him a torch. Dexter turned to everyone, instructed them to stay back and, holding the torch, calmly walked over to the car. He seemed relaxed but Jane's heart was pounding. 'The Long Walk' seemed to be happening in slow motion.

No one spoke as they watched Dexter peering into the car. He didn't attempt to open the doors as he moved around the car, which was parked with the boot facing the low brick wall. He crouched down by the driver's door and shone the torch around the rim of the door and the rubber seals before peering into the door lock. Gently, he eased the key into the door and slowly turned it, causing the push button lock to pop up. It was as if he was counting down time to himself as he carefully opened the door two inches and again checked around it before opening it further.

Stanley whispered to Jane, 'He's got nerves of steel.'

Dexter adjusted the two front seats as far forward as possible so he could get better access to the small rear section of the vehicle.

'What's he doing?' Jane asked.

Crowley whispered, 'The car could be rigged to explode so he's checking as he goes. The best way to examine the boot lock is to enter from the inside . . . If it's rigged, he can detach any tripwires connected to the boot lock before opening it.'

Dexter leaned into the car and removed a travel rug that had been spread across the back. Under the rug there were sticks of TNT, cling-film-wrapped gelignite, nails and other bits of loose metal. The upright section of the boot had already been cut away to allow the rear area to be crammed with explosives. He gently moved some of the explosives so he could shine the torch onto the boot lock.

The tension was palpable. No one could see clearly what Dexter was doing as he was crouched down looking inside the boot for what seemed like ages. Eventually he reappeared, walked back towards them, wiping the dripping sweat from his forehead.

'It's a big bomb, at least fifty pounds of gelignite and sticks of TNT attached to a clock timer that's ticking . . .'

'How long have we got?' Crowley asked.

'Don't know. I can hear the clock, but can't see it. It's inside a cigar box similar to the one I was testing at Woolwich. That helps in some ways, as at least I have an idea of its make-up. The back of the car is packed with nails and other lethal crap intended to cause as much injury as possible. The boot is booby-trapped from the inside so I can't open it with the key until I disarm the wires leading to the lock.'

Crowley was badly shaken. He looked, almost helplessly, at Dexter. 'Can you do this?'

'Yes. Just keep everyone away,' Dexter said. 'And get me some small sharp knives from the kitchen and wire clippers as quick as you can . . . We don't know when it's been programmed to explode, so every second counts. Is DS Lawrence here?'

'Not yet. He's coming but got held up at the lab examining the stuff from Wilde's flat.'

Dexter turned to Stanley as Crowley went back into the hotel to find the equipment Dexter had requested.

'You OK to work with me . . . hand me what I need?' Dexter asked.

'Sure . . . of course. But will you get it done before they serve the cheese and biscuits? My wife will be going ballistic sitting next to an empty chair all night.'

Dexter laughed. 'It shouldn't take long.' He turned to Jane. 'Go back to the dining room, Jane, it's too dangerous to be out here.'

'No, I'll stay here.'

'It's not necessary . . . go inside.'

'No . . .' she said, through gritted teeth, holding his jacket tightly.

Church pulled out his packet of cigarettes and lit one, passing it to Dexter who took it and gave him a smile of thanks. Church then shook a cigarette out for himself and Jane asked if she could have one. She took one and leaned towards him as he struck a match, using the same flame to light one for himself. Although the wait seemed interminable it was only five minutes before Crowley returned with some kitchen knives and a leather folding case full of tools.

'Found the tools in the basement maintenance office . . . they OK?' He handed Dexter the tools.

'Under the circumstances, they'll have to do.'

Jane watched as Dexter and Stanley conferred, checking over the tools together. Dexter looked round at the rest of them.

'If you insist on staying in the foyer then you should position yourselves further inside the entrance behind the pillars for protection . . .' He smiled. 'Just in case I cock up and it goes off.'

Grim-faced, Stanley took the torch and followed Dexter to the Triumph. Dexter handed him the tools and told him to place them on the front passenger seat and shine the torch inside the boot area. Stanley could now see the explosives. He was sweating as he crouched down next to Dexter and leaned forward into the cramped space.

Dexter grinned. 'Man, this bomb is a biggy . . . it would blow this car park and anyone standing in it to smithereens . . .'

'Let's hope not,' Stanley replied nervously. He could hear the clock ticking.

There were six wires running between the cigar box to the explosives and the lock of the boot. Stanley shone the torch around the boot.

Dexter grabbed Stanley's arm. 'Keep the torch steady on the cigar box, please.'

'Sorry. Why are all the wires the same colour? I thought they'd be set up like a plug . . . You know, red, green and brown? Or is the earth yellow?'

'They're deliberately all the same colour to make it more difficult for me to know what's what and which one to cut. Now, be quiet, unless you want to be blown up. Pass me the small paring knife.'

Easing the knife under the cigar box, Dexter lifted it a fraction and looked under it.

'Devious bastards!' he muttered under his breath. 'There's a small micro switch under the box so it will go off if I lift it . . . Get me a heavy spanner out of that tool kit.'

Stanley started to lift each spanner to feel their weight.

'The biggest one will be the heaviest, Stanley, so just hand it to me.'

Dexter took the spanner from Stanley then eased the knife back under the cigar box, to hold the micro switch down while he slowly lifted the cigar box and put the spanner down in its place. Next, he checked the seal of the cigar box lid and, satisfied it wasn't booby-trapped, opened the box. Inside there was an alarm clock connected to a battery and circuit board with the wires running from them. Dexter could see that he only had three minutes left before the big hand made contact with a piece of metal attached to the clock, which would then detonate the bomb.

'How long have we got?' Stanley asked, his hand shaking.

Dexter lied. 'Plenty of time. OK Stan, my man, gimme the torch and tool kit. You go back and join the others. Tell them all to go to the banqueting hall . . . just in case the bomb goes off.'

Stanley hesitated. 'No, I'm OK.'

'Well, I'm not. You've got a wife and kids, so just do as I ask.'

Stanley got out of the car and passed the tools and torch over to Dexter who carefully propped them up inside the boot. He then chose various clippers and scissors, and two Stanley knives from the tool kit, placing them next to him so they were easily to hand.

Stanley walked back into the hotel foyer and spoke quietly with Crowley, explaining that Dexter wanted to work alone and that it would take some time to defuse the device. Crowley dragged on his cigarette, his nerves on edge.

DCI Church peered around a pillar. 'What could you see?' he asked Stanley.

'There's an alarm clock and battery in a cigar box with wires leading to the explosives and the boot lock. He said there's plenty of time left, but we should get further back in the hotel to the banqueting room . . . It scared me half to death.'

Inwardly Crowley knew something wasn't right. Dexter had not made the booby-trapped car boot safe so he could get better access to the bomb. This could only mean he was running out of time.

Dexter picked up the wire clippers and, opening them, held them between one of the wires leading to the battery, but as they were all the same colour he wasn't sure if the timer was rigged so that when he cut the wire the detonator would activate. He looked at the clock and saw that he only had one minute left. There was no time for indecision. His heart was beating like it never had before. There was only one course of action he could take, but whether it would work or not was in the hands of the gods.

He put the clippers to the wire attached to the detonator that was embedded in the explosives. With thirty seconds to go he closed his eyes and cut the wire. When nothing happened, he breathed a huge sigh of relief and, after removing the initiator by hand, cut the battery wires to the alarm clock, finally making the bomb safe.

Dexter switched the torch off, slowly got out of the car and began placing the tools he had used back into their holder. He shut the driver's door, turned towards the expectant watchers and smiled as he held up the offending alarm clock. Crowley let out a sigh of relief.

'He's bloody done it!'

As Dexter joined them they crowded round him, but he simply waved his hand at them and placed the tools and torch down on the reception desk. He handed the clock to Crowley, as if he had won an award.

'Job done . . . now I need a large drink and some food. And I want to win the crate of Moët in the raffle.'

Jane handed him his jacket.

'I need to take a leak and clean myself up . . .' he said.

'We're so proud of you, Dex . . . Congratulations! We were all so tense, willing you to succeed . . .' Church clapped him on the shoulder.

'Oh, come on . . . enough of all this . . . I want to get into that banqueting room. I'm starving!' As Dexter walked away, jacket slung over the crook of his arm, he appeared nonchalant, but Jane could see that his shirt was soaked through with sweat.

DCI Church clapped his hands.

'OK, everyone . . . show's over! I suggest that we all do as our hero suggests and get back to enjoying the evening.'

As Jane accompanied them back into the reception she overheard Crowley speaking with Church.

'He's got nerves of steel . . . I'll speak with DS Lawrence about having the vehicle removed to the explosives lab.'

As they headed towards the dining room it was clear that the word had got round and some detectives, flushed from the evening's booze, were joking that the phrase 'the party went off with a bang' had nearly come true.

The frill at the bottom of Jane's skirt was still trailing as she headed for the powder room in the hope that there was a cloakroom attendant who might have a needle and thread. There was a large cloakroom next to it, with rails of coats and jackets belonging to the female guests. A woman in a hotel uniform was standing behind the counter.

'Do you have a needle and thread? I've had a bit of a problem with the edge of my dress.'

'Just wait here, dear . . . I'll see if I can find one for you.'

As she left the cloakroom, Alison, Stanley's wife, barged into the cloakroom. She was obviously very angry as she began to search for her coat.

'Alison . . . are you all right?'

'No, I'm not. First, I am collected to be brought here, then I have to sit throughout dinner with his empty chair next to me. Then in he comes with his shirt filthy, having lost his bow tie and a gold cufflink, and starts asking for dinner. I'm getting a taxi home!'

'Don't go, please . . . I don't know how much I can tell you about tonight, but if it wasn't for your husband I could have been killed. He's incredibly brave, and hopefully eventually he can tell you about it himself . . .'

Alison bit her lip.

'Besides, there's still the raffle, and –'

'That's been going on for ages.'

'Well, then there's the band . . . All I can say is that your husband really is a very special and very brave man . . .'

Alison hesitated, then turned and headed out of the cloakroom. Jane went into the powder room. There were large mirrors hanging on the walls and Jane gasped at her reflection. There was a nasty red welt around her neck. She washed her hands, then opened her small evening bag and took out her powder and lipstick. She dampened some tissue paper and wiped her face, then dabbed powder around her neck to try and hide the mark, but it was still red raw.

As she went out she found the cloakroom attendant had returned with a needle and black cotton thread. Kneeling beside Jane she began to attempt to stitch the frill back in place.

'I'm just going to do big hem stitches for now, but you need to get a professional seamstress. It's delicate silk and some of the lace is torn.'

'I'm so grateful . . . if you could please just do what you can so I don't trip up again . . .'

In the dining room, standing on the small raised platform, two rather drunk officers were digging into a box of raffle tickets and shouting out the numbers using a microphone. There were cheers as the lucky ticket holders jumped up from their tables to claim their prizes. They were mostly bottles of gin, whisky and brandy, with a few more feminine prizes for the female guests; bottles of perfume and bath salts. As they were reaching the end of the raffle, Stanley was tucking into a large plate of cheese, biscuits and grapes, accompanied by a glass of red wine.

Alison sat down beside him as the last but one ticket was pulled out of the box.

The prize was dinner for two at the Savoy Hotel, and there was a loud bellow as Blondie Dunston stood up waving his winning ticket stub. He received a slow handclap as he went to collect the gold envelope. As the band began to set up, the last major prize was drawn: the crate of Moët & Chandon champagne.

'Ticket number 409, ladies and gentleman . . . number 409. Donated by Minstral's Wine, a crate of vintage champagne hand-delivered to your door . . .'

Dexter rose to his feet and waved his ticket stub as the room erupted into yells of 'FIXED . . . FIXED!' but he danced his way up to the platform. Crowley was up on his feet clapping and cheering and the insults turned into a stamp and handclap of applause as the flushed and smiling Dexter took the microphone.

'I would like to hand over my winning ticket to a man who has proved himself above and beyond the call of duty tonight . . . my friend, DS Stanley. And now – let's dance!'

There were a few loud and abusive remarks as Stanley stood up at his table. His face was like a young boy's as he held his arms above his head and cheered. The band struck up and the small dance floor was cleared as guests started to move from their tables to dance.

Jane had arrived in the dining room in time to see Dexter pass his prize ticket to Stanley. Alison was smiling proudly as he guided her onto to the dance floor. They immediately collided with Edith, who was being whirled around by Maynard, his bow tie undone and his shirt tails hanging out of his trousers. Edith was wearing a black velvet sequinned gown with long strands of pearls that she continually swung around her neck. Together they looked like an overgrown schoolboy dancing with the inebriated school matron.

Jane was at a loss as to where she should sit, but just then DCI Church left his table with Crowley and Maynard, and their guests.

'Come on, we've got some food at the table for you.'

She followed him to a large round table. It was full of used napkins and empty wine glasses but there were two fresh bottles of white and red wine. Jane sat down as Church pulled out a chair for her in front of a setting of salad, cheese and biscuits.

Church poured her a glass of red wine. Crowley was sitting beside her, next to a large woman in a sequinned jacket who was obviously rather tipsy. Opposite them were two forensic scientists she knew by sight from the explosives lab who were also clearly enjoying themselves, as were most of the other rowdy guests. Couples were dancing and throwing themselves around as the band struck up 'Rock Around the Clock'. Suddenly the net above the dance floor was released and red and white balloons cascaded down from the ceiling, along with streamers and confetti.

Jane sipped her wine and cut a small slice of cheese as Crowley leant towards her.

'I'm proud of you, of what you have done. You are a brave young woman. Believe me, it won't go unnoticed.'

Jane nodded gratefully as he topped up her wine, then he gestured towards the woman in the sequin dress, who was knocking back her drink.

'That's my wife, Margaret . . . and you know those two rogues from the forensic science lab.'

He then almost turned his back completely to Jane as he suggested to his wife that they should be leaving. Church bent his head towards Jane and whispered.

'She's three sheets to the wind, and the forensic guys are plastered as well. You can relax, Tennison . . . everything is safe now, thanks to Dexter . . .'

'Am I all right, sir?'

Church tilted his head to one side. 'This is not the time or the place, Tennison.'

'I know I have been a bit of a liability . . .'

'That is putting it mildly, Tennison. Come in and see me tomorrow at midday, and we can talk everything over. Now, would you like to dance?'

'Could I just have a few minutes, if you don't mind? I'm really quite hungry.'

'It's a lucky escape, to be honest . . . I've got two left feet!'

Jane scoured the dance floor and the surrounding tables for Dexter. She eventually caught sight of him on the far side of the room, sitting at a table full of men. He was rocking back and forth in his chair, laughing.

She jumped as there was a tap on her shoulder. She turned to see DS Lawrence standing behind her, looking very smart in an elegant dinner jacket and a frilled shirt.

'Hello, Jane. I just got here – missed all the action by the sound of things. You look lovely . . . which is more than I can say for Edith. I think a couple of guys had to help her out, after she attempted to rock and roll with Maynard!'

Jane laughed softly as Lawrence pointed across the room to the dance floor.

'You seen Timex? He looks like an emperor penguin in that gear.'

Shepherd, known as Timex because he was always checking his watch, was the only man wearing a white tuxedo jacket with black trousers.

'That's his wife with him. Absolutely stunning, isn't she? No wonder he always wants to clock off at five sharp and get home ASAP,' Lawrence remarked. He leaned over to speak with Crowley, giving him an update on his work. The Triumph Herald had been double-checked before the car was towed away and it was all clear. Lawrence moved away from the table as Jane ate another slice of cheese.

DCI Church was now busy talking to Crowley and had left his packet of cigarettes on the table. Jane took one and picked up a box of matches that had been left next to the overflowing ashtray. She inhaled deeply as the band started playing 'Blue Moon' and the lights were lowered.

'Ladies and gentlemen ... the next song will be the last waltz. We hope you've all enjoyed your evening, and we wish you a safe journey home.'

Jane sat, smoking, and wondered if they had arranged a car or taxi to take her home. She stubbed out the cigarette and suddenly sat bolt upright as she felt a tingle down the back of her neck. Dexter leant down towards her, running his finger down her nape.

'Can I have the last waltz?'

Jane nodded. He drew out her chair and took her hand. She felt herself blushing as Dexter guided her forwards and then slipped his arms around her.

'You look lovely! Is your dress fixed? We don't want you to fall arse over ...'

'Yes, the cloakroom attendant sewed it up for me.'

He held her tighter, his face close to her hair. Stanley and Alison danced next to them. Alison seemed to have forgotten her anger and had her arms around her husband's neck, resting her head on his shoulder. She was quite a few inches taller than him.

'She's going to need you tonight, Dexter . . . she's got twenty-five buttons at the back of her dress, and there's no way she can undo them herself,' Stanley said.

'How do you know?' Dexter asked, grinning.

'I got her into it!'

Alison looked up from Stanley's shoulder and shook her head. 'Honestly, you say the rudest things! What if she doesn't want him to go home with her? Mind you, if it was me I'd jump at the chance.'

'ALISON!' Stanley said, whisking her away as she laughed and said she was only joking.

Dexter tilted Jane's chin up and at the same time ran his hand down the back of her dress.

'Do you need me to help you out of this?'

'Yes, I do . . .'

They didn't wait for the waltz to end. In the car park, the blue Triumph Herald was being loaded onto a flat-bottom truck under Lawrence's supervision. Seeing Jane, he waved her goodnight.

Dexter kept his arm around her shoulder as they headed into the road and hailed a taxi to take them to her flat.

'Well, that was certainly some event,' he said, casually.

'Yes, I won't forget it for a long time . . . I still can't believe it all happened.'

'Without you, Jane Tennison, it wouldn't have been nearly as exciting, never mind conclusive.'

'It was exactly as you told me . . . you know, remembering him from Covent Garden. When I did recognise him, I just froze.'

Dexter stared out of the window and said quietly that he didn't want to talk about it. He sat slightly apart from her as she tried to think of something to say to him.

'That was so nice of you to give Stanley your raffle prize.'

'It was all down to Crowley fixing it for me to win . . . He's an odd man . . . doesn't know how to look you in the face and show you his appreciation, but basically he's an all right old so-and-so.'

'He told me tonight that he would look after me . . . Church wants to see me in his office tomorrow.'

'You should get a commendation for what you've brought to the table, never mind what you were subjected to by that two-faced bitch. She'll be under tough interrogation . . . But when she finds out her bomber pal is mincemeat she might crack and give details about their cell, and name other IRA members.'

'You don't think it will go against me that I was so taken in by her?'

Dexter shrugged, not wanting to say that it very well could be an issue. Instead he pulled his wallet out of his jacket and took out some money to pay for the taxi. They drew up outside her flat and Jane unlocked the main front door, hitching up her long skirt to walk up the stairs as Dexter followed behind her.

On entering her flat she switched on the hall lights and tossed her evening bag onto the breakfast bar in her kitchen.

'Would you like a coffee or anything?'

'No thanks, nothing . . . unless you have any brandy?'

'I'm afraid not . . .'

'That's OK . . . Let's get you out of that dress.'

They went into her bedroom, which was still untidy from the search for her necklace. Jane quickly replaced the cushions on the bed and rearranged the valance where Stanley had lifted it and found the detonator underneath.

'Stanley had to hide in the wardrobe in Pearl's old room. Natalie really sent shock waves when she rang the doorbell.'

'I'd say our pal Stanley has probably done a lot of nipping into wardrobes when taken by surprise!' He laughed.

Dexter took Jane by her shoulders and slowly turned her around so that her back was facing him. He began undoing the tiny buttons, and as he did so he bent his head and kissed her bare back, loosening one button after another.

'My God, these are fiddly! Some of the buttonholes are really tight.'

By the time he had undone them, the top of her dress had slipped down, revealing her black strapless bra. She caught it in her hands, embarrassed.

'Well, that was a job well done!'

'Thank you . . .'

Dexter sat on the edge of her bed as she stood in front of him wanting, more than anything, for him to take her in his arms.

'I need to be straight with you, Jane . . . I think you're sweet, and sexy, and I would like to stay here with you all night. I think that's what you want as well. I could be wrong, and maybe that's my ego talking, but, like I just said, I want to be straight with you. I really like you, but if I sleep with you tonight it will be harder for you to understand that that is all it would be. I don't want a relationship.'

'I understand,' Jane said, close to tears.

Dexter stood up and cradled her in his arms. 'No . . . don't say that . . . don't make it any harder. I'm going to go, Jane.'

Dexter held her at arm's length and looked at her through what suddenly seemed like cruel blue eyes.

'You don't understand, Jane . . . I need to get fucked tonight . . . fucked rigid . . . because it's the only way I'm going to release all the pent-up shit inside me. And I'm not going to use you for that, because you are worth far more.'

Dexter walked out of her bedroom, and Jane slumped down on her bed as she heard the front door close behind him. She felt as if her heart was breaking as she reached for his faded James Dean T-shirt and held it to her face.

Dexter lit a cigar as he stepped into the phone box. He took some change from his pocket and dialled a number, waiting for it to be picked up. It was after midnight but he knew she would be up. Her husky, laconic, bedroom voice answered.

'Pauline, it's me.'

'You're lucky I got a good memory for voices, Dex. You think all my clients say "it's me" and expect me to know who it is? What you want?'

'Two of your best. Send them over in about half an hour, all right?'

'Cab fare on top, darlin' . . .'

'Yeah, OK.'

Dexter hung up and stared at his reflection in the small square mirror above the phone. He looked haunted and there were deep circles beneath his pale blue eyes. The incredible adrenaline he had felt that night had left him mentally exhausted and now he needed to feel the same way physically. Pauline's girls would ensure that, and when they left him he would sleep.

Jane was surprised that she was able to switch off, and when her alarm clock rang in the morning she could hardly believe she had slept so deeply. Her dress was still on the bedroom floor where she had stepped out of it, and there was a trail of underwear from the bedroom to the bathroom.

She pulled on her old towelling dressing gown and went into the kitchen to make herself some eggs and bacon. She was ravenously hungry.

By the time she had tidied her bedroom, showered and dressed, it was almost nine o'clock. The phone rang in the hallway.

'Hi there . . . it's Michael. Are you still free tonight? I was wondering if you'd like to see a movie and then maybe have dinner?'

'You know, I would really like that.'

'Great! Do you want me to choose which film, or do you have one you'd like to see?'

'No, you choose.'

'Done. Let me pick you up at around seven . . . does that suit?'

'Yes, that's perfect.'

'See you later. Is everything all right with you?'

'Yes, Michael, everything's fine . . . I'm really looking forward to seeing you.'

Jane replaced the receiver and rested her hand on the telephone. Michael was very different from Dexter. He was nice and dependable, and obviously cared for her. Deep down she was certain that Dexter cared too, and that was the reason he had walked away. She caught sight of his T-shirt on the floor next to her bed, where she had thrown it down last night.

Picking it up, she put it in the wastebin.

Acknowledgements

My sincere thanks to Mark Smith, Kate Parkin, James Horobin for their strategy, vision and commercial acumen and all the staff at Bonnier Zaffre for their hard work on my behalf. Special thanks to Angie Willocks who has travelled all over the world selling *Good Friday* (are you ever home?), Nick Stearn for such an original and eye-catching jacket, and Ruth Logan for handling my foreign rights sales so brilliantly and for reaching territories my books have never been sold in before.

Robert Gorman, I thoroughly enjoyed our dinner in London, Jim Demetriou, Matt Hoy, Andy Palmer, Alexa Burnell and all the team at Allen & Unwin for their work marketing and selling me in Australia and New Zealand. I look forward to seeing you all next year.

Thank you to everyone at Jonathan Ball in South Africa, I could not have a better team working with me in SA. I would also like to give special thanks to Jenny Crwys-Williams, who has given me so much promotional support over the years.

My thanks to Callum Sutherland who has, as usual, taken so much of the weight from my shoulders regarding the in depth research required for *Good Friday*. He has become someone I rely on 100% and his guidance has proved to be invaluable. Specifically I am indebted to Callum's wife Anne, as she was a young uniformed WPC at Hackney Police Station, so was able to give me authentic details of how a young probationary officer worked during the run up to her promotional exams. I would also express my sincere thanks to Dr Ann Preston who assisted with all the detailed forensic research.

I would also like to thank the team at La Plante Global who are constantly supportive and encouraging. Tory Macdonald I thank wholeheartedly for her dedication and to Veronica Goldstein who has recently become part of the team.

However, I have saved my biggest thanks and appreciation to Nigel Stoneman, Head of Development at La Plante Global. Nigel has continued to be supportive and encouraging throughout the process of bringing the character, Jane Tennison, through three successful novels, his genuine enthusiasm for future novels on the life of Jane Tennison and his ability to bring in a terrific shepherd's pie for lunch!

Turn the page for the first chapter from the next
book in the brilliant Jane Tennison series,
Murder Mile.
Coming August 2018.

CHAPTER ONE

Jane Tennison, recently promoted to sergeant, looked out of the passenger window of the CID car at the snow, which was falling too lightly to settle. It was 4.30am on a freezing Saturday morning in mid-February 1979 and recently the overnight temperatures had been sub-zero. The weather reports were calling it one of the coldest winters of the century.

Apart from a couple of minor incidents, Jane's CID night shift at Peckham had been remarkably uneventful, due to the bad weather. She looked at her watch: only another hour and a half to go before she finished her week of night duty and could get home to a warm bath, good sleep and some time off. She'd be back at Peckham on Monday for day shift.

Detective Constable Brian Edwards, an old colleague from her Hackney days, had been her night duty partner throughout the week. He was so tall he had the driving seat pressed as far back as it could possibly go, but his knees were still almost touching the steering wheel.

'Can you turn the heating up?' she asked, as they drove along East Dulwich Road.

'It's already on full.' Edwards moved the slider to be sure, then glanced at Jane. 'I meant to say earlier – I like your new hairstyle . . . sort of makes you look more mature.'

'Is that a polite way of saying I look older, Brian?' Jane asked.

'I was being complimentary! It goes with your smart clothes, makes you look more business-like . . . especially now you've been promoted.'

Jane was about to reply when Edwards suddenly slammed his foot on the car brake bringing it to an abrupt halt. They both lunged forward, Edwards banging his chest against the steering wheel and Jane narrowly avoiding hitting her head on the windscreen.

'What – what's up?' Jane asked, startled, staring at Edwards.

'A rat . . . A bloody rat!' He pointed at the middle of the road in front of them.

Illuminated by the car headlights was a massive rat, a piece of rotting meat between its sharp teeth. The rat suddenly darted off across the road and out of sight. Edwards shook his head.

'I hate rats. They give me the creeps.'

'Well, that's obvious! And yes, thank you, Brian, I'm OK – apart from nearly going through the windscreen.'

'I'm sorry, Sarge . . . I didn't mean to hit the brakes so suddenly.'

'I'm just touched that you didn't want to run the rat over, Brian,' Jane said.

Edwards pointed over towards Peckham Rye to a pile of rubbish-filled plastic black bin and shopping bags. They were piled up five foot high and stretched over twenty feet along the side of the park. The stench of rotting rubbish slowly permeated its way into the stationary car.

'It's thanks to Prime Minister Callaghan and his waste-of-space Labour government that the bin men and other public-sector workers are on strike,' grumbled Edwards. 'Everyone's dumping their rotting rubbish in the parks and it's attracting the rats. No wonder they're calling it the "Winter of Disconnect".'

'It's "Discontent",' Jane corrected him.

'You're quite right – there's not much to be happy about! Mind you, if Maggie Thatcher wins the next election we might get a pay rise. She likes the Old Bill.'

Jane was trying hard not to laugh. 'It's the "*Winter of Discontent*"! It comes from Shakespeare's Richard III: "*Now is the winter of our discontent, made glorious summer by this sun of York . . .*"

Edwards looked sceptical. 'Really?'

'I studied Richard III for A level English.'

'All that Shakespeare lingo is mumbo jumbo to me. I left school at sixteen and joined the Metropolitan Police Cadets,' Edwards said proudly.

'I didn't know you'd been a "Gadget",' said Jane, somewhat surprised. A 'Gadget' was affectionate force jargon for a cadet.

'It was all blokes when I first joined the Gadgets,' Edwards went on. 'We lived in a big dormitory and got work experience on division alongside the regulars. It gave me a better understanding of police work than your average ex-civvy probationer who went to Hendon – no offence intended,' he added hastily.

'None taken. If I'd known what I wanted to do at sixteen I'd probably have joined the cadets – though my mother would have had a heart attack.' Jane liked Edwards, but he wasn't the brightest spark. He'd been transferred to various stations and hadn't lasted long on the Flying Squad. In her estimation, he'd likely remain a DC for the rest of his career.

'Tell you what – head back to the station so we can warm up with a hot drink and I'll type up the night duty CID report,' she said.

Edwards snorted. 'That shouldn't take long – we haven't attended a crime scene or nicked anyone all night.'

Their banter was interrupted by a call over the radio. 'Night duty CID receiving . . . over?'

Jane picked up the radio handset. 'Yes, Detective Sergeant Tennison receiving. Go ahead . . . over.'

'A fruit and veg man on his way to set up his market stall has found an unconscious woman in Bussey Alley. Couldn't rouse her so he called 999. There's an ambulance en route,' the comms officer said.

'That's just off Rye Lane.' Edwards made a sharp U turn.

'Yes, we're free to attend and en route,' Jane confirmed over the radio, switching on the car's two-tone siren.

'If she's been out drinking she's probably collapsed from hypothermia in this bloody weather. Or maybe she's been mugged?' suggested Edwards.

'Let's just hope she's OK,' Jane said.

Rye Lane ran between the High Street and Peckham Rye. In its heyday it had rivalled Oxford Street as a major shopping destination and was known as the 'Golden Mile'. It was still a busy area, with a large department store, Co-op and various small shops and market traders selling home-produced and ethnic goods from their stalls. During the 1970s, Peckham had gradually become one of the most deprived areas in Europe, with a notorious reputation for serious crime, especially muggings, which were a daily occurrence.

Jane and Edwards arrived at the scene within two minutes. A man who looked to be in his mid-fifties was standing under the railway bridge at the entrance to Bussey Alley, frantically waving his hands. He was dressed in a dark-coloured thigh-length sheepskin coat, blue and white Millwall football club scarf and a peaked cap. Edwards pulled up beside him and opened the driver's window.

'I thought you might be the ambulance when I heard the siren.' The man crouched down to speak to them. 'Poor thing's just up there. She's lyin' face down and ain't moved. I put one of me stall tarpaulins over her to keep off the sleet and cold. I was hopin' she might warm up and come around . . . '

Jane put on her leather gloves, got the high-powered torch out of the glove box and picked up the portable Storno police radio.

'There's quite a lot of rubbish been dumped on one side of the alley, just up from where she is – be careful of the rats,' the market trader said as they got out of the car.

Jane grinned at Edwards. He hadn't looked too happy at the word 'rat'. 'You get the details,' she said. 'I'll check on the woman.'

She turned on the torch, lighting up the dingy alley. The narrow path ran alongside the railway line. In the arches underneath were small lockups where the market traders stored their stalls and goods. Jane walked at a brisk pace, until about forty feet along she could see the green and white striped tarpaulin. Crouching down, she lifted it back and shone the torch. The woman beneath was wearing a thigh-length blue PVC mac, with the collar up, covering the back of her neck.

Removing her right glove, Jane put her index and middle fingers together, and placed them on the side of the woman's neck, in the soft hollow area just beside the windpipe. There was no pulse and the woman's neck felt cold and clammy. Jane felt uneasy. She stood up and slowly shone her torch along the body revealing dried blood smears on the back of the blue mac. The woman's knee-length pleated skirt was hitched up to her thighs revealing suspenders and black stockings. Near the body the torch beam caught three small shirt buttons. Peering closely at one of them, Jane could see some white sewing thread and a tiny piece of torn shirt still attached. It looked as if the button had been torn off, possibly in a struggle.

A little further up the alleyway Jane noticed a cheap and worn small handbag. Wearing her leather gloves, she picked it up and opened it carefully, looking for any ID. All she found was a lipstick, handkerchief, a small hairbrush and a plastic purse. Inside the purse were a few coins and one folded five-pound note. There were no house or car keys inside the handbag or purse. Jane picked up the handbag and placed a ten pence coin down on the spot where she'd found it; it would go in a property bag later to preserve it for fingerprints.

Next, Jane shone the torch around the body. It was strange: she couldn't see any blood on the pavement around or near the victim, or on the back of her head. She crouched down and slowly lifted the collar on the PVC mac back, revealing a knotted white rope round the victim's neck and hair.

Shocked Jane got to her feet and pulled out the portable radio.

'WDS Tennison to Peckham Control Room. Are you receiving? Over.' She spoke with confidence and authority, despite the fact she'd only been promoted and posted to Peckham a few weeks ago.

'Yes, go ahead, Sarge,' the comms officer replied.

'Cancel the ambulance . . . The woman in Bussey Alley appears to have been strangled. I've looked in a handbag for possible ID, but can't find any. I need uniform assistance to cordon off and man the scene at Rye Lane, and the far end of Bussey Alley, which leads onto Copeland Road.'

'All received, Sarge. A mobile unit is en route to assist.'

Jane continued. 'Can you call DCI Moran at home and ask him to attend the scene? I'll also need the laboratory Scene of Crime DS here – oh, and the Divisional Surgeon to officially pronounce life extinct . . . Over.'

The Duty Sergeant came on the radio. 'Looks like a quiet week just got busy, Jane. I'll call Moran and tell him you're on scene and dealing . . . Over. '

Jane ended the transmission and replaced the tarpaulin over the body to preserve it from the sleet that was still falling, although not as heavily. Then she walked back to Rye Lane.

Edwards was still speaking to the market trader, and making notes in his pocket book. As she approached him, she gave a little shake of her head to indicate this was more than a collapse in the street or hypothermia and went to the rear of the CID car. Taking out a plastic police property bag, she placed the handbag inside it.

'Is she all right?' the trader asked.

She shook her head. 'I'm afraid she's dead, sir. Did you see anyone hanging about or acting suspiciously before you found her?'

The man looked shocked. 'No, no one . . . Oh, my – the poor thing. What's happened to her?'

'I don't know, sir, I'm afraid. Further investigation is needed,' Jane did not want to reveal more.

'Can I get me gear out the lockup and set up for business?'

'Sorry, not at the moment, but maybe in an hour or two,' she said. 'We'll need to take a more detailed statement off you later.'

Jane took Edwards to one side.

'I take it you're thinking murder?' he whispered.

Jane nodded. By now their hair was soaking and their coats sodden. 'Looks like she's been strangled and maybe raped. I've spoken with the Duty Sergeant who's informing DCI Moran. The market man's up a bit early – does his account of how he found her sound above board to you?'

'Yeah. His name's Charlie Dunn, he's sixty-two and he's been working the markets since he was twelve. He's always been an early bird. He said he's just been over to Spitalfields fruit and veg market to get fresh stock for the day. That's his white van under the railway bridge. He was unloading it to his archway lockup in the alley when he saw the woman on the pavement. I checked his van, it's full of fresh goods. He also showed me the purchase receipt for the fruit and veg and his market trader's licence. He sounded and acted legit to me.'

'Well, she's stone cold, so it looks like she's been dead a while anyway.'

'Any ID on her?'

'Nothing in the handbag I found, not even keys. I haven't had a chance to check her coat pockets yet. I want to get both ends of the alleyway sealed off and manned by uniform first – all the market traders will be turning up soon and wanting access to their archway lockups.'

Edwards nodded and blew into his freezing hands. He didn't question her authoritative tone; on the contrary, he liked the fact WDS Tennison was taking responsibility for the crime scene.

The market trader went to his van and returned with a Thermos flask.

'Hot coffee? You can have it if you want. I'm going to go home and come back later.'

'Thank you!' Edwards took the flask and poured some coffee into the removable cup and handed it to Jane. She took a mouthful, swallowed it, then let out a deep cough and held her chest.

'There's more brandy in that than coffee!'

Edwards promptly held the flask to his lips and took a large gulp.

'So there is,' he said with a grin.

'Put it in the car, Brian. We don't want Moran smelling booze on us – you know what he's like about drinking on duty.'

Edwards took another gulp, then put the flask in the back of the car and got a packet of lozenges out of his pocket.

'"Be prepared", as we used to say in the scouts. You see I remember some famous quotes as well.' Edwards took one for himself, and offered the packet to Jane.

'What are they?' Jane asked.

'Fisherman's Friends. They'll hide the smell of the brandy and warm you up at the same time. I take them fishing with me when it's cold like this.'

Jane reached into the pack, took out one of the small, light brown, oval-shaped lozenges, popped it in her mouth and immediately began taking deep breaths. The menthol flavour was so strong her eyes began watering, her nose started running and her throat tingled.

'They taste awful!' she exclaimed spitting out the lozenge and placing it in a tissue to throw away later.

Just then, two police constables arrived in an Austin Allegro panda car. They got out and approached Jane.

'What do you need us to do, Sarge?'

'I need the Rye Lane and Copeland Road entrances to the alley sealed off with tape and one of you to stand guard at each end.'

'Will do, Sarge.' They both set off and then one of them turned back. 'Oh – the Duty Sergeant said to tell you DCI Moran's been informed and is on his way with DI Gibbs.'

Edwards looked at Jane. 'I thought DI Gibbs wasn't due to start at Peckham until Monday?'

Jane shrugged. 'That's what I thought as well.'

'Maybe Moran wants him to run the investigation.'

'Why? Moran's the senior officer – he's in charge of the CID at Peckham,' Jane pointed out.

'Don't tell anyone I told you this,' said Edwards. 'But I was in the bog cubicle when I overheard Moran talking to the Chief Super. Moran said his wife was suffering from the "baby blues". Apparently, the baby was crying a lot and he didn't know what to do for the best. The Chief suggested he take some time off when DI Gibbs arrived – so maybe Moran's called Gibbs in early to familiarise himself with everything before he steps back to spend time at home.'

'I didn't know his wife had had a baby.'

'Yeah – about a month before you started at Peckham,' Edwards paused. 'I've not seen Spencer Gibbs since our Hackney days, but I heard he went off the rails a bit after Bradfield was killed in the explosion during that bank robbery by the Bentley family.'

Jane immediately became tight-lipped. 'I worked with Gibbs in the West End at Bow Street when I was a WDC and he was fine,' she lied. At the time Gibbs was drinking heavily to drown his sorrows, but managing to hide it from his other colleagues. She had always had a soft spot for Gibbs and didn't like to hear his name or reputation being tarnished. She suspected he must have overcome his demons, especially if he'd been posted to a busy station like Peckham. She also knew DCI Moran would have had to agree to Gibbs's transfer.

Jane and Edwards returned to the alley. Edwards went over to look at the body, while Jane picked up the coin she'd used as a marker and replaced it with the handbag, now inside the property bag. Then they both checked to see if there was anything in the victim's pockets to help identify her; there was nothing.

Edwards pulled up the left sleeve of the victim's PVC mac.

'She's wearing a watch,' he said. 'Looks like a cheap catalogue one, glass is scratched and the strap's worn. There's no engagement or wedding ring – they might have been stolen?'

'Possibly,' said Jane, 'but there's no white patch or indentation on the skin to suggest she was wearing either. Plus the handbag was left behind with money in it.' Jane got the radio out of her coat pocket and handed it to Edwards.

'Call the station and ask them to check Missing Persons for anyone matching our victim's description. I'll replace the tarpaulin, then we'll do a search further up the alley towards Copeland Road to see if there's anything else that may be of significance to the investigation.'

Edwards hesitated. 'What should I tell Comms?'

Jane gave a small sigh. 'Brian – just look at the victim and describe her when you speak to them, OK?'

'Oh, yeah. OK, I see.'

Jane watched Edwards disappear down the alleyway, leaving her alone with the body. It was still dark and now the initial adrenalin rush was wearing off she was even more aware of the cold. She stamped her feet and flapped her arms across her chest to generate some warmth. A sudden noise made her jump, and swinging her torch round revealed a rat scurrying from a pile of rubbish that had been left rotting in front of one of the arches. She thought about the woman lying on the ground in front of her. What had she been doing here? Had she been on her own, like Jane was now, or was her killer someone she knew?

Footsteps approached from the Rye Lane end of the Alley. Jane looked up, shone her torch, and saw Detective Sergeant Paul Lawrence from the forensics lab approaching. He was accompanied by a younger man in civilian clothes. Even if she hadn't seen Paul's face, she'd have guessed it was him. As ever, he was dressed in his trademark thigh-length green Barbour wax jacket and trilby hat.

Paul Lawrence was renowned as the best crime scene investigator in the Met. He had an uncanny ability to think laterally and piece things together bit by bit. Always patient and willing to explain what he was doing, Jane had worked with him several times and felt indebted to him for all that he had taught her. Now she felt relief at the sight of his familiar figure.

Paul greeted Jane with a friendly smile. 'I hear it's Detective Sergeant Tennison now! Well done and well-deserved, Jane. As we're the same rank, you can officially call me Paul.' He laughed. She had always called him Paul when not in the company of senior officers.

'You were quick,' Jane said.

'I'd already been in the lab typing up a report from an earlier incident in Brixton,' he said. 'Victim stabbed during a fight over a drugs deal. Turned out the injury wasn't as serious as first thought and the victim didn't want to assist us anyway, so there wasn't much to do. No doubt there'll be a revenge attack within a few days.'

Jane explained the scene to him, starting with the market trader's account and exactly what she and DC Edwards had done since their arrival at Bussey Alley.

'Good work, Jane. Minimal disturbance of the scene and preservation of evidence is what I like to see and hear. Peter here is the Scene of Crime Officer assisting me. He'll photograph everything as is, then we can get the victim onto a body sheet for a closer look underneath.'

The SOCO set to work taking the initial scene photographs of the alleyway and body. He stopped when the Divisional Surgeon appeared. Although it was obvious, the doctor still checked for a pulse on her neck, before officially pronouncing she was dead. As he was getting to his feet, Detective Chief Inspector Moran arrived, carrying a large red hard-backed A4 note book, and holding up an enormous black umbrella. Dressed smartly in a grey pin stripe suit, crisp white shirt, red tie, black brogues and thigh length beige camel coat, he nonetheless looked bad-tempered and tired.

'So, DS Tennison,' he said. 'What's happened so far?' He sounded tetchy.

Jane had worked with DCI Nick Moran when she was a WPC at Hackney in the early seventies, and he was a Detective Inspector. She knew to keep her summary brief and to the point so as not to irritate her superior.

'The victim was found in here by a market trader. Edwards spoke with him and is satisfied he wasn't involved. I called DS Lawrence to the scene and the Divisional Surgeon who's pronounced life extinct. From my cursory examination it appears she's been strangled and may have been sexually assaulted. I haven't found anything to help us identify who she is, though a handbag was nearby which I checked – '

Moran frowned. 'I had expected you to just contain the scene until I arrived. It's my job to decide who should be called and what action should be taken. You should have left the handbag in situ as well. It's not good to disturb a scene.'

Jane felt Moran was being a bit harsh. She, like everyone else, was working in the freezing cold and soaking wet. He should have realised she was trying to obtain the best evidence and identify the victim. She thought about saying as much, but wondering if his mood was connected to a sleepless night coping with the new baby, decided to say nothing.

Lawrence looked at Moran. 'It's standard procedure for a lab sergeant to be called to all suspicious deaths and murder scenes at the earliest opportunity. Preserving the handbag for fingerprints showed good crime scene awareness by WDS Tennison.'

Moran ignored Lawrence and spoke to the Divisional Surgeon. 'Can you give me an estimation of time of death?'

The doctor shrugged his shoulders. 'There are many variables due to the weather conditions, breeze in the alley and other factors which can affect body temperature. It's hard to be accurate, but possibly just before or after midnight.'

Just about managing to keep his umbrella up, Moran wrote in his note book. Jane could see Lawrence was not pleased. She knew his view was that Divisional Surgeons were not experienced in forensic pathology or time of death and should confine their role to nothing more than pronouncing life extinct.

Lawrence looked at Moran. 'Excuse me, sir, but now the sleet's stopped, it would be a good idea to get a pathologist down to see the body in situ. He can check the rigor mortis and body temp – '

Moran interrupted him, shutting his umbrella. 'The weather's constantly changing, and more snow is forecast, so I want the body bagged, tagged and off to the mortuary as a priority for a post mortem later this morning.'

Lawrence sighed, but he didn't want to get into an argument about it. Opening his forensic kit, he removed a white body sheet and small plastic ring box and latex gloves. Using some tweezers, he picked up the three buttons beside the body and placed them in a plastic property bag. Then he unfolded the body sheet and placed it on the ground next to the body.

Lawrence looked up at Jane and Edwards. 'I want to turn her over onto the body bag. If one of you can grab her feet, I'll work the shoulders. Just go slow and gentle.'

Jane took a step forward, but Edwards said he'd do it and grabbed a pair of protective gloves from Lawrence's forensic bag. As they turned the body over, Jane shone her torch on the victim, lighting up her contorted face and the rope round her neck. The strangulation had caused her tongue to protrude and her eyes were puffed and swollen. The victim wore little makeup, and looked to be in her late twenties to early thirties. She was medium height, with brown shoulder length hair parted down the middle, and was wearing a pink blouse, which was torn, and her bra was pulled up over her breasts.

Lawrence pointed to the pavement area where the body had been lying. 'It's dry underneath her,' he observed.

'The sleet started about 3a.m.,' Jane said.

'Then it's reasonable to assume she was killed before then.'

'How can you be sure it was 3 a.m., Tennison?' Moran snapped, tapping the ground with the steel tip of his umbrella.

Jane got her note book out of her inside coat pocket. 'We'd just stopped a vehicle and I recorded the details and time in my note book. I remember the sleet starting as I was taking the driver's details . . . Let me find it.' She flicked through the pages. 'Ah – here it is. Time of stop, 3.03 a.m.'

'Well, I want it checked out with the London weather office in case it becomes critical to the case,' said Moran. 'The body is a stone's throw from Peckham Rye railway station. She might have been out late Friday night and attacked in the alleyway if using it as a cut through to Copeland Road.'

Lawrence shrugged. 'She might have thrown it away, but there was no train ticket on her. She may have been walking from the Copeland Road end and heading towards Rye Lane. The fact there were no house keys on her could suggest she was returning home and expecting someone to let her in.'

Moran nodded. 'We can put out a press appeal with the victim's description and ask if anyone recalls seeing her on the train Friday night. Also we can run a check with Miss Pers for anyone matching her description.'

'Already in hand, sir.' Jane said, without receiving so much as a thank you back. She glanced at Edwards, reminding herself to check exactly what description he had given to Miss Pers.

Lawrence crouched down next to the body, looked at Moran and pointed to the victim's torn blouse. 'There's four buttons missing. I only recovered three beside the body and there's no more underneath her.'

Edwards raised his finger. 'Tennison and I had a good look up and down the alley before DS Lawrence arrived and we didn't see any more buttons.'

Lawrence stood up. 'Best we check the soles of our shoes in case one of us has accidently trodden on it and it's got lodged in the tread. It won't be the first time something has unintentionally been removed from a crime scene in that way. When you see the market trader who found her, check his footwear as well.' Everyone checked the soles of their shoes.

'Someone tread in dog shit?'

Jane turned around. Spencer Gibbs was wearing a trendy full-length brown sheepskin coat. His hands were deep in the pockets, pulling the unbuttoned coat around his front to keep out the cold. He had a big smile and Jane could instantly see he was looking a lot better now than when she last saw him, almost younger in fact. His hair had changed as well. It no longer stood up like a wire brush, but was combed back straight from his forehead.

Gibbs' smile widened when he saw Jane.

She held out her hand. 'Hello, Spence, you look well.'

'Jane Tennison – long time no see!' He pulled her forward to give her a hug.

Jane noticed that DCI Moran didn't seem too impressed and wondered if Gibbs' jovial mood was due to drink, although she couldn't smell any alcohol.

Gibbs walked over to Moran. 'Good morning, sir,' he said, and they shook hands. Gibbs' coat fell open to reveal a blue frilled shirt, tight leather pants, blue suede shoes and a large 'Peace' sign medallion. Everyone went quiet.

Moran frowned. 'So you really think that sort of outfit is suitable for a senior detective, DI Gibbs?'

'Sorry, guv. I did a gig in Camden town with my band last night then stayed at the girlfriend Tamara's pad. Thankfully I'd added her phone number to my out of hours contact list at the old station. I didn't want to waste time by going home to change when I got the call out, so after a quick dash of Adidas aftershave, I came straight to the scene by cab.'

Gibbs' looks and patter had become even more 'rock and roll' than they used to be.

'Your band do Glam Rock, guv?' Edwards asked trying not to laugh at Gibbs' dress sense.

'No, we're more progressive . . . Serious rock and roll. Girlfriend's in the band as well, looks like Debbie Harry from Blondie – she's a real stunner.'

'Well – you look like a real poofter in that gear,' Edwards replied, earning a playful slap on the back of his head from Gibbs.

Moran coughed loudly to get Gibbs' and Edwards' attention. 'Show a bit of respect you two. We're supposed to be investigating a murder, not discussing bloody music!'

'Sorry, sir,' they said in unison.

'What have you got so far?' Gibbs asked Moran.

Moran frowned. 'A murder, obviously. I want you to organise house-to-house enquiries DI Gibbs. Start with any flats in Rye Lane, and all the premises in Copeland Road. Tennison and Edwards can return to the station to write up their night duty report then go off duty.'

Jane knew that organising house-to-house was normally a DS's responsibility and she was keen to be part of the investigation team.

'I should have the weekend off, sir, but I'm happy to remain on duty and assist the investigation. You've got a DS on sick leave, one at the Old Bailey on a big trial starting Monday, and one taking over nights from me tonight. House-to-house is normally a DS's role so I could – '

Moran interrupted her. 'I'm aware of all that, Tennison. If you're willing to work for normal pay and days off in lieu, as opposed to costly overtime, then you can head up the house-to-house. Edwards, same rule goes for you if you want to be on the investigation.'

Jane and Edwards agreed. Earning extra money was a bonus, but never a big deal when it came to a murder enquiry; it was more about being part of a challenging case.

Moran closed his notebook and put his pen back in his jacket pocket. 'Right, DI Gibbs will be my number two on this investigation. We'll head back to the station. I'll get more detectives in from the surrounding stations and contact the Coroner's Officer to arrange a post mortem later this morning. Tennison – you head back to the station with Edwards. Do your night duty report first, then prepare the house-to-house documents and questionnaires. You can get uniform to assist in the house-to-house, as well as the Special Patrol Group. DS Lawrence and the SOCO can finish bagging the body and examining the scene. If possible, I'd like to know who the dead woman is before the post mortem.'

'I'll take a set of fingerprints while I'm here. Uniform can take them straight up the Yard for the fingerprint bureau to check. If she's got a criminal record they'll identify her,' Lawrence said.

Moran nodded his approval. As he walked off with Gibbs, Edwards turned to Jane.

'He could have poked someone's eye out the way he was swinging that umbrella! I reckon he's in a mood because the baby kept him up, and his wife gave him a hard time about being called in.'

Jane said nothing, but she suspected there was some truth in Edwards' comment. Just as she was about to follow him back to the CID car, Paul called out.

'Can you grab the large role of sellotape from my forensic bag?'

He and the SOCO had wrapped the body in the white body sheet and twisted each end tight. Jane knew the procedure and helped by rolling the tape several times around each twisted end to secure them. She always found it surreal that a bagged dead body ended up looking like an enormous Christmas cracker.

'Thanks, Jane.' As the SOCO moved away, Lawrence asked, 'Is Moran always so tetchy these days?'

'Wife had a baby recently; sleepless nights are probably getting to him.'

'Well, he was wrong to have a go at you and ignore my advice. He should have called out a Pathologist.'

'He was probably just asserting his authority to let us know he's boss.'

'He might be in charge, but he's spent most of his career on various squads like vice, so he's not had a lot of experience in major crime or murder investigations.'

'He did solve the Hackney serial rape cases and that murder committed by Peter Allard the cab driver,' Jane pointed out.

'Yes – but I also recall he was accused of faking Allard's confession. If it hadn't been for your dogged work in that case, he wouldn't have solved it. He showered himself in glory because of you, Jane. He seems to have forgotten that you stuck your neck out for him that night in the park acting as a decoy. You were the one that got attacked by Allard, not him.'

'I know, Paul, but I think he's mellowed since our Hackney days. Apart from this morning he's been OK towards me.'

'Well, I'd be wary of him, Jane,' warned Lawrence. 'He likes to think he knows best, which puts not only the investigation at risk, but the officers on it as well.'

This was not the first murder. The body count began to mount, the killings became more gruesome, no suspects and no witnesses, and all within a stone's throw of each other.

Readers' Club

If you enjoyed *Good Friday*, why not join the LYNDA LA PLANTE READERS' CLUB for exclusive writing, giveaways and news from Lynda La Plante by visiting www.bit.ly/LyndaLaPlanteClub?

Dear Reader,

Thank you very much for picking up *Good Friday*, the third novel in the Jane Tennison thriller series. It's been great to see how excited readers have been to discover how the Jane Tennison of *Prime Suspect* started her police career, and I have loved the chance to delve deep and bring her challenging earlier story to life. I hope you have enjoyed reading this book as much as I enjoyed writing it.

What I wanted to do with the Jane Tennison series was to explore the influences that made Jane the iconic character she becomes in *Prime Suspect* – and to do that, I had to go back to the very beginning of her story. Jane is a rookie police detective in the 1970s and even for those of us who can remember it, it seems like another world. She must battle not only her parents' expectations of what is and isn't a suitable job for a woman, but the ingrained sexism of the Metropolitan police. However, from her early twenties we see the grit and determination that Jane will show in her later career – and the flair, instinct and empathy that will mark her out as an exceptional detective.

If you have enjoyed *Good Friday*, then please do read the first and second novels in the Jane Tennison series, *Tennison* and *Hidden Killers*, which are now available in paperback and ebook. And you might like to know that the fourth book in the series, *Murder Mile*, will be published in hardcover this year. It's set in Peckham, in south London, in 1979. A series of murders take place within a one mile radius of each other. The Metropolitan police can find no pattern or connection linking the female victims. Then another victim is found, this time a young male, can Jane Tennison fit the pieces of the jigsaw together in time to stop the murderer from striking again?

And in the meantime, I'm very excited about a brand new series that I'm working on. I won't reveal much about it now – but if you would like to hear more detail, or about the Jane Tennison thriller series, you can visit www.bit.ly/LyndaLaPlanteClub where you can join the My Readers' Club. It only takes a few moments to sign up, there are no catches or costs and new members will automatically receive an exclusive message from me.

Bonnier Zaffre will keep your data private and confidential, and it will never be passed on to a third party. We won't spam you with loads of emails, just get in touch now and again with news about my books, and you can unsubscribe any time you want.

And if you would like to get involved in a wider conversation about my books, please do review *Good Friday* on Amazon, on GoodReads, on any other e-store, on your own blog and social media accounts, or talk about it with friends, family or reader groups! Sharing your thoughts helps other readers, and I always enjoy hearing about what people experience from my writing.

Thanks again for your interest in this novel, and I hope you'll return for *Murder Mile*, the fourth in the Jane Tennison series.

With my very best wishes,

Lynda

TENNISON

The first book in the sensational Jane Tennison series

The Kray twins may be behind bars but the streets of London are still rife with drugs, robbery and murder.

1973, in the East End of London, a young WPC Jane Tennison joins the toughest ranks of the Hackney police force as a probationary officer.

When her first case comes in, a woman savagely beaten and strangled to death, Jane is thrown in at the deep end. But the victim's autopsy is just the beginning of Tennison's harsh initiation into the criminal world . . .

Praise for the Jane Tennison series:

'Classic Lynda, a fabulous read'
MARTINA COLE

'La Plante excels in her ability to pick out details that give her portrayal of life in a police station a rare ring of authenticity'
SUNDAY TELEGRAPH

'A terrific, gutsy back story for the heroine of TV's *Prime Suspect*'
WOMAN & HOME

HIDDEN KILLERS

The second brilliant crime thriller in the Jane Tennison series

When WPC Jane Tennison is promoted to the role of Detective Constable in London's Bow Street CID, she is immediately conflicted. While her more experienced colleagues move on swiftly from one criminal case to another, Jane is often left doubting their methods and findings.

As she becomes inextricably involved in a multiple rape case, Jane must put her life at risk in her search for answers.

Will she toe the line, or endanger her position by seeking the truth?

Praise for the Jane Tennison series:

'An absorbingly twisty plot'
GUARDIAN

'Enthralling'
HEAT

'Vintage La Plante'
INDEPENDENT

Want to read
NEW BOOKS
before anyone else?

Like getting
FREE BOOKS?

Enjoy sharing your
OPINIONS?

Discover
READERS FIRST

Read. Love. Share.

Sign up today to win your first free book:
readersfirst.co.uk